# Evan stared. Brennan stared back.

"Hi, Evan," Brennan nodded in greeting. "For what it's worth, I'm sorry about this."

"No man, I'm sorry. You know, for your loss and all."

Brennan, peering out from behind delicate, silver-framed glasses, watched Evan with something too close to pity for his liking. It was already more horrible than Evan thought it would be, with Brennan's smooth, perfectly shaved jaw, his flawless, blemish-free skin and longer, stylishly cut, dyed-blond hair. Everything about Brennan seemed perfect. He was the person Evan should have been.

"She was your mom, too," Brennan said quietly.

Something dark and bare moved behind Evan's eyes, but he masked it before Brennan could try to tell what it was.

"Yeah, well..." he pushed the screen door open. "Come on in. Mi casa es su casa and all that."

Evan stepped aside to let Brennan in, and was startled when Brennan suddenly hugged him after coming over the threshold. Stiff and uncomfortable, Evan clapped him on the back and tried not to notice how good Brennan smelled or how nice it was to simply be touched by someone who was not looking to either kick his ass or suck his dick, both regular occurrences in his life.

# Also recommended...

You may also enjoy these other Forbidden Fiction works:

**Twin Ties 2: Twin Affairs by Lynn Kelling**

All Evan Savage wants is a quiet night at the bar, waiting for his boyfriend, Alek Popović, to finish his shift; what he gets instead is a nightmare. If Evan thought his life was complicated when his biggest problem was his tangled, complex sex life, it becomes infinitely more so once one selfless act ends in terrible violence. With life hanging in the balance, closely guarded secrets about the nature of Evan's relationships, not only with Alek, but Luka and Brennan, are threatened. Family is notified. The four young men's relationships with each other begin to unravel as carefully drawn boundary lines are crossed again and again. (M/M+)

http://forbiddenfiction.com/library/story/LK1-1.000168

**His Whipping Boy  by J.A. Jaken**

Cedric de Breos was an average son from an average farmer's family before he was chosen — by royal decree — to befriend Alain Tomolia, the solemn, enigmatic crown prince of Dunn. As Cedric dutifully pursues their strange friendship, he finds that Alain is haunted by a dark secret, one with its roots sunk deep in the crown prince's past. Cedric also discovers that his intended purpose is not only to serve as companion to the crown prince but also as his surrogate in the whipping yard, being punished for Alain's misdeeds. Cedric must come to terms with the resentment, pity, curiosity, and reluctant attraction he feels toward the crown prince. (M/M)

http://forbiddenfiction.com/library/story/JAJ-1.000182

# My Brother's Lover

## Twin Ties: Book 1

### Lynn Kelling

**ForbiddenFiction**
www.forbiddenfiction.com

an imprint of

**Fantastic Fiction Publishing**
www.fantasticfictionpublishing.com

**MY BROTHER'S LOVER**
A Forbidden Fiction book

Fantastic Fiction Publishing
Hayward, California

© Lynn Kelling, 2014

**CREDITS**
Editor: Rylan Hunter, D.M. Atkins
Cover Design: Siolnatine
Cover photo: Migfoto at Dreamstime
Production Editor: Erika L Firanc
Proofreading: JhP323 and Kaye O'Malley


SKU: LK1-000154-02 FFP
ISBN: 978-1-62234-144-3

Published in the United States of America

# DISCLAIMER

This book is a work of fiction which contains explicit erotic content; it is intended for mature readers. Do not read this if it's not legal for you.

All the characters, locations and events herein are fictional. While elements of existing locations or historical characters or events may be used fictitiously, any resemblance to actual people, places or events is coincidental.

This story is not intended to be used as an instruction manual. It may contain descriptions of erotic acts that are immoral, illegal, or unsafe. Do not take the events in this story as proof of the plausibility or safety of any particular practice.

For Raine.

# Contents

# Chapter 1

# Stranger with the Same Face

It was going to be the worst day of Evan Savage's life. Or, at least that's how he saw it. At only nine twenty-three in the morning, on August thirteenth, of course, nothing was set in stone yet, but the signs were all there.

Things had been going so well. Evan was officially eighteen years old, finally on his own, no more dad breathing down his neck, no more playing the outcast at school, no more hassles. Then life gave him a hard kick in the ass with a twist of fate he never saw coming. An identical twin brother Evan never met and only recently found out he had was coming to live with him, encroaching on this newfound freedom. He was expected to arrive at any minute, in fact.

*That*, Evan thought sarcastically, *is fantastic.*

Evan took another drag off of his cigarette, burned down all the way to the filter. Then, he crushed it under a boot heel before letting the smoke slip out in a twisting tendril over his full lips surrounded by unkempt, blond stubble. Vibrantly blue eyes ringed with long eyelashes squinted out into the blazing morning sun, keeping watch for a rental truck on the horizon, finding none.

The loneliness which had defined Evan's existence for as long as he could remember complicated things. It had always been just Evan and his dad, no other relatives meriting anything more than an annual greeting card around Christmas. And even Evan's dad, Charlie, had been vanishing for longer and longer stretches of time. Work out on the road, wherever he could find it, was the excuse but not necessarily the reason. Evan had been quietly debating the true cause for Charlie's wandering for years. Maybe it was simply part of who Charlie was, unable to stay anchored down, unwilling to stick around when things got tough. Evan had always wished for more, though — more family, more friends, or more people to count on. Charlie left Evan emotionally out in the cold at home while bullies put Evan constantly on the defensive at school. In theory, it was nice to be getting some company at long last. But living in isolation had taught Evan how difficult it was to trust, to hope and open up even in the most dire of circumstances.

There was plenty of cold beer in the fridge, thanks to an older acquaintance who kept Evan well-stocked. Unable to think of anything he'd enjoy more, Evan rose from his seat on the front stoop of his cottage-sized, beat-up old house. He pushed in through the screen door. It closed behind him with a loud slap. As he wandered back to the kitchen, he walked through the center hall, his boots click-clacking over the dust-bunny laden floor. Evan scanned the recently tidied rooms flanking the hall on either side with weary eyes, disturbed by their barrenness. His very bones ached at the memory of moving out so many of his things. It had all gone into storage — all of the stuff belonging solely to Charlie and anything else that Evan didn't want touched or seen by the stranger invading his home. The extra bedroom, usually kept ready in case Charlie found a need to come back to their rural hometown of Whippoorwill, Pennsylvania, was now completely bare, waiting for its new occupant to fill it up.

Evan grabbed a beer and popped the top off with the thick silver ring he wore on the third finger of his right hand. The first three swallows went down smooth and cool, refreshing him in the stifling heat of the house, but he wished the beer was something stronger, something that might do a better job at banishing the sick tickle of foreboding in his belly. Ever since he got the call from Charlie explaining who Brennan Holt was (and, in hindsight, Evan realized what a shitty way that was to find out about long-lost family, to be told over a bad cell connection from clear across the country) Evan had had a sense that he was being royally screwed by fate. He would have escaped it if he could, but it was impossible. It was too late.

Evan had only seen a handful of photos of Brennan, his secret identical twin, and only spoke to him on the phone once, but he did know a few basic facts about the guy. They were raised separately—Brennan by their mother, Maggie Holt, and Evan by their father, Charlie Savage. According to Charlie, who did everything he could to avoid explaining himself, the divorce had been messy, bitter, and hate-fueled. Maggie had gotten pregnant when they were both still teenagers, and the marriage happened out of a sense of obligation more than anything else. In the small collection of months between conception and birth, Charlie and Maggie realized their personalities clashed too much for them to try making the relationship work, even for the sake of the babies. But that still left them with a hard choice to make. Stubborn as hell when he wanted to be, Charlie wouldn't consider letting Maggie take off with both of the twins, leaving him with nothing. Joint custody would have meant regular, vitriolic, unbearable contact between people who had grown to lose all tolerance for each other. It had seemed kinder at the time, or so Evan had been told, to raise the boys as strangers to one another from the start rather than inflict any of that bitterness on them.

Kinder for whom, though? Resenting the decision that had robbed him of a brother and a mother, Evan also, grudgingly, understood the rationality behind it. His parents were too young, immature, and misguided. They weren't the first people ever to make a bad decision and they wouldn't be the last. He suspected it would soon become a lot less easy to act the part of the impassive bystander to his family's history once he came face-to-face with a person who was made up of the very same essence as himself.

Right in that moment, leaning inside the front door's frame and sipping his beer, Evan couldn't give a shit about Brennan Holt. But soon, possibly as soon as the coming night, or in only an hour's time, whether he liked it or not, that would all change. He would see something in Brennan he never wanted to acknowledge about himself. It would be like living with a walking, talking, breathing mirror, showing all of his flaws and quirks. Brennan wasn't just a new houseguest, he was a warped mirror; the perfect reminder of everything Evan had done wrong and would never be. They had avoided each other for eighteen years, existing in entirely different worlds through the concerted efforts of their mother and father, so why did it all need to change? Evan had no say in the decision, no ability to keep out his eighteen-year-old counterpart without becoming the bad guy.

"Fuck you, Dad," Evan scowled, letting that sweet sentiment float away on a warm summer breeze.

A yellow truck finally rolled into view, which Evan acknowledged immediately.

"And fuck you too, stranger," Evan added bitterly, taking another sip, tilting the mouth of the bottle toward the oncoming vehicle in salute.

It was a small moving truck. A kid with honey-blond hair was behind the wheel. The truck rolled up in front of the small house with its small front yard and even smaller driveway. Evan's stomach swooped and sank like a stone. The driver's door swung open and the kid hopped down. He left the truck behind and approached Evan with an expression colored with relief.

Not looking up until the last second, when Brennan was only a few feet away, Evan finally managed to lift his gaze from the dirty stoop. First, he saw Brennan's clean, crisp clothes, perfectly tailored and pristine on a body of a size and height nearly perfectly equal to his own. For a split second he was distracted by the particulars, like that Brennan appeared to be built slightly leaner than Evan was. Then he saw Brennan's face—*his* face.

Evan stared. Brennan stared back.

"Hi, Evan," Brennan nodded in greeting. "For what it's worth, I'm sorry about this."

"No man, I'm sorry. You know, for your loss and all."

Brennan, peering out from behind delicate, silver-framed glasses, watched Evan with something too close to pity for his liking. It was already more horrible than Evan thought it would be, with Brennan's smooth, perfectly shaved jaw, his flawless, blemish-free skin and longer, stylishly cut, dyed-blond hair. Everything about Brennan seemed perfect. He was the person Evan should have been.

"She was your mom, too," Brennan said quietly.

Something dark and bare moved behind Evan's eyes, but he masked it before Brennan could try to tell what it was.

"Yeah, well..." he pushed the screen door open. "Come on in. Mi

4

casa es su casa and all that."

Evan stepped aside to let Brennan in, and was startled when Brennan suddenly hugged him after coming over the threshold. Stiff and uncomfortable, Evan clapped him on the back and tried not to notice how good Brennan smelled or how nice it was to simply be touched by someone who was not looking to either kick his ass or suck his dick, both regular occurrences in his life.

"Thank you," Brennan sighed, filling the awkward hug with what seemed to be sincere relief. After a pause, releasing Evan from the embrace, he added, "I didn't know where else to go."

They locked eyes, each of them seeing things strangely familiar. It had only been seconds and it already felt like they'd known each other their whole lives. Evan's stomach swooped again.

"Let me show you your room. It's over this way," he said, ducking his head and gesturing with the beer. "Oh. Um, you want a beer or something?"

"I don't drink," Brennan politely replied. "But water'd be good."

"Course you don't," Evan muttered to himself. "Water it is then."

He headed to the kitchen and returned a moment later with a glass filled with ice cubes and water from the tap. Brennan gave it a quick glance, conveying to Evan that maybe he expected a bottle of filtered spring water instead, so Evan explained, "This is all I've got."

"Oh, that's fine. Thanks. I was planning to go grocery shopping once I unload the truck. I promise not to steal your food or anything."

They were standing in the empty bedroom with its muted sage-hued walls and well-worn dark wooden floor. There was a small closet and one window.

"This was my dad's... er, *our* dad's room," Evan explained. "But he's gonna be up shipping freight in Alaska for a while, so it's yours now. You said you had your own furniture, obviously, so I cleared it out yesterday. Bathroom's in the hall. There's only the one. I don't really have the place packed full of stuff, so you can put your things anywhere in the house that makes sense and, yeah...." Evan stuffed his hands in his pockets and let the sentence hang between them, unfinished.

"Okay." Brennan nodded. "You have to get to school or work or anything? 'Cause I think I'm good. The room is perfect. I think I'm just gonna dive right into unpacking."

"Nah, I told my boss I'd be out today."

"Oh. Cool. Where do you work?"

Evan ran his hand back through his short hair, a dirty-blond color, darker than Brennan's since he didn't dye it or spend enough time in the sun for it to lighten naturally. Most of Evan's time was spent in darker, shadowy places. After hesitation, he admitted, "There's a garage down the street. Mike's. I work there. Mechanic, or grease monkey. Whichever you prefer. You said you were headed to school?"

Brennan bit at his lip, pacing across the space and back, restless. "Yeah, that was the plan. Is the plan. But I just can't really get my head around it yet. There's been so much going on, changing. I mean, I didn't apply anywhere because I was taking care of Mom full-time for a while after they said it was terminal and then she... well. So I never contacted any schools. But I have savings. Inheritance. So I can handle my share of the rent. Don't worry about that."

"Rent? You don't need to pay any rent." Evan scoffed, offended.

"No, I do. I'm already barging into your home, the least I can do is compensate you."

"Save the money for college. Charlie has this place mostly paid for anyway." Evan cleared his throat and folded his arms over his chest. He knew there were things he needed to say, no matter how uncomfortable it was to voice them. He owed Brennan explanations for some of his choices, especially given their family's history of making shitty choices. The last thing Evan wanted was to start things off by being a disappointment. "Look, I'm sorry I didn't make it to the funeral. It was just, I didn't even know I *had* a mom until, like, two months ago and with the cost of flying out there, and —"

"Don't worry about it," Brennan said seriously. "You don't need to apologize. I mean, it's not like we asked for any of this."

Evan softened a little at that. "I hear ya. Hey, can I ask you something? Feel free to tell me to shut up and mind my own business, but why didn't you have anywhere else to go? It's not like I'm the most attractive option here as far as living arrangements."

Brennan smiled, but it was sad and strained. "Let's see.... Our house was rented. We sold our real house a while back and moved closer to the cancer treatment center. Then she died and the lease was up, and there weren't really any other choices. Mom was an only child. Grandmom and Grandpop are in one of those senior living communities with strict rules about who lives there. It'd be weird to move in with one of Mom's friends. I could've gotten my own place, but I wanted to get out of there. Make a fresh start. It felt like the right thing to do, coming here. And I don't really do well alone. I didn't really want to, you know, be alone right now."

His jaw clenched and he tossed his hair back off his forehead with a flick of his head, looking annoyed with himself as his eyes filled with tears. Evan felt like he should hug him or something, and he might have actually done it if not for the fact that they'd just met each other. So, instead, he just stood there awkwardly.

"That makes total sense," Evan blurted to fill up the subsequent prolonged silence. "Hey, let's get your stuff in here and then we should probably try to get to know each other, since clearly our parents were lacking with the information distribution."

Brennan smiled again, and with true happiness. "Yeah," he agreed. "That sounds great."

They headed outside and Evan watched as Brennan took a deep breath of the fresh air. They unlocked the back of the rental truck and opened it up. The inside was packed with boxes and, behind those, some furniture. Brennan grabbed a stack of two boxes and paused, turning to Evan beside him, who was also grabbing boxes.

"Listen, I should've probably told you this sooner, but before we begin unloading this, you should know, just in case—"

"What?"

"I'm gay. I mean, I'm out. Mom knew. Everyone at school knew. Is it going to be an issue?"

Evan just stared at him, expressionless. Disguising his instinctive reaction as best he could, he licked over his bottom lip and shook his head, pulling the two small boxes held clutched in his hands all the way out of the truck. As he headed back to the house, he said over his shoulder, "Nope. No problem."

"You sure?" Brennan called.

"Yep!"

Brennan added under his breath, "'Cause you kind of look like the type of guys back at school that would really get off on making me feel like shit about it, but maybe I'm wrong. I hope so."

He crossed paths with Evan on the middle of the lawn. "But I don't have a boyfriend or anything," Brennan assured him. "And I don't hook up a lot, so I won't be bringing anybody home either."

"Look, don't sweat it. It's cool," Evan told him, breathing heavier as he hefted a huge box.

Brennan dropped his boxes inside and waited while Evan set down the large box in a corner. "How about you? Girlfriend?"

"Nope," Evan sighed, brushing off his hands and heading back outside as Brennan trailed behind a step or two, watching him. "I'm not a relationship guy."

They got to the truck and Evan saw Brennan was still staring expectantly at him, so he elaborated with, "But I don't care if you bring someone home. I mean, I don't bring people home, but that's just a personal preference, and I guess a holdover from having Charlie breathing down my neck. But if you want to, go ahead."

"So it's the backseat and dark alleys for you?"

Evan chuckled. "Real romantic, huh?"

"Yeah," Brennan grinned, laughing with him.

"You a virgin?" Evan asked, not really knowing why. It was like spontaneous verbal diarrhea. He waited a half-second before glancing up at Brennan as he took hold of another box. Brennan's mouth was twisted up in a half-smile.

"No. You?"

"No," Evan said, thinking to himself, *Well not technically, but he doesn't need to know that. I kind of got it in her even though I was barely half-hard. It counts.*

It took a few hours to get everything out of the truck and the furniture in place in Brennan's room. Most of the larger things wound up staying in the bedroom: a four-poster antique bed, a wardrobe and a chaise. An overstuffed chair and ottoman was placed out in the living room. Evan couldn't wait to try it out, it looked so comfortable. The quality of Brennan's possessions was slightly amazing to Evan, as someone who was used to roughing it and making do. It made him curious to see what was hiding in the many boxes still to be unpacked, if there were any valuable treasures or mysteries. He was unpacking a stack of plush towels when he saw a small, very low table, which Brennan lifted from the box and tucked away in a corner of the room.

"What's that?"

"Hmm? Oh, my meditation altar."

"Meditation altar?" Evan squinted with confusion.

"Yeah. I meditate and do yoga every morning. It shouldn't affect you, though. I'll keep my door closed when I do it and I don't play music or chant or anything weird like that."

"Eh, you don't need to hide. Do it wherever you want to. Doesn't matter to me."

Brennan blushed, smirking. "Well, I usually do it naked, so...."

Evan turned and looked blankly at him. "Why?"

"I don't know, it feels better? I was taking a class for a while but when we moved I just started doing it on my own at home." He shrugged.

"Yeah, keep the door closed, then."

Brennan laughed. "Okay. How about you? Any weird habits I should know about?"

"Um," he thought it over. "Well, I smoke, but usually not in the house. And drink. And I keep a gun under my bed for protection. Sometimes when I go out I carry it on me, just in case. Dad taught me to shoot when I was really young. During hunting season we'll always have fresh meat. You're not a vegetarian or something, are you?"

"Sorry," Brennan squinted.

"Seriously?" Evan groaned.

"Yeah. But I'm not militant about it."

"Jesus Christ. So you're a gay vegetarian with nice clothes and nice furniture who does naked yoga and shit."

"And you're an über-macho tough guy that smokes, drinks, loves guns and kills his own food."

"Yeah, that about sums it up," Evan sighed, nodding. "We really have nothing in common, do we?"

"Well we both have blue eyes and freckles," Brennan pointed out.

"There is that," Evan agreed. "We'll have to work on this whole 'identical' thing."

Brennan smiled. "I really do appreciate everything, Evan. Thank you."

"Ah, stop it. You're my brother. Family should take care of each other." Seeing the touched expression on Brennan's face, Evan quickly held up a hand, "But don't even think about hugging me again."

# Chapter 2
# Jailbait

It had been hours since Evan left the house. His brand spanking new brother was unpacking even more boxes and Evan's skin had been starting to itch with restless energy. He needed to get out and blow off some steam. Sure, he had work bright and early in only a matter of hours, but after such a momentous day, he decided he deserved a break.

Brennan seemed like a great guy, someone Evan could soon grow to love as he should have long, long ago. It was a weird thing to be a stranger to your own flesh and blood. The resemblance was too eerie, too dead on. But it was more than that. Yes, it was disturbing to be faced with someone that looked just like you, talked just like you with the exception being the slightest hint of a southern accent. What was more disturbing was being slapped across the face with the realization that your brother, completely unknown until very recently, was almost painfully beautiful.

It had hit Evan in different ways throughout the day: in a smile, a glance, in the soft sweeping curl of Brennan's golden eyelashes, in his dimples when he tried not to laugh, in his nervous tics and the calm wisdom in his fiercely intelligent eyes. Of course, it didn't really help either that Evan was almost drowning in the common teenage affliction of low self-esteem. But Evan's particular type of low self-esteem sprung from the more severe afflictions of self-hatred and depression. It taxed the mind to loathe and become awestruck at almost the very same thing.

So he searched out a bar a few towns over, in urban, more densely populated Mitchellsburg; a bar he'd never been to before.

After an hour or so of drinking without being carded (though he always carried a good fake I.D. anyway), he hung out by the pool tables, watching a particularly heated game between a pair of elderly bikers. Leaning against the wooden paneling on the walls, he nursed his beer. The small stash of cigarettes he'd brought had run out hours ago, and he wanted another one badly. He had dressed for comfort and labor, in old jeans worn too-thin in spots, a snug-fitting plain white shirt and, over that, one of his work shirts with the logo for Mike's on the pocket. The bar was hot, so he took off the work shirt, tucking one end of it haphazardly in his back pocket.

It took a while for him to realize he was being watched by Tall, Dark and Handsome over by the bar—a burly guy who was ripped, cute as sin and way too old for him. Perfect. Evan caught the guy's eye once and didn't look away, just raised his bottle to his lips and sipped, letting the cool, rounded glass rest against his plump lower lip. He knew what he was doing, and at the same time he had absolutely no idea what he was doing. Calm and collected, he slid a hand down into his jeans' left front pocket, nudging the bulge of his crotch through the fabric.

Tall, Dark and Handsome got up from his seat at the bar, took one last, long drink of his poison and walked swiftly to the back of the room. Evan watched him go, not moving a muscle until the older man turned his head, looking squarely at Evan over his shoulder, no mistaking intent, and pushed into the men's bathroom. The door swung shut behind him.

"Okay. Okay," Evan murmured, setting down his beer and sparing the briefest glance around. No one was watching him. He made a beeline for the bathroom and went inside.

There was someone at the urinal and the dark-haired, god-like, broad-shouldered guy from the bar was washing his hands at the sink. Evan hesitated, then went to the sinks, too. After another pause, he turned on the tap and rinsed his hands. The man at the urinal finished and went back out into the bar. As soon as the door swung shut, Tall, Dark and Handsome moved.

He straightened, wiped his hands with a paper towel before tossing it in the bin and looked right at Evan, stepping closer, closer, and closer. Jaw clenched, Evan let the guy back him up to the tile wall between the sinks and the door. The guy's hand came up. He rolled the pad of his broad thumb over Evan's full lower lip. His chest was rising and falling noticeably with quickened breath, his hazel eyes dark and hungry. Evan sighed soundlessly at the touch, his eyes starting to close. Before they did, he caught a brief glimpse of the guy's arm reaching out to lock the door, keeping anyone else from coming in. It made Evan's stomach flip. This was really going to happen, he realized nervously.

There was a murmured greeting of, "Hey." A big hand cupped under his jaw, and another hooked over the ridge of his hipbone, the thumb brushing up under the fabric of Evan's shirt and skimming over the bare skin of his abdomen, touching him like this guy had every right to touch him wherever and however he wanted. There was no hesitation at all.

"Hey," Evan replied, his breath catching when the hand on his hip rotated, dragging down to brazenly palm his groin. Suddenly, the hand grabbed hold of him, firmly, squeezing around the hard line of Evan's dick through his jeans and not letting go. Hips canting forward, Evan felt the guy tracing him, measuring him, and rubbing a little. Evan's heart pounded in his chest, so loud he was sure the guy must have heard it.

Closing his eyes more tightly, Evan parted his lips when he was kissed, tasting alcohol on the guy's tongue, letting him push his way into Evan's mouth. The hand on his jaw slid back to cradle behind his head as his mouth was plundered roughly. His bottom lip was sucked on and the guy moaned a little. Evan didn't realize his pants had been unzipped until there were fingers pushing down inside the front of his briefs, seeking then pulling out his dick.

His head fell back against the tile with a swallowed, apprehensive groan. His eyes shot open with his surprise, finding passionate, determined, hazel ones staring down at him. Shifting his stance wider, he didn't protest as his pants were pushed down past his hips, down almost to mid-thigh, along with his underwear. It was intense. The guy stared down at Evan's cock, cradled in his hand. Slowly, he started stroking Evan hard.

"So fucking sexy," the guy growled, unzipping himself too. It made it a little easier to be standing there, fondled by a stranger with his pants down when he wasn't the only one with his cock out. Evan expected to get jerked off, maybe kissed some more, maybe sucked, but then the guy pinned their hips together and palmed Evan's ass with both hands. Their mouths crashed together again, soft lips on lips, sucking and biting. Evan thrust, his cock sliding alongside the thick, long length of his companion. The friction was unbelievable, and he moaned softly. He thrust again, building a rhythm.

The guy was still staring at him. His large hands squeezed the muscle of Evan's ass cheeks. Then, they pulled him open.

Evan became still, his eyes widening slightly. The guy grew even more watchful, inches away, not kissing him for a moment as he dragged the middle finger of his right hand down Evan's ass crack.

Too startled to speak, Evan muttered, "Um...."

The fingertip rubbed lightly over the pucker of his asshole, and circled gently around the rim. He tried not to clench up, but he was honestly afraid of being breached, so it was pretty impossible not to. The finger traced around and around the wrinkled spot. Then it settled right over his hole, pressing lightly.

"Um...."

He thrust again, despite himself. It was stuttered and followed a moment later by yet another needy push.

The guy said to Evan, "Use your hand. Go on. Don't be shy."

Evan did it only because he had to. His dick was so hard it felt like it was going to explode if he didn't get some relief, so he tried to fit both his cock and the other guy's in his right hand, tugging them simultaneously.

"*Mmm*, yeah, just like that," the guy sighed. His finger wriggled at Evan's hole, teasing it open and Evan's lips parted around a soft gasp. Evan hung his head to hide his reaction. But the guy caught on and he teased a little harder, parting Evan's pucker, pushing hard enough to begin to fit his fingertip inside the ring of muscle. Evan whimpered.

"So, Jailbait, you're eighteen, right?"

Evan glanced up, eyes blazing, trying to regain control. He sealed his lips and quirked his eyebrows in a non-committal response. It was enough to give the guy pause. The determination on his gorgeous, chiseled face mixed with trepidation.

"Yeah. Don't sweat it," Evan answered finally. "I'm legal."

"You sure?" The finger jabbed at him, breaching him dry and popping through his rim.

Evan cried out softly, his lower lip quivering slightly. He bowed his head again and, with his hand, pumped faster at the pair of cocks trapped in his grip. The guy, clearly savoring his revenge after the scare Evan just gave him, fingered him possessively, rubbing around inside his rim and keeping the tip of his finger wedged inside the clenched ring of muscle. He dipped his head to catch Evan's mouth, sucking soft kisses to his lips and swallowing Evan's small gasps.

"You're tight like a virgin. You a virgin, Jailbait?"

"No."

The finger pushed just a little bit deeper, then tugged out completely. Evan whimpered again, frowning heavily. The tip of the guy's tongue trailed up through the divot in Evan's lower lip.

"Mm, I like that, those sweet little sounds you're making. And that was only my fingertip. I think you're lying about that cherry being popped."

Suddenly, the guy was going down on his knees. He rolled a condom onto Evan and opened his mouth, rubbing the underside of the head of Evan's cock over the flat of his tongue before sealing his lips around it, just behind the ridge, and sucking it back into his mouth. It might have been the hottest thing Evan had ever seen, this Adonis who could have had anyone he wanted blowing him like *he* was the lucky one, like Tall, Dark and Handsome was grateful just to get the chance.

Evan gritted his teeth and closed his eyes tightly. The guy took him deep, giving him the most suction Evan had ever felt, coupled with wickedly talented tongue movements, curling, wrapping, wriggling, and licking. The finger fit back onto his hole. Evan bit his lip to stay quiet as it forced its way back up into his ass to the first knuckle before tugging oh-so-slowly back out. He was fucked like that, shallowly, out and in, with slow then fast pumps of the finger, twice as fast as the sucks to his cock.

"God, I'm... I'm gonna...." The rest was lost in a deep moan. He chanced a look down at what was happening to him.

Hazel eyes flicked up at him, knowing and devious. Evan's

cock was instantly deep-throated. The finger in his asshole thrust in harder than ever, burrowing all-at-once much too deep. Evan's hips thrust desperately forward.

Evan choked out a startled, broken sound and came in a flood, spilling hot into the condom.

The stranger pulled off with a slurp. "Can I fuck you?"

Evan forced his brain to work, every nerve exploding and his knees weak. He was deeply unsettled by how far up his ass the finger still was. It felt really weird. He felt intensely vulnerable. He clenched up but all the good that did was get the finger moving, fucking him in slow, smooth thrusts as he kept coming down.

Putting some iron in his voice with effort, Evan said, "Whoa, um. Easy there, tiger. Maybe another time, okay?"

"That's a damn shame," he tsked. "But you're cute as fuck when you're cocky."

Tall, Dark and Handsome stood and freed the damned finger. Evan couldn't look him in the eye, so he took his cue from body language. The guy took a half-step back, put another condom on himself, then circled the base of his own dick with a hand. He laid a hand on Evan's shoulder and pushed him down. Evan went to his knees and opened his mouth willingly. Bracing a hand on the guy's hip, he moaned softly when the thick cock was thrust between his lips. Holding Evan's head between both hands, the guy rode Evan's mouth, pushing in as far as he wanted. Evan fought not to gag, failing only twice, but at least the guy gave him a second to recover before resuming his thrusts. Taking every push, saliva running down his chin, eyes and nose watering, he did his best, using every trick he knew. Mostly he was nervous, but he palmed himself when he realized how much he was getting off on the rough treatment and the feel of a cock sliding on his tongue. He didn't even really notice the way the guy's fingers carded gently through Evan's short hair, or the deep, guttural moans Tall, Dark and Handsome was helplessly making, shattering some of his cool façade.

Evan glanced up, his eyes big and innocent. He suckled just the head of the thick, steely member as the guy feverishly pumped the shaft with a hand, hissing and straining, his cock flushed a dark red as he came.

Somehow, Evan stood, wiping his lips, tucking himself away. He zipped up and found his way to the sink. Splashing water over his bruised, swollen lips, swishing some around his mouth to wash away the taste of latex before spitting it back out, he watched the mirror.

"I'm Alek. You got a name? Maybe a phone number?"

It was asked with sincere hopefulness, and even a hint of self-consciousness like Alek was putting himself out there in a way he didn't do often or ever. It made Evan pause. There was a note of possessiveness there too, though, in the way Alek was looking at Evan, which decided him.

Evan grabbed a paper towel and dried his face.

With an apologetic expression, he backed up a few steps to the door and unlocked it. "Sorry. This was fun though."

He left quickly, wanting to get away before Alek could come after him. He jogged through the bar and out to his car. Gunning the engine of his Chevy, he tore out of the gravel lot, kicking up rocks behind him as he went.

It wasn't until he was shifting into park in the driveway of his house that he realized his work shirt, the one with the logo for Mike's Garage on it, was no longer tucked in his back pocket.

# Chapter 3
# Allure of the Illicit

Alek felt empty. But it was the best kind of empty, because he knew what was missing. He knew what his missing piece was, where it was, and how to get it. He felt somewhat blank, too, like someone shook up his life like it was an Etch-a-Sketch toy. Everything that mattered before he came into the bar's bathroom, hoping the hot young guy would follow, was gone, cleared away to make room for something completely new, something he couldn't make out the shape of just yet.

Clearing his throat, Alek excused himself politely, apologetically, as a barrel-chested biker with a pronounced scowl pushed impatiently past him into the previously locked bathroom. Alek headed back to the kitchen, his heart still beating too fast, wholly unaware of anything but the thing held wadded up in a ball in his left hand, and, maybe, the ghostly touch of sinfully luscious lips and nervously skittering fingers moving over his body.

Alek could still feel him, whatever his name was, and the heavy weight of the gorgeous cock that was so recently riding his tongue. And, more than that, he could still feel the wet soft heat of that pretty mouth willingly taking every fevered rut as Alek chased the best orgasm he'd had in almost a year.

As soon as he was through the kitchen's swinging door, he sighed and leaned back against the nearest counter.

From his right, a soft female voice purred, "Well, well."

Katie Cooper, Alek's friend and co-worker, sidled up to him.

"You dirty old man."

Alek complained, "I'm twenty-five!"

"But in *comparison*. I can't believe you. You *actually* screwed him in the bathroom, didn't you?" She folded her arms under her breasts and glared at him like she was his mother or something.

"No," Alek frowned with lame defensiveness. "Not really. It was just, you know, oral. And some other stuff on the side."

"He's a person, sweetie, not a menu item."

Alek made a frustrated grunt and flapped his arms in defeat. "Hell, Katie, he's so fucking pretty. You saw him too, I mean, come on. How could I not go for that?"

"You could have asked him on a date instead of treating him like a fuck toy."

"But he's the best fuck toy *ever*."

"Alek," she called when he started to space out, his lips sore and slightly kiss-bitten, his hair tousled, not combed carefully back like it usually was. "Earth to Alek."

"He has the softest lips," he murmured. "And his *eyes*. God, I just want to lick his eyelashes."

"Alek?"

"What?"

"What's in your hand?" She gestured to the balled-up dark blue fabric held in his closed fist.

He hid it behind his back. "Nothing."

She tilted her head and cocked out her hip. "Really?"

Alek straightened up and put on his 'stern' face. "I'm heading out. See you tomorrow."

"You on kitchen duty or security detail?"

"Kitchen," he said, standing half outside the back door. Mosquitoes zipped around his head in dizzy circles.

"Cool. See ya then. Don't do anything stupid."

He rolled his eyes and waved goodbye. The door slammed shut.

Evan tiredly shuffled into the house with just enough sense left to know to try to be quiet. He'd started to fall out of practice with slipping inside late at night without being detected, not that Charlie ever went out of his way to give Evan a hard time about breaking rules. To get to his room, he had to walk past Brennan's room first. The door to Brennan's bedroom was mostly shut. Instead of going right by, tiptoeing around the squeaky boards, Evan pushed it open a few inches. Inside, he saw Brennan sprawled on his stomach across the big four poster bed wearing only a dark pair of low-slung boxer briefs. Instinct told Evan to indulge in enjoying the fascinatingly taboo sight of a near-naked body — whether it was a relative or not — overriding any moral responsibility to give Brennan his privacy. Evan tried to force himself to stop staring at the set of dimples denting Brennan's lower back.

*I wanna lick those. Or maybe just fit my thumbs right in there to hold him and just —*

He broke the thought off right there. The dimples were right above the tight swell of what might have been the most perfect ass Evan had ever seen.

*Stop looking you perv, it's your brother. He's your goddamned brother, and worse, he's your twin brother. What the fuck's wrong with you?*

But it was just looking after all. He wasn't hurting anyone by lingering and making sure Brennan was all right, or so he told himself. For some reason it hit Evan how incredibly young Brennan seemed with his face soft and peaceful with sleep. It made Evan wonder if that was how people saw him, too.

The word 'Jailbait' rang in his head, affecting him in a plethora of different ways. *That's not who I am,* Evan thought. Or maybe he was just in denial. Most of the people in his life had no idea he was gay and he intended it to stay that way. But he couldn't help but enjoy the way it made butterflies knock around in his stomach, remembering how it felt to have Alek call him Jailbait and treat him like someone unspeakably desirable. That wasn't the first time he had let someone fuck around with him just because it seemed like fun at the time. It *was* the first time he really enjoyed it, though.

He went into the bathroom and grabbed his toothbrush. After brushing his teeth, cheeks and tongue long enough for some of the lingering guilt to wash away, and trickle down the drain, he got in the shower and began scrubbing his body clean.

Limbs heavy, head foggy, he fell into bed and was out like a light.

The next morning he woke early, thanks to the shrill tone coming from his alarm clock. In the kitchen he found the pantry, countertop and fridge all laden with food, which would have been purely good news except most of the food was fruit and vegetables.

"Oh, you've gotta be kidding me," he groaned, scanning Brennan's purchases.

The door to Brennan's room was firmly closed. Evan stared at it for a second, wondering what could possibly be going on behind it, until he forced the thought away. Ignoring the tiny voice at the back of his mind that told him to go over there and maybe put his ear to the door, Evan headed out the back of the house.

The walk to work was a quick one, but on the way he called his neighbor, good friend and beer supplier, Jimmy Bennett.

"Hey, I know it's early. Can I swing by later? After work?"

"Sure. Everything okay with the new arrival?"

"Yeah," Evan said shortly. "So you'll be home? Around four?"

"I'll be here."

"Cool. Thanks, Jimmy."

"Sure thing. Later, Ev."

They hung up and Evan set his sights on the garage just ahead, thinking of coffee and the attractive distractions of manual labor.

In a mobile home only a half-mile away, Jimmy Bennett gazed out of the small, curtained window over his sink and tried not to overanalyze Evan's brief call. He couldn't help but feel responsible for the kid—who was more than a few years younger than him—especially with Charlie gone again. A deeply pious man at heart, Jimmy sent up a little prayer.

"Please God, watch over him. He needs You. Help open Brennan's eyes to who Evan really is and help open Evan's heart to receiving such a gift as a brother in his life. I believe they can be a blessing for each other, Lord. As long as they don't keep their heads buried in the sand," Jimmy sighed. "In Your Name I pray. Amen."

His thoughts went there again, to that field of tall grass, four years in the past. It seemed like it was just yesterday. There was sunshine, with a light breeze making the supple blades wave and dance. It was such a beautiful day. All he wanted was a walk to ease his mind and to listen for God's voice in his heart. Jimmy listened, all right, and the warm, bright day was turned black and cold in a matter of moments, finding what he did cradled on God's living canvas, nestled in the green-gold grass.

"Oh, Evan." Jimmy rubbed his eyes and went to fill the coffee pot.

As usual, Alek's late night was followed by a late morning. He rolled out of bed around eleven, got dressed and headed downstairs with the work shirt discarded by the sexy, beautiful teenager from the bar's bathroom crumpled in his hand. His first stop was the kitchen. The house was quiet. Carter Raed, one of Alek's three housemates, no doubt was at work. Presley Owens, another housemate, was probably working too, being one to favor the early shift over the late one. Alek could hear the television in the front room, and that was probably Luka, Alek's twin brother, either passed out or watching ESPN.

After being in the same large circle of friends in high school as Presley and Carter, they'd migrated toward one another the older they got, growing closer after graduation, and agreeing to chip in on rent in order to gain their independence. It was all done without any of them coming out and saying it was because of their sexual orientations, even though that was the case. Even in such a crowded school as theirs, it was still rare to find guys who didn't self-identify as being straight, and who were open-minded enough to know when to look the other way, or live and let live. They never talked about it when they agreed to live together, and years later it was a conversation that had never quite happened. Alek and Luka never tried to hide who they were when at home, though. Presley and Carter's tolerance for the twins' lifestyle had, in turn, earned them respect and willingness to overlook some of the other strange things happening behind closed doors.

Noting the recently emptied coffee pot with only a few drops scorching the bottom of the glass, Alek sighed, "Thanks, Luka," and decided to hit a coffee shop on his way that morning.

He pulled the phonebook from the cabinet and looked up Mike's Garage. He knew it sounded familiar but when he saw the address listed, he instantly remembered the place—a beat-up but long-standing business in Whippoorwill, way out in farm country but a short enough drive from Mitchellsburg.

"Awesome," Alek grinned, teasing his bottom lip between his teeth.

Taking the shirt with him, he made for the front door. Passing through the living room, he saw his brother, but someone else, too. A petite brunette wearing only a t-shirt and panties was seated comfortably on Luka's lap. Luka's left hand was slipped down between her thighs. His right was wound around her in an embrace while Luka's thumb stroked idly against the under-swell of her breast through the thin cotton.

"Hey, Jackie," Alek sighed, half-smiling out of politeness. He was used to finding her around sometimes. She and Luka had broken up a year ago but there had been booty calls ever since. Luka was a big fan of casual sex with old flames.

"Hey, *Alek*," she drawled back with a wicked smirk.

*Wow, do I want to get out of here*, Alek thought. Jackie had never quite given up on trying to get both twins into bed with her, no matter how fervently Alek declined her advances. He had never been able to figure out if part of Jackie's appeal for Luka was her ability to annoy Alek so intensely. Alek couldn't tell Luka who he could and could not have sex with, though. He could only try to be there to steer his beloved brother toward the best, healthiest path available. Ensuring Luka's wellbeing always came first for Alek, no matter what, prioritized even over his own happiness.

His hand was actually resting on the doorknob when he heard in that eager, persistent tone, a voice that was tonally identical to his own, just slightly, constantly, more chipper, "What're you doin' up?"

"Need to go somewhere," Alek told Luka with a pointed look that basically said, 'Stop bothering me.' "Don't worry about it."

Which, of course, to Luka meant, 'Keep bothering me, please.'

"Go where?" Luka perked up with suspicion as he asked, intrigued by Alek's vagueness.

"I said don't worry about it."

Catching the heated look exchanged by the two men, Jackie decided to butt in, stroking Luka's chest. "You want some more coffee, babe? Babe?"

Luka ignored her and squinted suspiciously at Alek.

Alek held Luka's stare as he grabbed his keys and left without another word.

"Aleksy!" Luka bellowed as the screen door slammed. "Alek!"

"Let him go," Jackie said softly, soothingly. "What's the big deal? Just let him go."

"I know that look," Luka huffed. "He's up to something."

"You know what this looks like, don't you? It makes you look desperate. And pathetic."

Alek turned the worn fabric of the work shirt over and over in his hands as he sat in his truck, parked in the front lot of Mike's Garage. He could see people moving around inside, and someone that could have very well been the person he was looking for.

*Those lips, that haunted look in his blue eyes, the way he whimpered, like he was scared by how good it felt, the way he tasted, how goddamned tight he was....*

He'd always been prone to over-thinking and worrying. His brother, Luka, was often the focus of his preoccupation. There had always been an invisible, unbreakable tether between the twins, linking them in perpetuity. If Luka went one way, Alek was helpless but to follow. Every feeling or problem, joy or danger, shivered the line connecting them to each other. Information traveled both ways, but Alek could always sense Luka there with him, even when alone. It was both a comfort and a burden.

Usually, when Alek hooked up with someone, it meant nothing. There was no connection, no reason to go back or stick around. It wasn't because he was coldhearted; he was simply looking for something worth investing his emotions in. There was a lot of competition for his attention. He would feel Luka pulling him somewhere else, and, because in so many ways, Luka—who had endured so much already in his life—was the owner of Alek's heart, Alek would gladly go without a second thought. But that teenager—*he* was different. There was something there, Alek could feel it, the same kind of way he could feel Luka. Part of him was terrified of that feeling, and of the fact he was sitting in his truck, worrying about a nameless kid who owed him nothing. It was like the barb had already snagged inside him, hooking another one of those tethers to the core of his being. If he started to care about this guy, it was just more to scrutinize, to obsess over and open himself up to. Luka had always chided him on living too much in his head, on assuming responsibility he didn't need to carry. But sometimes, if you didn't bother to care, no one else would either.

Alek was out of the car before he realized it, smoothing down his hair which came almost to his chin, tucking it behind his ears and walking up to the garage. "You're just returning the shirt. Get your shit together. And stop talking to yourself like a crazy person."

Seeing a flash of vibrantly blue eyes, and the mouth-watering sight of full lips formed in a natural pout, Alek almost tripped over his own feet for a second before he did get his shit together and headed over to the young guy in the far corner of the garage.

"Can I help you?" A startled look was the only thing betraying the teenager's vibe of cool disinterest. When Alek got a little bit closer, only a foot or two away, the kid's voice got much quieter as he growled in that gravelly, fucked-out, sexy tone which Alek got to first enjoy the night before, "What're you doing here?"

"Just returning your shirt," Alek explained, unable to stop staring. He stood towering over the younger man and felt a rush of blood surge to his dick because... *Jesus*. It wasn't just that he was hot; it was the air about him of seeming wholly untouched and unspoiled. The lure of possibly getting to seduce again someone who hadn't already seen and done it all was too powerful to resist.

Someone called from the front office, "Evan, you okay over there, buddy?"

The kid—Evan—replied, raising his voice, "Yeah! I got this one!"

Alek handed over the shirt. Evan took it, blushing. The sight of that blush made Alek's mouth water, wanting to lick every inch of the rapidly heating skin. He shoved a hand into his front pocket to help conceal his growing hard-on. When Evan's eyes went right there at the gesture, and fixed on Alek's crotch for a beat, Alek's lips twisted up in a small, victorious smile.

"That's your name, huh? *Evan*. I like it."

Evan frowned, nervously scratching the nape of his neck. "Look, I can't do this here. You have to leave."

Alek searched for an excuse to pull sweet, pretty, fuckable Evan aside. "My truck's been acting up, won't start on the first try. Maybe you could look at it for me? I'd really appreciate it, *Evan*."

"Fuck," Evan groaned under his breath. There were a couple of men watching them curiously from the office. "Yeah, c'mon."

He led the way, hot-footing it out of the garage with Alek on his heels. Alek jogged to catch up and pointed to his black truck.

"'Kay. Um. Open her up," Evan muttered, tucking the shirt in his back pocket like he'd done the previous night.

Alek repressed a smile, reached into the truck and popped the hood. There was nothing wrong with the truck, and he suspected Evan knew it.

Evan planted his hands on the frame and leaned over the engine. "Start 'er up for me."

"Why?" Alek asked with a glimmer in his eye.

Evan flushed a darker pink under countless faded freckles — each one of which Alek wanted to trace with the tip of his tongue — and hissed, "Because my boss is watching."

Chuckling, Alek sat behind the wheel and turned the key. The engine came to life right away. Getting back out of the vehicle, he went around to where Evan was hunched over, his toned arms flexed. Alek's gaze slipped down the gentle curve of Evan's back leading from strong, broad shoulders to where his spine dipped to his narrow, tapered waist and hips. He was all muscle, put on from hard work, not the gym, and he was gleaming with a slight sheen of sweat.

"Damn, I bet you look fantastic naked," Alek rasped, leaning against the truck.

Evan pretended to ignore the comment, but Alek was pretty

sure Evan was hunched over the engine for more than one reason. He glanced down at the bulge in Evan's jeans and fought not to just start humping his ass right there like a dog in heat. "What are you doing here?"

"I want to see you again. Soon."

Evan bit his lower lip. He wouldn't look up at Alek's face; wariness taking over, like Evan was suddenly in wildly unfamiliar territory. He leaned farther over, fiddling with things in the truck as they talked.

Finally, Evan sighed, "How soon?"

"When's your lunch break?"

Evan hesitated, so Alek pushed on, lowering his voice and letting all of his growing, dark, simmering lust seep into every word. "C'mon, Jailbait. I just wanna suck you... *everywhere*... and then, you know, we could go get coffee or a couple of steaks or something."

"I'm pretty sure the fucking comes *after* dinner on dates usually," Evan retorted, swallowing thickly and shooting a sideways glance back to the building.

"Not when you're this hot," Alek grinned, predatory and determined as a shark surging in for the kill. "Look, I'm not the kind of guy that messes around like this. I swear. Last night it was right after my shift and when I saw you, I had to go for it. But I'm here now because I want more than one night with you. I want to get to know you."

"No, you don't. You're just sticking around until I put out, then you'll be gone."

"Try me. You got a *last* name, Evan? And how about that phone number?"

Evan cursed under his breath and straightened. Alek got out of the way and Evan slammed the hood shut.

"Okay, first off, you can't come to my work like this. Ever."

"Okay," Alek nodded. "I get it. You're trying to pass. I still want to see you later."

Evan's eyes slipped shut. Alek got the feeling like maybe if they weren't being watched, or if he had parked around the corner instead of out front, it would be a whole different story—that Evan would open for him like a flower and the tough-guy act would disappear.

"Goddamn you're persistent. Fine. You know Cedar Mill Road? Out on Route 73? Follow it until the asphalt turns to gravel. I'll meet you there. Five o'clock."

Alek smiled, his deep dimples perfectly framing his mouth.

Evan cleared his throat, "I've gotta get back to work but, um, you got a last name, Alek?"

"Popović." When Evan cocked an eyebrow at him, Alek explained, "It's Russian. You?"

Evan threw him a sly, sexy twist of a grin and turned back toward the garage, letting Alek stare at his ass as he walked away. "Savage."

"Evan *Savage*. How appropriate, since I'm pretty sure you're gonna be the death of me."

Evan laughed, "Dude. That was *so* cheesy." His jeans, loose and low, hung on the top swell of his ass. The muscle there shifted with every step and Alek was too hypnotized by the sight to think of a comeback. His retort turned into a low moan. He checked his watch once Evan was gone from sight, counting the hours until five.

# Chapter 4

# Restless and Hopeless

Brennan got through his morning routine just fine. He meditated for a full hour, trying to release some of the torrent of emotion and tension inside him. The weird blend of excitement and fear caused by the drastic shifts the course his life had taken left him feeling restless and un-tethered. He did yoga too, but it wasn't enough. After making a smoothie out of an assortment of vegetables and fruit, using the blender he brought from home since Evan didn't appear to have any sort of useful kitchen appliances, Brennan strolled through the small house, getting a feel for the place.

There were a couple of messages on his phone when he woke up—from Tommy and Charlie. He hadn't wanted to listen to either of them. Tommy, his ex, was the past. It was over, and Brennan appreciated that Tommy still cared enough to check on him, but he couldn't go backward anymore. He needed to move on. And Charlie....

Brennan sighed, thinking of his biological father, the mastermind behind the current state of affairs. Charlie had orchestrated the move, wanting to bring his sons together at last. He had asked Brennan to move in with Evan, offering Brennan the chance to finally get to know his twin and have a place to live at the same time without having to worry about Charlie being there to butt in very often. It was a tempting offer, and one Brennan couldn't refuse. The opportunity to get to know Evan seemed priceless, but Brennan still resented the hell out of Charlie. Charlie was a stranger. He was the guy who never bothered to visit or call for Brennan's entire life. His meager attempts at kindness were too little, too late.

Sometimes the sheer, sudden absence of responsibility Brennan now enjoyed raised his spirits. The possibilities seemed endless after having assumed the role of caretaker at such a young age. Now he was free of all of that, but what was he left with? Not much, it seemed. The pain drew him down. His heart ached with such loss and grief that it more than overwhelmed him most of the time. All Brennan wanted was to see his mom once more, and it was never going to happen. She was really gone. He told himself she was in a better place, that she wasn't in pain anymore—no more chemo, no more doctors or hospice. She was free. But he was only eighteen after all, and being on his own, *really* on his own, was a reality so suffocating, Brennan didn't know how to claw his way out.

The bedroom was tempting. He could just go back in there and keep on crying and feeling sorry for himself. It would be so easy. Instead, he wandered into Evan's room and sat on the bed.

The room was sparse. Besides some battered concert posters and postcards tacked to the wall, there wasn't much in the way of decoration. A few framed four by six photos lined the one shelf—pictures of Evan as a child, hunting with his dad. Or, rather, *their* dad.

Brennan lay down with his head on the pillow, curling up and trying to imagine growing up there, how it would have changed who he was to be raised by a father rather than a mother. It was too hard to manage. He couldn't make the mental leap. He'd never had a father, so he couldn't begin to imagine what it would have been like. Then, he realized, not for the first time, that Evan never even got to meet their mother, and ached for Evan; he never got to know her, the angel of Brennan's life.

A tear slipped down his cheek and he angrily wiped it away. Staring at one of the faded, glossy photos of father and son, Brennan asked the empty room, "Why'd you do it? How could you do this to us? We should have been a *family* instead of torn in half."

Before he got to Whippoorwill, he thought it was no question that he'd had the rougher deal, having to nurse Maggie on her deathbed, but after seeing Evan, Brennan realized maybe it wasn't true. Alone in this dark, empty house, with such shadowy emptiness hiding behind his eyes, Evan struck Brennan as a wounded soul from the moment they were face-to-face at last. And Evan seemed like a stranger. Expecting something from the meeting—recognition, revelation—there had been nothing, only fascination and a sad sense that there was going to be very little the twins would have in common with each other. Evan was a man's man—tough, strong and fearless. Brennan felt like none of those things. He felt only left behind, shattered and terrified.

Maybe he should have called Tommy back. Maybe he should have listened to Charlie's message.

He didn't do either.

Restless energy and cabin fever were the only things he could identify in the churning of his thoughts. So, he grabbed his laptop and looked up the nearest yoga studio. The closest one was a few towns away. He didn't have a car, so he decided to borrow Evan's and fill up the gas tank in the old Chevy as payment for the loan. Yoga clothes in hand, not bothering to check a mirror before he went, knowing he'd see only his sunken, baggy eyes and bitterness, Brennan headed out into the sunshine all too aware of the storm cloud following along over him.

Presley and Luka leaned casually against the end machine in a long line of ellipticals on the ground floor of Sweat gym. It was mid-day. Presley's shift was winding down while Luka's was just getting started. It was a slow time of day—right between the lunch rush and the after-work surge.

"What the *hell* were you doing to that poor woman last night, man?" Presley asked. "I had half a mind to come up there and save her or something with all the hollering goin' on. I mean, *damn*."

Luka rolled his eyes and he couldn't help but grin.

Presley *tsk*ed at him.

"It was just Jackie. She was in the neighborhood. You know."

"'The neighborhood' my ass. You two might as well be dating again with how much time she spends in your bed." Presley folded his muscular arms over his broad chest, watching a man a few feet away struggle with a loaded leg-press.

"Oh," Luka chuckled. "I see. *You're* gonna start lecturing *me* on spending too much time in bed with people I'm not dating? That's just not ironic at *all*."

Luka's expression lost its amusement as he pondered Jackie. His levity drained steadily away until all that remained was an unhappy pout. "No. Last night was it. I'm done. Shit with her is getting *way* too complicated. She's starting to think there's a chance for us. Hell, I apologized to her this morning, you know. Told her I was a jackass for using her like I did, when there was no way it could ever work between us."

"Yeah. Then you kicked her ass out. Didn'cha?"

"Whatever."

Presley *tsk*ed again.

"Stop that," Luka scowled.

"*Boundaries*, Luka. Say it with me. *Boundaries*. You gotta set rules and then not break them, no matter how horny you are."

"Easier said than done," Luka muttered quietly.

"No shit. You, of all people, have crossed some *major* fucking boundaries. Haven't you learned your lesson yet? There are some people you cannot fuck. Can-*not*."

"Prude. Just because our particular society currently frowns upon certain predilections doesn't change how people feel. And it doesn't make them bad people for feeling that way."

"Okay. Then how about, to start with, you pick a gender and stick to it. Women, men. I'm tellin' you, though, women are *not* worth the effort sometimes. No matter how good the pussy is. They start talking about commitment and *babies*."

Luka stared at him. Presley looked like he just sucked on a lemon. "You have something against propagation of the species?"

Presley turned to face Luka, lowered his brow and widened his stance. "I do when propagation is spelled D-E-N-I-A-L. Look, I'm not judging you. You know I love you like family. I just think you're a very confused person and, as your friend, I'm gonna just say one more thing. One."

He held up one long digit. Presley, with his flawlessly perfected, lean and toned body, captivating hazel eyes and skin like coffee without the cream, was not someone you ignored when he demanded your attention.

"What?" Luka blinked, leaning toward him a little.

Presley promptly smacked him upside the head. "Use your head."

"Ow!" Luka complained, rubbing the back of his skull. "Excuse me, I'm gonna go find someone less mean to hang out with."

He made a big, dramatic show of turning his nose up at Presley, still leaning there like a handsomely chiseled statue decorating the gym rather than a person working in it. Instead, Luka headed over to the hallway that ran by the enormous exercise room he was currently in, connecting the locker rooms to the pool entrance and yoga studios.

All of a sudden, someone went past, moving across the doorway from right to left—someone blond, model-gorgeous, slim and toned, wearing only a pair of form-fitting black yoga shorts which hid absolutely nothing.

Luka stopped in mid-step, gobsmacked.

"Did you *see that*?!" he hissed over his shoulder before literally bolting after the blond like a big, gangly, shameless oaf.

"Luka! *What* did I just say to you?!" Presley shouted after him. "Hopeless."

Luka caught up to the blond, getting a quick eyeful of honey-colored hair streaked with lighter bleached strands, longer at the top, shorter around his ears and in the back. But it was the guy's face that wiped all sense and intelligible thought from Luka's mind. Ridiculously defined cheekbones, cleft chin, strong jaw, lips so plump they almost didn't make rational sense, but really it was the eyes—a bright, startling blue and framed with long eyelashes, eyes that were almost feminine and delicate despite the very masculine body accompanying them—that sealed Luka's fate.

"Uh," Luka said stupidly in greeting. He realized he had grabbed the guy's arm and thought to himself, *I should let go.* But found he couldn't. His brain and body were not communicating well enough to accomplish that. "Hi."

"Hi." The blond tossed his hair back out of his eyes and smiled with those plump lips, and it was such a breathtaking sight that Luka actually whimpered a little. Audibly.

"Jeez, I'm sorry. What's the matter with me? I'm Luka. I work here, and damn. You've probably got a girlfriend and I'm probably an ass, but can I buy you a drink sometime?"

The blond chuckled; his smile got wider and more heartfelt. "You're cute."

A huge, dimpled grin of pure delight transformed Luka's face and he straightened, recovering in an instant thanks to the compliment. "I can work with cute."

"Brennan. I'm, um, I'm Brennan." He extended a hand and Luka shook it with both of his, amazed at how comfortable Brennan seemed in his own skin even with such insignificant clothing on. He radiated calm confidence.

"Very nice to meet you, Brennan. Don't take this the wrong way, but I mean, you probably just saw me run out here to catch you just to introduce myself, but it would just make my day. Hell, it'd make my *month* if you'd say yes to that drink. I swear I'm not a freak or desperate, but you are just... wow."

The reply was simply, "I don't drink. I'm eighteen." Luka's expression fell so drastically and so fast that Brennan quickly added, "But maybe coffee? Or dinner?"

"Wow. I'm an idiot. You do look young, but you don't *seem* young, if that makes any sense. So I thought... but, awesome! Yeah! Dinner. Thank you. What do you like? I know this great French place. Or Thai? Maybe, um, Moroccan, or just steaks. I mean, I can cook an awesome steak but you probably would rather go out somewhere."

Brennan pursed his lips in an indescribably hot expression, his lips framed with his own smaller dimples right at the corners. Luka actually leaned in slightly, and brazenly took a half-step farther into Brennan's personal space. He made himself comfortable there, standing almost intimately close. Luka's lips parted softly, and for a second Brennan gazed expectantly up at him, thinking perhaps Luka was going to kiss him, right there in the middle of the Sweat gym hallway, which reeked of chlorine and body odor.

There was a half a beat where Luka paused to take a breath and Brennan laid a hand lightly on Luka's defined chest, perfectly outlined by his skin-tight, black, sleeveless tank with the gym's logo on the front. "Why don't I just give you my number and we can work out all of the details later? I literally just moved here yesterday, so I'll follow your lead."

Luka's hands went immediately to his pocket-less pants. "No pen. Damn. Wait here one second. I just need to grab a pen and one second, okay? My memory is like a sieve or else...."

Brennan nodded, grinning as Luka ran down the hall, through the door and came back seconds later, not even out of breath, but a little more flushed for his efforts. He scrawled Brennan's number on his hand. "Are you sure you're eighteen?"

"Yeah, fairly sure," Brennan said, holding Luka's gaze as he inched steadily back into Brennan's space, not even completely realizing he was doing it.

"I really should get back to work and let you go. You'll be around later? If I try your number?"

They were barely inches apart. A chestnut-hued tendril fell forward and Brennan reached up, pushing it back behind the shell of Luka's ear. His hand lingered there, on the ridge of Luka's jawbone and he tilted his head back a little, his full lips supple and parted. Luka exhaled, surged forward and closed his lips around Brennan's.

"Mm," Luka hummed, tilting his head and catching even more of Brennan's lips on his second try. He forced himself to break contact, stepping back and clearing his throat.

"Later?" Brennan said, taking one more long look down and back up Luka's body, turning toward the smaller studio spaces in which the yoga classes were held.

Luka's gaze fell from mouth to shorts and everything they barely concealed. "Uh-huh."

Then the angelic specimen was gone. Brennan pushed through a door and stepped out of sight. Luka fell back against the wall and moaned, clutching his heart.

Presley appeared back by the doorway to the exercise room. "What did you do?"

"Died a little, I think."

Presley blinked at him. "That's... I don't know what to say to that. But, you know. Walk it off, son. You'll poke someone's eye out with that thing and there's ladies present. Ladies with mustaches and Adam's apples, but ladies all the same."

"Hmm?" Luka looked down at himself. "Oh."

Rolling his eyes, Presley left him there. Luka shuffled back to the locker room to do a lap or two to recover.

# Chapter 5
# Not so Harmless

Evan stood on the dusty ground in front of the steps leading up to Jimmy's door. The house was technically a mobile home, given foundation and rooted between a long, winding road leading back into the same open wilderness that was also beyond Evan's home, and acres of grassy fields. If you were facing away from town, there was nothing but earth and sky for as far as the eye could see. It was one of Evan's favorite places in the world, even more so than his own home. It was the only place where he could be himself and be completely honest about absolutely everything. Even the bad memories lent the spot a bittersweet, comfortable air.

He scuffed his toe over a patch of thin grass and cracked, dry earth. It looked so harmless, so much like every other patch of ground. But it wasn't.

The door opened behind him; he heard it creak on the hinges. Jimmy stood there, watching Evan take a step, centering himself directly over the patch.

Evan took a deep, steadying breath and released it back out with a sigh.

"I died here," he said with some awe.

"Just for a couple of minutes," Jimmy added softly. "I'm glad you can say that aloud now. That's a good sign. Kinda wish you didn't sound so happy about it though."

Evan shook his head. "It's just weird. Sometimes it feels like that was another life, like I came back as someone else."

"Maybe you did." Jimmy stepped aside and waved Evan over. "Come on in. You hungry?"

"Yeah," Evan smiled while brushing his dirty hands futilely over his grime-smeared arms. His second appointment of the evening came to mind. "And can I grab a shower too? Just, you know, while I'm here."

"Sure."

Once Evan had scrubbed off the engine grease and emerged from the bathroom both looking and smelling much cleaner, the two men sat down across from each other at Jimmy's table. There was a big plate loaded with salad and a sandwich set out for Evan, so he dove in.

"What's up? Why aren't you at home, eating with Brennan?"

Evan shrugged, taking a large bite of bread to avoid having to verbally answer.

"What's he like?"

"Hmm, well...." He thought about it for a long moment. "He's a twink. Bleached hair, dainty little glasses. The whole nine. One of the first things he told me was that he's gay. He asked if it was gonna be a *problem*." Evan huffed out a laugh and took another bite when the chuckle twisted and turned cold.

Jimmy sighed, his face a picture of concern. "I'm sorry."

Evan's brow furrowed and he bowed his head, chest heaving with emotion.

"Does he know?" But it only took one look at Evan's face to make the answer clear. Jimmy answered his own question, saying, "Of course not. Maybe you should tell him. He's going to find out anyway."

Defensively, Evan barked out, "Says who?"

"He's your twin brother, Evan. I understand having a sibling is a new concept for you, but Brennan will be able to read you, especially living together in such close quarters. It could help you two get closer."

"I don't want to be closer. I didn't ask for this. I opened my home to him because he had nowhere else to go, but it doesn't mean anything. He's a stranger."

"You don't think that he could *possibly* understand where you're coming from? Hmm?" Jimmy suggested, glaring at Evan.

"He's nothing like me," Evan spat. "He likes who he is. He's proud of it."

"Do you resent him? For being proud of himself? For getting to be with Maggie?" Evan set down the sandwich, shutting down, turning off. "He didn't ask for this either. He's just trying to survive and grieve, same as you."

"Whatever."

"Hey, if you wanna try again, I'm sure there are enough pills in the medicine cabinet to do the job. I won't interfere this time."

Evan sat back in the chair, hugging himself and scowling, gazing blankly out the window.

"Go on. What're you waiting for? You still wish I'd left you alone?"

Breathing shallowly, watching a flock of sparrows take flight over the swaying grass, Evan didn't answer right away. Then, reluctantly, he grunted, "Sometimes."

"Then why are you here? Why are you telling me all of this stuff about Brennan?" There was a pause as Evan answered Jimmy's questions silently, to himself, only. "Have you talked to Charlie?"

"No."

"You should. He loves you."

Evan scoffed. "Sure." Standing, grabbing the sandwich to finish off on the walk to Cedar Mill Road, Evan mumbled, "Thanks for the food and the shower. I've gotta go. Got a hot date."

Jimmy stood with him, walking Evan to the door. "Use protection."

Evan laughed, hastening down the steps and hurrying away. "Why bother?"

Jimmy grunted with frustration, his hands balling up into fists. "Evan!"

"'Bye, Jimmy."

Alek's truck rolled to a stop at Cedar Mill Road. His tires crunched over loose gravel, leaving the asphalt behind. Awaiting him on the edge of the woods, Evan was laid out on a blanket and gazing up at the fading daylight.

Reclined on his side, Evan sipped a beer, propped up on an elbow with a faraway look in his eyes as his thoughts went to places his body couldn't. Cutting the engine and hopping down from the truck, Alek headed right for Evan. Pulling his shirt off as he fell to his knees, Alek lowered himself down on top of Evan, who grinned slyly and set his beer down in the grass.

*At least he's not expecting a talk first,* Evan was glad to see.

He let Alek guide him onto his back and ran his fingers up into Alek's soft, dark brown hair. Growling with lust, Alek started kissing. He latched onto Evan's jaw, sucking bruises along it and down the column of his neck. He began grinding his pelvis down against Evan's, their stiffening cocks rubbing together through the coarse fabric. Evan pushed up into Alek's slow thrusts and let his head fall back to expose more of his neck. Reaching down, Evan popped the button on his fly to give Alek the hint.

*Just keep going. Get off and get gone. No questions, no explanations, just take what you want and go.*

It worked. Alek's lips left Evan's neck, the new trail of bruises nestled among smatterings of faint freckles. He tugged down Evan's fly, and pushed at his pants. They shimmied down over Evan's hips, taking his boxers with them, exposing a bare swath of skin, the cradle of his hips and the long, swelling length of his cock.

Heart pounding, running away with itself, Evan distracted his nerves by removing his own shirt. He hadn't wanted to have a big conversation before doing this, pretending they were going to be friends or more than friends, so he was glad Alek seemed to be of a similar mindset, but once they started, Evan was more than a little anxious about what Alek was expecting from him. Alek planted his knees between Evan's thighs, yanking Evan's pants the rest of the way off and nudging Evan's legs farther apart. When Alek brazenly grabbed him loosely by the balls and tugged, Evan fell back down flat on the blanket. Tilting his hips up into Alek's hand, he bit at his bottom lip. Alek hummed and reclaimed his place on top of Evan's body. He stayed propped up on his knees, braced on one hand, allowing room for his other hand to roam over Evan's skin.

"Is this okay?" Alek asked. The tension in Evan's face and body was unmistakable. Evan nodded, holding his tongue. "Been thinking about you all day—how incredible and sexy you are. I can't get you out of my mind. For hours I fantasized about all the ways I want to touch you. And God, when I saw you this morning, I wanted to bend your ass over that truck and fuck you right there."

Alek leaned in closer, taking a moment to inhale deeply through his nose. Lips skimming lightly along Evan's neck, Alek gently scraped his teeth over the skin. Evan grunted and twisted his hips reflexively as Alek gently rolled his balls in a closed palm and stroked around the base of Evan's shaft with a thumb. Alek's lips sealed over Evan's pulse point in a brief kiss. Anxiousness clawed at him for being so naked, in more ways than just the obvious one, but Evan pushed it down. He tried to remind himself he could handle it if things got out of control, that so far he was fine, just really nervous and self-conscious, but it was normal to feel that way.

"You smell fantastic. Thought you'd come right from work and be all sweaty and greasy, but you snuck in a shower, didn't you? Wish I'd been there to watch."

"Yeah, I was pretty filthy."

"So? I like the thought of you all dirty. But... mmm..." he sucked his way down to Evan's collarbone, then across his chest to the dark, peaked nub of his nipple, dragging the tip of his tongue over it. He flashed a mischievous grin, peering up at Evan's face. "This is good too."

Alek slowly stroked Evan's cock a few times. It was already full and heavy, straining up against his pale, taut belly. Letting it go, his hand moist with Evan's pre-come, Alek rubbed two of his fingers down underneath Evan's balls, over his perineum to the clenched pucker of his hole.

As soon as he touched there, though, Evan tried to close his legs. But he couldn't really close his legs, not with Alek's whole body positioned between them. Evan's thighs hugged Alek's sides and Alek gazed patiently at Evan's face, which was creasing with tiny frown lines at odds with his youth. Evan's eyes widened the more scared he became. Alek teased his fingers experimentally at the center of the wrinkled knot, and Evan gasped.

*Say something. Open your damn mouth.*

"Can we not... I mean, I'm not ready to, um...."

"Hey, it's all right," Alek told him, repositioning his hand, bringing it back to Evan's shaft and rubbing over it. "There's other stuff we can do, right?"

"Yeah," Evan sighed, relieved. "It's just, no offense, but I just met you."

"I'm not gonna pressure you, Evan. If you aren't ready, you aren't ready."

"I want to, you know. I do. But I'm just not. Yet."

Evan hoped he wasn't coming across as young and naive as he felt. He also tried to figure out the particular expression on Alek's face as his piercing hazel eyes darkened rapidly.

"What?"

"It's really hot that you're actually a virgin. I love that no one's had you yet. Means you're pristine, unspoiled. And, just so you know, I'm definitely willing to stick around whether you eventually decide to let me fuck you or not. It's a bonus, but it's not everything. What have you done? Besides, you know, what we did yesterday," Alek smirked.

Overly aware of Alek's hand which was currently wrapped tightly around Evan's shaft, Evan wriggled a little, feeling trapped, not wanting to say anything at all, to just get off and get out of there.

He wasn't sure why he answered honestly, but he did. Maybe it was the kindness etched in Alek's face, behind the predatory stare. Or maybe Evan just didn't care enough anymore to keep his secrets. "Not much. Handjobs, BJs."

"Have you ever been with a girl? I have, but I knew it wasn't what I wanted after I tried it."

"Yeah, me too," Evan agreed, some of the pressure taken off by Alek's commiseration. "I thought it'd be easier if I could just get interested in girls, but no dice."

"You are interested in fucking, though? Any preference between top and bottom? You wanna be the giver or the receiver? I'm flexible, so it'd be your call."

Evan licked his lips and closed his eyes. Alek released him, quickly unzipped his own pants and pulled out his dick. Evan peeked at it through his eyelashes. Alek smiled. Lying down flush atop Evan's leaner frame, propped on his elbows, Alek pinned their hips snugly together and thrust, squeezing their trapped dicks between them in a slow push-pull, building a gentle rhythm.

It felt really good so Evan sighed out a low moan and undulated, rocking up, counter to Alek's movements. He wrapped a hand behind Alek's neck and drew him down, shuddering and trying to buck up against Alek's massive, immaculate, tan and toned body bearing down on him. Alek's cock felt so thick, riding through the hollow of Evan's hip. There was no question what Evan wanted, what every fiber of his being was silently screaming out for. If there had ever been any doubt in Evan's mind about what his preference was when it came to sex, it was utterly gone as he focused on Alek's girth nudging at him, ready and eager.

"Bottom," Evan managed in a whisper. "Is that okay?"

Alek moaned, snapping his hips. "Okay? That's the best news I've heard all fuckin' day. There's nowhere in the entire world I want to be more than inside you. Trust me."

Evan grabbed onto Alek's waist, holding there, his fingers denting the skin as he pushed up desperately, needing more. Then, hesitating a little at first, his hands slid lower, cupping Alek's bare ass, feeling the thick, round muscle clench with each thrust.

"This is new for you, too. Isn't it?"

"Yeah." Evan chuckled shyly, trying so hard to swallow back the sounds bubbling up from low in his throat—embarrassing mewls and gasps. Pressure built, making it impossible not to thrust, grinding against Alek.

"God damn you're sweet," Alek moaned. "You close? 'Cause I am."

Evan nodded, palming Alek's ass, sucking a kiss to Alek's throat as he thrust hard, stiffening as his balls drew up tightly and he got ready to unload. Alek's fingers carded over Evan's body, scratching lightly, leaving more marks.

"*Fuck*," Evan keened, voice breaking, fingertips denting the smooth curve of Alek's ass. Alek ground down harder, in fast, shallow pulses. Their dicks were squeezed between them with all the weight of Alek's body, sliding side-by-side, rubbing together. Both of them were panting and sweating lightly.

Evan's lower lip quivered and, instantly, Alek leaned in to suck on it. The world whited out with a frantic last burst of rutting and Alek groaned loudly, spilling hot and messy over their abdomens as he came.

Moaning Alek's name, Evan wrapped a leg up around Alek's body and convulsed, his back curving, coming up off the ground as his spend mixed with Alek's. Soft, wet sounds filled the air as they kept rocking lazily against one another, coming down.

"That? I'm never gonna get enough of that," Alek panted, caressing Evan's throat. Evan was breathing hard and the world spun around them.

Long minutes passed. The sun sank lower in the sky — the blues shifting into purples and oranges in wide bands of color. Feeling sticky and embarrassed, Evan would have loved to be long gone and showering already, but he couldn't move. Moving would have meant letting Alek see him covered in semen, completely naked and with no possible way to hide. And also no way to clean up. He realized he should have thought this through a little more.

But Alek wasn't moving either. As soon as the thought flashed through Evan's mind, though, Alek rolled off to lie on his side instead. Evan wanted to melt and disappear into the ground underneath him.

Gazing up and down Evan's body, Alek asked, "So, Evan Savage. Eighteen years old. Working a hard-ass job. Hanging out in bars. Tell me something about yourself."

"Why?" Evan asked. "What difference does it make?"

"I'm asking. I'm interested." Alek's thumb skimmed through the hollow of Evan's jaw. "Just tell me something. Anything."

"Like what?"

"Like why are you so defensive?" Evan's brow creased in a deep frown and Alek said, "You want me to start? Okay. I work at that bar as a short-order cook and sometimes I do security on rowdier nights. Been there for a few years now. I live in Mitchellsburg with my brother and two roommates. Haven't had a relationship for years. I'm picky. I don't hook up with just anyone." He locked eyes with Evan, who was still half-scowling, half-pouting, but not turning away from the gentle strokes of Alek's thumb.

"Your turn."

Evan sighed, "Fine. It's been a bad week. I'm a little stressed. Someone... important to me... died. And now, I don't know. Things are complicated. I needed a distraction so I went to your bar and I guess I was looking to hook up. I wasn't really thinking about it."

"I'm sorry for your loss. You want to talk about it?" Alek said, looking worried.

"No," Evan replied instantly. "No, I really don't." He rolled his eyes with bashfulness. "And I've never been in a relationship. I know, really lame, right? But it's true. You were asking."

"How are you so damn sad for someone so young? Has life really been that hard for you?"

Evan's jaw clenched and he turned away.

"Talk to me," Alek urged.

"You don't even know me," Evan retorted.

"Hey, I'm trying to know you. I like you. Let me know how to help. What do you want?"

"I want to stop talking about this stuff and forget everything for a little while."

"I can help with that. Definitely."

"And I feel pretty gross right now, so a shower's kind of what I want most."

Alek smirked, his hand trailed down from Evan's face to his navel, stroking through their come smeared on his skin. "Why do you feel gross? Because of this? This isn't gross."

Evan didn't believe him at all. In what seemed to be reaction to Evan's disbelief, Alek scooted down lower on the blanket, settling back between Evan's thighs.

"What are you doing? Alek?" Evan asked, startled.

Throwing Evan a wicked smile, Alek quickly hooked both of Evan's legs over his shoulders and took Evan's spent cock between his lips, kissing around it and slowly taking it back into his mouth. He licked it clean, then sucked and swallowed it all down without any hesitation. When Alek let him slip free, he began to lick Evan's pelvis and belly clean, too.

By the time he was done, Evan's whole body was pebbled with goosebumps and he was hard again. Alek played with Evan's erection, chuckling at Evan's restless twitching and writhing. Slapping the head against the flat of his tongue, Alek waited until Evan was watching before he deep-throated him, taking him down his throat all the way to the root before swallowing and pulling off. Then he wriggled the pointed tip of his tongue at Evan's slit. Evan moaned loudly and dug his heels into Alek's back, thrusting impatiently up, wanting more. Alek complied, sucking him again and again with deep, slow pulls until Evan was shuddering, nearly ready to come for the second time already.

But then Alek slowed down and stopped altogether. Taking hold of Evan's legs, Alek pushed them back, curling both toward Evan's chest by holding them behind the knees. Evan cursed and grunted with tense, nervous frustration as he was folded into the new position until Alek licked a wide, wet stripe over Evan's balls. Evan gasped then gritted his teeth as Alek sucked on his sac as intensely as he just did Evan's shaft. It was about all Evan could take and he was about to jack himself off if Alek didn't get back with the program.

Then, throwing Evan off completely, Alek held Evan's legs in place, keeping him folded nearly in half, and licked deliberately, firmly, right over Evan's asshole.

A wild moan broke free from deep in Evan's chest. "Oh god, *Alek*! What're you...."

"Feel good?"

"*Yeah*, but—" The words broke apart as Alek did it again and again, then pressed gently with his pointed tongue. The ring of muscle began to open for him and Alek's tongue pressed harder to get inside.

"Oh Jesus," Evan moaned, palming himself, tugging against the swell of coiling pressure in his balls as Alek oh-so-slowly, breached him with the thick, wet, tapered muscle, forcing it through the clenched ring.

Humming with pleasure, letting the sound's vibration tickle up through Evan's body, sucking on Evan's rim as he tongue-fucked him very shallowly, Alek didn't look at all surprised when Evan's hand started to pump more furiously. He was about to come. Alek withdrew his tongue and kept licking, but inserted his middle finger in one smooth stroke, up to the hilt, right as Evan climaxed.

Utterly taken by surprise, Evan's orgasm was instantly magnified and he almost managed to escape Alek, flying a few inches up the blanket and shouting hoarsely. Hooking a hand around Evan's right thigh to keep him from getting away, gripping hard enough to bruise, Alek fingered him through the rest of his orgasm, twisting and rubbing against his inner walls.

"Good, that's it. 'S okay, I gotcha," Alek said softly.

Clawing at the blanket, Evan whimpered and sobbed a little, just coming and coming and *coming*, every nerve in his body sizzling, his whole being tuned in to the digit moving inside him.

He wasn't even starting to recover when Alek suddenly crawled up Evan's body. Alek left a trail of bites, light scratches and licks with the tip of his tongue from Evan's hips to his chin. Then he shifted farther up, so his knees were planted under Evan's arms, his lower legs gripping Evan's sides. Alek guided his straining, massive cock to Evan's mouth and Evan opened wide for it instantly. His lower lip must have been dry, because he felt it split. Ignoring the small pain, loving the way he could still feel the trails left all over his skin from Alek's fingernails and teeth, Evan slipped his tongue out to catch Alek. His hands took hold of Alek's hips. Alek set a quick pace, growling softly. He moved shallowly at first, but lost control a few times, going too deep and provoking small, plaintive whimpers from Evan.

Tingling, aching and exhausted, Evan was in a daze when, almost an hour later, they had finally gotten dressed again. Folded blanket tucked under an arm, Evan stood there while Alek said goodbye, needing to leave for a shift at work. He hooked a finger under Evan's chin and tucked the folded scrap of paper with Evan's phone number deeper into his front pocket. Kissing Evan, Alek licked over the tender, swollen split in Evan's lower lip. After their second orgasms, they'd kissed, groped, scratched and nipped at each other, making out and rolling around on the ground for a long time. It had been passionate, not gentle, so Evan's lip, as well as a few other places, felt sore.

"Sorry about that."

"'S'okay. Really," Evan murmured, feeling dizzy and sated.

"I won't get home until late tonight, but can I call you tomorrow?"

"Yeah," Evan nodded.

"Perfect. Take care of yourself. Maybe get some ice for your lip." Alek kissed him lightly again. "God, I miss you already."

Evan fought futilely against a rising blush and muttered, "Me too."

"Sure I can't give you a ride?"

"Nah, I'm good. It's a short walk."

Watching Alek carefully drive back down the narrow lane, Evan smiled despite himself. He turned to cut across the field, back toward home.

# Chapter 6
# Out in the Open

Evan had hoped Brennan would be in his room, or the kitchen, or pretty much anywhere but the front hallway when he got home. But, no. He was there. Right there in the foyer, no way to avoid him. Then Evan had a half-second to hope the light was dim enough, or maybe Brennan was distracted enough not to pay him much mind.

Evan wasn't that lucky. He saw his brother's eyes fix onto his mouth and groaned inwardly. Then Brennan actually stepped closer and seemed to take a deeper breath than necessary—like he was sniffing for something.

Deflating, ready to walk around Brennan and flat-out ignore the guy if he had to, Evan set his jaw and moved to the side. "Excuse me."

Brennan laid a hand flat on Evan's chest, standing right in his space, eye-to-eye.

Then, Brennan asked him, "Are you okay?"

Evan knew what he looked like, or had an inkling at least. The initial split of his lip had been an accident, but the blowjob he'd given Alek, and the prolonged, rough kissing after, during which Alek had kept biting Evan's swollen lower lip, probably had him looking like he'd been punched in the face. Add in scratch marks and love bites all over his body, cover it all in sweat, dirt and grass stains, and it didn't make a pretty picture. And he knew he smelled like sex, and semen. He was pretty much covered in a thin film of it from his chest to his thighs.

"Excuse me," Evan repeated, spreading his arms and looking directly down at the hand planted on his sternum.

"What happened?" Brennan's gaze skittered over Evan's face, like he was taking in every little detail.

"I was on a date. Now I'd like to shower, if you'd get the hell out of my way. Please."

"A date," Brennan repeated, sounding like he wasn't buying it one bit. "Wow. He must have been a real nice guy."

Evan snarled, "Shut up!" He drew an arm back to punch Brennan square in the mouth just as Brennan grabbed it, holding Evan back and pushing him into the closed door behind him.

"What's his name?" Brennan yelled. "Where is he? I'm gonna kick his fucking ass!"

Evan recoiled like he was slapped. "What?" he said softly, all the fight draining out of him and transferring right into Brennan.

"Where is he, Evan? Who did this to you?" Brennan's eyes blazed behind the lenses of his glasses, his perfect, straight, white teeth grinding together.

"It wasn't... I mean, he was... it was... What happened to my lip wasn't his fault. Nothing was forced. He apologized for getting a little rough."

Brennan scoffed and held up a finger. "Stay there. Or, no, I'll meet you in the bathroom. Gimme a sec."

He jogged down the hall toward the kitchen. Evan, moving in a haze, went to the house's only bathroom and stood in front of the mirror over the vanity, contemplating the idea of locking Brennan out. Both of his lips looked raw and bruised just like the spots on his neck, not to mention some small welts from scratches or the blood-red cut running up the center of his lower lip. His skin was smeared with sweat and dirt like he'd been wrestled down to the dirt and held there. No wonder Brennan had overreacted.

Brennan appeared over his shoulder, a double of his reflection only cleaner, better — purer. Evan watched the person he felt deep down he should have been gently press a thin towel wrapped around ice cubes to his lip.

Brennan looked him over, asking with heavy implication, "Are you injured anywhere else?" "No," Evan insisted. "I'm fine. Really."

"God, he didn't even use protection, did he? Maybe I should

take you to the hospital to get evaluated," Brennan said distract-edly.

"What? No. Listen, this isn't the first time that... I mean, I know the guy. So it got a little intense. So what? Relax, okay?"

Brennan sighed, pulling the towel away to inspect the wound. He took the bottle of hydrogen peroxide from the shelf and got a tissue to apply it with. Dabbing the cut gently with the liquid, then putting the ice back on, Brennan said quietly, "You need to use pro-tection, okay? I know everyone thinks it can't happen to them, and they won't catch anything but that's wrong and dangerous. It can and it does. People get sick all the time. They die and the people who care about them are the ones to suffer. And I mean, we're iden-tical twins, Evan. It has occurred to me that we might have this in common, and maybe you just didn't want to admit it. Most identi-cal twins have the same sexual orientation. You can trust me, you know. I wish you would have told me."

"Tell you what?"

Rolling his eyes, Brennan then raised an eyebrow at his brother. "Don't play dumb with me. I know you're not stupid."

"This is my personal life. It has nothing to do with you."

"I'm your brother, who also happens to be gay."

"Yeah, my brother since what? A few weeks ago? You have nothing to do with me or my life."

Brennan huffed, shaking his head. "You don't get it, do you? I'm not a distant relative. I'm not a step-brother or a half-brother. I'm your *identical twin*. That means we were once the same person, until we split in two. We're the same, Evan. I mean, I don't understand why you don't need glasses like I do, but clearly, other than that we have more in common than we thought."

Evan pushed Brennan's hand away and stepped back, his gaze locked on his feet. "I used to need glasses," he murmured. Brennan seemed confused by that but Evan pressed on, "Look, can I take a shower in peace? I mean, thanks for the..." he gestured at the ice, which Brennan handed over.

"No problem. Are you sure you're okay?"

"Yeah. It was actually a pretty good day."

"All right then. You want some dinner? I made eggplant parmesan. There's leftovers."

Doubtful, Evan scrunched up his nose. Brennan chuckled, "It's good. I swear."

"Yeah, you said you were one of those vegetarians or something, right? I saw some of the weird shit you got from the food store."

"Well, I'm pescatarian, actually."

"Excuse me?"

"Never mind. Yes or no to the food?"

"Sure. I guess it won't kill me."

Shaking his head, Brennan left the bathroom. Even more bewildered than before, Evan peeled off his dirty clothes and cranked up the hot water in the tub.

Alek got home fairly early that night. Katie thought she smelled gas in a back room off of the kitchen so they closed up until the threat of a gas leak could be ruled out. It was just shy of eleven thirty when he kicked off his boots and shrugged out of his button down shirt, leaving him in a tank top, jeans and not much else. He headed through the kitchen in search of a beer when he crossed paths with Carter.

"Heads up, your boy's in a good mood," Carter rasped conspiratorially, taking a plate laden with reheated steak to the table where Presley was sitting, focused intently on his phone.

Alek ignored the warning, understanding everything it implied, and opened the fridge. "Little late for supper."

"Yeah, well, it's gonna be a late night. Jamie's pickin' me up in ten for practice," Carter explained. He sawed away at the slab of beef, glancing up when Luka bounded into the room.

In a pair of loose shorts and bare-chested, Luka tackled Alek from the side, jumping on his back and trying to steal his beer.

"Getcher own," Alek complained, holding it out of his reach. "Pest."

"Oh, I'm a pest, am I?" The hand Luka had hooked over Alek's shoulder in a half-hug slipped lower, his thumb dragging deliberately over Alek's nipple. It was discreet, and the others didn't seem to notice. Alek did though.

Under his breath, Alek asked, "What are you doing?"

"Me? Nothin'." Luka chuckled darkly. Pulling his hand away from his brother's nipple, Luka squeezed Alek's shoulder instead. But before Luka finished backing away and detached his chest from Alek's back, he caught Alek's earlobe between his teeth and tugged.

It sent a pleasant shiver racing down Alek's spine, and he shook Luka off.

"Why the good mood, then?"

"He met someone," Carter offered, stabbing a chunk of steak and popping it into his mouth. "He won't shut up about it. Has a date with a pescatarian. Pres had to look it up for him, so he could book a reservation at the appropriate restaurant."

Luka wagged a finger at him. "You're making fun of me. Unless you want Icy Hot in your underpants again, I suggest you be nice."

"Ooh, I'm scared," Carter said in a sing-song tone, pretending to shake in his seat.

"Dude, I don't think he's kidding," Presley muttered under his breath, adding even lower, "And the last time he did that, you were hollerin' like a little girl."

"Did I ask you, smart ass? Did I?" Carter shut up, though, stuffing his mouth full of steak.

Alek sat on the beat-up old couch in the space adjoining the eating area. Sipping his beer, when Luka flopped down beside him, Alek threw an arm around Luka's shoulders and let his legs fall open comfortably.

For a few minutes they just sat there, side-by-side, relaxed and happy. Carter ate; Presley clicked away at the tiny buttons on his phone and crickets chirped outside. Then, Luka's hand shifted from where it had been curled up in his lap, crossing over to Alek. He rubbed up Alek's thigh and palmed the bulge of his brother's crotch briefly before sliding the hand under the waistband of Alek's pants.

Alek exhaled loudly and his head fell back against the couch cushions, his eyes closing. Luka wrapped his fingers around Alek's shaft, making a tight circle with his thumb and index finger. He squeezed up to the ridge, holding there as he licked his lips, avidly watching the effect he was having on Alek. Alek hissed a little, his flesh still slightly raw and tender from his earlier escapades with Evan.

"Girl or guy?" Alek grunted in question. Luka's fingers went to work, seeking out Alek's trigger spots. Alek loved the particular way Luka's thumb dragged over the head of his cock. Luka knew Alek's body at least as well as he did, after all. It was his body, too. No one had ever touched Alek the way Luka touched him. Each time, it felt like Luka had been studying the best ways to make him feel good for twenty-five years. Tilting his hips, Alek pushed against Luka's hand but he wasn't hard yet. Soreness was making it more of a challenge than it would be otherwise. But he appreciated the effort Luka was making.

"Guy," Luka grinned. "Hell of a guy. I think I'm in love."

"How sweet," Alek cooed sarcastically. He grabbed Luka's face, hooking a hand around his brother's jaw, fingers sliding back into his long hair, and chased after his mouth. Their kiss was rough right from the start, with teeth biting at lips and tongues twisting together, pushing hungrily into each other's mouths. Alek tilted his head to get farther inside, ignoring the rattling clink of silverware against china as Carter dropped his fork.

Once the four of them began living together, it quickly became clear to Carter and Presley what the nature of Alek and Luka's relationship was, but they also knew how it began. Drugs played a part, and what started as fooling around, kissing and groping each other for shock value at rowdy parties, was pushed far over the line with one incident of non-consensual sex. An older man with sicker tastes than they'd thought coaxed them in a moment of extreme intoxication and it changed the nature of Alek and Luka's closeness forever. Things got worse before they got better. They had each struggled with guilt and remorse, and they still did. But, thanks to the support of devoted friends Carter and Presley, the brothers worked to get sober and began to strive to protect each other rather than use danger as a way to soothe old hurts. And, somewhere along the way, the shock value started to wear off. It had been a long time since Luka or Alek bothered to hide what used to stay behind closed doors.

Alek heard Presley clear his throat and spied him over Luka's shoulder as he averted his eyes, or pretended to anyway. Carter stared for a long minute before shoveling another piece of food into his mouth and lowering his gaze to his plate.

Luka kept diligently fingering Alek's dick but it was futile so Alek pulled Luka's hand out of his pants and grabbed him instead. He quickly discovered how hard Luka was and finally figured out what was going on. His little brother was all wound up over his date with a severe case of blue balls.

Breaking the kiss with a growl, Alek pushed Luka down sideways on the couch and twisted his own body around to face him. Without ceremony, he yanked down the front of Luka's pants. His cock sprung free. Alek grabbed it by the base and lowered his mouth down onto Luka.

Luka moaned with exaggerated relief, palming the back of Alek's head as it bobbed in his lap.

At the table, Presley was dumbstruck, gawking at his roommates without shame. A piece of steak fell from Carter's lips as he gaped. Alek watched them both with amusement from the corner of his eye. It said a lot, in Alek's opinion, that neither Carter nor Presley left the room or exclaimed protests. He never asked for their approval and those moments of public displays of intimacy were the brothers' way of challenging their roommates, daring them to voice their outrage if they truly felt any at all. Plus, it was their home. If Presley and Carter didn't want them there, they would have said so years ago.

Though society marked twin incest as taboo, literature and mythology were littered with it, from the Bible to modern day television shows. There had been studies done on genetic sexual attraction, and how people tended to rank faces similar to their own as more attractive or trustworthy. They preferred mates with similar interests and traits to their own. All of these factors, compounded with the mysterious closeness that was always there between twins, naturally opened doors the world liked to pretend were tightly shut.

"Damn," Presley cursed, standing to get a better view. His chair almost toppled over as it got shoved back.

"Sit down," Carter hissed at him.

"Nuh-uh," Presley mumbled, raising his phone, probably intending to record the action for posterity.

Carter did a double take before trying to grab the thing from Presley's hand. "Gimme that. What's the matter with you? Don't encourage them."

It didn't take long for Luka to come. He was really wound up and, thanks to experience—as well as his familiarity with Luka's body, a mirror of his own—Alek knew just how to finish him off quick and easy. Just the right amount of suction and speed, pressure by rubbing his tongue just so, and he pushed all of Luka's buttons.

Luka's brow and nose scrunched up. His mouth fell open and he bucked up into Alek's mouth, crying out in a building crescendo. He made a choked-off, hard grunt, thrusting one last time before becoming instantly boneless on the couch, letting go of Alek's head and just lying there as Alek sucked him soft.

Pulling off with a wet, obscene slurp, Alek wiped his chin. He noticed Luka's peaceful, sated expression and, seeing his work was done, Alek helpfully tucked him back into his pants. Sparing his other roommates a brief, disinterested glance, Alek grabbed his beer and moved to stand. As Alek leveraged himself off the seat and straightened, Luka's left hand swung around, directing a firm, stinging slap to the thickest part of Alek's ass.

"Good job!" Luka praised Alek deliriously, slurring a little.

"Yep," Alek agreed, bowing slightly to his captive audience, finishing his drink and swishing the beer around his mouth to wash down the remnants of Luka's come. The empty bottle was tossed into the bin as Alek shuffled tiredly through the door toward the stairs.

Presley, still standing dumbly by the table, watched Alek until he was gone from sight. Then his gaze slid right back to Luka. Carter snorted, chuckling, "Good job," shaking his head and taking a last bite of food.

Right at that moment, Jamie knocked twice on the back door. Without waiting for an answer, he pushed the door open and stuck his head in. "Hey, Raed, you 'bout ready to go? Wanna get there by midnight. Raed?" He looked around, saw Luka sprawled on the couch and called happily, "Oh, hey, Luka."

"'Sup, Jamie," Luka mumbled with the same loud, dazed enthusiasm, raising an arm and throwing him a peace sign without looking up or moving a muscle.

"Presley. How's it goin?" Jamie said, saluting the statuesque black man standing for no apparent reason with a horrified yet enchanted expression. "Raed. Hey, Raed!"

"Huh?" Carter muttered finally, gradually returning to his senses.

"Let's go!" Jamie shouted. "Grab your guitar. Move it!"

"Sure," Carter grunted, scooping up his plate and high-tailing it out of there before any more weird shit could happen.

When they were gone, and it was just Presley and Luka, Presley said sternly to his friend, "I am truly ashamed of you, man." His voice wavered slightly.

"Oh, me too," Luka agreed, flapping a hand at him. "Totally. I feel really, um," he yawned. "Really guilty about that." He bowed his back to stretch out a kink in it and rubbed a hand down over his shorts, adjusting himself through the material. "That was... *mm*... terrible. From now on, *pfft*! Just say no to awesome, random blowjobs." His hand sliced through the air, definitively. "Done." After a moment, he added, "You get any of that on the phone?"

"Yeah. Don't tell Carter," Presley murmured, tucking it into his pocket and walking away.

"Cool. Send it to me," Luka shouted after him, settling into the cushions and giving in to the pull of sleep.

# Chapter 7
# Wake Up Call

Evan poked at the bizarre looking but fantastic smelling food on his plate and tried to become invisible through the sheer force of will.

It didn't work. Brennan was still standing there, mostly naked, wearing only a ridiculously tiny pair of shorts that were probably what he exercised and did yoga in when he wasn't doing it bucknaked.

*And please, God, let me not imagine that,* Evan prayed.

Brennan was leaning back with his hands braced on the countertop's edge beside his slim hips. One foot was propped against the cabinet under the sink, and he was watching Evan like he was a newly discovered, exotic species or something. Evan just hoped Brennan wasn't expecting to bond over their shared love of cock since, hey, it appeared they had that in common, too.

"If you have something you need to do or whatever, don't let me keep you," Evan muttered, taking a bite.

"What could I possibly have to do?" Brennan asked with a smirk.

"Watch TV? Put some damn clothes on? I don't know."

"How is it?" Brennan asked, nodding at Evan's plate.

Evan grunted. "Edible. Kinda wish you'd stop staring at me, though."

Evan tried to keep his eyes trained on his plate, because each time his gaze drifted upward it caught right on the fine dusting of golden peach fuzz covering Brennan's bare right hipbone and the shallow dip just inside the protrusion and a sick part of Evan, some facet of his libido he didn't know was so incredibly perverted, really couldn't stop wanting to lick *right there* and feel that soft, fine hair against his lips.

*It's your brother. He's your goddamned brother, Evan. Stop it. Now.*

Trouble was, brother was just a word to Evan, not a reality or a feeling. It was a label. It meant next to nothing without any history there to back it up.

Brennan said softly, "How long have you known?"

"That I'm queer? A long time. But I'd appreciate it if you didn't tell anyone. Ever."

"Why? It's nothing to be ashamed of."

"Oh, here we go," Evan groaned, dropping his fork and rubbing both hands over his face.

It seemed like because he was trying so hard not to think of Brennan in sexual ways, his brain was providing filthy thoughts and fantasies much more readily. It was similar to how, if someone told you not to think of an elephant, an elephant was the first thing you thought of.

The dirtier his thoughts got, the more clipped and angry his tone became. Unable to make sense of his reactions, his feelings or what the hell was going on with him, Evan hid behind his fingers and thought, *Bet he has more of that peach fuzz trailing down his ass crack. Bet if he turned around, you could see some of it, catching the light right between those fucking dimples and leading down under those tight little black shorts and what would he taste like if I licked there, just buried my face between his butt cheeks and just —*

He cut off the thread of the thought cleanly and said, "Spare me the pep talk, please."

Evan realized he had lost his appetite—for food, anyway.

"Okay. No problem. Change of subject, then. Why don't you wear glasses anymore? Do you have contacts? I didn't see them on your eyes, but—"

"*No*, okay?" Evan replied too abruptly, too defensively. "I don't have contacts. I had laser eye surgery when I was fourteen."

"Wow. Really? You just don't seem like the type to—"

Evan cut him off. "I don't want to talk about it. I really don't. It's a long story. But hey, when you meet Jimmy, feel free to ask him. I'm sure he'll tell you anyway sooner or later, whether I like it or not."

He stood and brought his plate to the sink. "Thanks for the food. I'm going to bed."

For a few seconds they were very close to each other, since Brennan was leaning by the sink and Evan reached past him to drop his dishes there. Evan's nose filled with the warm, clean, fresh scent of Brennan's skin and he ground his teeth together, hating himself for liking it. But the downward twist of the corners of Brennan's lips and his hunched posture conveyed crystal-clearly Evan had said something wrong, or maybe had just been too cold and too damn mean. Guilt softened him, so he asked, "You need anything before I go? I don't know if I'll see you in the morning, since, you know, I leave early when you're probably, um.... Anyway. Did you make out all right today?"

"Yeah. Fine. I went to a gym. Kept me busy."

"Good. Well, 'night then."

"'Night," Brennan murmured.

Brennan stared up at the light hanging from the ceiling as Evan's footsteps padded softly away toward his room. Biting his tongue, Brennan fought hard against the tears that were always there now. Not getting along with Evan at all was just too disappointing and painful a reality when Brennan had been hoping so desperately for a kind, welcoming presence in his new life. There was so much Maggie couldn't understand about what Brennan went through in his adolescence, things Brennan's friends and boyfriends couldn't relate to either—being an only child of divorced parents, being gay and living every day with that profound feeling of wanting more of things he may never have, not ever. Everything that made Brennan feel like a freak were the same things he had in common with Evan, and he didn't understand why Evan couldn't see that too. Everything that made Brennan hopeful he'd found a kindred spirit at last after searching for one for the entire span of his life, were the things Evan ran from, unwilling to face them let alone talk about them or confide in Brennan. Together now, it was possible they could begin to make those feelings of being abandoned lessen with each other's companionship. Brennan could have someone to talk to about losing Maggie, of the struggle to grow up without a large support system to rely on, and learning to depend on one's self to survive. But Evan wouldn't talk. Evan wouldn't let him in.

Brennan missed his mom so profoundly, it was often suffocating. The dad he never knew was somewhere far away, trying to help somehow despite the distance. The brother he'd been so excited to meet was a sullen, closed-off, repressed jerk. Knowing he was just going to go hide in his room some more, but not quite ready to give in to such a childish reaction just yet, Brennan hand-washed Evan's dishes and tried to stay positive. The thing standing out the most to him was Luka—how nice and funny he was at the gym, not to mention sexy, gorgeous, tall and distracting in all the best ways.

*Maybe*, Brennan thought, *being around Evan makes me feel weak and pathetic just because of how gruff and strong Evan is on the surface. On the inside, though, I'm guessing it's a whole different story.*

Determined to learn more, Brennan gathered his strength and tried to overcome the temptations of self-pity. He would do anything to get closer to Evan, to become part of his life in any way Evan would permit. Maybe expecting to feel like brothers was too much to hope for. Even if Brennan had to settle for something else, he would take it in an instant, if only he could figure out a way to get Evan to let him in.

The next morning, Evan got dressed and grabbed a quick breakfast consisting of a few handfuls of dry cereal and a can of soda, hoping the little bit of caffeine would wake him enough to get his ass to work. On his way out, he passed by Brennan's room. The first instinct was to block out any sounds coming from within, picturing acrobatic, naked bending and twisting, probably accompanied by grunting and other things he didn't want to encounter. But his feet stopped outside the bedroom door anyway. The regret for his harshness the night before when Brennan had been so kind to him plagued Evan still. When he heard nothing but silence from beyond the closed door, Evan took another step closer.

There was a sound after all—the soft hitching of the last remnants of gut-deep sobs. Not thinking, just acting, Evan raised his fist and knocked twice.

"Hey. Bren? You okay?"

Muffled, he heard a groan and a choked, "Perfect." Then louder, "I'm fine, Evan. Go to work." And softer again, "Leave me alone."

Evan tried the knob. It turned and he tentatively pushed the door open a few inches.

Brennan was curled up in bed with the curtains drawn, the room in shadows. He was under a bed sheet that was pulled up to his waist. Clutched in one hand was a small framed picture depicting a smiling, blonde-haired woman. It lay there limply, facing up toward the ceiling. Brennan wasn't looking at it. He wasn't looking at anything.

Brennan's expression shifted from impassivity to anxiousness and he whined, his voice thin and raspy, "Just leave me alone. I don't want you seeing me like this. So pathetic."

"It might help to talk about it," Evan offered, stepping into the room, hands in his pockets.

"Not with you. You don't care. Nobody cares. *Nobody remembers her* but me." He took a stuttering breath and held it.

The words hit Evan like a punch to the gut. Stricken, he said quietly, "I wish I did, you know. Don't you think I wish I remembered her? She was my mom, and I never got to hug her, or see the look on her face as she recognized me..." *or see if she would have been proud of me.* "She's just a picture in a frame to me. She's a name. You are *so lucky*, Brennan, to have gotten to be with her for *so long*. Don't you know that? That's a blessing. You have all of these memories I wish I had and she didn't... she didn't even *know me*. I'm her son too, and she didn't know anything about me."

Then Evan was crying, too, and he felt like his heart was ripping into shreds. He turned away and covered his mouth with a hand, wondering why he said all of that, and why it bothered him so much to hear those things said aloud.

Suddenly, he was being pulled around again and Brennan was hugging him. The side of his face pressed against Brennan's soft, tear-damp cheek. Arms wrapped around him, a perfect fit, and

Brennan rubbed his brother's back.

"She knew you. She loved you," Brennan whispered. "She told me that, before she died. How sorry she was for doing this to us, and you. You should've had a mom. It was cruel to take that away from you."

Evan moaned softly, grabbing on to Brennan tightly. The only thing separating them was the ache in Evan's heart. But it was a good ache. It was real and powerful and when Evan nuzzled against Brennan's neck and let out a small sob, Brennan didn't let go. In fact, he held on tighter.

"I'm sorry," Evan gasped. "I'm sorry for being such a dick to you. I just thought you were this guy I had to put up with."

"I know. It's okay."

"No, it's not. What you must be going through right now, and the way I've been acting... It's selfish and shitty." He breathed hot against Brennan's neck, then tilted his face up and pressed his lips to Brennan's cheek with eyes squeezed shut. His breathing settled down and the well of tears dried up. His hand was wrapped around the back of Brennan's head, tangled through the strands of his blond, slightly longer hair.

*Let go. Let go of him now, Evan.*

He couldn't though. He needed the contact too much and he knew once they broke apart it might be too difficult to find this again. It would hurt to give it up and relinquish the comfort.

The darkness in Evan recognized this and decided for him, choosing pain.

He let go. He stepped back and cleared his throat. The hole in Evan's heart ripped back open. It made him stronger, feeling it there, festering.

"It's the worst in the morning," Brennan admitted, oblivious to Evan's inner battle. "I wake up here in this place, this room, and for a second I forget. For a second I don't remember where I am or that she's really gone and then it all hits me all over again like the first time."

"Will you tell me about her? Later tonight after I get back?"

Brennan smiled and it was such a beautiful sight that Evan felt dizzy from how much he loved Brennan already. "I'd like that. Yeah.

It's a plan."

Making a difficult decision, suddenly, Evan grabbed a pad of paper on the desk and scribbled down a rough map. Then he handed it to Brennan.

"Here. This is the way to Jimmy's place. It's a short walk. He's an old friend of the family and, well, I guess he's my best friend, and he knows all about you. He'd love to meet you. Just, you know, if you're bored."

Brennan nodded, biting his lip. "Thanks. Yeah, maybe I'll go say hi."

Evan turned and headed to the door, stopping on the threshold. Without looking back he added, "And if you see him, tell Jimmy I said it was okay to tell you. He'll know what it means."

Brennan frowned, opening his mouth to ask something, but Evan left before he could. The house's front screen door slapped shut and quiet settled once more.

The alarm's buzzer was shrill and, when it went off, Luka jumped like he was zapped with electricity.

"What the fuckin'..." He grunted, pushing up off the bed without letting go of Alek. He cracked open an eye and complained, "Eight forty-five! It's still the middle of the night! Why is your alarm going off in the middle of the night?!"

Alek sighed, slapping the button to quiet the buzzing. Groggy, he reached for his wallet and phone and glanced first at the sunshine streaming in through his windows, then over his shoulder at the man-child attached to his back like a parasite.

"Here's a better question. Why are you in my bed?" It was purely rhetorical, as Alek knew exactly why Luka was in his bed. It was the same reason Luka slept beside him their entire childhood and adolescence, even though they had separate beds. Luka hardly ever used his. He simply craved comfort and the touch of someone who loved him unconditionally, and he was only ever going to find that with Alek. So Luka held on to Alek, literally and figuratively. When your own mother couldn't stand the sight of you, it affected you on a deep level. Alek knew it was no excuse for the things he'd done, and especially the things he'd done to Luka, but it was the start of it all.

"I was lonely," Luka pouted, covering his head with a pillow and burrowing in under Alek's shoulder.

"Oh Christ."

"And you're all warm and snuggly."

"How old are you again?"

"Five minutes younger than you," Luka retorted, but it was heavily muffled.

Alek forced himself the rest of the way awake, woke up his phone, too, and dialed the number from memory, even though it was the first time he'd ever called it. Before he hit send, he warned, "Swear to me that you will not say a *word* while I make this call. You owe me. I'll install more locks on my doors if you screw this up for me."

Luka gasped, offended. "You wouldn't!"

"Shh!"

"Fine. I'm goin' back to sleep." He turned over onto his stomach and yanked the covers up over his head.

A few seconds later, the phone started to ring. It was picked up on the third one.

A low, hushed voice said with audible confusion, "Alek?"

"Yeah. Good morning." Alek grinned, just from the sound of Evan's voice.

"I thought you were gonna call later. I just got to work."

"I know. This is just good morning. What's your favorite thing to eat for breakfast?"

There was a pause. "Why?"

"Don't over-think it, just answer."

"Coffee and donuts I guess, but I already had some cereal and—"

"Cereal?" Alek *tsk*ed. "Oh, a friend's band is playing at my bar tomorrow night. I wanted to ask if you'd go with me. It'll be a blast. They're really good. Food and drinks are on me."

"I don't know," Evan said, hesitating, but Alek heard the smile in his voice.

"Please," Alek beseeched. "It'll be fun. I miss you like crazy. No pressure. We can just hang out in a dark corner and enjoy the music by ourselves. Please?"

"Okay," Evan relented. "But I've really gotta go."

Now Alek could really hear Evan's smile, put there by him, and it made his heart swell with pure joy and pride.

"Of course. Have a good day. I'll call you after work."

"Okay. Bye."

Alek ended the call and fished his credit card out of the wallet, ignoring Luka, who was propped on his elbows and gaping at him.

"Who—?"

"Shh!" He nudged Luka and dialed again. "Hi, yeah, this is an order for delivery. I need three dozen donuts. An assortment of everything you've got. And two boxes of coffee. This'll be on my credit card." He recited the card number and the address of Mike's Garage.

Once the phone and wallet were back on the nightstand, Alek flopped back down onto his side and shut his eyes.

"Oh, no you don't!" Luka exclaimed, rolling Alek onto his back and sitting on top of his thighs. "What was that?! You just ordered breakfast for somebody! That you called! And flirted with! And 'miss like crazy!' What the hell? I thought you don't do relationships!"

Each exclamation point was accompanied by a swat of Luka's hand to Alek's arms, as Alek attempted to deflect the blows from his grinning, giddy sibling.

"Stop! All right!" Alek complained. "What happened to sleeping?"

"You're not even denying it! You're dating somebody! This hasn't happened in, like, *ever*!" Luka bounced a little on Alek's legs.

"Stop," Alek groaned. "I really have to take a leak and that's not helping. I have so dated people before."

"Fuck and run is not *dating*."

"Well, there was, um... Drew," Alek floundered.

"Drew was a series of fuck and runs. Not a relationship. Doesn't count. Since, you know, he was fucking both of us, sometimes at the same time, and you never even asked what his last name was."

Alek frowned pensively, squinting. "I thought his last name was something like... Johnson."

"Or maybe you're just projecting because the most memorable thing about him was the size of his johnson," Luka offered. "Stop changing the subject. Who is he? Tell me!"

"No! Not yet. You'll scare him off."

Luka softened, lying down on Alek, cradling his chin on a hand, the elbow braced on Alek's chest. "Aw, so he's delicate? How delicate? Super twink? The really nervous, swishy, wallflower type? That's unlike you, I must say."

"No!" Alek hooked an arm around Luka's neck, flipping him over and swatting him with a pillow. "Go back to sleep."

Luka was quiet for a while, spooning up against Alek again, which was unsurprising. He couldn't really help himself. Sleep always came easier for Luka when he could feel he wasn't alone. It was part of how Alek took care of his beloved brother and the job he had assigned himself—providing what Luka needed to be happy, whatever it was, even if making Luka happy meant sacrificing things Alek craved. Luka's well-being was more important to Alek than his own. Things would have been much different for them if they had a real family, and parents that loved them. But you couldn't choose the fate you were given, you just had to make do with what you had. And Luka had Alek. It hadn't always been perfect. They'd each made mistakes and hurt each other in terrible ways, but they belonged to each other, and that tether linking them would always keep them joined in inexplicable ways. Maybe Alek cared about Luka too much, but he wouldn't have it any other way. He'd never cared as much about anyone as much as he cared for Luka, but maybe that could change. With someone like Evan, it seemed possible, as scary as that was for Alek to admit, even just to himself. Caring about Evan as much as he cared about Luka was a daunting prospect; it was scary, thrilling and irresistible all at the same time.

Alek was half-asleep himself when Luka whispered to him, "How about we barter? Detailed information for sexual favors?"

"No!"

Luka huffed, and gave up. He was clearly not winning that battle.

Fifteen minutes later at Mike's Garage, a delivery van pulled up. The table in the garage's back room was laid out with the free food and coffee, which the boss signed for. No one had any idea who sent it, except for Evan who couldn't stop smiling no matter how hard he tried, but Evan wasn't saying a word. All day long he smiled, sometimes chuckling softly to himself, even when Jason accidentally spilled engine grease on Evan's boots. All in all, it was a very good day; one of Evan's best, actually, just from knowing someone cared and was thinking about him.

But all of that changed when Brennan appeared, seething, crying, and furious. Visibly enraged, he stormed into the garage, searching out Evan and shoving him violently backward when he found him.

"*How could you*?! How could you do that, you *selfish* fucking ass-hole?! Fuck you! Fuck you!"

Evan tried to grab him, and talk him down. "Bren. Brennan, listen to me. Let's go outside, okay? We can talk about this —"

A sharp, precise left hook connected with Evan's jaw. Pain flared up, hot and blinding, through Evan's skull as he almost toppled over. Some of the guys came to his aid, but he waved them off.

"It's fine. He's my brother. And I had it coming." He took Brennan's arm as Brennan shrunk in on himself, the anger draining away, replaced quickly by heartache. "C'mon. I'm due for a break anyway. Let's take a little walk."

# Chapter 8
# Life After Death

*One hour earlier*

Brennan found Jimmy's place easily, shortly after lunch. Jimmy was in his mid-thirties from the looks of him, with dark, tousled, short hair and twinkling green eyes. He was an inch or two shorter than Brennan and just as lean. His smile was warm and welcoming, and he ushered Brennan inside, seeming very glad to meet him just as Evan promised. At first they talked about Brennan, his life growing up with Maggie in Louisiana and his journey up to Pennsylvania once she'd succumbed to a particularly malicious, terminal case of breast cancer. Jimmy assured Brennan he would always be there to talk if Brennan was so inclined, explaining how he used to be a preacher until he decided he could do more good working in social services with people truly in need.

Purged of his somewhat sad story and feeling lighter for having told it, Brennan told Jimmy what Evan had said to him, relaying the cryptic message.

Jimmy hummed, rolling the news over in his head. His easy, pleasant smile faded, his expression becoming troubled. Through the window beside where they sat, a flock of brown speckled birds swooped and dove in the field, searching for something unknowable in the tall grass.

"He should have told you himself," Jimmy muttered. "It's only right. But maybe it's too much for him. Laying it all out plainly is something he's never been able to do. Hey, at least he wanted you to know the truth. It's something."

"I don't understand," Brennan confessed, totally lost.

Flattening a hand on the tabletop, Jimmy held Brennan's gaze and said, "I know you're in the process of getting to know Evan right now, but I don't think he's going to make a whole lot of sense to you until you realize where he's coming from. I don't even understand him sometimes, though the revelation of your existence certainly cleared up a lot."

With a sigh, Jimmy confided, "My theory — which could be total crap, by the way — is that Evan, in his heart, always knew you were out there. He knew on a soul-deep level that he was missing you, his other half, and his mother. He was... incomplete... and the saddest kid I've ever met. He was picked on in school, teased for being quiet and awkward, and because of things like his glasses, his appearance. Then, as he got older, he was teased for being gay. There was never any proof of him being gay, of course, it was just kids being kids, labeling someone who maybe looked too long at other guys and wasn't as into talking about girls as much as the other boys were.

"Evan came home with black eyes and bruises and a bloody mouth all the time. Charlie tried to teach him self-defense, but being able to fight back didn't really affect the source of the problem."

Jimmy bowed his head, bracing it on a hand that covered his eyes.

"What?" Brennan murmured.

"This is really hard to say," Jimmy admitted. "Makes me understand why Evan wanted me to tell you for him. "He seemed to be having an easier time of it. There weren't any warning signs. That's the scariest part. Charlie felt confident enough to go on a long cross-country freight run, leaving Evan alone for a few days during spring break. He was only fourteen. I went out for a walk to clear my head and to pray. I found him, lying in the grass with pill bottles — empty ones — scattered around on the ground and a bottle of cheap, strong gin right by his hand. He was... gray... and I called 9-1-1. I tried to carry him back here to my place to wake him up."

Jaw clenched, Jimmy glanced away.

Brennan stared at him, not really breathing, his heart beating at a frantic pace, everything in him focused on what Jimmy was saying, the words themselves not really processing yet. When Jimmy started talking again it was with the saddest, most pained vestige of a smile Brennan had ever seen. Jimmy's voice wavered as he said, "Evan wasn't breathing when I set him down on the ground outside, right over there by the door. He was gone.

"He'd ground up the pills into a powder, they told me, and mixed it with the liquor. It entered his system fast and he went into shock. Then his heart stopped."

Brennan hunched forward, trembling slightly, his forehead resting against his folded hands. Everything else ceased to exist but Jimmy's voice and flashes of images provided by Brennan's imagination. That familiar sense of loss, of losing something or someone without being able to stop it or hold them there was so intense, it jarred him to the core.

"I did CPR on him until the paramedics got here. They'd been close by at the time. It was lucky. One more minute and he wouldn't have come back. They shocked his heart. He started to throw up once his heart was beating again and at the same time tried to suck in some air. He almost suffocated on his own vomit."

Jimmy shook his head as if to clear it. "He came back though, that's all that matters. The coma lasted about a month. When he finally woke up from it, that was a good day. That was a miracle. But Evan wouldn't talk about any of it. He wouldn't admit to trying to kill himself and he wouldn't even acknowledge it had happened. I mean, he wasn't really talking much at all, but especially about that. So Charlie checked him in to a psychiatric hospital about an hour away from here for evaluation and so that he could be kept on suicide watch. That lasted a couple of months."

Brennan moaned softly, denying it, all of it.

Continuing, Jimmy said, "One day, Charlie changed his mind, out of the blue. He took Evan out of there, brought him home, and gave that boy every single thing he could ever want. Anything. He was just doing everything he could, trying to give Evan reasons to live. He bought him that car. He paid for the surgery on his eyes so he wouldn't need the glasses anymore—for his self-esteem, you know. He homeschooled Evan as long as he could to get him out of that school and taught him to hunt, taught him to work on cars. That's Evan. He's still too sad, too quiet, and in too much pain. But he's great at his job. He's a loyal friend—to a fault. Every other weekend he works with me down at the homeless shelter and everyone there is always so happy to see him."

Jimmy took a deep breath and laid a hand on Brennan's arm. There were copious, silent tears streaming from Brennan's eyes. "The resemblance between you is haunting. I am so grateful for you being in Evan's life now. It truly is God's will that you have each other for comfort and strength. It's the best thing that's ever happened to him, in my opinion, rediscovering you. And *please*, try to forgive him, Brennan."

Brennan looked up, eyes ablaze. He sucked in a rough breath and, trembling, stood up. "I have to go. I have to, um... Where's Mike's?"

"Down the road. Three blocks to the south, towards town," Jimmy told him.

"Thanks," Brennan whispered, and then he was running — out the door, down the winding driveway.

"That year, when I was fourteen, was the worst year of my *life*," Brennan spat at Evan.

They were standing together outside, behind Mike's Garage. Evan was sucking hard on a cigarette, staring off into space.

"I had these panic attacks for no reason," Brennan continued wildly. "I'd feel really suddenly, really strongly, like something was wrong, *really* wrong and I didn't understand it. Mom started to drink out of the blue. She drank all the time and was fired from her job. She left me at her friend's house for a few weeks right when I was feeling the worst and I was so goddamn *mad* at her for that. My stomach hurt and I felt groggy and upset and like I was going crazy. And it was *all your fault*, wasn't it?! That's why I felt so sick, why Mom was out of her fucking mind. Charlie must've told her what you did. She must've visited you in the hospital."

"No," Evan muttered, shaking his head, blowing smoke out of the side of his mouth. "She couldn't have."

"Why? You were unconscious! You wouldn't know."

"Neither would you," Evan retorted doubtfully. "You didn't

even know I existed."

"Maybe part of me did. They say twins have a weird connection to each other sometimes. Maybe that was why I was so freaked out," Brennan accused.

Evan chewed his lip and held Brennan's hurt, cutting glare for a fleeting moment. "Look, I've gotta get back to work. Can we talk about this later?"

Brennan didn't say anything and didn't blink. He folded his arms more tightly over his chest and dug in his heels.

"If you're waiting for an apology, you ain't gettin' one," Evan told him. He took one last drag from the cigarette before dropping it and crushing it out.

When Brennan still didn't respond, Evan sighed, walked past him and headed back to the garage. It was a long time before Brennan was able to move. Scared, lost and lonely, he walked away and didn't bother looking back.

Evan got home around five o'clock that evening. Brennan was in his bedroom. Walking past his doorway, not looking in, Evan went to the darkened living room and sat on the couch. Folding his hands between his knees, he took a deep breath and let the eerie stillness relax him. He heard soft, padding footsteps approach and didn't look up as Brennan hovered a few feet away.

"We don't have to talk if you don't want to," Evan said when Brennan simply stared at him. He could see that much with his peripheral vision and not much else.

"Why did you let me find out that way?" Brennan asked. His throat sounded like it'd been scraped raw from crying. There was so much hurt there that Evan winced as some of the pain sifted through the air between them, seeping in through the pores in his skin. "That was a really shitty thing to do."

Evan turned his face away. Restlessly, he rubbed a hand over the back of his skull, hunched forward, then sat up stock-straight. "I don't talk about it. I don't talk about it and I'm not gonna talk about it. We were gonna talk about Mom. We...."

He stood, wanting to bolt from the room. Brennan stepped in his path and stared hard into Evan's eyes.

"I don't want to talk about it, okay?!" Evan barked.

He infused the outburst with as much anger and coldness as he could manage, but it didn't have the desired effect. Brennan wasn't put-off at all. He actually stepped closer and softened. Hooking his arms under Evan's and around his back, Brennan wrapped him in a gentle hug—their third hug, not that Evan was counting or anything. His face pressed gently against the side of Evan's face and Brennan whispered, "I'm sorry."

Evan's arms hung limp and he blinked rapidly to clear his eyes. Every complicated feeling that rose to the surface was pushed immediately back through sheer force of will, out of self-preservation.

"I'm sorry," Brennan repeated, pressing his lips against Evan's jaw, hissing the words. "I don't want to lose you. I just got you back. I've lost too much already."

Evan's expression crumpled as it became too much for him—the kindness and caring, the realization that Brennan needed him already—but Brennan didn't see. Tensing more rather than relaxing, Evan fought not to give in to the urge to hug Brennan back and said, "Wow, you sure do like to hug a lot, don'cha?"

Brennan rolled his eyes and stepped back, releasing him. "You're family. I'm allowed to hug you."

"Is that so?" Evan challenged, his lips pursed with determination. Brennan's gaze slid down from Evan's eyes to his mouth and for a dizzying split second, just a split second, Evan was sure Brennan was going to kiss him.

*Do brothers kiss each other? Is that something that people do? I know hugging is fine, but kissing?*

He wracked his brain, sifting through everything he'd observed of other families, his eyes widening a little in startled uncertainty.

"You're cute," Brennan grinned.

"Shut up," Evan frowned. "That's a really weird thing to say."

"It's true. You come off so tough, but you're not so tough, are ya, Evan?"

"Clearly," Evan retorted.

Brennan's small smile disappeared. He pressed lips together

and folded his arms. "Is this why Charlie wanted me to move in with you? He's worried about you?"

Evan huffed, folds his arms too, mirroring Brennan perfectly without intending to. "No. Moving in was your idea. And he agreed because he was worried about *you*."

"How could it have been my idea? You really think I'd just invite myself to live here?"

The words sank in, and the more they did, the more disturbed Evan became by what they implied. Brennan quickly added, "Maybe he's worried about both of us."

*He thinks I'm going to do it again. He sent Brennan here to make sure I don't try to kill myself. He doesn't think I'm getting better. He thinks I'm getting worse. Am I getting worse?*

Evan's chest heaved and he blinked more as his vision blurred. He focused on a spot on the wall just to the right of Brennan's head and sighed. "Can we just, um... I mean, I hate this shit."

Brennan nodded, saying nothing. They each took a seat, lost in their own thoughts in silence.

The clock on the wall ticked loudly. Eventually, Brennan spoke up.

"Did you want him to do all of that? Charlie? Did you really want the eye surgery and the car and everything, or was he just trying to change you?"

Staring at Brennan, at first Evan couldn't answer. "I don't... I don't know. I mean, I knew there was stuff wrong with me, so I was fine with it all. It was good to get rid of my glasses and I dug the car and, I don't know."

"There's nothing wrong with you, Evan," Brennan told him softly. "If he made you feel like there was stuff wrong with you, that's awful. You didn't need to be fixed by changing what you looked like or taking you out of school, away from people who could have been your friends, or trying to toughen you up so you wouldn't leave him. Haven't you thought about this stuff? Charlie doesn't know you better than you know yourself. It's your life; you should be making the decisions about it. You're strong and beautiful, and perfect, just the way you are. You should know that. Don't let anyone try to change you. Not even him."

Evan was looking down at his hands and Brennan's words washed over him. Some of the message behind them sank in, but some didn't process at all. He was unable to believe Brennan thought that highly of him, that he was beautiful and perfect. It didn't make sense. If anything, he was just saying what he thought he should say, not what he really meant.

Just needing to shift the focus off of him, Evan asked, "Have you talked to him? Charlie?"

Brennan cocked an eyebrow, cleared his throat. "No. He's left messages, but...."

Cracking a tiny smile, Evan bowed his head to hide it. Maybe they were twins after all.

"But what?"

"I don't know," Brennan sighed. "I haven't been in the mood to talk to him. Don't really know what to say to someone I've never met."

"Well, I don't know what to say to him either and he's been my only kin my whole life. So there ya go," Evan offered. He shuffled his feet and mustered some courage. "So, w-what was she like?"

Brennan slouched back into the cushions. "Honest. Or at least honest about most things. Obviously she knew how to keep a secret, too. Hard worker. Quiet. Sad. Treated me like I was all that really mattered. Every day was a gift to her. The little moments were what she liked. Money, possessions, status — none of that was worth anything to her. She was a great mom. She tried to make a good life for us. She had the best smile. It made her whole face light up. And she smelled like lilacs." Expelling a rough breath, he complained, "God this sucks. Why did this happen? Why did any of this happen? Why couldn't we just have been a family? Or normal? Nothing makes sense anymore."

"For what it's worth," Evan said in his low, gruff voice. "I'm glad you're here."

Brennan peeked up, and grunted, "Huh."

"Huh?" Evan mimicked. "That gets a *huh*?"

Brennan broke into laughter. "I'm sorry, *thank you*, Evan," he said melodramatically, with dripping sarcasm.

"Jesus Christ," Evan sighed, shaking his head and standing. "I need a fuckin' beer."

As Evan walked back into the kitchen, Brennan watched him go while chewing on his thumbnail. The instinct to soothe, learned from caring for Maggie, kicked in sometimes when Brennan was with Evan. He wanted to care for Evan in ways he'd never wanted to care for anyone before, because it wasn't about sickness or anything temporary. Echoes of how it felt to be with his mom shook Brennan gently when he was around Evan, but it was different. It was like Evan was something Brennan had needed, had been missing, and needed now to continue on. He wouldn't make it without Evan. Now that Brennan sensed it, how being with Evan made him feel more whole than he'd ever been before, he realized, slowly, how to ever be apart from Evan would only magnify the empty place Evan filled up. They were part of each other. They belonged together. Maybe if they'd always been together, some of the worst things in their lives would never have happened.

The need to hold on to Evan, to keep him as close as possible, kicked in strongly for Brennan. And he meant it when he said Evan was beautiful. Sometimes Brennan couldn't stop looking at him, even when he tried. The similarity, the weird sense that when Brennan helped Evan, he also helped himself, since Evan was an extension of him, underlined the unmistakable desire to extend kindness and love to him. But Evan was still a mystery. He didn't feel like a brother, or even a distant relative. He felt like Evan. Beautiful, heartbroken, quiet, sad, strong, wonderful Evan.

If all Brennan needed was someone to care about, someone to love, Evan was someone who needed love, validation, and a sense of belonging in his life. And that Brennan could give him. They were like two pieces to a puzzle. They fit together in all of the right ways, or so Brennan was beginning to see.

# Chapter 9

# First Date

It was the night of Brennan and Luka's first date. Sitting at a small table tucked away in a corner of one of the nicest restaurants in town, the only illumination by which to see each other and eat their meal was from the candle flickering between them and the dim golden light from a decorative hanging lamp above. It was quiet and comfortable. They dined on fish—the freshest in the area—accompanied by a nice sparkling cider for Brennan and some wine for Luka.

Luka did most of the talking at first, his mouth running on with nervous energy at the intoxicating sight of Brennan in glasses and dressed to impress. Brennan was wearing a blue striped button-down shirt, ironed perfectly smooth and fitted to his lean frame, the crisp sleeves rolled up to his elbows. The top button was undone at the collar, revealing a small triangle of lightly freckled, golden skin. Unable to stop remembering the sight of Brennan in his miniscule pair of shorts, his body tight and toned, Luka helplessly undressed Brennan with his eyes throughout their dinner. He tried to let his natural chattiness drag his thoughts out of the gutter and back to polite conversation.

"So," Luka said, taking a sip and letting the heady, sweet taste of the white wine roll over his tongue, "What brings you to Whippoorwill? It's not exactly the most glamorous place to move to, and if you came all the way from Louisiana, that's quite a haul."

"Is my accent really that bad?" Brennan grinned, swallowing his mouthful of food and washing it down with a drink from his own glass.

"Bad? No. Sexy as hell? Yes," Luka winked. "And you're avoiding my question."

"It's just a long story."

"I've got time," Luka prodded, pleading shamelessly with his eyes. "Try me."

Brennan nodded once, almost in surrender. Sitting with his hands folded in his lap, he straightened a little and said softly, "Okay. Well it's only fair for you to know this anyway. I've not really been myself lately, so in the interest of full disclosure I should probably come clean. But I'm not looking for pity or expecting anything of you. I mean, we just met. I honestly didn't even want to say anything in case it made things too weird."

Luka's tensed and braced himself. Brow furrowed, he sat forward, leaning in. He reached out and took Brennan's hand when it skirted the table's edge, claiming it and holding on to him. "What's the matter? What is it?" It was the nervous edge in Brennan's voice as much as his words that worried Luka.

"Well, okay. I was raised by my mom. She was a single mother, my only real family and my best friend. It was always just the two of us against the world."

Brennan didn't move, didn't look up. Luka's thumb stroked lightly, gently back-and-forth over the back of his hand. Sighing, Luka echoed a single word, "...Was...."

"She died a few weeks ago. Breast cancer."

"Brennan," Luka ached. "My god. I'm so sorry."

"Don't," Brennan objected. "Don't. Please. I don't want you to feel sorry for me. I just want to enjoy our dinner and your company. I don't want this to be about that. So, to answer your initial question, I moved here because I just found out that I have relatives here."

"That's a good reason to come," Luka agreed, full to bursting with concern and sorrow. His grip on Brennan's hand tightened slightly.

Looking resigned, Brennan quietly suggested, "Look, if you want to call this off, I totally understand. I'm not exactly good company right now. Maybe this was a bad idea."

"No," Luka said determinedly. "No way. I think you're great company and we're not calling it off. I like you. I want to get to know you better. Talk to me. I'm a good listener."

"Honestly, talking isn't what I'm interested in right now," Brennan said, finishing off his cider. Pushing the elegant crystal goblet away, he grabbed the napkin from his lap and asked, "What do you say we get out of here and go back to my place?"

"Is that a good idea?" Luka asked, knowing Alek would be flabbergasted to hear Luka question such an offer.

"I might be young, but I'm old enough to know what I want," Brennan retorted. "What do you say? Wanna keep me company?"

"Yeah. You know I do," Luka admitted, logically wanting to say no for Brennan's sake, but wholly unable to.

"Good. C'mon. Let's go."

Luka drove them in his truck over to Brennan's place. It took about ten minutes to make the trip, during which Luka tried to think of ways to get out of the situation he found himself in. As soon as they were out of the truck and he had Brennan ready and willing in front of him, there was going to be very little chance he would be able to stop at that point. His trademark lack of willpower would kick in and he would do what was easy, and what felt good. Usually, Luka wouldn't even question it. It would hardly occur to him that there might be alternate choices. He'd be all about hooking up just to hook up. Brennan was a sure thing, he said as much, and why wouldn't Luka go for that?

But something *had* caused Luka to begin to rethink his approach. Something....

*Brennan's mother. Brennan lost his mother and now he's all alone. He has no one, not even someone like Alek to watch his back. He's just a kid; a scared kid needing some kind – any kind – of physical comfort to dull the hurt eating him up from the inside out. Even if it's sex, even if it's sex with a stranger, even if it's not really what Brennan wants, even if it gets to the point of no return where it's too late to say stop and he says stop, please don't hurt me, please stop... and it happens anyway... Brennan is going to do this. He's going to go out looking for someone to make him feel, to fill the cold, desolate emptiness inside where unconditional love should be and isn't in any way he can manage. I've gotta stop this. I can't let it happen to him, too. I just can't. I'd never forgive myself if I enabled this or worse, turned my back when Brennan is so clearly crying out for help. Where would I have been if Alek hadn't been there for me? Would I even be here right now?*

Something was making that night vastly different than every other date Luka had ever been on. Luka did *not* want to take advantage of Brennan. The thought of doing so turned his stomach. Luka really did like him and wanted more than a quick fuck. A lot more. Brennan was the sweetest, most intriguing, most gorgeous person Luka had met in a long time. The more he learned about Brennan, and now finding out about the recent loss of his mother, the more it made Luka want to actually do the right thing for once.

It was clear Brennan just happened to be in the middle of some hard times. He didn't really understand how he was hurting himself more by inviting relative strangers into his bed. Luka was slightly terrified of being the jackass he usually was when it came to matters of the heart. What if he screwed things up and lost his one chance at something amazing and real? But the temptation was undeniable. It was there, merely smoldering, though ready to ignite and incinerate every good intention crying out in Luka's heart.

*Am I really going to be that guy? Have I truly gotten to that place where I have become that which I despised for so long — someone who preys on the weak and naïve for their own pleasure? Have I become the same as those men who used me and then threw me away so easily, like I wasn't a human being with feelings at all, just something to fuck?*

Feeling torn and a little bit overwhelmed, Luka parked in front of Brennan's house. An old, refurbished Chevy sat in the driveway.

They got out of the truck and Brennan led Luka inside the quiet, darkened house, bringing him directly to his bedroom located just to the left of the foyer. He closed the door behind them. Stepping up to Luka, Brennan breathed in deeply as if trying to catch Luka's scent and slipped a hand up under the hem of Luka's navy polo shirt. The moment shifted from innocent to not in a flash as Brennan's fingertips connected with Luka's abdomen. Shivers of excitement and want radiated from the spot. Stroking over the taut skin just to the inside of Luka's left hipbone, Brennan watched Luka with an upward glance. A small line of tension creased Luka's brow right between his eyebrows. Licking his lips, Brennan tilted his head up, obviously waiting for Luka to act and kiss him.

Embroiled in a mostly-hidden but raging inner battle, Luka

cradled Brennan's jaw in a hand and dipped his head, getting closer, tingling all the way down to the pit of his stomach at Brennan's feather-light touch moving over his skin, slipping now around his waist. Luka was hard and aching but, thankfully, his brain was still functioning.

To anchor himself to his good intentions, Luka spoke up, asking, "Have you ever been in love?"

Breathing out a soft chuckle, Brennan hummed and answered after a thoughtful pause, "Almost. Not really. You?"

"Yeah. I was," Luka murmured. "A long time ago. But she dumped me and broke my heart." Brennan stretched up on the balls of his feet and simultaneously guided Luka down by gripping behind his neck. Softly, experimentally, Brennan kissed Luka's lips.

"So you're bi?"

"Yeah," Luka nodded. His fingers positively itched with need to touch Brennan, to grab his ass and throw him down on the large bed helpfully located only two feet away. He wanted to strip Brennan naked and devour every inch of him, very, very slowly. But he settled for pushing in for a deeper kiss, tasting Brennan's tongue and moaning softly into Brennan's mouth as those sinful, plump lips parted for him so easily. Knowing they were about to cross a line when Brennan's hand slid farther up Luka's torso and the pad of his thumb rolled over the peaked nub of Luka's nipple, Luka instantly pulled back. Steadying himself with effort, he cleared his throat and opened his eyes.

"Wait. I can't do this. I feel like I'm taking advantage of you. I mean, damn, I want you *so badly*, Brennan, but it's too fast. This may be the first time in my life I've said this to someone, but I like you way too much to settle for a one-night stand."

They locked eyes. Brennan clearly heard him, but it didn't seem to change his mind and he didn't back down. He surged forward, sucking on Luka's lips. Pinching Luka's nipple, Brennan hungrily swallowed Luka's instant low groan. Brennan followed up this small victory by grabbing Luka's backside and fitting their hips together, rocking deliberately against the hard, thick line of Luka's cock straining against his slim-fitting pants. Luka's cock jumped and he was radiating heat from head to toe. Growling back in his throat,

Luka stroked a thumb through the hollow of Brennan's cheek, caught Brennan's lower lip between his teeth and tugged.

Then he made himself stop, breaking the kiss, but Brennan wasn't backing off or letting go.

"What are you doing?" Luka managed.

"Fuck me. C'mon. I need it. It's been too long and *god* you're hot. I'll beg. You want me to get down on my knees and beg for you to fuck me?"

"Wow, you are like... evil. And possibly the only person on Earth hornier than me, and that's saying a lot. I'm *trying* to do the right thing here. And also? How long could it have been? You're practically a *child*."

"You can do the right thing and still fuck me," Brennan teased, palming Luka through his pants before Luka knocked his hand away, pointing a finger of accusation at him.

With a stern expression he growled, "Stop it."

"Make me," Brennan smirked.

"Fucking hell! Okay, you asked for it." Luka quickly crouched down, slung Brennan over his shoulder, took two steps forward and tossed him down onto the mattress only to climb on top of him, kneeling there and straddling his thighs. He grabbed Brennan's wrists and pinned them down to the bed on either side of his head.

Not wasting a second, Brennan, flexible as he was, curled his legs up, slipping them out from between Luka's legs to hook them around Luka's waist. Grunting with effort, even though Brennan was a few inches shorter as well as slimmer than Luka, he twisted and rolled them so he was on top.

"How did you even *do* that? You're so small!"

"Oh, I'm small? Really?" Brennan quickly guided Luka's hand to his crotch and dove in, sealing their mouths together and licking back over Luka's tongue.

"Mmm," Luka hummed, kissing him back and rubbing along Brennan's erection. Frantically, Brennan fumbled at the fly, pulling it open to give Luka more access. Luka's hand slipped in under the waistband of Brennan's underwear and closed up around his shaft. Brennan was *throbbing*, slick and wet with pre-come and moaned loudly, pushing into Luka's hand as Luka started to pump him. Shuddering and thrusting desperately into Luka's fist, Brennan planted his hands on the bed and closed his eyes.

Luka stared up at Brennan. Stroking a fingertip over Brennan's quivering lower lip, he steadily increased the speed of his tugs, watching Brennan come more apart with every second that passed. Then, his body tensing, Brennan stopped riding Luka's hand and he bit down on his lip, frowning. A strained whimper sounded back in his throat and he exhaled sharply through his nose.

"So sweet," Luka sighed, cupping Brennan's face.

"Slow down... you have to... I'm... *fuck....*"

Luka ignored this and dragged Brennan down by the back of his neck, sucking his lower lip and jacking him hard. Shuddering, Brennan came, spilling over Luka's fingers, and over both of their shirts. He tried to pull back but Luka kept him there, worked him through it, humming with pleasure at each wrenching little cry that passed through Brennan's lips and into Luka's mouth.

"I'm sorry," Brennan rasped when he was finally allowed to pull away. He was blushing fiercely and, for the first time since they met, had gone shy, not meeting Luka's eyes. "Told you it's been a while. I shouldn't have—"

"Hey," Luka hushed. "You needed it. And I wanted to."

Brennan seemed to process this and nodded slowly. "Okay. So, what do you want? I could suck you or you can—"

"No," Luka interrupted. "Not tonight. I meant it when I said I want to slow down."

Still with lowered eyes, Brennan said softly, "Oh. You know, when you asked me out I thought it was because you wanted to screw around."

"I did. I *do*. I mean, yeah, that's usually my style, and wow, I never realized how terrible that is until now and I don't know. You deserve better than that."

"You don't know me well enough to decide what I deserve," Brennan accused.

"Hey, I'm trying to."

Hope shone from Luka's eyes. The honesty in it seemed to seep through Brennan's defenses and soften him.

"I think I need to get cleaned up," Brennan said, looking down at himself. "I'm sorry about your shirt."

"Don't sweat it," Luka told him with a small smile. "Go ahead. I'm not going anywhere."

# Chapter 10

# Caught in the Act

"There's a sink in the kitchen at the back of the house if you want to get washed up there. There's only the one bathroom," Brennan apologized.

"Okay," Luka grinned. He watched Brennan go, his button-down shirt all rumpled and damp in patches, his pants hanging open in the front but his underwear at least protecting his modesty. "You were right about that 'small' thing by the way," he called. "I totally take it back."

"Thank you," Brennan smirked, disappearing into the dimly lit hall. A light blinked on, shining from the bathroom, then was blocked as the door shut. Struggling up off the bed, taking a moment to try to tame his raging libido, Luka attempted to wilt his huge hard-on by thinking about the nasty, sweaty, stinky people from the gym that morning.

Long moments later, he headed out into the hallway. The bathroom door was open again but no one was inside.

Moonlight filtered through the windows and it was just enough to see by. Luka could just make out the kitchen in the distance, so he turned to go that way when someone stepped into the hall a few feet ahead of him.

It was Brennan but he was wearing other clothes now — a snug-fitting, worn t-shirt and jeans. And his hair was different. It looked... shorter.

"Brennan?" Luka squinted.

"Alek? Shit, what're you...."

Baffled, Luka repeated, "...Alek?"

"Luka?" Brennan said, appearing from behind the door to the linen closet. "I just needed to grab a clean towel... oh. Hey, Evan."

"*Evan*? No. Wait. You're... Evan," Luka pointed, looking between the perfectly identical pair. "Whoa. Oh my god. Oh my god, *you have a twin*!? What the fuck!? This is... incredibly... insanely... Whoa. You didn't *tell me* you have a twin! Well, I didn't tell you I have a twin either, so I guess I really have no room to complain."

Brennan's eyes widened. "Wait, what? No way. You have a twin, too? No. Okay, now I know you're fucking with me."

"I'm not fucking with you!"

"Evidence suggests otherwise," Evan muttered, glancing at Brennan's come-streaked, falling-off clothes and unzipped pants.

"Shit. Yeah. Christ. Excuse me. Luka, you'll be cool for a minute if I, um..." Brennan fumbled, gesturing to the bathroom.

"Yeah. Yeah! Go ahead. I'll just stare awkwardly at Evan or something. Probably."

They stood there as Brennan hurried back to the bathroom with the towel. Evan chewed at his lip, hunching over like he wanted to disappear, and swirled the half-empty beer in his hands, glancing up through his long eyelashes at Luka who was indeed staring awkwardly at him, as promised. Evan looked exactly like Brennan, so much so that Luka had an overwhelming desire to stand them next to each other so he could compare and contrast. Their features were the same, right down to the placement of freckles. It was everything else that was different.

"That's so weird," Luka gushed. "Oh man. This is how I've been making people feel all my life, isn't it? I've never met identical twins before, besides, you know. Myself. And Alek. Obviously."

"So, you wanna borrow a shirt or something? 'Cause..." Evan nodded, tipping his beer toward the wet spot on Luka's polo shirt.

Looking down at himself, Luka shut up quickly and ran a hand back restlessly through his hair. "Yes. Please. That'd be appreciated."

Evan turned, walking into a darkened room located off of the center hall. Luka followed along behind him like a dog with its tail between his legs, embarrassed and confused. He accepted the shirt Evan handed over with a low, muttered, "Thanks. I'm sorry about that with your brother. Who is awesome, by the way. I swear I'm not just here to perv on him. It's not just, you know, what it seems."

"No problem," Evan said, digging down into his pocket and coming out with a cigarette. His hand trembled slightly as he placed it between his lips and he seemed pale but Luka wrote it off to the shock of walking into the scene he just had. "You mind if I?"

"Nah. Your house, man."

Evan nodded, lighting the cigarette and walking with Luka to the kitchen as he changed shirts, sitting down at the table and picking restlessly at his beer label. "Have a seat. Beer's in the fridge."

"Sure," Luka agreed, sitting across from Evan. They were in better light, so he was able to study Evan closer, and the differences between him and Brennan. Luka found Evan's hair was cut shorter and styled differently than Brennan's, not to mention darker in color. Evan's posture and body language, his expression and build were all wildly different too, but there was also so very much of the same. It was a little spooky. "Sorry for staring, but this is really fascinating."

"What?" Evan shifted in his chair, sucking hard on the cigarette, blowing smoke out the side of his mouth.

"Well, you look like you should be the bad twin, with the cigarette and the beer and mild surliness and all. You know — the angel and the devil, that whole thing. It's kind of this theory I have. Alek thinks I'm crazy. But anyway, I think Brennan is definitely the bad twin. I think you two got your disguises mixed up or something to throw the rest of us off."

"Hmm. *Brennan's* the bad twin?" Evan echoed, squinting at Luka, flicking ashes into the ashtray in the center of the table.

"Why, you don't agree?"

"I don't know." Evan shrugged, "Don't really know him that well but I'd disagree from what I've seen."

Utterly baffled, Luka blurted, "What do you mean you don't know him that well? He's your identical twin brother! How could you not know him?"

"Long story. Just met the guy a few days ago."

"No shit?"

"No shit."

"Fuck."

"Yeah."

"Huh," Luka grunted thoughtfully, considering this new information. "Well then, trust me, Brennan is the bad twin."

"I still disagree. He's as dangerous as a cupcake."

Luka snorted, "Cupcake. Ha! That's totally gotta be his nickname from now on. But I've gotta warn you, Evan, beware of that cupcake." He thumbed back over his shoulder at the bathroom, raising his eyebrows and nodding once for emphasis.

"Will do."

"Wait," Luka frowned. Finally, he realized one thing he almost missed, something that only sparked upon replaying the incident in the hallway over in his head. "You called me Alek. You thought I was him. You know Alek?"

"I guess," Evan said evasively.

"Huh. Small world."

Evan chuckled, sucking hard on the filter of his cigarette, filling his lungs with smoke and holding it there a second. Then he breathed it out and shook his head. "Yeah, tell me about it."

When Luka heard Brennan emerge from the bathroom, he excused himself, bid Evan goodnight and went to meet Brennan. He found Brennan seated cross-legged on the bed, wearing only a thin, silky-soft pair of white drawstring pants. His tan skin, flushed pink from the quick shower he just took, glowed in contrast. An easy smile spread across his face and he bowed his head bashfully.

"So, seems you may have been right about the not-knowing-you-that-well thing," Luka said teasingly.

"You really thought he was me?"

"Just for a second there," Luka admitted, stepping closer, the fronts of his thighs resting lightly against the edge of the high bed's mattress. He slipped a hand around one of Brennan's calves, the desire to touch too intense to ignore.

"What's your brother's name?"

"Alek. He's older. More of a stick-in-the-mud. Scowls a lot. Not *nearly* as attractive."

Brennan laughed brightly at that and Luka sighed, "Wow, you have the most beautiful smile I've ever seen. Makes me want to keep on making you laugh so that I can keep enjoying the view."

Brennan rolled his eyes, but the smile stayed.

"So, now what?" Luka wondered aloud. Brennan's hand came to rest atop Luka's laying on his leg and weaved their fingers together.

"Sleep with me?" he asked softly, some deep-seated, underlying hurt and fear showing in his face. Then, to clarify, he added, "Just sleep, I mean. I have a hard time sleeping these days. Having company helps."

Luka grinned, his cheeks dimpling. He tucked a lock of dark hair behind his ear and pursed his lips to try to hold in some of his overpowering joy. "Yeah, I'd love to."

In the kitchen, Evan stubbed out his second cigarette and finished off his beer, too.

They weren't enough. He was still rattled. Sure, he'd heard the sounds from Brennan's bedroom, the moaning and heavy breathing and had figured out pretty quickly what was going on, but the last face he expected to see emerging from there was the one *he'd* been fantasizing about and obsessing over since the night at the bar—Alek's face. Now all Evan could think of was everything he'd done with Alek, only replacing himself and *his* lover with their doppelgangers. It hit too close to home. It underlined everything Evan didn't like to face about himself, making him queasy but also, horribly, turning him on more than he would have liked to admit.

He realized he was the only one who understood; who realized Brennan was screwing Luka while Evan had been screwing around with Alek at the same time, totally oblivious. What it said about the similarity of his and Brennan's sexual preferences, about the way their minds worked and how alike they were was all too much for him.

Evan had done a better job than Luka at not gawking, because he really didn't want to know just how alike Luka and Alek were, so he mainly kept his eyes trained on his hands, but it was impossible not to mentally compare and contrast. It was fascinating to him, the difference in Luka's personality, how light-hearted and easy-going he came off versus Alek.

He was due to meet Alek for their quasi-date soon. Alek's friend's gig at the bar where they first met was scheduled for midnight so Evan had merely been lounging in the dark, biding his time until then, and, of course, trying to block out the moaning coming from across the house. Now he couldn't bear to be in the house at all, not with Brennan and Luka both back in the bedroom doing god-knows-what. So he got up, grabbed a pack of gum to freshen his breath, pocketed his keys and went outside.

The idea was to get in the car and drive around for a while to kill time but, as Evan walked around the side of the house, he couldn't help noticing how Brennan's window was wide open. Evan's feet took him over to it silently, without any instruction from his brain. Once he was there, right by the window's edge, he crouched down. Resting his back against the house's siding, he dug a third cigarette out without thinking about that either.

He could hear them. There was the soft rustling of bodies and bed sheets, the creaking of floorboards and mattress springs. They were getting into bed. Evan imagined them sliding in under the covers, touching each other or maybe not, and wondered what they were wearing, if anything.

"I gotta warn you, I'm a natural cuddler. It can't be helped. Is that gonna bother you?"

"No, I don't mind. And if you change your mind, we can still always... you know. I still want you."

It was Brennan's voice, but it was nothing like how Evan was used to hearing him. It was scratchy, raw, and aching, and goddamn but it was making Evan hard. Hating himself for it, he palmed himself and shut his eyes, letting the smoke burn at his lungs, letting himself choke on it a little.

There were soft, wet, suckling sounds of kissing and Evan knew he shouldn't be hearing them, but his body wouldn't move.

"I want you, too. But let's at least save that for our second date, okay? I wanna take my time with you, really savor it, and right now, just holding you feels perfect."

*Damn, Bren's a slut,* Evan thought with astonishment. It did nothing to cool his interest but it did help lift from his shoulders some of the guilt he'd been carrying about wanting to have sex with Alek. If Brennan wanted it, and was so very bluntly vocal about wanting it, maybe it was okay if Evan wanted it, too.

There was more rustling; more smooching sounds too, then a low, choked moan. Brennan.

"You better cut that out if you don't wanna fuck me."

A lightning bolt of pure want shot down Evan's spine, lighting him up from inside. He willed Luka to go through with it. Evan wanted to hear it happen. He wanted to be sitting there, right under Brennan's window while they fucked.

The cigarette burned at his fingers, so he dropped it, grinding it out with his boot heel.

"Mm, sorry. You just taste *really* good, pretty much everywhere."

Evan's mouth watered. His skin prickled and his cock ached, wanting to feel Alek's mouth sucking kisses down his body, too.

"You're not stopping," Brennan pointed out, gasping. Then he moaned like the cry was startled out of him.

"That didn't really sound like a complaint."

Soft suckling, small growls and grunts mingled with the faint sound of flesh slapping and rubbing against flesh. Evan palmed himself, needing relief.

"I think *you're* the evil one. Fucking teasing bastard."

"Nope, I'm the good twin," Luka interjected after a particularly wet slurp.

"My ass," Brennan huffed.

"Mm, yeah, love your ass."

Brennan snorted with laughter and Evan shifted. It was quarter of, he realized. Damn it. Time to go.

He scrambled away, crouched low until he was well clear of the view from the window. Then he jogged to his car and got inside behind the wheel. There was a dirty rag on the floor in front of the passenger seat and Evan grabbed it. Tugging down his zipper, he pulled out his dick and wrapped the rag around it, beating off fast and hard, gasping and chasing his release.

Inside the house, Brennan put a hand on Luka's shoulder. Luka was busy sucking on Brennan's left nipple and palming his ass through the thin pants but he stopped when Brennan hissed, "Wait. Shh!"

"What?" Luka said, looking up through fallen hair, pupils blown wide and black, lips fuller from all of the kissing.

"I heard something. Hold on a sec." He unceremoniously pushed Luka off, darted to the opened window, and looked outside into the gloom. The light by the front door illuminated enough to begin to make out shapes. The scent of cigarette smoke lingered in the air. His eyes adjusted, helping him pick out more detail. Behind him, Luka groaned in protest and flopped belly-down onto the bed.

The first thing Brennan saw was the still-smoldering cigarette butt crushed into the dirt inches from the house, right by where he was standing. Then, he looked up to see Evan sitting behind the wheel of the Chevy, head thrown back against the headrest, mouth fallen open and brow furrowed. One of his arms was moving....

"Oh my god," Brennan gasped, embarrassed. Pivoting on his heel, all too aware of the pronounced tickle that stirred low in his gut, the unexpected, somewhat disturbing swell of heated lust, he returned to the bed.

"What?"

"Nothing."

"Nothing *my* ass," Luka retorted. "*What?*"

Brennan gave him a doubtful glance, sat down on his 'side' of the bed and leaned back against the pillows. He bit his lip and picked at a nail. Curling his legs up to his chest as Luka propped himself up on his elbows, Brennan muttered reluctantly, "He was outside. Evan. He heard us."

"How do you know?"

"I just do."

"Do you know if he liked what he heard?" Luka asked, low and gravelly. It made Brennan's already restless stomach flip-flop more. Brennan scooted down under the covers and turned his back to Luka, nestling into the pillow.

"Ooh, that's a yes," Luka said with sly amusement. He rubbed a hand down around Brennan's body, cupping the straining line of his dick. "Want me to take care of this?"

Seeing nothing but the after-image of Evan jerking off in the car, beginning to imagine sound effects to go along with it, Brennan blurted, "Nah, I'm good."

"You sure?"

"Yep. G'night."

Luka curled up around Brennan, spooning him from behind, being careful to keep his hips tucked back in what seemed a genuine attempt to honor Brennan's request for sleep. Brennan whimpered anyway. It was very quiet, but loud enough for Luka to hear. He palmed Brennan's flat stomach and nuzzled into the nape of his neck.

"If you need anything, I'm right here," Luka offered gently.

"'Kay," Brennan rasped. "Thanks."

# Chapter 11
# Getting Heated

The band, Raed, was already performing when Evan arrived at the bar. Spotting Alek immediately, Evan made a beeline for him, weaving through the dense crowd to where Alek was waiting in the back corner of the room, hunched over a pair of beers.

Thanks to everything else that had already happened that night, Evan felt more relaxed and confident than he had thus far around Alek. Evan walked straight to him without first glancing around to check if they were being watched by anyone else. One thing that did catch Evan's attention, though, was the band's singer when he stepped out of the spotlight to take a drink of water. The guy flashed a knowing sort of grin in Alek's direction and winked before he went back to the microphone.

The bar was packed. People were dancing and singing along, crowding in between the tables since all of the seats were filled up. Evan weaved between patrons and finally got to Alek. The slightly secluded spot Alek saved for them had a poor view of the stage and was totally out of the bartender's line of sight, so it was the least stuffy place in the whole room. Feeling even more brazen than when he'd joined Alek in the bathroom that first night, Evan beckoned to Alek seductively without saying a word, needing him like Brennan needed Luka. Hair mussed like he just rolled out of bed, his t-shirt formed to the slight curves and hard planes of his body with a light layer of sweat from the humidity, Evan knew he looked different than before, and not just because of the heat of the room.

He slid up next to Alek, leaning forward and bracing his forearms on the table beside him, giving Alek a sleepy, sideways grin.

Claiming the full beer as his own without asking, Evan took a drink from the bottle. In a husky voice just audible under the din, he said, "Hey Alek. How's it goin'?"

"Pretty good, now that you're here. Wow. You look...."

"Fuckable?" Evan supplied with a slightly wider, suggestive smirk before hiding it behind the mouth of the bottle.

The glass bottle clinked down onto the tabletop, slipping free of Evan's grasp when, in a flash of movement so fast Evan didn't anticipate it at all, Alek's finger hooked in one of Evan's belt loops and yanked him around, spinning him. The move put their mouths maybe an inch apart. It gave Evan an up-close, clear view of the fire he was playing with, dancing in the darkness of Alek's eyes. Half-expecting Alek to bare his teeth and bite down on his neck like a wild animal, Evan chuckled nervously and added, "Well, not right now though. Rather have the mob watching the band, not me bent over the table takin' the ol' love-salami."

The words had no effect at all, and Evan only had time to think, 'Uh-oh,' before Alek's teeth really were coming at him, nipping at his bottom lip hard enough to hurt before licking back over the wound, into Evan's mouth, cradling his head with one hand and backing him up to the table's edge. It was very dark and no one was paying them any attention, but it still rattled Evan when he felt Alek's huge hand blatantly palm his ass and squeeze.

His face and neck flushed as blood rushed under his skin and surged downward like a rocket to his cock, leaving him dizzy and dazed. Alek's eyes were open, watching Evan intently as one long finger rubbed, hard, down the center seam in the seat of Evan's pants. Evan undulated forward at the intimate touch, his hands splayed on Alek's chest to brace himself. He had nowhere to go, held tightly in Alek's arms, and gasped against Alek's mouth, very much aware of where they were and how many people could be watching his first real public display of affection with another guy.

"You're really gonna let me have you, Jailbait? Hmm?"

Evan exhaled roughly, swallowing back a broken sound. His head fell downward in a semblance of a nod.

"Was that a yes?"

"Later," Evan croaked. "Yes."

Alek rubbed over the curve of Evan's ass. Hooking a thumb in the waistband of Evan's jeans, which were riding quite low, Alek delved underneath, stroking gently. There was nothing there but skin, since Evan chose not to bother with underwear.

"You go commando a lot? I like it. Easy access." Alek's lip caught between the points of his teeth, rolling it, making him look as hungry as ever. "I would, you know. I'd do you right fuckin' here. Or maybe at least pull you into the kitchen first so there'd only be... hmm... three witnesses instead of two hundred."

"Gee thanks. How thoughtful."

Alek smirked wickedly, then got suddenly serious, asking, "What changed your mind?"

"You. Er, well, it's just time. I know I want it. I want you to be my first. I'm ready. But I'd like to have an actual, you know. A date. First. Please."

Alek was looking at him closely, like he was trying to read Evan's expression. But there was so much churning inside him, Evan wasn't sure what Alek saw. Alek brushed the pads of his fingers over the ridge of Evan's cheekbone and sighed his name.

Shrinking under the scrutiny, Evan's eyes fluttered closed. He frowned oh-so-slightly, knowing he was choosing to cross a line, that even by standing there, being held as he was by Alek, he'd gone farther than he ever had before. There was no turning back. The noise of the bar thundered all around them, rattling his bones, thumping under his skin, blending together. Heat radiated from hundreds of bodies, but it was only the two of them. No one else mattered.

"And, yes, I know how stupid that sounds," Evan admitted when Alek didn't say anything else, detecting something like concern in Alek's eyes. Alek immediately shut him up with a tender kiss.

Resting a hand in the small of Evan's back, Alek gave him a little space and guided him to a barstool.

"You hungry? Want something other than this?" He clinked Evan's beer with his own. "We make a mean burger here if you're interested."

"Nah," Evan replied. "I'm good."

Trying to keep his eyes on the tabletop and the beer bottle, Evan couldn't help noticing also that there were people looking at them. Specifically the bartender and the band's singer on stage were watching them, not to mention random people in the crowd. Alek slid his stool closer to Evan. One of his hands fell onto Evan's thigh, the fingers curling around to the inside, wedging between Evan's legs possessively. Sipping from his beer, Alek glared right at one guy who dared to look too long at Evan. Evan caught it and hid a grin.

Time slipped by. They talked about their jobs, which, it turned out, they were both devoted to. They also talked about hunting, something they each loved to do. When Alek realized they needed another round of beers, he gestured to the bartender, a lovely, dark-haired, keen-eyed woman who instantly started to make her way over.

"I want you to meet someone," Alek told Evan, sitting up a little straighter. The woman arrived at their table and rested her forearms on it, leaning toward them. The pose showed off her cleavage, and Evan couldn't care less. When he glanced sideways at Alek, he was happy to see Alek wasn't ogling her either. In fact, for the first time Alek seemed to have lost some of his plentiful confidence and looked a little unsure. Evan had no time to ponder this as the bartender spoke up, looking Evan over.

"Now, aren't you just the cutest thing. Good thing you've got this big puppy dog to protect you in this crowd. 'Fore ya know it, you'd have some cougar or a dirty old man trying to hump on you in the bathroom."

Evan choked a little on his beer. When he glanced sideways, he saw Alek purse his lips, lowering his eyes to the table. "Evan, this is my friend Katie. She's got a big mouth."

Katie flashed Alek her sweetest smile and eye-groped Evan some more.

"Katie, keep your paws off of him."

She meowed, then giggled. "So Evan, this is the first time Alek has ever introduced someone he likes to me, in all the years I've known the guy. You must be somethin' special." "Could we get another round please? Without the commentary?" Alek asked pointedly.

She eyed Alek's hand, clamped around Evan's upper thigh, and asked Evan, "He treating you okay, hon?"

"Yeah," Evan smirked. "He is."

"Good. Well, if he gets too fresh with ya, gimme a shout and I'll give Aleksy a little refresher in how to be a gentleman."

"Yes, ma'am."

She slinked away. Alek cleared his throat and told him, "Sorry about that. She's a little forward sometimes, but she means well."

They got their beers and the night slipped by. The music was good and Evan was having a great time just hanging out with Alek and listening. He chuckled at the way the singer kept flirting with the women in the front row, at one point singing right to a redhead and grinding up on her a little.

When there was a sudden outbreak of shouting and commotion from the far end of the room near the door, the rest of the crowd fell quiet. After another minute, the band's long-haired singer, the same one who was eyeing them earlier, stopped playing, motioning to one of the bouncers by the exit.

Two men were brawling, Evan saw. A tall, muscular, dark-skinned guy pulled them apart only to get a sharp left hook to the mouth for his trouble.

Before Evan realized he was going, Alek was up and darting across the room in a flash. He pushed through the throng and swiftly manhandled a stocky, bearded guy, who was still throwing punches, out the door. Evan stood; trying to see over people's heads what the hell was going on but couldn't make out much. He was just beginning to wonder if Alek was okay, if he should have gone after him when the crowd parted, letting Alek and the bouncer through.

Alek, scowling but otherwise fine, led his companion by the arm to another barstool at their table, the one across from Evan. The guy's lip was split and bleeding.

"Sit!"

The bouncer protested, saying angrily, "I ain'tcher dog, Alek. I'm fine! Seriously!" Alek stalked over to the bar, pushing through the crowd to take a towel wrapped around some ice from Katie. Turning to Evan, the newcomer held out a hand and said, "Hey. I'm Presley. I'm one of Alek's roommates."

"Hey. I'm Evan." He shook Presley's hand as Alek reappeared, still raging and incensed. Teeth gritted, eyes burning, body tensed and ready to fight, the sight of him so wound up was more than a little hot and Evan couldn't look away. He just replayed in his head how easily Alek threw the brawler out, like he was a ragdoll instead of a two-hundred-plus pound guy.

"Good. You've met," Alek said, nodding. He glanced around threateningly at everyone staring at them. "Oh, here we go," he groaned, retaking his seat as the singer from the band darted through the crowd toward them.

Once he got to their table, the long-haired man yanked Presley around in his seat and grabbed his chin, forcibly tilting Presley's head back to get a better look at his split lip. "I'll fucking kill 'em."

"Let go of me! Kill 'em for what? Being drunk? I'm fine. Calm down."

"This is Carter. He's my roommate," Alek explained to Evan.

"Another one?"

Carter frowned heavily at the sight of blood on the ice pack from Katie, his hackles evidently rising again.

"Carter, man. *Be cool.* Go finish your set," Presley insisted, all-too-aware of how many people were still staring at them.

Huffing, Carter glanced back at the exit like he intended to go after the guy who punched Presley.

Presley shouted, "Carter!"

"Fine. Two more songs and I'm taking you home," Carter said, pointing a finger at Presley who rolled his eyes and seemed kind of pissed off at the implication he couldn't take care of himself. Then Carter appeared to realize he hadn't acknowledged the other two men at the table. He turned to Evan and offered a hand.

"Hey, sorry man. I'm Carter."

"Evan," Evan nodded, shaking Carter's hand.

"Excuse me, I've gotta," he thumbed back over his shoulder at the stage and took off.

Alek leaned closer to Presley, telling him, "It's just 'cause he feels responsible."

"I know that. Still doesn't mean he can treat me like his bitch," Presley seethed.

Alek sighed, sitting back. He took a deep pull from his beer, then turned to put his lips right by Evan's ear, confiding, "Carter asked Pres to handle security tonight, just in case, as a favor."

"Oh. Are they...." Evan glanced down at Alek's hand fitted intimately between Evan's thighs.

Alek caught his meaning but didn't reply right away. Dropping his gaze, fingering drips of condensation on his beer, he replied, "No."

"Huh. Coulda fooled me."

An hour later, Presley and Carter shuffled into the house. Presley headed straight for his room. Once inside, he dropped his keys and wallet on the bureau. Carter went to his own room across the hall and lingered in the doorway, half in and half out, tracking Presley from the corner of his eye, watching as Presley pulled his shirt over his head and tossed his knit hat onto a chair.

Presley could feel his friend's eyes on him, but ignored it as long as he could. When his hands went to the button fly of his jeans, he hesitated for a moment. Then he went ahead and took the pants off, leaving his boxer briefs on and grabbing a pair of sweats to sleep in.

Carter was still watching.

Presley, sighing, finished pulling the sweatpants on and rubbed a hand wearily over his face.

"Go to bed, Carter."

"Not sleepy."

"Yeah, well, I'm not really in the mood right now."

"Bullshit," Carter growled, sounding like he was still riled up from the gig and the fight. After a beat he added, somewhat more gently, "Let me make it up to you."

The soft sound of footsteps could be heard over their heads. It was Alek and Evan walking around on the second floor. Presley gazed pointedly up at the ceiling. Carter was unmoved.

"I think they're a little preoccupied right now," Carter told him. "And who cares anyway." *It's not like they don't know*, he didn't need to add. Presley got the gist anyway.

As he was generally in a withdrawn mood, Presley gave in very reluctantly. Carter stepped aside to let him through the doorway, closing it behind him.

The light in Carter's room was dim but, on top of the dresser, Presley could see a gleaming white slip of paper with some girl's phone number scrawled on it, lying right beside Carter's discarded wallet.

Carter turned to face his friend, getting an eyeful of dark, glistening, chiseled muscle. He planted a hand on Presley's sternum and pushed hard, sending him falling backward onto the bed. Greedy and unhesitant as ever, Carter sank to the floor and had Presley's cock pulled free and wrapped in a tight fist in one fluid movement, stroking him hard. Carter's shoulder-length, light brown hair tickled as it brushed lightly over the exposed skin of Presley's hip.

"Anything you want. Anything at all," Carter promised, licking his lips moist, trying to talk Presley down, to tempt and lure. A wicked grin teased at the corners of his lips, lighting up his face.

Presley tried to shift his gaze, fixing it firmly to the ceiling, listening for more sounds from above, but there were none. Then he gazed down his body at Carter kneeling between his spread legs.

Opening his mouth, Carter extended and curled his tongue, licking a thin, wet stripe up the underside of Presley's shaft, then over the tip of the rapidly thickening flesh cradled in his hand before simply engulfing it completely. His lips, sealed tightly, kissed around the girth, his cheeks hollowing out as he sucked. Presley hissed, grabbed a handful of Carter's hair and thrust up into him.

"Anything," Presley echoed, letting the offer sink in, knowing what it meant and what Carter was asking for. He swallowed back a groan that rose up from low in his throat as Carter's warm, wet mouth worked on him in an intense, long pull from root to tip and right back down again. The blissful sensation wiped out all thought or protest and left him wanting, just like he knew Carter intended.

Carter always knew just how to play him, and Presley let him. There was really no point in resisting anymore. Presley hooked a thumb under his sweats and underwear, pushing at them to shift them lower, exposing even more skin. Carter's eyes flicked up to Presley's face, eagerly. Since he knew Presley liked to watch, Carter tried to make it look good, letting the dark length of Presley's shaft slip out from between his stretched lips so he could suck and lick just at the head. Stroking over a fat, throbbing vein, Carter kept an eye on Presley's hand on his pants. He took the hint and grabbed hold of the fabric, yanking it roughly down even farther.

Presley asked, "You got stuff?"

"Mm." Carter moaned as he pulled off with a wet slurp. A thin, gossamer string of saliva and pre-come stretched out between his lower lip and Presley's cockhead. "Hell yeah, I do. That a yes?"

"Just get it," Presley answered quietly, giving in, kicking off the rest of his clothes.

Finally getting permission, a switch flipped in Carter as he focused on getting what they needed so they could get on with it. He rifled like a madman through his top drawer, searching, palming his very obvious erection through his pants.

Heart hammering in his chest, Presley knew how wrong it was to let Carter pressure him into having sex, especially when it never seemed to mean anything to Carter, or lead to anything more than an orgasm. Realizing he should respect himself more than he did, Presley took a deep breath, getting ready to hold on and let it happen. Because it didn't matter how wrong it was. It didn't change the fact, naked and alone with Carter in that bedroom, seeing the passion burning in those grey eyes for him and only him, that Presley wanted it too.

# Chapter 12

# Surrender

"You want a drink? Maybe something stronger?"

They were standing in Alek's room by his bed. Alek was right in Evan's space, breathing hot against his neck, fingers tickling through the divot inside Evan's hipbone. Evan's head lolled to the side and he exhaled through his nose. The buzz from five or six beers was more than enough to take the edge off. Any more would just cloud his senses and he wanted to remember everything that happened come morning.

"No, thanks. The hard stuff and me don't really get along anymore." Evan sighed, leaning back against Alek's bulk, letting it prop him up as long fingers slipped down inside the front of his pants, grabbing a handful and kneading, pulling gently on his sac and cock.

"Shit," Evan said on a sharp exhale, reaching back over his head for purchase, finding a cascade of Alek's dark, shaggy hair to hold on to. Alek's mouth closed up around Evan's neck, under his jaw and on the left side of his throat, sucking the blood to the skin, leaving a bruise there as he yanked gently again, evidently liking the way it made Evan twist and shiver.

"God, you make me so hard," Alek growled. "Gonna take it slow, okay? Make sure you enjoy it, too. Want you begging for more when we're done."

Alek's free hand stroked up slantwise across Evan's torso, moving across his chest, and pushing up under his shirt. His fingers sought out and tugged on Evan's nipple, twisting it sharply as Evan gasped and undulated. Holding him flush to his body, Alek kissed in a line up to Evan's ear.

"Look, I know you're nervous, but I'm gonna take care of you. You trust me?"

Evan shivered again as Alek twisted his nipple the other way. Evan's cock pulsed wetly in Alek's hand, twitching and almost fully erect.

"Mmm," Evan grunted.

"Say yes," Alek breathed against the shell of his ear.

"...Y-yes," Evan rasped.

"Again." Pinching, squeezing, kneading, fondling.

"*Yes*," Evan whimpered, pulsing pre-come again, and every inch of him flushing pink.

Alek impatiently pushed Evan's pants down. They caught and puddled around his knees because of his wide stance. Alek released Evan's cock, let it arch up snug to his belly and pulled at Evan's shirt, getting it up, over his head, and off. Rubbing a flat hand down the front of Evan's body, over the firm muscles of his stomach, skirting down around his cock to his hip, down his thigh, Alek commanded, "Get on the bed for me. Lay down."

All Evan had to do was turn around to face Alek and sit down on the mattress' edge, which was right beside them. They had come up a back staircase into the house which led right to Alek's bedroom door. Alek told Evan that it used to be rented out as a separate apartment before he moved in, hence the private entry.

They had migrated over to the bed once Alek had turned on the stereo and lit a few candles for ambiance. The heavy, humid warmth of the room helped Evan relax a little as he sat, leaning back with his hands braced on the bed behind him as Alek tugged Evan's jeans off and climbed on top of him.

At first Evan just went with it, laying back and letting Alek settle there. He nudged Evan's legs apart with a knee, hooked an arm under one then drew it up to wrap around his lower back. Alek surged in, kissing Evan deeply. Caressing down Evan's inner thigh, Alek hummed and suckled at Evan's full lips, teased the tip of his tongue.

Alek's eyes were open, taking in every little thing. Alek hadn't removed any of his own clothes yet, maybe to help reassure Evan he wasn't in a rush. The leg slung around Alek's body tensed more the farther up Evan's thigh Alek's fingers got. Pivoting his wrist, Alek rubbed lightly over the underside of Evan's ass and played up through his crease. Watching his face, kissing him through it, Alek circled the pucker of Evan's hole with his thumb, making Evan want to squirm.

Evan whined in anticipation when the thumb circled in a gradually smaller and smaller spiral, finally coming to rest right on the center. Alek rubbed gently with Evan's bottom lip trapped between his in a tender kiss. He broke the kiss right as he pushed through, breaching Evan dry, popping his thumb through the outer ring then deeper, pushing in all the way to the hilt. A startled, tiny grunt escaped Evan's fallen-open mouth before he sealed his lips, squeezed his eyes tightly shut and pressed his face against Alek's neck to hide it from view.

Stroking gently over Evan's inner walls, with Evan's body clenched like a vice around the intrusion, Alek whispered, "Evan, baby, let me see you."

"I can't," Evan gasped. "You watching me while you.... I can't do it this way."

"You wanna flip over? That be easier?"

"Yes, please."

Alek sighed, kissing Evan breathless, not letting him stop even to gulp down some oxygen, cupping his face in his free hand.

"Okay. I just wanted to be able to kiss you. I could kiss you for hours."

He gave Evan some space and used the brief reprieve to find lube and a condom. Returning with them as Evan scooted a little farther up the bed, their eyes locked as Evan gazed over a shoulder.

"This is a first for me too," Alek confessed as he knelt on the bed behind Evan, who was now up on his hands and knees. "I've never been with a virgin before."

Evan, looking forward now, rolled his eyes as a pang of embarrassment ripped through him. "Sorry."

"Sorry? For what?" Alek draped his huge body over Evan, kissing the nape of his neck reverently. "You're gonna be so *tight*. I don't know if I'm gonna just lose it before we even really start. I can't wait to be inside you. Been fantasizing about this since I first laid eyes on you, before I even found out how amazing you are. There's nothing to be sorry about."

Evan clung to the small hope it might be over fast, but didn't tell Alek that. He was convinced it was going to hurt. He knew about prep and all of that, but he just couldn't imagine it not hurting at least a little bit. And the whole thing was beginning to cause something like an identity crisis in Evan.

This was it. This marked him as something he always knew he was. After he let Alek screw him, there would be no more pretending. He'd just be a faggot. No going back. No more lying to himself that maybe he was just going through a phase and he'd get over it. Maybe he'd meet some girl that turned him on as much as Alek did. Maybe he didn't have to be such a freak, beating off to daydreams of getting butt-fucked by a broad, ripped, towering guy like Alek.

But it was just not so. All of those kids who loved to kick his ass and send him home bloody were right about him. And not only that, it seemed Evan was developing a crush on his own brother.

*What a swell guy I am, huh?*

He got a flash of memory of what Brennan and Luka sounded like through the open window, making out, and quickly pushed it away.

*What's wrong with me? What the hell is wrong with me?*

But Alek felt good—solid, strong and real. Evan held on to that, how safe he felt with Alek's left arm circled around his chest, holding him in an embrace.

"You can lie down. You might be more comfortable that way. This might take a little while and I want you as relaxed as possible."

Evan turned his face toward Alek, almost looked back over his shoulder at him again but not quite and murmured, "Okay."

He settled himself down on the worn, soft nest of Alek's black sheets. Alek quickly got undressed, grabbed a pillow from near Evan's head and said, "Lift your hips for me."

Evan complied, his stomach restless with nerves as Alek slid the pillow under him. It forced Evan's back into a curve, his hips and ass tilted up. His legs were only slightly parted and he wondered if that was okay, but wasn't really in a hurry to further expose himself.

"This is gonna be a little chilly," Alek warned. "I just wanna make sure I use enough."

Something cold was squirted up Evan's ass, and he made a surprised little grunt, clenching up reflexively, but tensing did no good. The cold spread deeper. He was concentrating on the foreign sensation when a slippery but thick-as-ever finger popped through his sphincter and corkscrewed up into his rectum, rubbing through the slick, smearing it around inside.

Hands planted by his shoulders, Evan gaped, open-mouthed, burying his face in the bed to stifle a wrenching moan as Alek added a second finger, too. The stretch was intense and Evan pushed his ass even farther up off the bed to try to relieve it. Alek moaned Evan's name and lay down half on top of him, half on the bed, thrusting and twisting his fingers inside Evan.

Sucking light kisses down the back of Evan's shoulder, Alek worked to coax the muscles loose, prying Evan open.

Evan bit off the hard grunts he began to make despite trying to be quiet and breathed hard through his nose. With his face turned away from Alek, he softened a little when Alek nuzzled into his neck and thrust gently against Evan's hip. The impossibly thick line of Alek's dick nudging him distracted Evan and reminded him of Alek's desire for him. The proof of it was right there.

Alek's index and middle fingers pulled apart as he withdrew them from Evan, spreading him, widening the opening. Then they were free and Alek squirted on more lube, rubbing it around in his hand to warm it before spreading the fluid onto then into Evan. He rubbed through Evan's rim and pushed in as far as he could reach. Alek finger-fucked him like that a few times, half of his hand disappearing into the yielding passage with each thrust. Evan arched his back, adjusted the angle his hips were tilted at and gasped against the bedding. He was flushed a darker pink and sweating. His fingers were clawed around handfuls of the sheet.

Exhaling roughly against Evan's neck, Alek rasped, "Goddamn, I hope I fit in you." Bending the fingers nestled in Evan's ass, Alek hummed hungrily at Evan's next wrenching moan. Evan undulated, moving his ass in a gentle, rocking motion to try and find a more comfortable position. Alek just chased in farther, bent his fingers more, and rubbed his knuckles along the passage with little twists.

"A-Alek. *Alek*," Evan whimpered. His hips snapped as he thrust against the bed, trying to relieve some of the pressure building in his balls. "I-I guess I should've picked some pencil-dicked guy instead of you, huh? With the goddamned baseball bat between his legs."

Alek growled and pivoted his wrists, stroking around inside Evan. "Too late. You're all mine now. Gonna fuck you wide open. Gonna watch you take my fat cock, and come so hard in your ass."

As Alek triggered his prostate, Evan cried out, the sound shattered at the edges. He shuddered. Alek bore down on him, held him there and did it again.

"Ahh, *shit*. Alek, please."

The muscles were looser and Evan was rocking back gently against Alek's hand, so when Alek slipped in a third finger, it went in easily.

Evan moaned at the further stretch and rocked sharply against the bed.

"You wet? You wanna come? You wanna hump the bed and come just from having three of my fingers fuckin' your sweet ass wide open?"

Evan's eyes rolled back in his head and he spread his legs farther apart. His ass pushed up in invitation, accepting each pump of Alek's fingers prying him wider.

"No. Not yet," Evan murmured.

"You could though, couldn't you?"

"Yes."

"'Cause you love it. Don't you, Jailbait?"

"Fuck yes," Evan begged, "Alek, *please*."

"You ready for my cock? It's gonna be a hell of a lot more than this. You want it?"

Alek shifted and grabbed the condom, tearing it open with his teeth and rolling it on. Then he got up on his knees between Evan's legs.

Evan grunted out a sound. It was muffled by the bed, though, so Alek growled, "I need to hear you say it. No messin' around. Yes or no."

"Yes," Evan choked out, hating how close tears were. The salty, bitter wetness stung his eyes, flooded his vision as psychological pain ripped into him.

"Good, baby. Now get your knees under you again for me. This'll be easier on you that way. Show me you want it."

Questioning everything, sure of nothing, Evan's heart raced. His blood surged in a raging tide under his skin. He was overheated, panting for air, as he slid his knees up under him. Then he pushed his ass up. Both of Alek's hands instantly palmed his cheeks, pulling them apart. The warm air of the room kissed Evan's wet, throbbing asshole and he started to clench up in embarrassment and nervousness when Alek just pulled harder.

"Relax. Don't be ashamed of this. You're so fucking beautiful. Every part of you, but especially this part of you. Now if you need me to stop, you say stop."

"Okay," Evan managed, trembling now.

One of Alek's hands fell away. Then there was pressure. Something broad and unyielding pressed at him. Evan's arms were circled loosely around his head on the bed and he stopped breathing, just waiting for it to happen, wanting to get it over with. Alek fit his body more snugly to Evan, leaning over to get closer to him, not entering him yet, just feeling him out. He caressed tenderly up and down Evan's body, stroking along his sides, down his legs. He fondled between Evan's legs, grasped his cock and tugged gently on it while simultaneously kissing behind Evan's ear.

Evan sighed and some of the tension melted away. That's when Alek increased the pressure and began to enter him, forcing the thickest part of his cock through the narrowest part of Evan as slowly as possible. Evan's outer ring of muscle resisted at first, then yielded, letting Alek in. Alek's crown popped through, producing a hurt little keening whine from Evan as ache flared in his body.

"Shh," Alek soothed, nuzzling the side of Evan's face, damp now not just from sweat but tears, too.

Evan hiccupped and let out a shaky breath to breathe through the pain. Alek waited and pushed again, sliding deeper, inch-by-inch. Evan's mouth fell open widely. Gasping, lips quivering, Evan stayed as still as possible except for a hard shudder that tore through him.

Behind Evan, Alek let out a thunderous, gut-deep moan.

"Oh sweet Christ, *Evan.*"

Evan could sense how restless Alek was, though he stayed still, giving Evan a moment to adjust.

Another teardrop slipped down Evan's cheek when the pain didn't fade or become easier to handle. Finality settled on him like a weight and a tiny sob slipped free. Hearing it, Alek pressed his lips against Evan's temple.

"Did I hurt you?" he asked fearfully.

"No. It's not that."

"You promise?"

"I promise," Evan grunted, sniffing and groaning out another low sound.

"Thank god. I'd never forgive myself if I hurt you."

"Move, Alek, you gotta move. It's too much," Evan gasped weakly.

Alek didn't answer, he just complied and moved, tugging back out until he caught on Evan's rim.

Evan gasped audibly and twisted his clenched fists in the bedding as Alek pushed back in. His back arched. Eyes wide and mouth working soundlessly, Evan essentially shut down as Alek made love to him for the first time. He could feel Alek's thickness splitting him open, dragging over his prostate and filling him up so full that Evan couldn't help or even hear the small cries he made as their bodies slapped together faster and faster, chasing to a climax.

Alek's hands moved restlessly over Evan's body, scratching, grabbing, kneading, caressing. His hips pistoned and his dick was like a battering ram slamming home and jolting Evan forward each time. It continued to hurt but not enough to make him open his mouth to ask Alek to stop. There was pleasure, but not enough to keep Evan hard. He was overwhelmed by what was happening, what he was allowing Alek to do to him and how it felt to be so full and so intimately used.

Alek's hand was on Evan's cock, stroking him as they fucked, and it helped distract from the ache, but made Evan feel even more vulnerable, too. Thinking he was probably such a disappointment to Alek, unable even to stay erect, Evan was a little surprised when Alek's thrusts quickened. Moaning like he was dying, Alek drove desperately into Evan, filling the condom with a few uncontrolled convulsions.

Overwhelmed, heart pounding, body throbbing, and breathless, Evan almost didn't hear Alek's aching whisper by his ear.

"I love you. It's never been this way. Ever."

Sighing, Alek didn't pull out but wrapped Evan in his arms and rolled them onto their sides. They lay there like that, just breathing, joined so intimately, having both given away precious parts of themselves too fast. Alek's hand shifted back to Evan's dick, pumping so gently, and he was finally able to react to the stimulation. Fighting it at first, writhing slightly in Alek's embrace, he was soothed by kisses along his shoulder and neck and careful, patient touches. It took a few minutes for Evan to become fully erect and begin to want to push into Alek's hand. But, once he did, he couldn't stop. Eyes closed, gasping softly, clenching up around Alek's flesh nestled inside him, he rode out the good feelings, leaving the bad behind. Soon he was coming, shuddering, and letting Alek work him through it.

He didn't let Alek know he heard what he'd said, as he was a little startled by the confession. He wasn't sure if he believed it was true or how he felt about it until Alek leaned over to kiss Evan's cheek, and Evan smiled — *really* smiled. Once he let himself open up to it, he could feel honest affection exuding from Alek. Alek saw Evan's grin, propped up just enough on the pillow nestled under his head.

"You should smile more," Alek told him. "You have possibly the best smile in the whole world, and it's selfish of you not to share."

Evan smiled wider and tried to turn away. Alek just snarled playfully and nipped at Evan's earlobe.

And that was when Evan realized how happy he was. In that fleeting moment, he wasn't regretful or sorry. He was just happy. Sure, his ass hurt, he was sticky with come, very sweaty and felt gross, but he was tangled up in Alek's arms and *happy*.

It was such a foreign feeling to him; he instantly tried to squelch it.

"I should probably get out of here. Let you have your bed back."

"No way," Alek frowned, tightening his hold. "I don't want you to go."

"Why?"

Alek hesitated, then said, "Because I haven't really ever felt like this before. Everything just seems perfect, and that's all because of you. I'm not ready to let you go. *Please* stay, Evan."

Evan's face crumpled, the tears chasing up from his gut, taking him by surprise. He sobbed and quickly attempted to swallow back the sound, nuzzling against Alek's arm and trying to make himself stop.

"Evan," Alek sighed, kissing his jaw and hugging him tightly. "What's wrong?"

"Nothing. I'm fine. Just tired I guess. But I'll stay if you want me to."

"I want you to," Alek insisted gently, sounding like he was getting choked up from Evan's sudden, overpowering tears.

"Okay then." Evan closed his eyes; his arms overlaid Alek's which were wrapped possessively around him. He was asleep in seconds.

# Chapter 13

# Aftershocks

Sometime just before dawn, Alek woke up to find he was still inside Evan and still wearing the soiled condom. Grimacing, he carefully tugged free, hoping not to wake Evan.

He wasn't successful. Evan roused with a startled groan. "What the...."

"Sorry," Alek apologized, pulling off the condom, tossing it in the trashcan and grabbing for a wet wipe to clean off a little. He did it as fast as he could before turning back to Evan. "I didn't want to disturb you."

"Yeah, well, you just pulled your massive cock out of my ass. That's probably gonna wake me up."

Alek grinned. "Probably. Unless you're a heavy sleeper. My brother's a heavy sleeper."

"Okay," Evan laughed. "Interesting context to mention your brother, but no, I'm not a heavy sleeper."

"Good to know," Alek smirked. "Did I tell you I have an identical twin brother?"

"No, you did not," Evan said, matter-of-factly. "Brother, yes. Twin, no."

"I could be wrong here, but you don't seem overly surprised by that."

"That's because I met him yesterday."

"You met Luka?! How? Where?"

"Well, he was with *my* twin brother."

"Okay, now you're just making shit up. Are you making fun of me?"

"No!" Evan laughed, wriggling when Alek started tickling him. It was quite easy for Alek to do, as naked as they were.

"You can't have a twin brother, too! You didn't tell me you have a twin brother!"

"Well, neither did you!" Evan yelped. Alek eased up on the tickling. They'd rolled so that Alek was lying on top of Evan and he held Evan's arms down, caressing along them.

"So you really have a twin brother?"

"Yes. So I've been told. It's kind of new information for me, too."

"What?"

"I never knew about him. We were raised separately, without any knowledge of each other's existence and just met a handful of days ago. Long story. Basically my parents are psycho. Did you know our twins are dating?"

"They're dating?!"

"Huh. They didn't tell you they're dating either?"

"Okay, you really have to be making this shit up. Is this weird payback for mentioning my brother in bizarre context?"

"Why do you think I'm lying to you? I'm being serious," Evan laughed.

"Well, because it's ridiculous."

"You know what's ridiculous? Trying to take a nap only to wake up and find *your* mirror image and *my* freshly-fucked brother wandering the halls. *That's* ridiculous."

Alek gasped. "He told me he had a date with the, um, pescatarian, but that's all he told me, he... wow. And they were fucking *already*? It was their first date!"

"I know!" Evan exclaimed in mock horror. "The sluts."

"How are you feeling? Sore?"

Evan's gaze darted away. He bit his lip and shrugged. Alek wondered if he should back off, give Evan time and space to recover or at least sleep it off a little more, but when he brushed his hand down the side of Evan's slim, nude body, Evan's lips parted. His eyes slipped closed and he reached up to pull Alek in for a kiss.

A moment later, Alek backed off a little to say, "We can talk about it, you know. There's no reason to be embarrassed."

"Don't wanna talk," Evan murmured, breathing heavier against Alek's skin, arching into every touch. Experimentally, Alek rolled to lay more on top of Evan and felt Evan's dick nudging him. He rocked against it and Evan sighed with pleasure. It was the same reaction Evan had that night in the field, on the blanket out on Cedar Mill Road. He was shy about talking and embarrassed by the come on his stomach but reacted readily to Alek's continued attention. Now here he was after having sex for the first time, unsure what to say or do, but willing to let Alek be with him and showing every sign of enjoying himself. Trying to puzzle it out, to do the right thing and not take advantage, Alek tried to tread carefully.

Evan said softly, "Hey, since we're up, and since *you're* up...."

"You noticed that, huh?"

"It's jabbing my balls. Yes, I noticed. Anyway, so, you wanna?"

"Do *you*?"

"Just kiss me," Evan pleaded, sounding so young and out of his element.

Alek response was to dive in and start sucking on Evan's Adam's apple.

The last thing Alek wanted to do was take advantage of Evan. He knew the right thing to do was say they should go back to sleep, but his willpower was about nil. Evan spread and wrapped his legs around Alek's waist without prompting, making it even harder for Alek to put on the brakes. Alek's fingers went right for Evan's hole, needing to feel how stretched he was. Evan exhaled sharply through his opened mouth when Alek made contact with his opening. It was slightly swollen and sticky from the lube, but he parted around three fingers easily enough, undulating up into Alek's body with a soft gasp at the probing touch.

"This okay?" Alek asked.

"Yeah," Evan nodded, closing his eyes again. He wasn't frowning, which Alek took as a good sign. He looked for signs of pain in Evan's expression and found none.

"You want this?" Alek asked again, to make sure.

"Come on. Yeah. Yes." Thrusting lightly against Evan's erection, Alek watched him react. His lower lip quivered, he threw his head back, stretching his neck and moaned.

"Damn, I wanna do you bareback. We need to get tested or something, 'cause *damn*." Alek lunged for another condom, rifling in the nightstand for a minute before finding one. He had it rolled on in seconds, impatiently fisting on a palm-full of lube and, before Evan could think to get resituated, Alek bent Evan's legs back until his knees were in his armpits, lining up and pressing very slowly in.

The position was completely different and Evan's breath was stolen by how deep Alek went on the first push. He moaned loudly and grabbed his knees.

Alek let go of Evan's legs, pressed down into him, and braced his arms on the bed beside Evan's head. Starting to move, he fucked Evan's tender orifice as gently and carefully as he could.

Staring down between their bodies, Evan was watching what he could of Alek's darkly flushed, fattened cock driving into him again and again. Evan's hand went right to his cock as it stiffened in seconds, dragging wet lines over his abdomen. The evidence of Evan's pleasure spurred Alek on.

There didn't seem to be much discomfort for Evan that second time. He moaned with pleasure, pressing down onto Alek and wrapping his fingers around his cock in an attempt to get off.

However, Alek batted Evan's hand away from his erection as soon as he started pulling on it. "No. Just let me."

"But, Alek," Evan complained.

"Just let me. Just enjoy it."

"I kinda *am*. That's... *Jesus*... kinda the problem here."

"No," Alek growled, taking Evan's wrists and pinning them in place, crossed above his head. He picked up the pace, pumping into Evan a little faster and harder than before, his pelvis slapping against Evan's buttocks. Evan's cock slapped against his belly with the force of Alek's thrusts, straining and getting darker, copiously weeping pre-come. Whimpering, Evan arched, taking it all. His eyes rolled back; his head tilted back into the pillow. Growling again, Alek surged down, sucking on Evan's pulse point.

Evan's cries got lower and rawer the longer it went on.

"Alek, *please* let me come."

"Goddamn, you really do love it, don't you? Look at you, begging to be touched. You love having your ass stuffed full of my cock that much?"

Evan moaned, rocking down against each of Alek's thrusts, rolling his hips.

Alek hissed out a curse and suddenly pulled out, stripping off the condom. "Hold your legs open!"

Evan grabbed his knees, pulling them open and apart. Alek fisted his dick, squeezing up to the tip only twice before he was coming hot and thick, spurting a huge load all over Evan's gaping, reddened asshole, over his balls and shaft. Gasping, tingling from head to toe, Alek smeared it all around on him once he was only pulsing dry, rubbing his spunk over Evan's ass, over his balls and up his dick with one slow, squelching squeeze.

Evan's body went tight as a rubber band and his hips snapped up into the touch. He was right on the knife's edge. Alek lowered his mouth onto him, kissing the head of Evan's cock, licking his own semen from it, then took Evan back into his mouth. One long, deep suck was all it took. Then Evan was unloading down Alek's throat, their come mixing together there. Evan cried out with his climax, and Alek drew it out for him as long as he could. Then he climbed back up Evan's body, cupped Evan's face with his hands and chased his mouth.

Evan reacted instinctively, as Alek knew he would. He opened right up for a kiss. Alek's tongue pushed past Evan's lips, feeding him the mix of their come, licking it back over Evan's tongue.

Evan's eyes shot open and he moaned, but Alek held him still, waited for him to swallow some of it and kept on kissing him until Evan was gasping for breath.

They broke apart and Alek wiped away a stray drop of milky fluid from the corner of Evan's mouth. Smiling and sated, Alek praised him with, "You're obedient. I really like that. It's sexy as hell. And I will never, *ever*, get tired of fucking you. I've never had better. I mean it."

Evan's eyes closed bashfully, his long eyelashes resting against freckled skin.

"Sleepy?"

"Yeah."

Alek sat up and grabbed another wipe or two to clean Evan off.

Lying down beside him when that was done, Alek reached between Evan's legs to finger him. He'd become more swollen. The delicate tissue of his rim was puffy and hot.

"Sore?"

"Yeah. A little," Evan admitted.

"Want some ice? A cool washcloth? I'll get whatever you want, if it'll help."

"Nah. Just wanna sleep."

Alek kissed Evan's temple and smiled when Evan pulled Alek's arm around him, cuddling it.

After drifting off again, Alek dreamt of Evan. But things kept getting confused as they each multiplied, doubling and tripling. More than two hands caressed over Evan's naked body, and Alek had two glistening bodies before him, each young, tight, and lean and dusted with freckles; two voices cried out, pleading and begging for him to devour and plunder.

# Chapter 14

# Come Morning

Luka was awakened little by little, pulled layer by filmy layer from his heavy, dreamless sleep by the gentle hitching of Brennan's chest and his soft sniffling. It wasn't unexpected, but expecting something didn't make it any less hard to face once it was actually happening. Years ago, when it had become horribly clear to him that he was on his own, with Alek being the only family left who mattered, Luka used to wake up crying a lot, too. Those painful, early morning revelations were what set him on the path to drugs, underage, sometimes-forced sex with multiple partners, incest, self-destruction—all sorts of demons he was still dealing with every day.

Wanting better, so much better than that for Brennan, wanting him to know at least that he wasn't alone, Luka tightened his embrace around Brennan before he was even conscious enough to open his eyes. Acting instinctively, Luka lightly brushed Brennan's skin with gentle back-and-forth strokes of his fingertips. He pressed his lips against the top of Brennan's shoulder and cracked his eyes open.

Brennan had the heels of his hands pressed hard against his eye sockets. His lips were turned down at the corners like he was trying not to cry. Small whines sounded back in his throat, coupled with sniffles and hiccups. It broke Luka's heart to witness.

"I'm sorry," Brennan croaked. "Christ, I thought it'd be different with you here, that I wouldn't act like such a baby for once. I'm so stupid."

"Don't you dare apologize," Luka hushed. "You don't have to explain anything. Not to me. You're *supposed* to be grieving."

"But it's not fair to you!" Brennan cried. "God, what must you think of me? It's just that there's been so much to process recently and I don't know what to do."

Brennan pressed back into Luka's embrace, burrowing farther into it for a precious second before changing his mind and rolling over to face him instead. With balled-up fists, Brennan pressed his face against Luka's chest and let out a long-held breath right before sucking it right back in.

"Bren, it's okay. It's gonna be okay. You'll get through this."

"Why did she have to die? Why did she just leave me here alone? I don't want to be alone."

"You aren't alone. You aren't."

Luka brushed the hair back from Brennan's face, determined to wait with him until the pain eased back.

It took a good fifteen minutes before Brennan had calmed down and was breathing more regularly.

It was more than the loss of his mother. It was the absence of his father and the near-loss of his brother, though Luka didn't know that much.

Brennan had a revelation, lying there in Luka's arms. He understood how depressed and confused Evan had been. He also understood the current stress that was affecting Evan, and could guess at how overwhelming it must have been for him—dealing with Brennan's sudden presence, having to confront the darkest aspects of his past, being judged, and being outed before he was ready. Brennan knew what he needed to do, for Evan and his own peace of mind.

Pulling free of Luka's encircling hold very reluctantly, he sat up and picked at his nails.

"Do me a huge favor?"

"Name it," Luka said.

"Is there somewhere I can store some stuff? Somewhere safe and private? It's important."

"Yeah. Yeah I think so. What's this about?"

Brennan tensed. He battled against the ever-swelling tide of grief inside and gathered his courage. Maggie might have been gone, but Evan was still there and Evan needed Brennan's help, whether he could admit it or not. Brennan had to look out for Evan. It wasn't even a choice, it was a realization. Maybe it used to be Jimmy who watched out for Evan in Charlie's absence, but Evan had more than that now. Brennan could read Evan better than Jimmy or Charlie ever could. Evan might still be tempted to hurt himself. Brennan needed to lessen Evan's ability to do so. Buoyed by the chance to make a difference and do something positive for Evan, Brennan explained, "I need to keep my brother safe. That's my job now. No one else is going to do it but me. I need to make sure he can't hurt himself anymore."

"Bren," Luka sighed.

"I have to! You don't know! I almost lost him! *Really* lost him, and I can't take the chance." Fear, stark and undiluted, radiated from him. In response, Luka took Brennan's hand in his own.

"What are you thinkin'?"

"Get rid of Evan's gun and any other weapons that are lying around. If I lock 'em up and don't tell him where they are, he can't do something stupid."

Dumbstruck, Luka rolled onto his back. He took a moment before suggesting, "Maybe if you talk to him, tell him how worried you are about him?"

Brennan shook his head. Evan would have never agreed to give up his gun or lock up the butcher knives in the kitchen. And Brennan wouldn't be able to sleep another night knowing that under Evan's bed lay the means to his end. One dark mood or one bad decision could permanently rob Brennan of the most important person left to him.

"Please, Luka. *Please* just help me with this. I'll talk to him too, okay? And you can't say a word to anyone, not even Alek. It'd be a breach of trust. Evan would *hate* me."

Crestfallen, Luka looked at Brennan with a cold, hollow sort of realization. "He tried to kill himself, didn't he?"

Brennan turned away, quickly losing the battle against the tears, not wanting to subject Luka to any more. He got off the bed and darted from the room completely.

"Brennan!" Luka called after him.

The handgun Brennan found right away. Then he searched Evan's whole room, top to bottom, for anything else. Luckily that was the only object of concern, so next Brennan hit the medicine cabinets and the kitchen. There wasn't much. Whatever he couldn't flush fit easily enough inside Brennan's backpack from high school.

Once he had it all in there, under his control, he felt better. He was more composed and calm. Luka got washed, dressed and ready to go. In a few more minutes, Brennan was, too.

With the backpack slung over his shoulder, Brennan ran his fingers back through his still-damp hair in a nervous gesture, pushing it out of his eyes.

"I'm taking you to my friend Jamie's," Luka said. "He's got a decent-sized vault in his place where he locks up his own guns and some other expensive shit. I just called him and he said he's fine with holding on to your stuff for a little while."

"Look, I'll make it up to you okay? The crying, the drama—whatever you want. Lap dance, massage, kinky sex...."

Up until this point, Luka's expression had been a sullen one, very uncharacteristic for him, but upon hearing Brennan's offer, dimples dented his cheeks. He bowed his head to hide what he probably felt was an inappropriate grin. Hair fell in front of his eyes. "Ahem. Okay, then. Gotta admit, lap dance got my attention but you really don't owe me anything, Bren. If I didn't want to be here, I wouldn't be here. Simple as that. Wanna pick up some breakfast while we're out?"

"Yeah, that'd be nice," Brennan smiled. His gaze drifted over to the meditation altar for a second as they both moved to leave.

"What?" Luka asked.

Brennan shook his head. "Oh, nothing. I just usually meditate when I wake up. Do some naked yoga. Feels weird not to, especially when I'm this off-kilter about everything."

Luka's eyes went wide, nearly bugging out of his head. He blinked. "Wow. Excuse me, I just got some *majorly* vivid... sorry, naked what now?"

"Yoga," Brennan supplied.

"Ooh! That's what I want. Watch you do some naked yoga.

Maybe if we hurry we could get to Jamie's and come right back so that you don't have to miss your daily, um, naked time. Is touching allowed? It would be awesome if touching was allowed. Minimal penetration, I promise. God, you are really just beating the shit out of my willpower, you know that?"

Brennan burst into bright laughter, doubling over and bracing his hands on his thighs. He straightened back up once he composed himself. "Did you seriously just promise me minimal penetration?"

"Or there could be *more*, if that's better. *I* think it's better. Wow, now I'm just thinking of all the ways I want to penetrate you. Um, yeah. We should go. Quickly. Or at least move out of the bedroom before the rest of my brain dribbles down into my dick. Have I told you how awesome you are? Because you are. Awesome."

"Well, you told me I'm evil."

"Oh, you're still evil."

"But also awesome?"

"Yes. Also awesome."

Planting his hands on his narrow hips, Luka gestured at the opened bedroom door expectantly. He cleared his throat loudly for emphasis and raised his eyebrows.

Brennan gave Luka's tall body a good long look, from his tousled bed hair to his insanely broad, thick shoulders to his tight stomach and tapered waist, down to his bulging crotch. "Maybe first I should check exactly how *full* your dick is. Maybe provide some relief for that."

"Stop it," Luka scolded, trying to shake off the words like they were a physical thing lingering on his skin.

"Why? What're you gonna do? Spank me?"

Luka whimpered, closing his eyes tightly. His lips moved silently in supplication.

"Would this be a good time to ask if you're doing anything later?" Brennan said in a mock-serious and overly polite tone, "Because I had a fantastic time last night on our date and if you're *at all* interested in a second...."

Luka pursed his lips. His eyes opened narrowly. "Gimme this. Thank you," he said too quietly, too calmly as he took the backpack from Brennan and hooked it over his own left shoulder. Then he proceeded to take hold of Brennan's bicep, turned him around toward the door and delivered a loud, stinging smack to his backside.

In mild shock, Brennan gasped loudly and clenched up. His mouth clapped shut to stifle any further exclamations.

Luka sighed happily, adjusting the pack. "Mm. Yeah, I feel much better now."

Brennan gazed back at him, lips pressed together, jaw set, eyes blazing, ass tingling and throbbing. The punishment had not worked very well since Brennan was still horny and willing as ever, but he did at least stop verbally torturing Luka.

His eyes flicked downward towards Luka's crotch.

"Don't. Don't even think about it," Luka warned, talking to him like he would a child.

The corners of Brennan's lips curled up.

"Okay, we're leaving. C'mon," Luka decided, grabbing Brennan's arm again and partially dragging him from the room.

Alek passed the bathroom where Evan was showering and continued on down the hallway, past Luka's room to the steps leading downstairs. He headed through the downstairs hall, past Presley's room, which was empty and the bed curiously un-slept-in, and past Carter's room on the other side of the hall. That door was shut tight, so Alek had no idea what might be going on inside. His feet kept him moving toward the kitchen and the scent of freshly brewed coffee.

Carter was there by the counter, wearing only a pair of boxers. There were a few dirty dishes by the sink, including a cup of coffee and a cereal bowl. The coffee pot was not quite full, like a single cup's worth had already been drunk. Alek bit at the inside of his cheek, trying to puzzle it all out.

Carter peeked up, half of his mane of hair tied back to keep it out of his eyes. "Mornin'! How's the kid? He enjoy himself?"

Alek gave him a sharp look, then decided to let it go. He didn't appreciate the 'kid' comment, but whatever. The skillet on the stove sizzled. Carter flipped over the ham, cheese and egg omelet and slid the plate closer to him, opening up a freshly toasted bagel. Scooping up the steaming pocket, he set it carefully on the bagel and went for a mug, taking it over to the coffee pot.

"Morning," Alek replied. "Yeah, Evan's fine. He's getting washed up. I'm gonna take him home in a little bit."

"So that's his Chevy outside? Nice. I am kinda surprised he's still here."

"Of course he's still here. You think I'd kick him out in the middle of the night?"

Carter shrugged and made a non-committal grunt. "Why can't he drive himself home?"

"Why isn't Pres in his room?" Alek countered, steering the course of the conversation away from himself in order to protect his and Evan's privacy.

"He got up early for a run," Carter said, adding extra sugar to the coffee he'd just poured. Alek noted this since Carter drank his coffee with only cream, no sugar, just like he didn't eat egg sandwiches either. But Presley sure did.

"Huh. So he's not here then?"

"Nope."

"Who's that for?" Alek asked, nodding at the food.

"A friend," Carter said shortly, mug and plate in hand. Alek was in his way, blocking the path back to the bedrooms, so Carter gestured past him and asked, "You mind?"

"Not at all," Alek replied, stepping aside.

With Carter gone, Alek went about fixing breakfast for two.

Up in the bathroom accessible from both Alek's room and the hallway, Evan reveled in the, albeit temporary, solitude. Bracing his hands against the tile and staring out into space, he let the lukewarm spray of water wash down his back, trickling down his spine to the crease of his backside, through it and down the insides of his legs. He was sore and aching. He felt empty and strangely vulnerable. Only one of the two doors to the bathroom was locked, the one leading to the hallway, so he was secluded enough for the time being.

An uncertain amount of time passed. The water grew cooler.

There was a knock at the door. He couldn't tell which one.

"Evan?"

Alek.

"You okay? I made some breakfast if you're interested. We can eat in here when you're done with your shower."

Evan opened his mouth to speak and at first no sound came out. He cleared his throat and tried again. "Thanks! Yeah, I'll be out in a minute!"

"No rush. Take your time."

"What am I doing?" Evan said quietly to himself. The whisper echoed off the porcelain walls and faded away. "What did I do? Why the hell am I still here? He probably thinks I'm the biggest idiot on the planet. A stupid love-struck kid. He probably only said that stuff 'cause I put out and now he feels like he's gotta make me breakfast as, like, payment."

He shut off the water and grabbed a towel from the small stack on the shelf above the toilet. Patting himself dry, he pulled open the shower curtain and buried his face in the terrycloth.

There was another knock on the door leading to the bedroom. Evan froze.

"Yeah?"

"Can I come in?"

At first he couldn't answer. His mind drew a blank. "Sure? One sec."

He wrapped the towel around his waist, holding it closed with one hand.

Alek opened the door the whole way and just stood in the doorway, blatantly looking at Evan's bare chest. Evan swallowed thickly and turned away toward the mirror to make sure his hair wasn't sticking up crazily. Fingering through the dripping-wet spikes, he didn't expect it when Alek came up behind him, pressing flush to his back. The hardness in Alek's pants pressed demandingly at Evan's tender ass through the towel. Hot, soft lips closed up around Evan's earlobe, tugging on it. He shivered violently and pulled tighter at the towel, afraid it would slip right off. Alek's fingers tickled over Evan's lower back, right above his ass.

"You know, you have the sexiest little dimples right here. And this golden peach fuzz that it's taking all my willpower not to just get down on my knees and scrape my teeth over," Alek rasped. "Drop the towel."

"*Alek*," Evan pleaded, his brow furrowing.

He looked up, watching Alek watching him in the mirror over the sink. Alek grasped the towel's edge and Evan let it go. It fell away to the floor. Alek instantly started to eye-fuck Evan's naked body in the mirror, so Evan looked away. A wide, strong hand rubbed over his chest. A thumb rolled over his left nipple just as another hand caressed over the side of his bare buttocks.

"I never got to see you in the light. I had to see you. Your body is just... sick. I'd fuck you again, right now. If I didn't care about you as much as I do I'd be fucking you already, even though you're sore and it'd hurt. That's the kind of guy I used to be. Real nice, huh? I'd stuff you full of my cock and if you cried out or, hell, just plain cried, it'd just turn me on even more."

Evan breathed heavily, gripping the sides of Alek's hips behind him, getting dizzy, getting hard.

"Are you sore?"

"Yes."

"Bet your hole is really hot and throbbing. Bet if I licked it, it'd cool it off really nice, though."

Evan moaned, almost too softly to hear.

Alek grabbed Evan's chin, and tilted his head around for him to catch his lips in a soft kiss. Evan hummed and kissed him back, tasting minty toothpaste on Alek's lips.

"I've been too careless with you, letting my libido obliterate common sense when it comes to safety, and I'm sorry about that. You should know I've always been really careful with my partners in the past, and I get tested regularly out of principle, but just in case, I want to go today to get tested for you, if you want to come with. After getting a taste of you last night, I need more. I want to have full access to all of you. No more condoms. No one else. Just you and me. Then I'll drive you home."

Confused, Evan blurted, "What? Well, you don't have to worry. You really don't have to do that, and like, go to the trouble. And I'm clean. Former virgin and all."

"But there's still a chance I might not be."

"I don't care."

"Well, *I* do," Alek argued. "You really don't care if we're safe or not? If I give you something? Don't you care if you get hurt because of me?"

Evan shrugged, dropping his chin to his chest, wishing he had the towel back.

It was all the answer Alek needed.

"Huh. Okay then. Guess I'll have to make it my job to look out for your well-being then, if you don't care enough to." His hands were resting on Evan's shoulders, heavy and firm, grounding him, trapping him.

Evan sniffed and tried to turn his face away from the mirror when tears stung his eyes. Self-respect was something that had eluded him for a long, long time. It was still hard to admit it to people who mattered to him, though. He angrily brushed away a fat teardrop that sprung from the corner of his right eye and avoided Alek's gaze.

Alek sighed against the side of Evan's face and kissed his temple, asking, "How do I fix this?"

"You can't. And you don't have to take care of me."

"I'm sorry, but it seems I do."

"How did I get here?" Evan murmured to himself as he detangled from Alek's grasp.

"What?"

"Nothing."

Alek followed as Evan went to grab his pants, stepping into the legs and shimmying them into place on his hips. He knew he was moving awkwardly, and grimaced a little when he bent.

"Come and eat," Alek urged. "I'll drive you right home if you want to go."

Evan hesitated in answering, pulling on his shirt. "I can drive myself. I'm not actually a child, you know."

"Tough shit. I'm driving you home. I want to make sure you get there okay."

Evan sneered and laughed bitterly. Alek stalked up to him and grabbed his wrist when he tried to twist away.

"Something is up with you, and I'm not going to make you talk about it if you don't want to, but it scares me that you care so little about yourself. I'm not letting you take off on your own right now until I know you're okay."

Breathing roughly, Evan yanked at his arm. Alek just drew him closer. Evan stared at Alek's mouth, feeling defiant and speechless and incredibly turned on. Pushing in suddenly, he stretched up on his toes and chased Alek's mouth, dragging the swell of his bottom lip over the cupid's bow of Alek's stubborn pout. A small, soft, breathy fragment of a grunt escaped Evan as he licked with the point of his tongue, teasing up the center crease of Alek's bottom lip and inside. Alek cupped the back of Evan's head, forced his jaw open wide and licked over his tongue.

Eventually they separated, dizzy but calmer.

"Sit. Eat," Alek commanded, pulling out a chair at the small table by the window, the platter of breakfast food laid out and ready.

"Okay," Evan relented, not quite believing the submissive tone in his own voice.

Sitting down across from him, Alek grabbed one of the two cups of coffee and sipped. "Thank you."

After their plates had been mostly emptied, Evan spoke up. "If we're taking my car, how are you gonna get home?"

"I've got it covered. Don't worry about it," he assured Evan who eyed him warily but didn't argue.

Alek asked, "What's your brother's name?"

"Brennan. He's basically the new and improved version of me, better in every conceivable way. Smarter, cuter, healthier, more common sense, less of a push-over."

Alek set down his napkin after wiping his mouth with it and rested his forearm on the table. "Don't say things like that. You're not allowed to berate yourself to me."

"Really?"

"Really. Out of everyone in the world, *you* are the one I most want to be with, and I find it insulting that you think so little of someone I care about."

Shifting uncomfortably in his hard seat, Evan kept his focus on his lap, popping the last piece of sausage in his mouth and washing it down with some juice. He apologized softly, saying, "I'm sorry." There was silence between them for a full minute. "What's Luka like? I didn't get to talk to him for too long. But he did seem different than you."

"He is," Alek admitted. "You know, if you'd be more comfortable on the bed, please sit there instead. I should've given you a cushion."

"I'm fine," Evan said, blushing. "Actually, I think I'll stand."

He got up and paced around Alek's room, drinking coffee as Alek spoke.

"Luka's a personal trainer. He's funny and laughs a lot. His hair is too long and he doesn't shave as often as he should. He wears lots of flannel shirts and likes to show off his body. He acts like my little brother, but I'm okay with that. I trust him with my life. He's part of me. He might be the best part of me, actually. I take care of him, too. All we have is each other."

"What about your parents?"

Alek tucked his hair over an ear and folded his hands on the table, leaning forward. "We were raised by our mom. Dad was pretty much a sperm donor. Never met him. Mom hated everything about the guy and never talked about him. We reminded her of him, so she didn't like us much either. She was a single mom with a brutal, thankless job, so I don't blame her. I just wished she cared more. When we were teenagers, she got remarried and had her 'real' kids who she loved. Luka and I were unwanted, so we left as soon as we could. Luka agreed to move in with Presley and Carter, and I followed him here. I went to college and got my degree in business management and finance. Luka worked to cover the bills so that I could stay in school. All the money I made bussing tables and slaving in kitchens went to tuition. I owe him so much for that. He wanted me to have a career, move to New York or someplace where I'd have better opportunities, but he needs me here, so I'm here. I won't abandon him after everything he's given me."

"I-I don't know what to say. I'm sorry. That's horrible, what you've been through. But I'm glad you've had Luka. He sounds like an amazing brother."

"He is," Alek agreed.

"I wish I had that too."

"You will. You said you just found Brennan?"

Evan nodded, his eyes still lowered.

"Then give it time. You two are connected in ways you can't even fathom. You share a bond that makes you closer than anyone else in the world."

Evan chuckled doubtfully. "I don't know about that."

"Trust me," Alek urged gently, and Evan finally met his eyes. There was hope there, and a hint of a smile.

# Chapter 15

# Back to Reality

The stop by the clinic took about an hour. Evan and Alek both decided to get the full work-up and get tested for everything. Evan let Alek drive him home afterward, feeling doubly violated after his time on the exam table. He was quiet but Alek held his hand the whole time at the clinic, and continued to do so in the car afterward, and that was nice. It was enough to help Evan keep himself together.

They pulled up to the house and there was a truck in the driveway. Brennan didn't have a vehicle and, for the first time, it really struck Evan how strange that was. He pushed the question away and refocused, getting out of the car.

Alek came around to his side and looped his thick arms around Evan's neck, resting them there. There was a small, happy smile on Alek's face as he leaned in closer and closer. Evan parted his lips, closed his eyes and hummed as the soft, hot fullness of Alek's lips brushed across his in a tease before pressing in more firmly. Evan grabbed Alek's belt and pulled his hips towards him, fitting their pelvises together, grinding gently against him as he licked back over Alek's tongue.

Evan didn't hear the house's front door open, or the two men come out of it.

Luka cleared his throat loudly to alert them to his and Brennan's presence. Evan jumped back from Alek instantly, as if shocked.

"Whoa," Luka blurted, looking between them. "*That's* who you've been flipping over? Evan?!"

Baffled, Brennan gaped at Evan as Alek reclaimed Evan's hand

and also encircled Evan from behind with his other arm for good measure. Evan began to feel like a deer caught in headlights but, fortunately, Alek reacted by doing his best to soothe Evan.

"Yeah. We're together. What're the odds, right?" Alek said easily enough. "You must be Brennan. It's nice to meet you. I'm Alek, but you probably already figured that out."

"Hey," Brennan waved, baffled. "This is so... I mean, out of all the people for us to each hook up with..."

"Is that all I am to you? A 'hook-up'?" Luka asked prissily, folding his arms.

Brennan rolled his eyes and nudged him. "You know what I mean."

"It's a small world, I guess," Alek offered. His fingers were dragging in gentle swoops over Evan's chest, over the hammering of Evan's heartbeat. "And I guess we have similar tastes. Makes sense when you think about it." He turned his mouth to Evan and whispered, "I'm gonna walk you inside, okay?"

Evan nodded, feeling very uncomfortable. His gaze skittered around, not focusing on anything.

As they passed between Brennan and Luka, Alek smiled, "Excuse us for just a second."

Once inside, Alek turned Evan to face him and said, "Hey. You're fine. Breathe."

Evan shivered and folded his arms. "I didn't think they'd be here. I don't know why, I just didn't. And we put on a nice little show for 'em too, didn't we?"

Alek pulled him in, hugging him to his chest. "You think *that* was a show? That was nothing. And I have news for you, Evan. I'm gonna be kissing you in public a lot, because yours is a mouth that should be always well-kissed, and if anyone has a problem with it, they can deal with me. But I can guarantee you that my brother and Brennan are absolutely not about to attack you for kissing your boyfriend goodbye."

Evan smiled despite himself and nuzzled against the heat of Alek's solid body before saying, "So we're... I mean, you said that you're my—"

"Boyfriend? Yeah, is that okay?"

Biting shyly at his lip, Evan nodded. Alek kissed him once more time, chastely, gently, then said, "I'll call you later. Or you can call me. I have to work for a couple hours tonight but I'd like to see you again tomorrow if we can work it out."

"Okay," Evan agreed, relaxing more and more as Alek's finger brushed against his cheek.

Alek left him rooting through his dresser drawers for some clean clothes, pulling the bedroom door closed before he headed back outside.

Smiling at Brennan, Alek took his hand to shake it, marveling at both the resemblance and differences between him and Evan.

"Is he okay?" Brennan asked quietly, nodding toward the house.

Alek nodded. "You guys just surprised him. He likes his privacy. So how'd the date go? I see it's gone into day two, so it couldn't be too bad."

Luka smirked and retorted, "I was the perfect gentleman. Ask Bren. But yeah, we had a great time."

"Hmm, so Brennan's your official new cuddle toy then, I see? Careful you don't smother him in his sleep, ya big monkey," Alek teased, liking the way it got Brennan to smile and laugh.

"You need a ride back home I guess?" Luka said, checking that his keys were still in his pocket.

"If you don't mind. Or I could text Carter."

Luka clapped Alek on the shoulder, leaning into him a little in his familiar, comfortable way. "Nah. I should go get freshened up anyway before date number two starts in a few more hours."

"Really?" Alek smirked slyly.

Brennan's gaze darted between the twins. He looked dumbstruck by their easy closeness, the way Luka was touching Alek like it was the most natural thing in the world. Alek couldn't help but sneak a few glances up and down Brennan's body, comparing it to Evan's and also simply appreciating how gorgeous Brennan was, too. One glance at Luka showed Alek that his brother was looking at

Brennan in a similar way. With both of the twins' attention on him, Brennan grew a little shy, but it just made Alek smile.

"Do me a favor?" Alek said to Brennan, his tone soft and sweet. "Take care of Evan for me?"

"Of course."

"Very nice to have met you." Alek took Brennan's hand in a lingering hold. Luka kissed Brennan goodbye, but didn't make a big production of it.

"I'll call in a little bit."

"'Kay. Thanks for everything. Really," Brennan told Luka softly.

"My pleasure."

Tugging down the long sleeves of his cotton shirt so they covered his hands, Evan sat cross-legged on his bed and brushed his fingers over the buttons on his phone. He was glad to have the bandage on his arm covered from where they drew blood, especially after wondering if Brennan noticed it, and he was glad to be alone, away from prying eyes.

Those were the only things he was glad of. The jittery, nauseated feeling hadn't gone away. Without Alek there to distract, Evan slipped farther and farther back into his ever-present fear and self-doubt. What happened the night before was too vivid, too raw. The things he'd let Alek do to him—the things Evan *enjoyed*—it was too much to process and be immediately okay with. The berating voices in his head niggled at him, picking apart his reasoning and excuses, leaving him only with guilt, regret, and self-hatred.

He dialed Jimmy.

From the other end of the line, he heard, "Hello? Evan?"

"It's me. Can you come over? Please?" He could hear how choked and weepy he sounded already and despised it.

"What's wrong? Evan, what's wrong?!"

"Just come over, okay?"

He hung up rather than face more questions.

Meanwhile, and not too far away, out on the front stoop, Brennan was listening to his voicemail just as a call started to come through. Groaning inwardly, he answered.

"Yeah?"

"Brennan? Thank god, I thought I had the wrong number. How are you? I've been trying to call."

"I know. Sorry, it's just been crazy, getting settled in and all. I meant to call you back. Look, it's not really a great time."

"Oh. Well, I was just calling because I wanted you to know, I've put in for some vacation time. In a couple of weeks I should be able to get down there to see you."

"Oh. Good. That's good. Does Evan know?"

"Not yet. Do you mind not telling him? I hate to get his hopes up in case my boss nixes the request and I have to cancel. When I know it's definite I'll tell him myself. I just wanted you to know that I'm trying my damnedest to see you, son."

Brennan cringed at the endearment. "Thanks, Charlie. I've gotta go."

"Okay. Can I call you later? Maybe we can talk?"

"Sure. That'd be great," he said. It came out sounding more hollow than he would have liked. The 'too-little, too-late' feeling he got whenever he talked to Charlie was there again, unshakeable.

"Bye, Brennan."

"Bye."

Jimmy *ran* to Evan. He burst through the back door without knocking, frantic, wild-eyed, panting, and searching, startling Brennan, whom Jimmy encountered in the kitchen.

"Where is he?!"

"Who?" Brennan asked lamely.

"Evan!" Jimmy shouted.

Brennan recoiled, stricken. From back toward the bedroom they heard, "In here, Jimmy."

Jimmy darted toward the sound of Evan's voice. His feet almost slid out from under him on the slick wooden floor. Grabbing the doorframe for purchase, he pushed into Evan's room only to see him sitting there on the bed — absolutely fine — or at least fine on the surface and not....

*Slowly getting poisoned to death, choking on his own vomit, turning grey, his blue eyes open and unblinking, not moving and not breathing, not breathing at all....*

...hurt.

Jimmy put a hand on his heart and tried to catch his breath. He roared viciously, *"You scared the shit out of me!"*

"I'm sorry," Evan breathed. The apology caught in the middle, his voice lilting as he fought through tears. He pressed his lips shut when they started to curl down at the edges and quiver. Then he just drew his knees up to his chest and buried his face in them.

*"Why would you do something like that to me?!"*

"I'm sorry, Jimmy," Evan whimpered.

Brennan appeared behind Jimmy, stepping into the room. He'd been lurking in the hall but couldn't take it anymore; curiosity and concern drew him in.

"Don't yell at him," Brennan admonished quietly.

Evan sobbed softly and curled farther in on himself.

The fight all-at-once drained out of Jimmy. He walked to the bed, sitting on the edge beside Evan, and placed a hand gently on his arm. Jimmy took a deep breath, calming down.

"I'm sorry. Forgive me. I thought you had—" he shook his head to clear it. "Never mind. What's wrong? Evan, tell me what's wrong."

Evan shook his head, hiccupping, whining back in his throat.

"Talk to me," Jimmy urged again.

Brennan hovered in the middle of the room, clearly not knowing what to do but making no move to leave either.

Jimmy pressed, determined, "What happened? Something happened."

Evan mumbled a reply, glanced up. His eyes fixed on Brennan and Evan moaned, covering his tear-streaked face with a hand.

Knowing he had no right to tell Brennan to leave, Jimmy waited, giving Evan some time.

When Evan started to talk, he talked right to Jimmy and very quietly, not looking at Brennan. He picked at the worn denim of his pants and scratched along the weave of the threads.

"I let him fuck me," Evan confessed. It was barely audible, but it hit Jimmy like a punch. The former preacher's hands curled into fists, like this was something he could possibly fight back against.

"Who?" Jimmy demanded. It came out sounding sharp, fierce.

"His name's Alek," Evan said, his voice still lilting. "He cares about me."

Confused, Brennan stared at Jimmy, who was so very angry, nearly boiling now.

"He forced himself on you."

"No," Evan frowned, still picking at the seam of his jeans. "I just... *let him.*"

Jimmy groaned, holding his face in his hands, rubbing over the skin. Of course this had happened. Jimmy wasn't surprised at all, just furious. Evan had always been easily moved or coerced. Charlie had been pushing his son this way and that for years, trying to shift Evan onto a safer path when all along he probably should have been helping Evan to make his own decisions about who he was and what he wanted. If Evan had learned to do that, maybe he wouldn't have been a pushover with some hardheaded guy looking to take advantage of someone so young and unsure of himself. "God help me, I want to strangle him with my bare hands. Did he know you were a virgin? Did he use a condom? Bet he's a lot older than you too, right?"

Brennan gasped. The naïveté of Evan's words were plain and terrible. Though Jimmy had tried to explain to Brennan who Evan truly was, Evan was showing his brother now what was hidden behind his thin, gruff exterior. This was the Evan Jimmy knew. This was the Evan Jimmy had constantly been afraid for. As Brennan sank into a chair, a tear spilled down his cheek. He curled up just like Evan, upset and trembling slightly. Then, they truly did look like twins.

"He knew," Evan whispered. "I told him. I just wanted it to be over. I wanted to get it over with." He looked up at Brennan for the first time, and seemed surprised at how upset Brennan was too all of a sudden. That's what got him to confess, Jimmy suspected—the pain on Brennan's face.

"You know, I heard you and Luka last night. Together. I know I shouldn't have listened. But you sounded really happy. I guess I kind of just wanted that, too. So, I told Alek I was ready."

"Were you ready?"

Evan shrugged, then shook his head no.

Brennan wiped at his eyes.

"When I realized I wasn't, it was too late. He was already, you know. It was too late."

Jimmy sighed, trying to be calm, trying very hard to be calm. "How did all of this make you feel?"

Evan bowed his head.

"Sad?"

There was no response, just a growing vacancy behind Evan's eyes.

"Angry?"

Jimmy set his jaw, pushed on.

"Did it make you want to hurt yourself?"

Evan averted his gaze. After a moment he nodded but it was barely noticeable. Evan appeared to become lost in thought but was yanked right back to reality, blinking and alert, when Brennan made a heartbroken, choked sound in the corner.

"But you didn't," Jimmy supplied.

"No," Evan said. "I didn't. Because... I don't know. Once it was over, Alek told me how much he cares about me, and he didn't kick me out like I expected him to. He just held me. Then I was happy. I was really happy. And it happened again, and the sex was better. It didn't hurt as much and I was still, you know. Happy."

Jimmy's eyes slipped shut and he murmured a prayer to himself, willing the violence in his heart, borne purely of fear for Evan, to drain away.

"Did I do the right thing?" Evan asked. He sounded so young and so lost that it caused a sharp pang in Jimmy's chest.

He reached out and took Evan's hand. "What do *you* think?"

"I think I did."

"Then you did. Do you feel better now? Having talked about it a little?"

Evan nodded, smiling slightly. "Yeah." He sat up straighter and said urgently, "Look, I'm real sorry for scaring you."

"That's okay. I shouldn't have assumed the worst. Just don't do it again, please. And don't you *dare* ever hurt yourself, you hear me?"

"Yeah."

"Promise me you'll call your father later. I know it helps when you talk to him. Maybe just tell him you had a tough day."

"Okay."

"He worries about you."

"I know."

"Well, I was hanging wash on the line and have a pile of wet clothes at home on the ground now so I should get going. If you need anything, you know where I am."

"Thanks. Really. Thank you," Evan said softly.

Jimmy smiled, squeezing Evan's hand once before turning to go. It was good Evan was able to talk about why he was scared and how he felt after making such an important decision for himself. It helped put Jimmy at ease about his young friend's state of mind. Evan was okay. He was overwhelmed, but okay, and that was the most important thing.

Jimmy hesitated at the door, glancing at Brennan, who was still crying silently in the chair in the corner. It had to be a lot for him, to be faced with his twin's troubles when he was already dealing with so many life changes of his own. But maybe it would give the brothers something to bond over. That hope was what moved Jimmy to leave them alone. He had a sense that it was better not to intervene more than necessary and let nature take its course.

"Are you okay?"

Brennan sniffed and nodded, not looking up. "Yeah."

Jimmy nodded, too, and left.

Minutes passed after the back door of the house clicked shut. The air was still. Neither Evan nor Brennan moved or spoke. Evan watched with rapt fascination as Brennan tried to stifle his emotions.

Then Evan told him with stark sincerity, "I lied to you. About a lot. I'm sorry about that. I was just embarrassed. You seemed so confident and sure of yourself and I just wasn't."

Brennan stared at a spot of the wall, his face betraying some of the battle for control going on in his heart. He just got sadder and sadder, looking younger and younger.

"Bren?"

Brennan's mouth closed in a battle to keep his lips from trembling. Evan couldn't watch him be that upset anymore and do nothing about it. He couldn't bear it. So he got up off the bed and went over to Brennan, standing in front of his chair. When Brennan still didn't look at him, didn't say anything, Evan took his hand and pulled at Brennan's arm.

"Come on. C'mere. C'mere," Evan coaxed.

Brennan slowly got to his feet. Then they were just standing there, inches apart. Brennan rubbed his hands over his arms and sucked in a rough breath.

"Bren," Evan sighed.

"I don't wanna lose you, too." It was the last straw; Evan pulled Brennan into a tight hug as Brennan broke apart in his arms.

"You're not gonna lose me," Evan hissed.

"I love you," Brennan told him, burying his face in Evan's neck and shoulder, his tears dampening the new shirt. "Please don't leave me alone."

Evan's eyes prickled. He breathed in the scent of Brennan's hair. "I love you, too. You're not alone, you hear me? You're not." He grasped the sides of Brennan's face and gently kissed his eyelids, brushing the tearstains away. Without opening his eyes, Brennan closed the miniscule distance between them and softly kissed Evan, once, full on the lips. Then he wrapped Evan's neck in a bruising hold.

Evan's lips tingled. The ghost of Brennan's kiss was still there. It was part of him now, that brief, intimate touch, just as Brennan was part of him, too. His life suddenly, miraculously fuller, richer, Evan felt his head spin and his heart begin to feel complete in a way he had never experienced before.

# Chapter 16
# Hard Up

Luka called Brennan once he got home, suggesting that for his and Brennan's second date, they go to a hockey game instead of staying in again. At first, to Evan's amusement as he eavesdropped, this made Brennan unhappy. Suspecting that the distraction of a game would help take his brother's mind off of everything, Evan wasn't surprised to discover afterward they had a great time. Once it was time to drop Brennan back at home, though, neither Brennan nor Luka was in much of a rush to separate again. When Brennan asked Luka to sleep over for a second night, Luka was easily swayed.

At around ten in the morning, Luka swiftly headed home to tackle some household chores that had piled up after a few days' neglect. Not wanting to seem clingy, Brennan didn't protest, though Evan knew Brennan really did want Luka to stay. Evan thought it healthy for them to have some time apart, too.

Evan, for his part, headed out at dawn with Jimmy to prepare and distribute breakfast down at the local homeless shelter. He crept from the house before Brennan and Luka were awake and returned after Luka left.

All was well as Evan began to gather dirty clothes to be washed and tidied his room, until he realized something of his was missing. Possibilities of what could have happened wove through his mind, but only one thing made sense: Brennan did it.

Furious, frustrated, but also confused at what the theft implied about Brennan's level of concern for him, Evan stomped over to Brennan's closed bedroom door, ready to really let him have it, only to freeze there, paralyzed by second thoughts.

"I can hear you breathing. The acoustics are insane in this house, but I guess you know that," Brennan murmured somewhat sullenly from inside the room. "You might as well come in."

"Are you naked?" Evan asked, pushing the door open anyway, provoking a quirked eyebrow of dull astonishment from Brennan. Stepping into the room, Evan crossed over to the bed on which Brennan was lying and, yet again, only wearing a pair of thin, clingy, white yoga pants.

"Yes. I'm naked," Brennan replied sarcastically. "Thanks for asking *before* you came in."

"You're welcome," Evan said distractedly, sitting on the bed. He positioned himself in grabbing range of Brennan. "So, I was curious. Why don't you have a car?"

"Excuse me?"

"A car," Evan repeated. "You drove all the way out here from Louisiana, to rural, east-bumblefuck Whippoorwill, Pennsylvania without a damn car."

"I hate cars," Brennan shrugged.

"You hate cars? What did they ever do to you?" Evan asked in amazement.

"I dunno," Brennan mumbled. "I'm just not a car guy."

"That's completely ridiculous, considering we share genetics and all. So, what? You just planned on bumming rides from hot guys you randomly meet or walking a lot?"

Brennan cracked a tiny smile. "Yeah. Pretty much."

"Slut."

"Why am I a slut?" Brennan laughed.

"Have you met yourself?"

Brennan narrowed his eyes. Evan fell quiet, pausing.

When he asked what he came in there to ask, it came out sounding deadly serious, in a vastly different tone than his first question. "Where the hell is my fucking gun?"

Eyes widening fractionally with what Evan decided was unmistakably guilt, Brennan slowly drew his legs up, pulling himself into a more upright position.

They were both very, very still for a long moment until Brennan quickly tried to dart from the bed. Evan grabbed him easily, pulling him back down, then held his brother to the bed by his arms, leaning over him when he tried to wriggle free.

"Where is it?! What'd you do with it?!"

Brennan looked gravely up at him. Twisting like a limber, very strong cat, he easily flipped them over so *he* was the one on top. Evan reacted angrily. Brennan acted fast, grabbing Evan's wrists, pinning them to the mattress by his head. Then he sat firmly atop Evan's hips, straddling him. Their faces were mere inches apart.

Evan fought back at first, writhing and bucking. It took all of three seconds before he realized how screwed he was. Not only was he unable to throw Brennan off, but he became keenly aware of how very thin Brennan's pants actually were. He himself was only wearing some old, worn sweatpants until the laundry was done. And Brennan's firm butt was perched perfectly atop Evan's cock.

All of Evan's rage about the gun, all of his righteous arguments about trust and respect were funneled down into an endless inner chant of, *Don't get hard. Don't get hard. For the love of Christ, don't get hard.*

"Lemme go," he managed.

"No," Brennan replied firmly and obliviously. "Give me a second to explain."

"Brennan, let me go," Evan repeated, swallowing a groan as Brennan shifted to get a better hold on him, the move causing him to grind down against Evan in what would otherwise have been a really fantastic way, if not for the whole, unfortunate 'brother' thing.

"Do you really think it's not irrational to give a gun to someone who could be suicidal or sometimes feels like he wants to hurt himself? Do you *really* think I might not take issue with that? I put it in a safe place, okay. It's not gone; it's just not *here* anymore. And I'm sorry for not trusting you and not talking to you first, but I did what I did, and I'm not changing my mind."

Very slowly, Evan's face and neck started to flush pink. He could feel it happening. Gnawing at the inside of his cheek, he tried to think of something gross, or get angry again, but it didn't work. Just worrying about getting hard with Brennan sitting on his lap was enough to get him going.

"You done?" Evan asked quietly.

"What, you're not even gonna talk to me about this?"

Brennan shifted again when Evan tugged at Brennan's unyielding hold on his wrists.

"Could ya stop wriggling like that, please?" Evan blurted out, exasperated at the whole thing.

Then, just when he thought it couldn't possibly get any worse, it did.

Brennan realized why Evan was blushing, why he wouldn't meet Brennan's eyes, why he was breathing roughly and trying to free his wrists. Horrified, Evan was helpless as Brennan tested his newfound theory by pressing down slightly harder down on Evan's pelvis, rolling his hips backward.

Evan tensed bodily, his fists balling up, sucking in a sharp breath through his nose. Yep, Brennan was definitely able to feel it now — the defined, long line of Evan's erection now fitted perfectly in the crease of Brennan's backside.

"Oh," Brennan said stupidly.

At the same time Brennan realized Evan was hard, he was also fully cognizant of the reason he was sitting on Evan in the first place — the gun. That was when Brennan began to get a little scared. He wondered, *What if Evan feels guilty about this? What if it sets him off and makes him want to do something horrible as penance?*

Brennan had always instinctively used sex to deal with stress and forget about his troubles — screwing around, seeking out and keeping around a 'boyfriend' who was convenient to fuck when life went rotten. Physical pleasure helped banish mental or emotional anguish. Relying on that had become a habit for him, and Evan was a relatively new presence in Brennan's life. He simply didn't *feel* like family, at all. He was just Evan. And Brennan loved Evan.

"Bren, let me *go!*" Evan cried, his voice breaking with the force of desperation.

But if he let Evan go, Brennan knew Evan would only take off and it would all get a hell of lot worse than a chance boner.

So, Brennan tightened his grasp, squeezing the bones of Evan's wrists.

"No."

Not able to make sense of the response, seeming purely ashamed, Evan half-whined, half-growled in reply. Brennan felt Evan's torment mixing with his own fear of allowing Evan to slip away. Evan couldn't be allowed to slip away. Brennan just had to hold on to him tighter, try harder to make Evan understand how much he meant to Brennan. No one else had tried to hold on to Evan like Brennan was holding him, and no one was as good as Brennan at keeping a loved one close, loving them through a tough time, come what may. Just like with their mother, it was a matter of life and death. Brennan had one chance to reach Evan somehow and let him know he was wanted, that Brennan wouldn't judge him or let him slip away like Maggie had, for any reason. Depression or cancer, they were both diseases ripping people out of Brennan's life, giving him no say in who stayed and who went. He would do whatever necessary to stop it. Evan was the embodiment of Brennan's hope that life could be better for both of them, and together conquer everything holding them back. All they'd ever needed was each other. Now they had the chance to reclaim everything previously lost. Anything was possible, if only Brennan could find a way to demonstrate to Evan how very much he was cherished and needed.

Brennan leaned down. Their foreheads touched together. "Hey, calm down. It's okay."

"No, it's not."

"You're human. It's a normal bodily reaction, not a choice." Tilting his head slightly to the side, angling his mouth closer to Evan's, centimeter by centimeter like he was moving in slow motion, Brennan told Evan matter-of-factly, "*This* is a choice."

Evan didn't try to pull back, not that he could if he'd wanted to, but he did go perfectly still as if he was afraid of provoking a wild animal with any sudden movements. The swell of Brennan's bottom lip brushed over Evan's bottom lip. It felt nice, more easy and comfortable than Brennan suspected it would. Brennan breathed softly into Evan's mouth, feeling the heat of him, the softness of his skin, tasting each quickened breath that slipped through Evan's lips. It wasn't brotherly at all, like their last kiss.

"What're you doing," Evan managed to mutter against Brennan's lips without moving his much, if at all.

There was no instinct to pull away. If anything, he became more determined that he was making progress in the right direction— calming Evan down, showing him he could relax and trust. Brennan's eyes slipped closed and he went for it, placing a gentle but deliberate kiss full on Evan's mouth. But he didn't stop. As goosebumps pebbled his skin, Brennan kept on kissing Evan, peppering his full lips with feather-light touches of his own. He slowly felt out the shape and flavor of Evan's mouth, and was able to gradually relax into the connection.

After the first few seconds, Evan started to kiss Brennan back a little. Brennan wasn't holding Evan's arms down anymore, but Evan seemed to be oblivious to the fact, even when Brennan wrapped his arms loosely around Evan's head, and idly twisted some of the tousled strands at the top of Evan's head between his fingers. Neither of them used their tongues, or moved against or touched the other's body. It stayed relatively innocent, technically. But it didn't feel innocent at all.

Brennan wasn't sure how long it went on, how many minutes exactly. When they'd stopped and Brennan was still fingering tenderly through Evan's short hair, looking affectionately down at him while Evan stared up into Brennan's eyes, his lips were tingling and hot.

It took about four different tries before Evan was able to come out with his very simple question. "Why?"

"Had to make a point," Brennan replied.

"...And that would be?"

"This isn't just about you, or something you did, or something you wanted to do. I'm involved, too."

"Whatever. You're still not getting off of me."

Brennan nervously bit at his bottom lip. "I don't want you to do something stupid."

"Bren, I do a lot of stupid shit. Sorry. It's kind of unavoidable."

"It didn't feel wrong to me," Brennan whispered, glancing between Evan's eyes and his mouth.

Evan closed his eyes. His face creased with pain. Brennan tried to soothe the delicate frown lines away with more of those tickling, light kisses—along the corners of his eyes, between his eyebrows, at the edges of his mouth. Sighing, Evan gave up the fight and circled Brennan's back in a loose embrace, holding Brennan flush to his chest.

About ten minutes later, when they still hadn't moved, Evan asked into the silence of the room, "So, can I have my gun back?"

"No," Brennan grunted into Evan's shoulder. "I also kind of hid those big butcher knives and flushed all the pills in the medicine cabinet, so if you have a headache or something, you're kind of shit out of luck."

"Brennan!" Evan scolded.

"Mm."

"You're fuckin' crazy."

"Probably."

"So, why does Luka keep sleeping over? You two screwing like bunnies or something?"

Brennan groaned. "No. He thinks if we have sex it's like he's taking advantage of me in my time of grief, so he keeps turning me down. We've just been sleeping. I think he has insomnia issues and likes the company."

"Huh. It all makes sense now."

"What?"

"Why you're so hard up you're kissing *me*."

Brennan sat up, squinting down at him. "Excuse me, *who's* hard up?"

"Date night?" Carter asked. It was Friday evening. He was seated at his kitchen table along with Luka, Alek, and Presley. They'd all been eating pizza in awkward silence and staring impatiently at the clock on the wall.

"Yeah," Alek grunted, distractedly.

"'Bout damn time. You two have been zombies the last few days. Maybe getting laid will help jump-start your brains. I think it's great you both found someone. You're moving in a healthier direction."

Luka and Alek exchanged a glance and wordlessly went back to eating.

Alek had been missing Evan desperately. The instinctive need to constantly make sure Evan was okay hadn't eased up at all. Just as Alek initially feared, the more he grew to care for Evan, the more intense his feelings became and the harder it was to be apart from him. They'd gotten into a habit of leaving each other messages, though. Evan started it, leaving a voicemail for Alek while Alek was at work at the bar Monday night. By the time Alek got it, it was very late and Alek's return call to Evan went right to voicemail, so he had left a message of his own, just to say hi and that he was thinking about him.

But that night, Alek had off from work. He'd been looking forward to having another real date all week long, and he knew just how he wanted to spend it.

That morning, Alek spoke with Evan over the phone as he walked to work, asking if Evan had anything particular in mind he wanted to do.

"Yeah. I want you. I wanna be with you tonight," Evan had told him. It was spoken quietly, like Evan was afraid of being overheard, and that sexy shyness was detectable in his voice, too. "No one else, okay? Nowhere public. Just me and you."

"When can I see you? How soon?"

"I get off at six. Gimme an hour to get ready, then you can pick me up. You can eat dinner before if you want, so we don't waste any time. Brennan and your brother are staying here at the house for their date, so I thought maybe we could go out?"

"Oh, yeah, Luka's really looking forward to that," Alek grinned. "No problem. I'll take you somewhere more private if you prefer."

"Thanks."

It all sounded pretty cut and dried. Alek loaded the back of his truck with an inflatable camping mattress and blankets, his plan perfectly formulated.

In the kitchen of Alek and Luka's house, both of them lost in their thoughts, the clock ticked steadily away. For each of them, it was all about the one person they were infatuated with. For the first time in their lives, everything seemed normal to Alek, like they'd finally found their way to the life everyone else had always thought they should have and discovered partners they could love and be committed to, without complications. Part of Alek wanted that desperately. But it was the rest of him that contributed to the strange, new silence between them, keeping the brothers from meeting each other's eyes lest they see something lurking there that might threaten to spoil their pure intents.

"How about you two?" Alek asked. "Any big plans?"

Luka and Presley locked eyes for a second, communicating without speaking. The trouble with this was that Alek knew Luka infinitely better than Presley and could read his thoughts as if they were his own. With a glance at his brother, he figured it all out.

"Nah," Carter said, shrugging. "Gonna stay in and hang out. Take it easy."

Presley purposefully didn't look at Alek. Luka saw Alek open his mouth to speak and nudged his leg under the table. Alek's mouth snapped shut. He decided to let it go. If they weren't ready to talk about what was going on between them, Alek wasn't going to force the issue. Presley had always been closer to Luka than Alek, and had his trust. It wasn't something Alek intended to step on.

Luka had wanted to see Brennan all week long, ever since they last saw each other on Sunday morning. Brennan kept deflecting requests to get together by saying he had some stuff to figure out, promising they could spend the whole weekend together if Luka gave him a few days to get situated. So they spoke on the phone daily. Talking to Brennan always left Luka smiling and happier than he was before. Doing without Brennan's company for so many days in a row decided Luka about how to move forward. If Brennan was still ready to take the next step physically, then Luka was too. Afraid of losing Brennan entirely if he kept saying no to sex, Luka thought that night might indeed be the night they got to be together for the first time.

He was beyond excited about it, but also wary. Luka's relationships in the past had been all about sex. Even when he was in love, and ready to make it about something more than getting off, for the other person, it never got that far. Even with Jackie, she never was interested in committing to him, and simply moved on to find someone new when Luka got too clingy. That was why it'd been nice to, for once, focus on other stuff with Brennan — getting to be friends first, getting to know each other as people before becoming lovers. Luka considered Brennan a friend, not just a maybe-boyfriend. That was an incredibly important distinction to Luka. And he'd do anything to avoid messing things up.

Luka and Alek had been maintaining a healthy distance from each other, too. Once Luka found out Alek got tested for STDs for Evan's sake, it made Alek off-limits for screwing around with. Happy for his brother, putting his own selfish needs aside, Luka let Alek make the rules. No sleeping together, no crossing the line like they'd always done. It had caused Luka heartache, but he knew it was the right thing to do. They hadn't even really discussed the incredible coincidence of them falling for another set of identical twins. Luka felt like they might jinx their good fortune if they put it all out on the table for dissection.

After their makeshift dinner had been cleared away, and when Alek went to brush his teeth and prepare for the date with Evan, Luka pulled Presley aside. Luka asked him discreetly, "So? Everything cool? He treating you good?"

Presley clammed up immediately. "Listen, man, I can't really —
"

"Yes or no. It's not that complicated."

"No, it *is* complicated," Presley argued.

"You deserve better than this," Luka frowned. "A lot better. He doesn't even respect you enough to acknowledge what you mean to him or what's going on!"

"That's because I ask him not to. It's personal. I don't need the whole world knowing."

"It's nothing to be ashamed about! If being with him makes you happy, then that's all that matters."

"I'm not like you. He's not my *boyfriend*, Luka, and I don't want him to be. He just fucks me for fun, okay? That's all it is. I don't try to fool myself into thinking it's more than that. Go on. Have your date with your little man-child and leave me alone, please."

Presley was gone before Luka could respond, leaving him standing alone in the front hall. With a glance up the steps toward where he knew Alek was, Luka pushed past his hurt feelings and slung his bag over a shoulder, with his toothbrush, a few changes of clothes, and some other supplies packed inside. Not able to wait a moment longer, or wanting to be in that house anymore, Luka went out to his truck, jumping behind the wheel and flooring it all the way across town.

# Chapter 17

# When it Feels Right

·

Brennan leaned inside Evan's doorway, watching him towel-dry his hair. "You don't have to leave."

Evan shot Brennan a look of mute disbelief. Though on the surface innocent enough, that one statement might have been the most shocking thing anyone had ever said to him. It meant Brennan wanted to be there, in the house with Evan while Evan was with Alek—a tiny house with ridiculous acoustics and practically no privacy.

He chuckled to break the tension and turned his back. "You gonna protect me, Bren? From my own boyfriend?" When there was no response, Evan added, "This is your big chance. You're finally gonna get to boink Luka, right? That's what he alluded to anyway, from what you said. You don't want us crowding you."

"Don't put words in my mouth."

"Then say what you mean."

"I mean this is your house. Your home. Maybe it's time to start bringing people home instead of acting like what you're doing is something that should be hidden and lied about. Why haven't you talked to Jimmy all week? He's been asking me what's going on with you, and why you've been so quiet. He's worried."

"He's always worried. And this has nothing to do with me being ashamed of Alek or hiding Alek from Jimmy or anything like that. I'm just figuring stuff out. I'd think you would understand why," Evan said pointedly, glancing over his shoulder at his brother. The reason Evan hadn't called Jimmy was the kiss he'd shared with Brennan. It wasn't about Alek. It was about Brennan. And Evan knew Brennan knew it was. It was the same reason they'd each avoided

Alek and Luka all week.

"Then what's going on?"

Evan chuckled coolly. "Don't be naïve. You aren't naïve, Bren."

Brennan seemed to digest this and, after he did, said firmly, "You don't have to leave."

"Yeah, I do."

"You don't trust me?"

*I don't trust* me, Evan thought, walking past Brennan to the bathroom. He closed the door once he was inside in order to block out the simultaneously alluring and distressing figure lingering in his bedroom.

For the next hour Evan cranked up his stereo and hid in his room once Brennan had given up on pestering him. He heard Luka arrive, letting Brennan answer the door and audibly tracking their footsteps which headed right into Brennan's room. After that, Evan switched to headphones in order to further inhibit his ability to overhear them.

That was why he didn't hear Alek's knock at the front door when he arrived for their date, or Brennan's annoyed shout of "Evan!" from the front hall. After Brennan let Alek into the house, he gladly showed himself to Evan's room.

Evan looked up, surprised, from where he was laying on his back draped slantwise across his bed, spacing out and turning over and over in his hands an old football he and Charlie used to play catch with out back. He yanked the headphones off and twisted around, almost falling over himself in his hurry to get upright and standing.

"Alek! Hey. Man, I didn't even know you got here. Sorry about that."

"It's okay," Alek grinned broadly, crossing the space and taking another look around Evan's fairly sparse room. Alek walked over to look at a small collection of postcards with scenic views taped up by the bedside. There were mountains, rivers, the ocean, blue skies, and open fields.

Before Alek could ask about them, Evan said, "What's in the bag?"

Holding out the white paper sack, Alek answered, "Cheeseburger. You said you usually don't get around to eating dinner 'til late so I figured you'd be hungry."

"Even though we said this wasn't a dinner date?" Evan retorted with a half-smile. He accepted the cheeseburger, which smelled delicious. "Thanks. You keep giving me stuff. Food. It's weird. But nice. So, thanks."

"Well, where we're going there's not a lot of dining options. You're welcome. We have plenty of time if you want to hang out here for a while. You can eat while it's warm."

Evan eyed the exit, "Bren and Luka are here. I don't know. I thought we were going out."

"We will," Alek assured him. "I don't think they care if we share the house with them. They're just watching a movie in Brennan's room."

Evan gave in and sat cross-legged on the edge of the bed. Alek lay down behind him, getting comfortable.

"I like your postcards. Someone send you those?" Alek asked, pointing to the wall.

Swallowing a bite of burger, Evan ducked his head and answered, "Yeah, my dad. He travels because of his job and sends me those when he can. I don't know why. It's not like we don't talk on the phone."

"Liar," Alek squinted. "You know why he sends them. You can tell me the truth. I won't judge. What do you like about them? I mean, you hang them up. They must be special to you."

"It's stupid." Evan rolled his eyes.

Alek softened his voice and said, "Tell me anyway."

"He says he wants to show me how amazing it is to be on the road and see all of these places, how beautiful the country is. He does it to cheer me up, to let me know he's thinking about me. I would love to travel like that someday. But my life is here right now."

Alek slid his hand over Evan's thigh, stroking in small arcs with his thumb. From his expression, it didn't seem like Alek thought it was stupid at all. He seemed touched. "Why do you need cheering up?"

Evan shrugged.

"You really love him, don't you? Your dad?"

"Yeah. He's all I've got."

"What about Brennan?"

Evan breathed out a half-hearted chuckle. "Well, he's kinda new." Through the open door, Evan could catch the low sounds of the movie playing in Brennan's room. He cleared his throat and set down the remaining half of his burger. "Hey, can I ask you something unusual?"

"Shoot."

"Okay. I'm really not sure how to say this without freaking you out or making you think *I'm* a freak, but, you're a twin too, so here goes. Last weekend, something weird happened with Brennan and me. But it started before then. It started when he got here and I saw him, I think. Anyway. I don't know what to make of it, and it's making me question a lot of things and, hell, I don't know."

"Just ask me," Alek urged. He was still stroking the top of Evan's right thigh and shifted so he was sitting up instead of lying reclined on the bed.

*Are you really going to tell him this? He'll think you're sick, perverted, and fucked in the head.*

"No, you know what? Never mind. Forget I mentioned it." Folding up the rest of the food in the wrapper, Evan moved to stand.

"Did you guys kiss or something?"

Sinking back down onto the bed, Evan looked quickly around at Alek. "How did you—? Yeah. He started it, though," Evan blurted, knowing it was a lie, but whatever.

"Yeah, Luka and I kiss, too."

"You do? But I mean, not like...."

"How much tongue are we talking?"

"...you're making fun of me, aren't you?"

"Do I look like I'm joking?"

And he didn't. That was the thing. Alek's face was as dead serious as Evan had ever seen it. Initially, he couldn't figure it out.

"I wouldn't joke about this, trust me. You aren't a freak, Evan. Don't beat yourself up over it. You're young. You're messing around. It's expected. Plus you two weren't raised together. You don't have a shared history giving you normal cues brothers usually feel. There are tons of people—siblings—who get adopted by different homes when they're kids but meet as strangers as adults, and wind up hooking up. We're attracted to people we relate to, right?"

"Are you mad?"

Alek's eyebrows rose. "Um, no. No, I'm not mad my hot boyfriend kissed his twin brother and liked it. You did like it, right?"

Evan repressed a smile but the glint in his eye answered the question for him.

"We don't have to talk about it if you don't want to," Alek told him quietly, brushing the back of Evan's neck as tension built there, like he sensed it and his instinct was to soothe it away again.

"Thanks."

Evan left Alek for a moment to go brush his teeth, and came back to catch Alek in the act, rifling through one of the drawers in Evan's bedside table. He worried maybe Alek would want to talk more about the kiss with Brennan, or be thinking about it at least, but the first thing Alek said told Evan plainly enough he'd moved on from the topic.

"Damn, I haven't found a single sex toy. You must have them really well hidden from Daddy."

"I don't have any sex toys," Evan scoffed, like the idea was absurd.

"Why not? I mean, yeah, virgin, but not even to play around, or... no? Wow."

"I haven't even seen one in person. What can I say? I live a sheltered life."

"Obviously," Alek muttered, sliding the drawer shut. "Luckily, I came prepared."

"Excuse me?"

Circling Evan where he was standing near the bed, Alek embraced him from behind, tucking his chin over Evan's shoulder and slowly rubbing a hand down the front of Evan's body. "So, what specifically did you want to get out of our date tonight? You've had all week to think about it. What's the verdict?"

Alek's huge hand palmed him through his jeans. Evan's cock twitched, jumping at the touch. Alek hummed by Evan's ear.

"Maybe a nice, slow, thorough BJ?" Alek suggested.

"Sure, as long as I get fucked too," Evan grunted.

"You're up for taking then? No pressure. It's your call."

"Believe me, I'm up," he said roughly. Suddenly, Alek tugged Evan's pants open and shoved his hand down inside. Once again there was no underwear to hinder them and Alek chuckled darkly, wrapping Evan in a hand and squeezing.

"Mm, almost." Alek pulled him out, pushing the pants down and out of the way. Stroking a flattened hand down the underside of Evan's swelling length, Alek grabbed a handful of Evan's sac, tugging on it, rolling Evan's balls in his palm.

Evan gasped. His knees went weak. Blood surged to his dick in a tidal wave.

"Can we not do this here?" *The bedroom door is wide open*, Evan thought. *Bren and Luka are just feet away.* "Maybe the truck instead?"

"Fuck the truck," Alek growled.

"No thanks."

"Smartass."

Alek let Evan go for exactly three point two seconds to grab the light jacket he came in with. He pulled a shiny red object from the pocket and handed it to Evan while he found lube.

"What the hell is this?"

"Butt plug. For you. The idea is to make the whole stretching process more fun. I'm gonna put it in you right now, then you're gonna wear it all night until I decide it's time to fuck you wide open, sloppy wet and make you come so fucking hard you'll feel like you're losing your mind."

Evan had barely glanced at the tapered, cherry red plug, but his skin was slowly turning quite a similar color. The stark reality of the toy and nervousness about what Alek intended to do with it overtook Evan's worries about the others in the house or being overheard.

"And now that we know we're both clean, we don't even have to worry about condoms. It'll just be me. In you. Can't wait to feel you like that." Alek slicked his hand and the toy too, taking it back from Evan. Pausing, he asked before proceeding, "Do you want it? Yes or no. I don't want to pressure you. There's lots of other ways we can enjoy each other, too."

"Yes," Evan moaned. "I want it."

*But they'll hear us....*

"Okay then. Bend over for me. Hands flat on the bed."

He did it—heeding the verbal command rather than his less tangible mental niggling—bending almost in half, his jeans down around his knees. Alek nudged Evan's feet as far apart as they'd go with his foot.

"Stick your ass out. Farther. Good. Stay just like that," Alek hummed, pushing his index finger and a thick glob of lubricant into Evan who instantly gasped and tightened up around the digit, but took it easily enough. Alek pumped in and out a few times, savoring Evan's ragged, gasping breaths.

"Feel good?"

"Yeah," Evan rasped.

Taking hold of the base of the plug, Alek touched the narrow tip to Evan's opening, right above his finger, still buried deep. Everything else fell away, everything but what was touching him and how, and why. The finger was extracted just as the tip of the toy was pushed in. An inch of it was fed inside him before it rotated, twisting it like a screw.

Evan cried out, then bit off the sound abruptly, arching his back more and moaning low in his throat as Alek penetrated him with the toy.

"Ready for more? Mm, I wish you could see this, the way your hole's stretched out around the red plastic." Alek tilted the toy, rotating it in gradually larger circles, using it as leverage to pry Evan open more, turning it around and around in his sphincter. It helped to get it a little further in, about two and a half inches, with the widest part still to go.

"You're fuckin' killin' me," Evan complained.

Meanwhile, just a few feet away, inside the small, one-floor house and outside the other bedroom door, stood Brennan, leaning against the wall in the hallway. Enraptured by the sounds, moans, and filthy descriptions coming from Evan's room, he was held captive, taking it all in, just like Evan was. The craziest part was he could *feel it,*

too—Evan's pleasure—like Evan was broadcasting on a frequency only Brennan could pick up on. Luka stood behind Brennan, nibbling at his earlobe, one hand circled around across Brennan's chest while the other steadily worked the drawstring of Brennan's pants open enough to slip his other hand inside.

Luka finally was able to manage it, finding Brennan fully erect and dripping pre-come. Dragging a thumb across the head, over the weeping slit and down over the bundle of nerves under the ridge, Luka chuckled softly as Brennan shuddered, then nipped harder at Brennan's earlobe. Luka hissed one word, low and secret, just between them, "*Listen.*"

"This is the thickest part," Alek said. "You can take it. It's only as wide as me."

Evan felt more pressure. The mattress's edge was digging in to the front of his thighs. His splayed hands were pushing against the bed to keep him upright. Straining his ears, he still could hear the movie, though it seemed fainter. He was able to lie to himself and believe that maybe, possibly, Brennan and Luka were too involved in their own intimate activities to notice or care.

Evan wanted to be quiet, he really did, but he was much more distracted by the way that the harder Alek forced the toy through his asshole, the stiffer his dick became. Trying to swallow back his long, unending moan, Evan's control slipped completely. The moan sharpened and shattered when the widest part of the plug popped through.

"It's in," Alek told him and Evan could hear the smile in his voice, as well as raging, possessive lust. Alek pulled back on the toy, holding it by the flared base, tugging it gently against the inside of Evan's sphincter. "It's in you. You feel it?"

"Yes! Stop pulling on it," Evan growled.

"Mm, I'm gonna have so much fun working that really slowly back out of you."

"Yeah, I bet." "Stand up," Alek instructed, pressing up flush to Evan's back and staring hungrily down at Evan's full, flushed, hard-on bobbing against his belly. Kissing the side of Evan's neck, Alek cupped a hand over Evan's abdomen, avoiding contact with his dick, and said, "I don't want you to come until I'm inside you. Can you do that for me?"

"You're still killin' me," Evan complained. "How am I supposed to walk?"

"I could always just sling you over my shoulder."

"No thanks. I'll figure it out."

Alek promised softly to him, "I'm gonna make this so good for you."

Once Evan was tucked safely away in his jeans again, they got ready to go.

In the hall, Brennan pried himself away from his spot, letting Luka guide him back to the bed. They didn't bother shutting the door either. Luka walked Brennan to the bed and waited for him to lay back before climbing on top of him. With one hand, he pulled down the front of Brennan's loosened pants again, exposing him. Wearing only soft, smooth, mesh shorts, and boxer briefs, Luka began grinding purposefully against Brennan's erection in long, deliberate thrusts which slowly quickened in pace. Brennan breathed more heavily and arched up into Luka, his eyes rolling back in his head as he finally got some relief. He hooked his right leg up around Luka's body, urging him faster, weaving his fingers through Luka's long hair and pulling his mouth closer to kiss.

"Could you picture it, Bren?" Luka whispered against his lips. "Evan taking that plug? Made you wet, didn't it? You want to watch Alek fuck him, don't you?"

"Hell yes, I do," Brennan moaned.

"Bet he'd purr really sweet. Bet he'd writhe and beg, trying to be quiet while Alek made him take his whole cock. Would you suck him? Would you suck Evan off as Alek plowed his ass? God, I'd love to see that."

"Fuck," Brennan whimpered, grinding against Luka's clothed erection.

Brennan and Luka lay in an undulating horizontal tangle on the bed when Evan and Alek walked by, heading to the front door. They paused, watching for a long couple of seconds as Luka fucked himself against Brennan. The pale skin of Brennan's hip was visible, and the side of his ass, too, especially when he drew his leg higher around Luka's back. The sound of Brennan's small whimper burned into Evan's brain and he shivered. He tried to bolt for the door, afraid he'd come in his pants right there if he saw or heard any more. It was too tempting, too vividly graphic.

Alek watched Evan's reaction, smiling wickedly.

Evan's movement caused the floorboards to creak. Flinching at the noise, Evan motioned to Alek they needed to go. A moment later, they were gone.

Brennan and Luka heard the floor creak. It wasn't enough to get them to stop though, or for Brennan to open his eyes and look. Brennan came in hot and messy ropes, followed quickly by Luka.

Entwined and happy, Luka nuzzled into Brennan, saying to him tenderly, "See? Nothing to worry about. He's fine. He's into it. He's good with Alek. And he *probably* just watched us humping, so... bonus? Maybe they did it on purpose, and wanted us to hear. Maybe next time we should go inside instead of lurking in the hall."

"Mm, I think I'm just fine right here, thanks," Brennan grinned blissfully, tensing the leg hooked around Luka's lower back, thrusting in a gentle tease up against him. "What'd I do to deserve you?"

Humming happily, Luka quieted him with a fervent yet unhurried kiss. It worked for a little while, but when they broke for air Brennan's expression was even more solemn. "Seriously, thank you. I don't know what I'd have done without you to talk to these past few days. Things with Evan can be intense. But with you, I just feel so comfortable and like everything's really going to be okay."

"Good. That's exactly what I want—for you to be able to come to me with anything that's on your mind or that you just want to vent about. I'm here for you. Always."

After cleaning up, they headed to the kitchen to get something for Brennan to eat. Luka was put to work chopping vegetables for a salad he promised to at least try for Brennan's sake, though he didn't seem too excited about it.

Dressed in his second outfit of the night, with his recently come-soiled clothes thrown in the wash, Luka was very much the source of Brennan's amusement.

"Why don't you just go nude? There'd be less laundry," he suggested.

"You're really in a rush to get me naked, huh?"

"It's been over a week! This is our third official date! So, take your damn clothes off already! Whip it out! Shake your ass! I can handle it."

Luka laughed.

"You aren't still trying to not disrespect me, are you? Because I'm can assure you I'm not gonna be shocked by the sight of your dick. Promise. You haven't even let me touch it yet."

"Stop pouting," Luka smirked, sprinkling some walnuts into the bowl in front of him and popping a few in his mouth.

"That's not an answer."

"Okay. Fine. It's just that when I was your age—"

"Oh, here it comes." Brennan groaned.

"*When I was your age,*" Luka pressed on, determined and talking over Brennan. "I was just like you, looking for distractions to keep my mind off of how much parts of my life sucked. I slept around, got high all the time, got involved with some very bad people, did stupid things, got in trouble. I regret that now. A lot. Maybe I want to protect you from that kind of regret. I'm trying to be smarter about stuff now. Cut me some slack and trust me, will ya?"

"Yes, Daddy." Brennan tried to hide his grin, but when Luka's eyes narrowed, Brennan didn't move fast enough to avoid a firm swat to his backside. "Ow."

"Oh please, that was nothing," Luka scoffed.

"Can I ask you something? I've been wondering," Brennan said, the tone of his voice shifting dramatically. "You know, since you told me how you and Alek mess around together...."

"Yeah," Luka said, stepping closer to him, leaning next to where Brennan was standing with his back to the sink, gripping the counter's edge. Brennan's eyes were downcast, almost like he'd gotten shy. It was unlike him, or at least unlike how he acted around Luka.

There was a pause. "How far has it gone? With Alek?"

"All the way," Luka replied instantly, unashamed.

"Anal?"

"Yeah."

"Who bottoms?"

"We switch it up. The first time it happened we were both on E and Alek topped. His boyfriend, who was older and also there, called the shots. It, well, let's just say it wasn't nice. They didn't exactly let me have a say in what was happening to me. But I forgave him. I love Alek, with all my heart."

Brennan stared at Luka with a look raw with concern. "Luka...."

Shaking his head, Luka pleaded with a quick glance for Brennan to let it go for now. So he did.

"And you two, you still—?"

"Yes. We do. But not often. It's been months since it's gone that far and we stopped screwing around after we started dating you and Evan. That's a given. We don't cheat."

"Wow." There was plenty of sadness and a strange sort of hope in that one little word. "Don't take this the wrong way, but is it weird if I kind of want to see that—you and Alek, having sex?"

"No, because I kind of want the same thing, with you and Evan. Does that freak you out?"

Brennan blushed, *really* blushed, and covered his mouth with a hand. "Wow. Maybe, but I would. I mean, I think I want to. Is that terrible? Maybe it's because we just met and there's no real, tangible history there."

"Doesn't matter. If it feels right to you, that's all that counts."

"There's a lot of people who would disagree."

"I don't judge them. They shouldn't judge me. Or Alek, or Evan, or you. What happens between consenting adults in the privacy of their bedroom is no one else's business."

"Does anyone know? That you and Alek —?"

"Presley and Carter do. They don't approve, but they don't turn away when they see us going at it either, so I don't care if they approve or not. Actions speak louder than words."

"How about your mom?"

"Don't really care what she thinks, either. She always thought Alek and I were too close. But what were we supposed to do when she ignored us all the time? People need love in their lives. Especially kids. So, I'll be the first to admit it probably started because of the emotional damage our childhood inflicted on us, like we were inappropriately overcompensating for parental neglect or some shit. But, you know, fuck it. We love each other. Alek was the only one who loved me for a long time. Being with him is one of the best things in my life. Always has been. I'm just really grateful I'm with you now — someone who knows exactly what I'm talking about firsthand. You really are a miracle, Bren. Evan, too. I've never seen Alek so happy or devoted. He's a better man since he's been with Evan. And he was a hell of a man before."

Brennan smiled and took Luka's hand, folding their fingers together. "I love you," he whispered for the very first time.

"I love you too," Luka sighed, kissing Brennan's forehead.

# Chapter 18

# Confessions in the Dark

Evan's elbow was perched on the window frame of the passenger-side door, the back of his hand resting against the cool glass of the window pane. His dark-blond hair was tousled in soft spikes, some curling down over his forehead. His eyes, thickly framed with long, golden lashes, kept closing, but not out of weariness, only to reopen darker with heat simmering there. His head kept falling back against the headrest as he arched his back slightly, though his gaze stayed locked to the rearview mirror as miles of road disappeared behind them.

Alek watched Evan's movements with intensity out of the edge of his vision, unable to keep his attention from drifting away from the tempting sight of his lover. Wanting to get to the look-out point, to be able to focus completely on Evan, Alek drove on. Fields blurred past on either side of the road which dipped and climbed with the rolling hills of the landscape. They got to a rare intersection and sat at the red light. Evan's legs shifted apart as he lifted his backside slightly off of the seat in order to find a better position. When he settled back down, Alek tried not to grin at the small groan Evan made.

He asked Evan impassively, without looking around, "You good?"

"Don't even try to pretend you aren't enjoying the hell out of this," Evan retorted. "I still can't believe you have a *bed* in the back of your truck. I mean, come on. Who does that?"

"Luka and I like to go camping, but he's not so keen on ground-sleeping. That was our solution."

He turned toward Evan, eyes flicking down to look when Evan slouched farther on the seat, trying to get the least cushion contact he could manage with the plug lodged in his ass. Though he was frowning something fierce, Evan seemed happy—truly happy. Sure, he was distracted and trying to be cool, but all of the physical stimulation appeared to be drowning out the sadness Alek always saw in the young man when his defenses were stripped away. Evan felt very much like a kindred spirit to Alek—facing the world every day knowing what a harsh and often cruel place it was, and the defensiveness that knowledge provoked, filtering into every inch of Evan's body, making him tense, wary. It was why Evan hid behind a façade, his armor protecting him from everything and everyone he encountered. All Alek wanted was for Evan to trust him enough to let the armor fall away for a little while, even though to take things to that level of closeness scared Alek too. When Alek loved someone—really loved them, as he did Luka—it was all or nothing. But what if he gave Evan everything and was left with nothing? Alek had been there too, and permanently lost people he vitally needed. He used to be strong enough to handle that, but now he wasn't so sure he could do it again.

Alek looked at Evan and thought of Brennan. He tried to imagine living most of his life without Luka by his side, and it was incredibly difficult to manage. But there was one thing he suspected was true.

"It must have been easier for you, before Brennan came here. I bet things were a lot simpler then," Alek said.

Evan's eyes shot open wide. "What?"

"I was just thinking about it, what it'd be like if I didn't have Luka to worry about all the time. It would be easier."

"Yeah," Evan murmured. "I guess it was."

"But I'd never want that," Alek continued. "No matter how easy it was, I'd rather have him in my life. I'm a happier person because of him, and how well he understands me. It's a wonderful thing, you know, to be truly understood. It's one of the great benefits of being a twin, which I suppose you'll find out soon for yourself."

Evan's innate sadness was suddenly there, right on the surface. They were driving again, so Alek only caught it in glimpses.

"Would you change things, if you could? Would you make it so that Brennan never came here?"

"No," Evan said quietly. "I could never go backwards like that. So much has happened since then. But, I don't know. Sometimes I'm just so overwhelmed by all of this."

"I understand," Alek said, meaning it completely. "He's yours now, though. You've gotta watch out for him."

Evan smiled, his lips curving and eyes sparkling for a fleeting moment, maybe realizing how true that was, that Brennan really *was* his now. As someone who knew well what it was to be lonely, and therefore counted as precious what love did come his way, Alek supposed Evan was of a similar sort. Living in such a rural town as Whippoorwill, where he was much more isolated than he would be if he lived somewhere like Mitchellsburg, Evan had also chosen a profession where vehicles and engines were his companions more so than people, plus he had an absentee father, a shockingly new brother, hardly any friends to speak of. Just looking in on Evan's life, Alek saw how strong and self-reliant it must have made him, and how Brennan's presence was shaking things up. But Brennan was a gift from fate, not only a companion but a soul mate. Brennan was what everyone hoped was out there, waiting for them somewhere, ready to be found.

"You're lucky."

Evan looked squarely at Alek at that. There was disbelief, wonder and pensiveness in his expression.

"Maybe I am," Evan allowed.

By the time they got to the spot Alek had in mind, the sun was heavy and low on the horizon, not yet set, but close. They were flanked by woods on two sides, the gravelly road on another, winding back a few miles to the highway. Behind the truck, parked on the crest of a hill, was a sprawling view of the hazy countryside. All around them was brush and tall grass. They climbed out of the cab and Alek dug a few citronella torches out, planting them in the dirt on either side of the truck and lighting them.

"Keeps away the mosquitoes," he explained, pushing the lighter back into his pocket and going for a small cooler next. Inside was beer and liquor. Alek put the cooler in the cab of the tuck, leaving the window slid open so that they could grab what they want, and motioned for Evan to hop up onto the air mattress and blankets.

Moving gingerly, Evan boosted up, groaning a little, because of the plug. He sat and watched Alek climb up beside him.

"So this is the plan, then?"

"Mm-hmm. Sunset, then we wait for the stars to come out."

"Then what?" Evan asked softly, desire roughening his deep voice.

"Then whatever we want."

Evan smiled and fell down onto his back, staring up at the wide, unblemished sky stretching out, limitless above them. Birds, or maybe bats, slipped through the air, chasing one another. The mattress was soft and comfortable beneath them. The night was warm, spiced now with the burning, light scent of the candles, casting an orange golden glow as the sun sank steadily lower.

"This is nice," Evan murmured. He turned his face toward Alek when he lay down too, on his side, facing Evan with his head propped on a hand. Alek's fingers twisted gently in the front of Evan's shirt. "Perfect, actually."

"You wouldn't prefer something more exciting? More dangerous?"

"This is plenty dangerous for me," Evan smirked.

For a while there was just small talk and long stretches of silence between them as they simply enjoyed being in each other's company. Alek itched to touch Evan and finally get his hands on him, but he was in no rush. They had all night. It was good to listen to him after waiting for Evan to be comfortable sharing more information about himself, starting to let Alek in a little more. Evan's trust in him was steadily growing. More of that closed-off exterior fell away and it only lured Alek in closer, daring him pull away like he always did and deny Evan's fragile faith in him.

*He could hurt you*, a warning voice whispered. *Your love for Luka has hurt you more than anything, save the woman you called mother. Caring about someone simply gives them more chances to rip your heart into pieces.*

But it really did feel like falling, to give into the pull of allure and connection, to dare to love. Once you leapt, there was no scrambling back over the safety of the precipice. There was only the rush, the wind, and the hope of a gentle landing.

Soon the sun was resting on the horizon and the bright blues of the sky were gone, shifted into dusky violets. Alek's fingers brushed idly through the soft hair at Evan's temple. Evan looked relaxed and comfortable.

Alek was trying to memorize the precise curves of Evan's profile when, with downcast eyes, staring right at the sinking sun, Evan asked, "What's the worst thing you've ever done?"

Alek blew out a breath. His fingers stilled their restless movements, his hand dragging down to rest flat over Evan's heart. He could feel it beating fast, thudding against Evan's ribs.

"Hmm. Wow," Alek sighed, thinking it over.

"Bet you a million dollars that mine's worse than yours."

Memory buffeted Alek, slamming into him. He knew what his worst thing was. It was the thing he'd been trying to make up for every moment since it happened.

"I don't think so," Alek retorted. It was obvious Evan had a troubled past, especially with the way they'd met, but Alek believed it wasn't possible for Evan to have committed a crime equal to Alek's own. But he wanted to know. Maybe if he got access to that part of who Evan was, more of his quietness, his seriousness and fragility would make sense.

Alek asked, "Do you want to go first or should I?"

"You first."

There was no easy way to say it. "Total honesty?"

"Please."

"Okay. I had a threesome with my brother when we were seventeen. The other guy, Marcus, was about forty. I was really into it. Luka really wasn't, but he went ahead with it because I wanted to.

"It went too far. Marcus tied Luka's arms behind his back, tied his ankles together too. He was on his knees between us on the bed. There was a blindfold on him, and a gag. Luka said no before the gag was pulled tight."

Alek gave it a second to sink in before continuing, watching Evan's reaction. "*He said no*, but we were both too high on ecstasy to be rational. Marcus was whispering to me, telling me how good it would feel, how hot it would be to fuck Luka. Luka heard all of it, and later, once it was over and I was untying him, I felt how soaked the blindfold was with Luka's tears. But, you know, I did it. I raped him. As much as I want to pretend otherwise, that's what happened. He could have fought more, he could have tried harder to stop me, but he didn't. And you know why? He *trusted* me. He bit his tongue and let me do that to him because he trusted me *that much*. We'd never done anything like that before. It had never gone that far. It was all always just a goof, messing around, kissing, heavy petting, using our mouths. Guys loved to watch that stuff."

Alek fell quiet. He had taken his hand back, and twisted his fingers together. Evan reached out and overlaid Alek's hands with one of his.

"It changed everything. It changed both of us, our personalities, our outlook on relationships and hell... *life.*" Alek set his jaw, and knew he couldn't hide how close tears were for him. "Nothing was off the table after that. We did everything with each other—drugs, extremely kinky, dangerous sex with people we barely knew—like maybe if we kept pushing our boundaries farther it would make what I did to him that night seem less horrible, but yeah. That's the worst thing I ever did."

His brow creased with his concern, Evan wrapped a strong hand behind Alek's neck and drew him down for a gentle but fervent kiss. Alek was the first to pull away, turning his face into the warmth of Evan's hand cupped against his jaw.

"Luka forgave you," Evan told him.

"Yeah, he did," Alek said sadly. "Doesn't change anything. Doesn't undo what I did, or what a horrible person I am, to do that to the one person who is my whole world, the only one that ever really loved me and believed in me."

"I believe in you," Evan said, dragging his thumb over the shaved-smooth skin of Alek's jaw line. "And everyone is allowed to make shitty choices sometimes. It's kind of expected. You're a good man. The fact that this still eats at you is proof of that."

"So did I win? Is mine worse?" Alek asked sorrowfully, thinking, *God, I hope it's worse.*

And, just like that, Evan started to recede, pulling away from

Alek mentally, emotionally, even physically. Alek didn't let him, though. He fearfully held on and put his hand back over Evan's jackrabbiting heart.

"*Evan*," he moaned.

"You gotta understand, I don't talk about this. I didn't even have the balls to tell Brennan myself. I made him find out through a stranger. My own father had me locked up in a psych ward for months, I was so unable to talk about it."

Cold, tight fear focused Alek. He put as much force into his voice as he could muster and said, "Tell me."

Evan said it in the simplest way he could. "I tried to commit suicide when I was fourteen. I was dead for three minutes."

The confession hit Alek harder than it might have otherwise. Already in an emotionally raw place from his own confession, the discovery that he almost lost Evan before he ever found him was like a razor-sharp knife to the gut. Envisioning Evan younger, desperate and dying, dead, if only for a moment, Alek gasped softly and fought with tears that sprang to his eyes. Then a sense of helplessness, anger and betrayal started to hit him next, but Evan just pulled Alek closer, not letting him leave him there alone when he'd just left himself so bare and exposed. Alek lay down half on top of Evan, arms wound around him in a wounded hug.

"Tell me about it," Alek murmured.

Evan took a deep breath.

"I never felt right. I always felt like something was wrong with me. Kids picked on me a lot. I wasn't as good at standing up for myself when I was really little and when they'd try to cut me down, it usually worked."

"You were naturally sensitive," Alek guessed.

"Yeah. And Charlie tried to help. He taught me to fight, so I fought. I fought all the time. And when I realized I was gay—that was long after kids were calling me homophobic slurs. But knowing in my heart that they were right? I thought that was what was wrong with me. I thought it was something shameful to be gay, so I hid it. I never told anybody, and pursued what I wanted, except with drunken strangers who I wasn't even attracted to and who pretty much pushed themselves on me. I didn't even tell my dad.

He still doesn't know I'm gay."

"But that's not what was wrong with you. Was it," Alek sighed.

"No," Evan said, choking on the words. "It wasn't."

*God*, Alek thought, *all that time and no one knew. No one could see it. And it's so obvious....*

"You needed him. You needed Brennan."

"What are you supposed to do, when you know in your heart you're missing something that big? The hole he left was like this wound that couldn't heal. But I didn't know I *was* missing him! It didn't make *sense*. They never told me about him! It would've helped. I would have made sense if I knew he was out there somewhere, that there was this person who used to be mine and then wasn't. I never made sense without him. It drove me insane. I decided it would be easier to be dead. I wouldn't hurt anymore. There would just be... nothing. No pain. No misery. I crushed up a couple of bottles full of these pain pills Charlie had a prescription for from when he threw out his back. I dumped the powder into a bottle of gin and drank it down."

Evan took a deep breath. Alek held him, caressed him tenderly and tried not to feel the rising anger at Evan's parents for depriving him of his other half and causing him such confusing, elusive heartache. "They told me Jimmy, my neighbor, is the one who found me. He's the reason I'm alive. He did CPR and called for the ambulance. They shocked my heart after it stopped. I upchucked some of the poison and almost asphyxiated on it. All of that just seems like a story about someone else. I don't remember anything after lying down in that field behind my house and falling asleep. I woke up a month later from my coma. Everyone wanted to know why. Why, Evan? Why would you do such a terrible thing to your father? I didn't leave a note, because I didn't even know how to explain it to myself let alone other people, so they were baffled. But...."

Alek murmured, "It didn't fix anything."

"Nope. I was still fucked up. Then I was this poor kid who tried to off himself and everyone felt sorry for me and scared for me, but I was still miserable. The stay in the mental ward didn't last too long. Dad was smart enough to realize it wasn't helping. So he tried to give me more reasons to be happy I was alive. It was crazy, how much stuff he did just for the sake of doing it. I mean, he didn't know. He was clueless. Sure, it sent some mixed messages, like he was changing all of this stuff about me and my life, so it just reinforced the idea that it was bad enough to warrant changing. But it was enough, I guess, to see how much he needed me to be there with him. He was so desperate to find some way to make me happy. And so what if he never did make me happy? He cared enough to try."

Evan told Alek about the Lasik, the car, the training in mechanics, the hunting license, and also the things Jimmy had given him, like helping Evan get involved at the homeless shelter, making an active difference in the lives of others much worse off than himself. Since Alek never had a parental figure go out of their way to try to make him happy, he could see how the affection in the act itself could lend comfort, even if the results weren't ideal. He would have loved for his mother to put a little more effort into showing her affection. But he wasn't sure he would ever trade Luka for his mother's love, if that was the only way to get it. Either way, it was a shitty situation.

Alek rolled off of Evan and grabbed a bottle of rum, opening it up and taking a long drink.

"Can I? Thanks," Evan said gratefully, taking the bottle from Alek for a small sip from the bottle's mouth. "That's the worst thing I've ever done. I think I win."

Alek frowned at him. Carefully taking the bottle out of Evan's hand, he set it aside and surged toward Evan, straddling his hips and holding down his arms. Kissing him passionately, with all the fear of having someone so precious and irreplaceable stolen away when he'd only just been discovered. Alek poured his heart into every moment, every touch, cherishing Evan, being grateful to have him. The fear did strange things to Alek's heart, though. It broke down walls he never wanted to have to do without. He could feel Evan getting inside him, changing Alek's heart and making a home for himself there. That was scary too, as wonderful as it was, but caused Alek to just kiss Evan more passionately. Needing to touch, to feel him, vital and alive, Alek's hands slid upwards. His fingers spread as they got to Evan's hands so they could lace between his fingers.

"Don't you dare even think about hurting yourself again, you hear me? It's selfish and stupid and the pain something like that causes in the people that love you — that's unforgivable," Alek said, trying to make Evan see how it wasn't just Charlie anymore who needed him healthy and living. There was an echo of panic as Alek imagined he knew why Charlie tried so hard to affect basic things about Evan's life, using pathetically material things to erase his child's soul-deep pain. Alek would do anything, too, to keep Evan from slipping away like he once did.

"Okay," Evan said meekly.

# Chapter 19
# Kindred Spirits

Alek asked, "Are you glad you told me?"

"Yeah, I kind of feel lighter," Evan admitted.

"You've gotta talk about things. Maybe if you'd talked more to Charlie, he would have told you about Brennan before it got that bad."

Realization lit Evan's eyes. Alek watched the look on his face as he realized for what seemed the first time that if he'd just bothered to say something to his father, his pain could have been vanquished before anything happened.

"Oh. *Oh.* I never really thought about it like that."

"So if something is bothering you," Alek cupped a hand over Evan's heart, beating more gently now. "Promise me you'll tell me, or Bren, or someone. Anyone. *Please.*"

"I promise."

"Is anything else bothering you?"

Evan blurted it out. "I feel guilty about being attracted to Brennan. He kissed me last weekend, like *kissed* me. I mean, he did it because I accidentally got hard when we were, um, wrestling a little bit, and he was afraid I was freaking out. I *was* freaking out, so he had reason to be concerned, I guess. But he kissed me. And I liked it. And I kissed him back. Now it's making me feel fucked up again."

"Did Brennan like it?"

"Yeah."

"Because I'm pretty sure he and Luka were in the hallway listening when I stuck that plug in you, tonight, and that they were going at it in the bed when we walked by because it turned them on. Clearly that's not a bad thing, Evan. I know our society frowns upon the whole incest thing, but then look at how much straight guys get off on the idea of dating female twins. Look at all of those people who fall in love and get married only to find out later they're long-lost relatives. It happens in every country, in every part of the world. The way the world works is never clear cut, black and white, no matter how much politicians or religious people want to believe otherwise. It's always shades of gray. People act on feelings, need, and instinct, not rules. If you're into it, and Brennan is into it, you're consenting adults. That's all that matters. Trust me, I know."

"So you're really not mad? I mean, besides the whole brother thing, I kissed someone else. I confessed I'm attracted to someone else, too."

"That'd be kind of hypocritical of me, don't you think? Luka and I have kind of taken a break from each other out of mutual respect for our new relationships, but if you want to mess around with Bren, I'm okay with that. Just use protection if things go that far."

Evan's eyes widened. "You really think they'd go that far?"

Alek shrugs. "You never know. Oh, and of course you have to tell me every little detail. Or let us watch."

Evan hummed. Alek felt Evan's dick twitch, nudging him, before Evan shifted to wrap his legs around Alek. Brushing his lips lightly over Evan's, Alek sighed and pulled Evan's left leg higher. He rubbed up Evan's calf, past his knee to the thick muscle of his thigh. The tip of Alek's tongue teased up the center of Evan's upper lip, which was warm, soft and tasted faintly of rum.

"Did he use tongue?"

"No," Evan answered. He swallowed a grunt when Alek's hand rubbed over the curve of his ass, stopping at the spot where the plug flared out, nestled snugly, flush against his body. Alek pushed firmly at the center of the plug's base with two fingers. Evan arched his back, his hips tilting in response to the added pressure, and he began breathing more roughly through his nose. Loving every little reaction, wanting to push each one of Evan's buttons, especially the ones he never knew he had, Alek focused his efforts. "Just lips. But it went on for a while. It was nice."

"I bet," Alek teased.

Hesitantly, Evan asked, "Can I be on top?"

"Sure," Alek said, amused. He sat back on his heels, letting Evan get up, lying down in his place. The sun had set and the sky was a riot of color and wispy clouds. The crickets were starting to chirp louder and the glow from the candles shone into the truck's bed.

Evan stripped off his shirt and opened his pants, too. As he pushed them down slightly, only to dip his head and shove Alek's shirt up and out of the way, he licked a wet stripe up the center of Alek's abs.

With a hum of pleasure at seeing Evan act rather than simply react, Alek observed, "Guess you're ready for this, then?"

"Yeah," Evan sighed, licking over to Alek's right nipple, flicking it with the tip of his tongue. The sensation made Alek's breath catch, especially because it was sweet, young Evan causing it. He pushed up into the wet, tickling touch, palming the back of Evan's head and pulling him in closer. Evan sealed his lips around the dark, peaked circle and sucked gently on it while his fingers twisted and pulled at Alek's fly, trying to get it all the way open.

Could it be that simply not being held down, being on top rather than underneath freed Evan's inhibitions that much? Alek was captivated, craving everything Evan wanted to give him.

He kissed his way back down Alek's torso, murmuring between sucking presses of his full, dark lips, "My ass has been throbbing for too damn long. Everything's really sensitive. All I can think about is getting your cock in me. And doing this."

He pulled Alek free of his underwear and licked greedily over the reddened, slick, plum-shaped head of Alek's huge cock. Closing his lips over it in an intimate, obscene kiss, he opened wider and let the silken, rock-hard member slide back over his tongue, taking as much in as he could, then sucking as he pulled back off.

"Fuck," Alek hissed, palming the back of Evan's head and thrusting back inside, pushing deeper. Evan struggled with it at first, his eyes tearing up, but then he relaxed into it, letting Alek pump in and out of his throat a few times before pulling off completely. "Take your pants off. C'mere."

Evan kicked the jeans away and settled atop Alek's hips, thrusting gently against Alek's thick, wet, dark erection to get some relief.

"Good. Now bend over a little more. Push your ass out for me."

Evan braced a hand on the mattress beside Alek, letting his other rest on Alek's broad, bare chest as he knelt over him, hovering above him.

"Yeah. That's it. Now just relax. Don't clench up."

Alek caressed lightly along Evan's sides, reaching back around his backside until he found the plug's base, grabbing the edge. He pulled at it with just enough force to get it moving, tugging against Evan's rim from the inside.

Evan shuddered.

"Feels big, huh? I'm just taking it out. Gonna go nice and slow."

Evan moaned wantonly as he was forced open wider and wider, pulled farther apart by the well-lubricated, tapered width of the plug being extracted. He fisted his cock, masturbating as Alek removed the plug slowly. Evan's moan sharpened when the widest part squeezed through, stretching him impossibly as it withdrew and then it was easier. His cries became softer. Alek pulled it almost all the way out then slid it back inside, fucking him shallowly with it while he watched Evan jerk off. Evan's eyes were shut tight, his lips parted and soft with his low moans. His back was arched with his pleasure, his body slick and glistening with sweat, his dick red, heavy and swollen inside his hand.

"Look at me," Alek whispered.

Evan's eyes fixed on him obediently, the pupils blown wide and black.

Alek dropped the toy, replacing it with his fingers. First he traced Evan's wet, stretched rim rubbing it, fingering just inside the tender pucker. Then he pushed three fingers deliberately in. Evan's mouth fell open wider and he choked off a deep groan as the digits slid in deeply, twisting as they went, up to the last knuckle.

"Feel good?"

"*Alek*," Evan gasped, tugging faster and harder at himself.

"Don't come yet. Remember what I said. I want to be inside you when you do."

Evan groaned and his hand fell away. Alek's head chased up off the blankets to catch Evan's mouth. Their tongues tangled together, tasting, questing, as Alek stroked at Evan's inner walls, pumping his hand in and out with slow snaps of his wrist. Evan started to push back on it, riding the fingers he was impaled on. At first the movements were subtle, restrained. Then he grew more brazen, lost some hesitation and bounced back against Alek's hand, breaking their kiss. On the in-stroke, Alek rubbed over Evan's prostate. It got Evan shuddering, trembling and sweating more. He arched his back like a cat, tensed his arms and rode out the sensations with low, rolling moans and animalistic grunts.

"Gonna fuck you now, Jailbait. Gonna feed your hungry hole my dick and stuff you full. You want it?"

"Yeah."

Alek withdrew his fingers, and guided the head of his cock to Evan's hot, throbbing open, fitting himself against the spot and steadying the shaft by gripping around the base. His other hand braced Evan by grabbing his waist, and Alek thrust inside. Evan buried his mouth in the side of Alek's neck and cried out sharply as Alek's long, thick girth popped through his rim and forced its way deep, deeper, deeper, inch-by-inch into him.

Gasping, Evan clung to Alek chest-to-chest, shifting his legs a little wider. Alek planted his feet on the mattress and pumped shallowly in and out of Evan, riding the fluttering contractions of his inner muscles from nerves and self-consciousness. He was a velvety, tight, hot glove constricting around Alek, a blissfully perfect fit. Alek could feel everything, absolutely everything, without the condom. It was all magnified, rawer, and exquisite.

"You feel so good," Alek moaned. "If Bren was here, I'd have him suck you while I rode your sweet ass. And maybe Luka could have your mouth."

Evan whimpered and grabbed his cock again, beating off frantically as Alek thrust harder, in longer, deeper strokes.

"Sounds good, huh?" Alek whispered, "think about it... how his mouth would feel, how he'd moan at the taste of you dripping down his throat...."

Alek pounded into him, knocking him forward with each slam of his hips against Evan's ass. Evan's body bowed, tensing up, his cock reddish purple and steely in his hand.

"I'd watch you come down Brennan's throat and then I'd come

inside you, shoot my load so deep inside you...."

Evan's body tensed, clamping like a vise around Alek's dick. A guttural groan broke off as Evan began to climax.

"Oh Jesus Christ, you're tight," Alek hissed, gritting his teeth, riding it out, right on the knife's edge.

Come erupted from the tip of Evan's cock, splattering hot all over Alek's body, over his chest and throat, even up to his chin. Trembling, Evan stroked himself through it as Alek bit down on Evan's shoulder and growled as he unloaded in Evan's ass, slamming into him, twitching against Evan's rim as Alek's mind whited out with the force of his orgasm. Everything in him pumped into Evan, making him wetter, soaking his insides in semen.

"You've got my seed in you now. You're *dripping* with it. Now you're really mine," Alek growled, licking over the bruise he's left on Evan's shoulder. "All mine." "I love you," Evan murmured, kissing Alek's lips desperately.

When he pulled back, though, he looked guilty and embarrassed.

"I love you, too," Alek assured him. "I'm gonna take good care of you, okay? Everything's gonna be fine. No more worries. No more secrets. No more pain."

"Alek," Evan moaned, delirious but smiling beautifully. "Alek...."

# Chapter 20
# Holding Out

Brennan and Luka were both still wearing most of their clothes, but were lying under the covers, comfortable and cozy in Brennan's bed. They were facing each other with pillows and their arms helping to prop them up. They were almost ready to cross the line into full intimacy once and for all, and go for it. It created an electric charge in the air. But wanting to ease into things, and also to know a little more basic info first, Luka started asking some questions.

"I'm impressed that you haven't jumped my bones yet. That's some major self-restraint you're showing tonight."

"Wow," Brennan said with wonder. "You are *so* full of yourself." Luka laughed brightly. Once he settled down, he asked, "Are we really gonna do this?"

"What? Hump? I hope so."

"Are you a top or a bottom?"

"Bottom," Brennan said without hesitation.

"Only?"

"Only."

"Hmm. You've never even *experimented* with?"

"Nope."

"Wow," Luka said with some awe. "So you love it?"

"I *love* it," Brennan said with passionate emphasis and a wholly not-angelic smile.

"Nice," Luka grinned, his interest piqued, approving of Brennan's position on the matter very much.

"You?"

"Eh," he shrugged. "Whatever. Both. Recently, I'm really just into being a top. For a long time I was only a bottom."

"So you're versatile."

"Yeah."

Brennan's eyes sharpened thoughtfully. "Tell me about your most recent ex."

Luka sputtered, "Why? There's a mood-killer for ya."

"I want to know. Hey, I waited a solid week of regular, daily conversation with you before coming out and asking, didn't I?"

"You first."

"Fine. His name is Tommy. He's tall, dark hair, perfect teeth."

Luka burst out laughing. "Perfect *teeth*? Really? *That's* what stands out to you?"

"Shh! Let me finish," he frowned. "Tommy's a total jock. You know, football, letter jacket, clean cut, momma's boy, too pretty for his own good — the total package."

"Why'd you break up?"

Brennan's gaze dropped, some of his smile faded away. "He cared way more about himself than me. I came second with everything, all the time. And he wasn't really mature enough to understand about Mom and what I was going through. It wasn't important to him until I stopped wanting to put out."

"That sucks." Luka took Brennan's hand like it could help to pull him out of the bad memories.

"Yeah. But you can't always expect mature reactions out of a high school senior who's never known real hardship in his life. Whatever. I dumped his ass. And he *still* tries to call me. Okay, now you go," Brennan sighed.

Groaning dramatically, Luka flopped onto his back and rubbed a hand over his face. "Can we not do this? Pretty please?"

"No way. Spill."

Knowing how miserable he sounded, Luka said, "Her name's Jackie. She's short, dark hair, perfect teeth."

Brennan swatted him with an extra pillow. "Ass. Your ex is a girl? Huh."

"Yeah. Like I said, I swing every which way. Like a monkey. Okay, *my* turn again. When'd you lose your virginity?"

Brennan rolled onto his back too, gazing up at the ceiling and twisting his fingers in the blankets. "Can you go first?"

Gasping loudly with shock, Luka instantly rolled back onto his side and propped up on an elbow to get a better look at Brennan's face, leaning down over him. "Is it *that bad*?!"

"Twelve?" Brennan said meekly.

"Brennan Charles Holt! You let some guy put his dick in you when you were twelve?!"

"I should never have told you my middle name," he sighed forlornly.

"How old was he?"

"...Eighteen? But c'mon! I was *obsessed* with him. He was super hot. I didn't regret it. It was totally worth it. Plus, he really was very sweet about it."

"What's his full name?"

Giving him a brief, sharp look, Brennan shook his head. "Nope, you've got that 'I'm about to kill someone' crazy look in your eye."

Luka squinted at him.

"Your turn," Brennan prompted.

"For what?"

"When did you lose your virginity?"

"Hmm. I was almost sixteen. I bottomed. First time I ever topped I was seventeen. It was with Alek. He was my first." Luka grinned fondly and happily at the memory.

The smile must have been contagious because it spread over Brennan's face, too.

"When's the last time you were with someone?"

"In what sense," Luka asked.

"I need to clarify that?"

"Yeah. Last person I was with period, besides you of course, was Aleksy. Blowjob. Awesome."

"How about sex?"

"That'd be Jackie then. Right before I met you. We ended it that morning you and I met, before I left for work."

"Wow. How about sex with a guy?"

"Hmm. It's been a while."

"How long's a while?"

"...Two and a half years? No, that's not true. Six months ago I

185

fucked Aleksy."

"Jesus. Are you sure you're gay?"

"My constant boner when I'm around you isn't proof enough?" Luka asked, wide-eyed with bafflement. His thoughts swung back around to something else, though. "I still can't believe you let that guy fuck you when you were a child."

It riled him, imagining twelve-year-old Brennan in such a situation. Luka wasn't a violent person at heart, but thinking of Brennan being so taken advantage of made Luka want to ring the eighteen-year-old's neck.

Brennan argued, "He wasn't even four inches! I barely felt it."

Luka masked his expression and asked seriously, "How do you know *I'm* not four inches? You could've just horribly insulted me."

"You aren't four inches," Brennan scoffed, shoving Luka's shoulder lightly.

"How do you know?"

"By calculating the angle your pants get tented at? By paying attention when you were grinding your meat against my hip? You're more than four inches. And, you know, you could always just whip it out and show me."

"Later," Luka replied, waving a hand to dismiss the suggestion. "There's stuff I'm still curious about. Like what do you want to be when you grow up?"

"Well, since I was pretty good at taking care of Mom through all the chemo and then in hospice, I thought that maybe I'd be a nurse?" He said it shyly, without looking up to see Luka's reaction, like he was nervous about him laughing at the idea. Of course, this meant Luka *had* to tease him about it.

"Aw, no way. I'm sorry, Brennan," Luka frowned, intentionally sounding like he hated to be the bearer of bad news. "You absolutely can*not* be a nurse."

Instantly hurt, Brennan asked softly, "Why?"

"Are you kidding? Because you'd be the hottest nurse *ever* and all of the doctors would instantly fall in lust with you and try to seduce you. You have to have heard about all the whoring around that goes on in the medical profession! You in scrubs would be like waving a juicy steak in front of hungry lions."

Brennan chuckled.

"Not to mention all the horny old gays you'd have to nurse who'd be grabbin' at yer tushie every time you walked by."

Brennan laughed even harder. "I really don't think they'd do that."

"Why not? *I* would."

"Are you a horny old gay?"

"Not yet," Luka said smugly. "That's what *I* want to be when I grow up."

"Not a personal trainer?"

"Nope, that's temporary. It's horny old gay for me. That's my supreme goal."

"I think you have that one in the bag, you big dork."

"Thank you!"

A few hours later, they were still laying in bed, talking and laughing. Evan and Alek had already gotten home, their footsteps clearly audible as they walked by, heading to Evan's room. The crickets outside the house chirped loudly. The wind kicked up, buffeting the walls from the east, making the old wood groan. It was dark and quiet. Luka was tracing patterns on the back of Brennan's forearm with his fingertip.

Luka knew why Brennan was looking at him the way he was, easily reading the beseeching, confused supplication in the depths of his eyes.

Luka said softly, "What's the rush, anyway?"

Brennan glanced away, looking like he felt rejected. "I just wanna make you happy."

"You don't have to put out to make me happy."

"But it helps, right? I mean, that's why guys ask me out. They don't wanna be my soul mate, they just want in my pants. It's fine. Sometimes that's all I want, too. And that's why I thought you asked me out. That's what I was expecting, anyway. You don't seem interested."

"Bren, you've got way more to offer than your body. Don't you know that?"

Brennan shrugged. "If you don't want to, you can just be honest and say so, you know."

"Did you just hear what I said? Am I talking to myself? Or are you just fishing for compliments again?"

Smirking, Brennan nudged him. Hurt lurked behind his eyes.

"Okay," Luka sighed, "C'mere for a minute, my sweet little Cupcake."

"I thought I told you never to call me that," Brennan complained, heeding Luka's request anyway.

Luka pulled him into his arms, spooning up behind him and curling his larger body around Brennan's, their legs entwined, Brennan's head pillowed on Luka's bicep.

"Lemme cuddle you for a minute or five and then it's on."

"Promise?"

"No doubt."

"Okay."

Half-a-minute later, Brennan was snoring softly. Glad the strategy worked, Luka kissed Brennan's temple and drifted off moments later.

Luka didn't typically wake early, especially on weekends, so when Brennan got out of bed soon after the sun began to shine through the room's single window, Luka was at first lulled back under the heavy weight of sleep tugging demandingly at his consciousness. He opened his eyes sometime later to feel the gentle caress of a morning breeze sliding over his cheek. The window had been opened wide. The thin curtain blew, dancing with the currents. Brennan was sitting on his heels by his altar, eyes shut, utterly relaxed and focused, his hands curled and resting on his knees. For a while, Luka simply stared at him, nothing but thankful Brennan seemed so peaceful and untroubled, not a sign or stain of tears on his delicate skin. His silver-framed glasses were perched on his nose, the lenses catching and reflecting shards of golden sunbeams.

Luka slipped back into dreamless sleep. When next he woke, Brennan was no longer meditating. He was no longer dressed either. It was fairly bright and comfortably warm in the bedroom. The morning light was rosy and soft on the contours of Brennan's skin, the contrast of deep shadows and golden highlights on his unmoving, perfectly balanced form made him seem not human at all but a living carving, a masterpiece of sculpture that should be studied and admired for the pure beauty in it. Actually afraid of disturbing him, Luka stayed as silent as he could, barely daring to breathe from his place in Brennan's bed. He watched for nearly an hour as Brennan bent and twisted like a pretzel, balancing impossibly, demonstrating keenly exactly how flexible he was.

At one point, Brennan was laying flat on his back on a purple yoga mat with his arms at his sides. Arching the middle of his body up off the ground from the tips of his toes all the way to his shoulder blades, he fit his hands against his lower back to maintain the stretch, his upper arms braced on the ground and arms bent sharply at the elbow.

That was the first pose, held for a length of time before continuing into another, lifting only his left leg upward until it made a perfectly perpendicular line to the floor with his body still dramatically arched. He paused, then shifted, pushing with his right foot off of the ground. His feet sliced through the air in a slow arc until the toes of his flexed left foot were touching the floor above his head; his right leg was pointed in a straight line that stretched in a ninety degree angle up to the ceiling. Most of his body, from his shoulder blades to the tips of his toes, was aligned at that perpendicular angle, braced only by his upper arms, his hands still braced against his lower back. From there, both legs came down to the floor above Brennan's head, curling his body in on itself, bending it in half. His legs spread as wide as they could go, toes touching the floor, held in place by straightened arms grasping the balls of his feet, his backside pointed up in the air.

Brennan took a break after that, laying flat once more, but then bowed his back in a beautiful curved line with the endpoints of the arc being the base of his spine and the top of his head. His neck arched back as well and his arms entwined, clasped over his chest, his toes pointed.

Entranced, Luka watched Brennan arch up into the same pose as before, pushing his behind up off the floor, staying up only with the tips of his toes and his shoulder blades. But this time he kept bending more and more upward at the middle, getting his feet flat on the ground. The top of his head and his flattened hands, splayed by the sides of his head, held the pose as he formed a sort of human table with his body from his knees to the bottom of his ribcage essentially being the tabletop. His buttocks clenched and arms strained. Then he got up onto the balls of his feet. Arching his spine, he pushed the curve of his body impossibly further until, with his hands clasped behind his head, he had his forearms braced on the floor. His chest and stomach were pulled tight, his leg muscles and buttocks clenched, his penis lying softly against his pelvis as he forced it up farther and farther into the air.

Luka was amazed as Brennan performed acrobatics with his lithe body that he'd never seen before. One moment Brennan was doing a handstand with his legs pointed out to the sides, nearly in a split in mid-air. The next moment he was folded cleanly in half with his face flush to his shins and hands clasped around the arches of his feet.

He was coiled like a cobra ready to strike. He was frozen in mid-lunge like a warrior who had just sliced through the air with his elongated, pointed arms as his swords.

By the time Brennan was done, and mopped some sweat from his face and chest with a towel, Luka was fully hard and aching for Brennan. His pulse raced; his breathing was roughened. He could hear, once in a while, someone moving around outside the room, possibly Alek, who was an early riser just like Brennan. But Luka tuned it out. All that existed for him was Brennan—not a child at all, but a young man with far too much worry and weight resting on his shoulders. He'd known loss, loneliness, trial, tragedy, temptation, so many things he should never have had to endure. It had granted him a maturity Luka not only admired but was intensely attracted to.

Finally, Brennan realized he was being watched. Taken aback by how awake Luka appeared, not sleepy at all, but alert and tensed, like he'd been enjoying Brennan's show for a very long time and was now more than ready to do... what?

"Morning," Brennan smiled. He glanced down at himself. "I guess you saw some of that. No more reason for me to be shy around you, then, I guess." He chuckled to disguise his growing blush, gaze darting around for the nearest clump of discarded clothes.

"Come to bed," Luka said. It was thick, low, and rough, like the words had been grated over stone. There was no joking in it, no lightness. Luka's gaze was as sharp as if he was a hunter stalking his prey.

"Maybe a shower first, I'm kind of...." He gestured at the drips trickling down his chest.

"Sweaty? Yeah. I know. Lie down."

Something sparked in Brennan's eyes—realization maybe, or self-consciousness. He set his jaw and bowed his head as a blush spread over his skin. After begging for sex for days, now that it was actually time and Luka was ready to have sex with him, Brennan seemed uncharacteristically timid and unsure. It just stoked the fire of Luka's need for him.

Brennan went to the bed and sat on the edge. "How do you want me?"

"Or your stomach. I'll give you a massage to relax you."

# Chapter 21

# Payback

Brennan's muscles were burning, sore in the best way from the exertion. He had been relaxed until deducing what was about to happen in that small bedroom with Alek and Evan somewhere very nearby. Tension spread across his shoulders, knotting muscles down his back, crawling up his neck.

He spread himself out on the middle of the bed. Luka made room for him, and stripped off his own shirt, leaving him wearing only a thin pair of boxer briefs.

"Spread your legs."

Brennan parted his legs, each foot pointing to one post of the bed. Luka guided his arms back along his sides, rubbing down them from shoulder to wrist a few times like he was wringing out the nervous energy collecting in Brennan's body.

Settling between Brennan's legs, Luka drew up a knee, nudging gently at the junction of them, forcing Brennan even wider. Brennan looked back at him, his breath catching, quickening.

"I'm not in a rush here. Is it okay if I play with you for a little while? We can go slow?"

"Yeah. Sure," Brennan rasped.

"I bought something. Wasn't sure if we'd be using it anytime soon, but if you're interested, I'll get it. Especially since you liked hearing Evan take the plug."

The heat in Brennan's expression seemed to be all the answer Luka needed. Luka's smile grew wicked, like he already knew he'd won.

Brennan asked, "What is it?"

"Well that's the thing. You don't get to see it; you only get to feel it. It's a surprise."

"...Okay."

Luka went to his bag and dug through it, finding what he needed. He returned to the bed with something hidden behind his back and a black leather blindfold dangling from a hooked finger.

Lust-drunk with anticipation, though still nervous as ever, Brennan's eyes slipped half-shut and when Luka leaned in to kiss him, Brennan hungrily kissed Luka back. His ribs expanded and contracted with every fevered breath. He lifted his head just enough for Luka to get the blindfold in place on him. Everything was blackened out by the mask, with only a soft glow at the edges from the radiant sunlight in the room.

Luka's butter-smooth voice by Brennan's left ear asked, "You hard yet?"

"Hell yeah," Brennan grunted.

"Good."

"You?"

Luka chuckled darkly. He took one of Brennan's hands and guided it to his crotch. Brennan instantly took advantage of finally getting permission to touch and fondled Luka through the cotton. Luka was hugely erect and bigger in circumference than Brennan had imagined, as well as bigger than Brennan ever had before.

Thinking he had disguised his trepidation and shock well enough, Brennan soon discovered otherwise. Luka nipped playfully at the shell of his ear and began massaging his shoulders, rubbing in firm circular motions, kneading the muscle with his huge hands.

"Can you take it? It's okay if you can't. We can improvise. I mean, you are pretty tiny."

"I can take it. And don't call me tiny. But Christ, Luka. Didn't really expect that."

"You sure?"

"Yeah. I'm sure."

"Okay. Well this'll help. You just lay there and stay loose for me. You don't have to do a damn thing."

"Mm, sounds good."

At first it was just a deep tissue massage. Luka worked at Brennan's shoulders, his neck, down his back along his spine, his flanks, arms, and thighs. It was divine and probably the best massage of Brennan's life. Luka avoided all intimate touching for a good twenty minutes. Then he generously coated the toy in his hand with lubricant and got ready to use it. Keeping his left hand busy grinding into the small of Brennan's back with his knuckles, he broke up a knot of tension there.

Distracting Brennan with the back rub, Luka surprised him by rubbing the pad of his thumb up over the smooth patch of skin of his perineum and up to his hole, then stroking over it with firm pressure in tiny circles.

Brennan's breath caught. His lips parted in a soundless exhale and he clenched his buttocks reflexively. Luka crooked the thumb and pushed, pressing deliberately though the ring of muscle, forcing his way inside. Brennan parted, hugged around the finger as Luka rubbed dry just inside Brennan's rim. The feel of it, especially after so long a wait, made Brennan's toes curl. He panted softly as Luka withdrew the thumb and rubbed over Brennan's opening, up through his ass crack and back down again. Without hesitation or restraint he plunged the thumb inside in one stroke, holding there and stroking over Brennan's inner walls.

Brennan moaned freely, the sound jolted from him. He shivered as goosebumps covered his skin from head to toe. The friction of Luka's gentle rubbing drew Brennan's blood right there, turning him on, making everything feel even better. Luka rubbed his left hand up the curve of Brennan's spine to the nape of his neck, then out over his shoulder.

Leaning in closely, Luka growled softly to him, "I'm gonna fuck you hard. Gonna make you take fuckin' all of me. You say you want cock so badly? I'll give it to you."

Brennan moaned and rocked down into the mattress to relieve some of the maddening pressure building in him. He greedily rubbed his erection into the bed, then pushed his ass back onto Luka's completely buried thumb.

"More," he begged, unashamed.

"Oh, I'll give ya more, babydoll. I'll give you all you can handle and then some." He tugged the finger out and replaced it with the tip of a toy, wriggling it teasingly at Brennan's opening, prying him apart with it as he worked it an inch or so inside.

Brennan choked off a keening cry, not holding back at all, just letting it all out. His fingers splayed wide at his sides, seeking for something to grab on to, finding nothing. He pivoted his wrists and grabbed at the sheet under him. Luka continued to knead the muscle of Brennan's shoulder, using the hold to simultaneously keep him pinned flat to the bed as he made Brennan take more of the tapered object. It was only about two inches in, but already had him pulled open wide, stretched tight around it. Luka twisted the toy and moved it shallowly in and out, working his way deeper.

"How's it feel?"

"Thick," Brennan croaked. He wasn't rocking against the bed anymore. It was all he could do to lay still and stay relaxed as the burning stretch of his sphincter demanded all of his attention. The toy was sliding easily enough, but it was the sheer size that was the issue. He couldn't believe Luka was still massaging him while he was inserting it. The combination of soothing, calming touch and intense, intimate violation was maddeningly arousing.

Once the toy was about four inches in, Luka let go of it, allowing it to protrude from Brennan's asshole as he went back to rubbing wide circles on Brennan's back and kneading down the backs of his thighs, one at a time.

Brennan was moaning and trembling slightly. Sweat beaded all over his body. Having the toy lodged in him, slipping slowly back out as he clenched in flutters around it, was driving him insane. As soon as it started to creep back out, Luka grabbed it and slid it back in as far as Brennan's body would let it go. When Luka started trailing the point of his tongue down the center of his back, licking up the salty beads and leaving a cool trail in his wake, Brennan started to beg wantonly.

"Luka... oh fuck... you have to... I can't take it..." he panted.

"I don't have to do anything. I'm just playing with you. You played with me for a long, long time, didn'cha? Trying to seduce me. Putting on that crazy-making show this morning, making me so hard I thought my dick was just gonna break off if I touched it. And besides, you said four inches was nothing. This is only four inches,

Cupcake. Can you feel it yet?"

"You dirty motherfucker. *You're* the evil one. You."

Luka laughed darkly. "No, this is just sweet, sweet revenge. I want you to know exactly what you get when you fuck with me and try to play your little games. I'm just gonna take it out of your gorgeous, luscious ass."

Shifting suddenly lower, Luka scraped his teeth over the firm swell of Brennan's backside, then sucked kisses to it, licked in wide stripes over it. He took his time working the toy back out, rocking it as it withdrew. Then he dropped it to the bed and formed his right hand into a tapered shape as well before he inserted three fingers in one stroke. They went in easily and Luka hummed happily, nipping love bites at Brennan's buttocks. He licked his way up to the dimples in Brennan's lower back and tasted those too.

"I think you're ready," Luka grinned.

"Oh thank god."

"So, any preference how we do this? Favorite position?"

Brennan, still blindfolded, got up on his hands and knees and moved closer to the headboard, feeling for it. He bent over sharply at the waist and listened to Luka rip open the condom wrapper. Grabbing his ass with both hands, Brennan pulled himself open and stuck out his ass, waiting and ready for Luka to put his cock in.

"Jesus *fuck*," Luka moaned. "Yeah, that's a good fuckin' position. Let's go with that one. Okay, Cupcake, show me what'cha got. I swear, you're the sweetest damn thing I've ever seen."

He lined up, the condom rolled on. As soon as Brennan felt him there, he pushed back onto Luka. All Luka had to do was stay right where he was as Brennan impaled himself on Luka's thick cock. Brennan braced a hand on the bed and moaned, the sound guttural and raw.

"So fuckin' huge," Brennan rasped.

Luka moaned freely, and goaded Brennan on. "Come on. Doin' so good."

Caressing lazily over Brennan's narrow waist and the sides of his ass, Luka growled when his nimble young lover started to fuck himself back onto his cock. He bounced shallowly on it at first, keeping a firm grip on the headboard, then when he found his rhythm and grew more comfortable, he sped up, moving faster, taking him in deeper, longer thrusts. Luka's girth slammed into him, but Brennan knew just what the angle should be to hit his sweet spot, just how to clench to make it better for Luka, too.

Luka released a shattered, powerful moan and growled even more loudly, breathing roughly through clenched teeth. "Not fair. So fucking not fair."

He lasted a few more moments, then pistoned forward, driving hard into Brennan's grinding thrust back onto him. Slamming into him up to the hilt, Luka then looped a hand around Brennan's pelvis to hold him there. Luka gasped, shuddered as he came, spilling into the condom and nuzzling the back of Brennan's neck. Brennan circled his hips slowly as Luka tugged shallowly out and pushed back in, riding it out.

"Okay? Hmm?" Brennan purred softly from over his shoulder. Luka found his lover's lips and kissed them tenderly.

"Yeah," Luka sighed.

"Lay down next to me. On your back. Gonna straddle you and feed you my cock, okay?"

Luka whimpered.

Taking off the blindfold, Brennan saw Luka clumsily—like his bones had been mysteriously replaced with spaghetti—get into the requested position. Then he guided Brennan into place, his knees planted right under Luka's arms. Brennan put on a condom and lowered his straining hard-on to Luka's eager, soft and supple lips. Luka gripped Brennan's hips, opened wide and took him back, lips sealed tight around him, frowning and moaning as he sucked and allowed Brennan to thrust as deeply as he wanted to go. Brennan tangled his fingers in Luka's long hair and rode his mouth, too desperate and worked-up to be gentle or hesitant. It was over quickly, but Luka didn't release Brennan until he was soft and too oversensitive to be able to stand any more stimulation.

Brennan shifted down and fell in a heap on top of Luka.

"I love you so fucking much," Luka panted, clinging to Brennan's smaller form.

"Ditto," Brennan agreed. "Tell me when the room stops spinning."

Seconds later, there was a knock at the door. It opened a crack and Alek said to them, "Hey. Bathroom's open. There are fresh towels in there and hot coffee and breakfast ready when you're out. I'm guessing you'll both need it after that performance. Very impressive, by the way."

"Thanks! You rock, Aleksy," Luka called, waving a hand deliriously.

"Yep," Alek nodded, retreating.

"Oh. Wow. That's... So they heard everything."

"Everything. I'm actually disappointed they didn't just come in and watch. Eh, maybe next time," he shrugged.

"When did life get so damn weird?"

"Mm. I love weird. But I love you more."

"See? We should have done this sooner," Brennan grinned.

Luka appeared to consider this then gave him a squeeze, "I don't know, the anticipation's half the fun. No regrets."

Brennan propped himself up and met Luka's gaze. "No regrets," he agreed.

"Brennan," he confessed quietly and sincerely, cupping Brennan's jaw, "I really didn't think I was gonna fall this hard."

Brennan exhaled sharply and fiercely held Luka's loving gaze. At first Luka seemed confused by his masked expression, but when Brennan angrily rubbed the heel of his hand at his eyes, wiping away gathering tears, Luka sighed and pressed a kiss to the center of his forehead.

"Baby, please don't cry. You're gonna break my damn heart."

Brennan sniffed and hid his face in Luka's expansive chest, waiting for the strong wave of emotion to pass. His gratitude was so profound, he couldn't process it. He couldn't even begin to try. "I don't know what I'd do without you. You're my best friend, but you're so much more than that. I'm yours, for as long as you'll have me."

"Then that makes me the luckiest guy in the world."

# Chapter 22

# Innocence Lost

Brennan waited in the hall by Evan's closed-over door with a hand braced on the frame. The back screen door slapped shut as Alek and Luka both headed outside. Absolute silence fell within the home.

There was a pull drawing Brennan to Evan, and it was part curiosity, part need and a vague sense Evan needed him too. He hoped it was true. Evan's innate ability to be loyal and heart-stoppingly sincere took Brennan's breath away. Evan was so different than any other guy Brennan had ever known. As soon as you were beneath the surface with him, you were cherished. You were important. Oh, how Brennan longed to be all of those things. The things Evan could give him would fill the empty places which had always left Brennan searching for love through casual sex. But there was nothing casual with Evan, and that was the best part about him. That was why Brennan was standing there—despite it all, despite the ways he knew the world worked and the warnings in his own heart—doing everything he could to get Evan to let him in.

After a beat, Brennan knocked gently. The bedroom door was slightly ajar, so the knocking was done more out of courtesy than necessity. Plus, he wasn't entirely sure Evan was even awake yet.

"Yeah. C'min, Bren," Evan murmured.

"How'd you know it was me?" Brennan asked, getting only a quirked eyebrow in reply. "Acoustics again?"

"Nah, you're the only one that'd bother to knock." Evan was curled up on his side in bed, lying under the sheet. He was bare-chested, gorgeous and groggy with sleep. Brennan had to make an effort not to stare and wonder if Evan was wearing anything on his lower half, focusing deliberately on Evan's face instead. But Evan was distracted, gazing intently at a scrap of paper, folded in half and left propped on his nightstand, placed just inches away from him. A duffel bag had been left on the floor between where Brennan was hovering in the doorway and the bed. Brennan figured it must have been Alek's.

Sidling slowly farther inside, Brennan brought to the bed a tray loaded down with nearly every food group and breakfast option known to man.

"Alek asked me to bring this to you," Brennan told him, leaving out the part about how much Brennan wanted to have an excuse to visit his brother. "He made all of it. The three of us already ate together in the kitchen. He said he was letting you sleep in."

Setting the tray safely out of the way on the floor, Brennan leaned over to peek at the note that had Evan's full attention. There was just enough time to make out 'good morning, sleepyhead,' before Evan's hand darted out to turn it facedown.

"You guys got to hang out a little then? That's cool." Now the note was hidden, Evan became fixated on the duffel, like he had to keep his eye on the evidence Alek had been there, and hadn't left yet.

"Yeah. You should have come out and joined us." Brennan sat on the edge of the bed, by where Evan's knees were curled up. Evan rolled self-consciously onto his back, putting a few extra inches of space between himself and his brother. He grasped the folds in the sheet, draped so everything from his navel down was covered and stared at his hands. He seemed quieter than usual, more introverted. It caused a prickling of worry. Brennan wondered what was going on, intrigued by the constant flickering of clouded thoughts in Evan's shadowed eyes. "Why didn't you?"

Evan shrugged. "I just woke up, and I didn't want it to be weird, I guess, with all of us in the same room. Plus, I've got a lot on my mind."

"I can tell. So does Alek."

Brennan got a quizzical stare at that and using Alek as bait seemed to work. Evan perked up and seemed to shake off whatever he'd been preoccupied with thinking about. "What do you mean?"

"He was quiet. It's weird, because he looks so much like Luka, but wow. Totally different. It was just so apparent out there. I could tell he was really unguarded and not putting on an act like he seemed to be when he dropped you off last week."

"But different how? Just because he's not as, like, bubbly as Luka, or what?"

"No. I mean, you're right about that too, but Alek's just more... I don't know how to put it. Sensitive?" Brennan struggled to explain himself better, looking for the right words. "Like if something's up he really takes it to heart and fights with the idea of stuff he can't change. Luka lets things go pretty quickly and moves on. He doesn't let himself get bogged down; he either reacts or dismisses it. Not Alek, though. You could see it in his face that he had a lot on his mind he was trying to come to terms with." Evan's lips pressed together and he stared off into space, giving a halfhearted effort to mask his reaction. But Brennan could feel Evan's reaction—no words or expression needed. Simple nearness allowed sadness and realization to radiate from Evan, soaking into Brennan with ease.

Giving Evan a leading look, trying to pull him out of his head, Brennan added, "He seemed upset."

Remembering how haunted Alek's eyes were, the signs of sleep lost and tears shed, of being plagued by some harsh reality all were there for Brennan to see, and easy enough to recognize for someone personally well acquainted with such things. As he ate breakfast, Brennan kept a wary eye on Alek who, like Evan, kept staring off into space, or falling perfectly still like he forgot what he was in the middle of doing or talking about.

"You told him what you did. Didn't you," Brennan said quietly. There was a measure of accusation there, but also understanding.

"Yeah," Evan nodded after a pause.

"How'd that go?"

"How do you think? He got upset." Evan shifted down lower on the bed, drawing his knees farther up. His gaze slid back over to the duffel, like he needed to make sure it was still there and not in the backseat of Alek's truck, on its way back home. "But it got more intense as the night went on, after I explained what happened specifically and why. We went to this lookout spot and were lying down, watching the sunset. After we talked, things got a little heated and we... um."

"Had sex? Made love?" Brennan supplied. Instantly, Evan bit bashfully at his lower lip and tugged uncomfortably at the sheet. Brennan smiled.

"Yeah," Evan agreed reluctantly. "Alek held me after that for, like, *hours*. And kept telling me he loves me, and that he wants to take care of me, and show me how to look at stuff in my life in more of a positive way."

"Evan," Brennan sighed, touched. "I'm so happy for you. So it was a good date?"

"It was a good date," Evan nodded, smiling despite himself.

"They're out cutting the lawn, by the way."

"What?!" Evan's legs fell flat to the bed and he shot upward a few inches in his surprise.

"Well, the grass *is* kinda long and after Alek did the dishes and took out the trash he grabbed Luka and recruited him to tame the yard."

"Why the hell would he...."

"Because he loves you," Brennan finished, smiling.

They locked eyes. A lot was said between them in that moment, with no words at all. It was as if Evan really believed, maybe for the first time, that Alek did care about him. It was more than simply wanting it to be true, it *was* true, and that truth was reflected in Alek's restless, urgent attempts to somehow be useful to Evan, to make things easier on him. Even if it was just cleaning the kitchen, or making breakfast, or doing yard work, Alek really was trying, because it was all he knew how to do in this situation. If he couldn't fix Evan's psyche, at least he could make a tangible impact in other ways.

Evan exhaled sharply in a rush. Brennan countered the glimmers of disbelief he saw in Evan, letting him know with unwavering confidence what he was saying was indeed true, and it was okay.

Evan started breathing a little more roughly, his chest rising and falling. Brennan glimpsed small love bites on it, and immediately got flashes of mental images of Alek sucking those marks to Evan's freckled, tan skin. It was a tempting fantasy, but reality and discomfort yanked him back to the present. Brennan didn't evaluate what he was doing or how Evan might read into it as he shifted so he could lie beside Evan. Evan moved over to accommodate him, but frowned with confusion and alarm.

"What are you doing?"

"More comfortable to lie down right now," Brennan admitted, resting on his side, facing Evan.

Evan's eyes grew wider. "Oh. Yeah. That was...." He glanced in the direction of Brennan's bedroom. "Extreme. At one point it sounded like you were actually killing him."

There was a second of silence before Brennan and Evan both erupted into laughter at the same time.

When they both settled down a little, Brennan sighed in agreement, "Yeah." Then they laughed even louder than before, snorting and feeding off each other's amusement.

After they'd stopped and fallen quiet again, Brennan asked, "So, you thought it was hot?"

There was no response at first. Evan looked to be doing everything in his power to not have a reaction to that question, which was a response in itself, Brennan decided. So he went with honesty and said the first thing that came to mind. "*I thought it was hot when Alek put that toy in you last night, how he just made you take it, and the way you sounded when you moaned. And just thinking about how you'd never played with sex toys before. Yeah. It was hot.*"

He expected Evan to get embarrassed again, so when Evan turned to look at him instead, his gaze skittering all over Brennan's face like it didn't know quite where to land or what to look at first, Brennan felt it like a tickle that went all the way to his gut. Evan was lying with his head cradled on a pillow, and Brennan was propped up on his elbow. They were mere inches apart. When Evan's gaze finally settled on Brennan's lips, Brennan took it as an invitation.

As he leaned in, Evan reached up and brushed his fingers lightly back around behind Brennan's head, cradling it and pulling him in. He was ready and kissed back as soon as Brennan's lips press gently against his. For the first few seconds, it stayed innocent, just soft, warm lips touching lips. But then the tip of Brennan's tongue touched the seam of Evan's lips and Evan made a soft, plaintive sound. He sighed out a sharp breath, gripped tighter at the soft strands of Brennan's hair and let his lips part at the same time. Evan tilted his head and Brennan teased his tongue back over the plump swell of Evan's lower lip. When Evan's tongue touched his, Brennan hummed softly and dove in. Quickly, Brennan became hard, and not for innocent reasons at all.

The tempting expanse of bare skin before him was too much to resist any longer. Brennan touched, then caressed over Evan's abdomen, over taut skin and smooth ripples of muscle. He felt Evan suck in his stomach in his surprise, then relax into it, too distracted by the ever-deepening kiss to pay much attention to where Brennan's hand was. Fingertips dragged up and down the center line of Evan's abs then up farther to his chest, tracing the muscles of his pecs before rubbing in small circles over and around the peaked nub and silky areola of Evan's right nipple.

Exhaling roughly, Evan gasped, "Bren."

Evan's eyes squeezed shut just as Brennan's popped open wide and watchful, taking in every detail as he brushed back and forth with the pad of his index finger over the erect flesh, feeling it get steadily harder. Gripping it between his fingers, he tugged and twisted. He was rewarded with an anguished, breathy whimper. Sucking lightly on Evan's lips, he pinched harder. It got Evan arching up into his hand and pulling gently on Brennan's hair.

"Bren," Evan whined more sharply.

All of Brennan's self-restraint tumbled away. All he wanted, all that mattered, was making Evan fall apart, getting him to let his carefully erected walls down and provoking even more of those lusciously wrecked sounds. Each one was like a jolt of electricity surging right to Brennan's dick, making him harder—his whole body buzzing. He realized he was panting and overheated. The light exercise pants and t-shirt he was wearing were too bulky, too heavy. His ass still throbbed from the rough sex with Luka that morning, but his cock throbbed even more. Needing in the most primal way to know if Evan was as hard as he was, Brennan's hand slid fast, stroking firmly down the front of Evan's body and grabbing on to the steely line of his erection, disguised poorly by the bed sheet. Brennan squeezed it once, stroked down and over Evan's balls then back up, tracing the outline with questing fingers before simply grabbing onto it again and tugging.

Evan shivered, his eyes opening at last as he gaped, choking off a jagged, thunderous moan.

"I'm so fucking hard," Brennan rasped, nuzzling Evan's neck.

Something, possibly his willpower, or his sanity, snapped in Evan then. He rolled them both with a lusty growl. Swarming in Brennan's head were arguments, voices that sounded like Jimmy or Charlie, telling him it was wrong, that it was forbidden. But then Evan was on top of Brennan, molding their bodies together from the hips down and trapping their erections between them. Brennan's hands were grabbing at and squeezing Evan's ass and Evan was thrusting against the proof of Brennan's desire, rutting desperately into it. Brennan wrapped a hand behind Evan's neck and yanked him down closer, latching on to a spot under Evan's jaw and sucking hard on it. Both of Brennan's legs were wrapped around Evan to hold him there. Undulating up off the bed, Brennan rocked into Evan's thrusts. Wanting to untangle Evan from the damned sheet, wanting to push his own pants out of the way and rub their cocks together without any barrier between them, Brennan realized there was no time. It felt too good, just pushing, pushing, *pushing.*

"I-I'm gonna come... Evan... oh *fuck....*"

Evan moaned and grinded down even harder, his cock sliding and rubbing alongside Brennan's and he was so close to the edge of release, it hurt. Brennan found Evan's mouth again and kissed him as he whimpered through his orgasm, twitching, pinning Evan so tightly to him that Evan would probably have the bruises for days afterward.

Keening, Evan kissed Brennan breathless. Three more hard thrusts and he lost it. He shot his load and suckled on his brother's tongue.

"Wait, I need to...." Brennan rolled them again, so that he was on top. Evan, still coming and completely dazed, stared up at Brennan with flushed cheeks. Brazen and wild, Brennan finally pushed the sheet out of the way and wrapped his bare hand around Evan's come-soaked shaft, stroking him through the aftershocks. "I need to touch you."

Evan's hips snapped, bucking into Brennan's hand, his lower lip quivering and head falling back. It was more than physical contact; it was Evan letting him in, deeper, maybe, than anyone had been before, even Alek. It felt like victory.

An hour later, they hadn't moved, and were still entangled and sticky. Evan had dozed off and awoke to find Brennan lying on him still, his head nestled in the crook of Evan's neck.

"We shouldn't have done that," Evan said quietly as Brennan stroked gently over Evan's chest.

"Then why do I want to do more?"

"Don't say that," Evan ached.

"Too late." Brennan's nose nudged Evan's cheek. His eyelashes tickled against Evan's skin. His hand lay hot on Evan's skin, their bodies a perfect fit, the contact soothing and comforting. "I love you so much. I just want to... you know... keep loving you."

Sighing, Evan wrapped an arm around his brother. His hand came to rest on the small of Brennan's back and his fingers slipped down under the waistband of Brennan's drawstring pants, grazing the top swell of Brennan's backside. They crept lower. Palming the muscle of Brennan's ass, Evan stroked his thumb back and forth over the skin. Brennan moaned very quietly and nuzzled against his brother's neck, asking, "Let's just stay here for a while, okay?"

"Okay."

# Chapter 23
# Fear of Falling

"You look how I feel."

"Hmm? You say something?"

"Exactly," Luka nodded, planting his hands on his hips. "Just provin' my point."

"What? What are you talking about?" Alek looked blankly at Luka. They were standing in the backyard, beside an old lawnmower they'd pulled from the shed but had yet to actually do anything with. It seemed like Alek was paying attention, but Luka knew Alek was only just barely humoring him; he was really far, far away, pondering whatever it was he was pondering and causing his deficit of attention.

"What's up? You look like horse shit."

Alek blinked. "Wow. Yeah, don't hold back on me, Luka. That's great. Thank you." He rubbed a hand roughly over his stubble-covered jaw, bloodshot, puffy eyes and sallow skin. Then he bent down to pull the cord and start the mower up.

"I think we all know *my* excuse for feeling like I just got my ass soundly kicked. Because I did. By a sweet little blond Cupcake who was sent to me by God as retribution for all of my whoring around."

Alek smiled at that, surprised into sudden amusement. He flipped his hair back out of his eyes and shot Luka a knowing look. "Yeah? What's the verdict?"

Luka clutched dramatically at his chest and feigned a heart attack, nearly falling over backward, his face contorted with glorious anguish.

"That good, huh?"

"No," Luka said seriously, with emphasis. "Better. So much better. Aleksy, he's like, *way* outta my league. I don't deserve him. At all. He's such a sweetheart and funny and sexy as fuckall, and good Christ I keep picturing him in a nurse's uniform and really, that's not helping at all. What do I do? I'm gonna fuck this up. I know it. I always do."

Alek got the mower's engine started and clapped him on the shoulder. "If you want it that bad, you'll figure it out," he shouted over the din before striding away, guiding the lawnmower in a broad path across the grass.

While Alek tackled the neglected yard, Luka trimmed the hedges along the house and chopped at some of the overgrown weeds. He finished off by using the weed-eater on the periphery of the property, pretty much doing whatever he could to be useful until Alek was done. The abrupt end to their conversation had only heightened Luka's already typically overwhelming curiosity, and he wasn't going anywhere until he wheedled out some answers. It was apparent to Luka that Alek was more than tired or cranky, he was unequivocally freaking out. It was in Alek's eyes, posture and attitude, and Luka would be doing Alek a disservice, as his only family, if he didn't do his best to get to the bottom of it.

When the yard work was indeed done, the pair of them sat on the back porch. Sipping cold beers pulled from the fridge, Luka sighed and patted Alek's leg.

"Tell me, oh wise one. Why did we just bust our asses doing the lawn of a house we don't even live at?"

Alek bowed his head and stared at the ground by his feet. "Because Evan's got enough on his mind without worrying about that, too."

And just like that, Luka remembered what Brennan confided in him about Evan. Aching for Alek, Luka fell quiet. But he knew he should act like he didn't know what Alek was talking about, so, when he was sure his voice would come out sounding normal, he asked, "What's up?"

Alek simply shook his head, and rubbed dirty fingers over his eyes. He braced his forehead in a hand, his elbow propped on his knee.

"Dammit. Aleksy, talk to me," Luka pleaded. He didn't like how Alek looked at all. He hadn't been this upset about anything since they were teenagers.

"It was just supposed to be a quick, dirty fuck in the bathroom. That's *all*. How did I get here? Losing my damn mind over some broken *kid*? I feel like he's under my skin or something. Like when I wasn't paying attention he got inside me and twisted everything up so I can't even tell up from down. He's all I see, all I can think about, and all I want. And knowing… what I know… what could have happened, what could still happen. I start to get this panicky feeling." Alek clutched his chest, frowning severely, "Like I can't breathe, like someone's squeezing my heart inside their fist. I didn't sleep much at all last night. There was no way I was taking my eyes off of him. And now I've gotta fuckin' go to work and deal with those drunken jackasses. I don't know. I don't think I can leave him."

Alek spewed this all out without thinking or censoring much. If he *was* thinking, he might have realized how little sense he was making, but luckily Luka knew Evan's secret already and read between the lines.

"I'll be here. I'll make sure he's okay until you get back," Luka said gently.

Alek's arm, the one holding his head up, started to shake.

"Aleksy," Luka sighed.

Looking sideways at his brother, Alek set his jaw with fierce determination, his eyes wet with tears.

"C'mere." Luka pulled him over, letting Alek lean on his shoulder and wrapping him in a lose embrace. "Maybe we're *supposed* to be here. Maybe we're supposed to look out for them. Like fate."

"You don't believe in fate," Alek murmured doubtfully, but lightening up nonetheless. "Or true love. Or any of that stuff."

"Well, I did say *maybe*."

"You're so full of shit," Alek grinned.

"Should we go check on the kids, old man?" Luka sighed, slapping Alek's knee.

"Why does everyone keep calling me that?" Standing, Alek cracked his back and hobbled wearily over to the back door.

Once inside, there was no immediate sign of Brennan or Evan. The house was quiet—too quiet. The Popović brothers stood in the kitchen and listened for any sign of their lovers. Then, Luka spied the iPod dock Brennan had set up on the counter for when he was cooking. Pointing at it, he turned to Alek. "I have an idea!"

"Oh no," Alek groaned. "Your ideas terrify me. What now?"

Luka fished his iPod out of his pocket and scrolled through his playlist until he found what he was looking for.

"They can't still be sleeping, right? I mean, we slept a lot when we were that age, but not for *this* long," Alek pondered.

On the other side of the house, Brennan paced agitatedly between his room and the bathroom with bare feet and a dressed in new change of clothes. Evan had been in the shower for a half-hour. He answered Brennan's shouted questions by telling him to go pee in the bushes outside if he needed to go so badly, or saying he was almost done time and time again, even though the water was never shut off, frustrating Brennan to no end. Evan went so far as to say that if Brennan was waiting so they could talk about what happened, he'd happily stay in there all day.

They had literally raced each other to the bathroom. Evan wanted it all to himself, unlike Brennan, so he could get thoroughly cleaned up without an audience, and since he happened to be laying a few inches closer to the door when they were in bed together, it gave him just enough of an advantage. He won the race and Brennan was forced to clean up with moist towelettes and tissues after Evan locked him out. It was clear enough from Evan's tone of voice that he was fine and simply seeking privacy, but Brennan was stubborn enough to linger anyway.

Luka, grinning like a cat, set the iPod in the dock and hit play, cranking up the volume. House music started blasting from the tiny speakers, thumping with a pounding beat. Alek cocked an eyebrow at his brother. "Seriously?"

"What? It's an experiment," he argued. "Hey, I was offered a lap dance earlier, so I just wanted to see if maybe.... Ha!"

Luka broke into delighted laughter as Brennan bolted down the hallway toward him, sliding gracefully on the wooden boards until he collided with Luka, who caught him to keep him from sailing right into the cabinets. Brennan laughed with him. Reaching up and hooking his arms over Luka's broad shoulders, Brennan began to swivel his hips along with the bass beat, keeping his body loose and fluid, his eyes locked onto Luka. Brennan teased his full bottom lip seductively between the points of his teeth and smiled wickedly. Holding on to Brennan by the waist, Luka started to lead, urging Brennan's movements on. Their bodies fit together, with Luka's thigh snugly nestled between Brennan's legs and Brennan rocking rhythmically against the thick muscle, riding it.

Alek watched them with amusement, but also kept an eye out for any sign of Evan.

After a few more beats, Brennan pivoted on a heel, leaning back into Luka's chest, shimmying and shaking his ass. Undulating against Luka's body, he raised his arms loosely over his head. Brennan's lips went soft and his eyes closed half-way over. Turning his head to the side, toward Luka, Brennan gave him a heated look. He rubbed a hand down the front of his body and pulled Luka's hand snugly around the front of his waist as he circled his hips in tight figure eights, dips and sways that had him rubbing right against Luka's crotch.

Alek just stared, completely captivated, murmuring, "Damn."

Unable to *not* hear the loud music coming from his kitchen, Evan let curiosity win out over shyness. Tugging a clean shirt over his head, he shuffled toward the source of the noise. He got as far as the doorway when he saw Brennan doing smooth hip-rolls and dry-humping Luka with movements perfectly synchronized to the thumping bass, wearing the sexiest pout Evan had ever seen and shaking his ass like a go-go dancer. Evan broke into a big, easy grin that took over his face, banishing all cares and worries away. He tried to hide it with a hand to his mouth, but it was too late, Brennan had already seen him and was bouncing his way.

"Should we just hang a cage in here for you to dance in?"

"Only if you promise to tuck some dolla' bills in my g-string," Brennan smirked.

"Oh my god," Evan chuckled. "You actually have one, don't you?"

Brennan winked at him. Grabbing Evan by the hips, Brennan fit their pelvises together with a hard tug, their legs interweaving as he palmed Evan's ass and guided him slowly into the dance. Evan gazed heatedly down between their bodies as Brennan rocked them with his thumb hooked in Evan's back pocket.

For the moment, Luka and Alek weren't even there. They weren't whispering in each other's ears and gaping at the arousing sight of the other set of twins dirty dancing together. It was just Evan and his seductive other half who had, not two hours earlier, made Evan come so hard he saw stars.

Brennan's free hand came up and cupped Evan's jaw, stroking gently over the bristles of his morning stubble. The guilt, built up in Evan's heart while he washed up, melted quickly away. He felt the heat in Brennan's stare, the soft warmth of his touch and the firmness of his lithe body. Evan closed his eyes and grabbed Brennan's ass, gripping it, feeling the muscle work as Brennan rotated his hips. Their cocks squeezed together through insubstantial layers of fabric.

The intimate, bold touch set something off in Brennan. He exhaled against Evan's skin and leaned in, mouthing over Evan in a feather-light brush of lips against lips. A shiver raced down Evan's spine and blood surged between his legs, making his cock swell and his balls ache. The moment went on and on. The almost-kiss dragged out.

He could tell Brennan was waiting for him to make the next move, but Evan couldn't do it, at least not until Alek came up behind him, trapping Evan between the two of them and dancing along with them. Then, the tip of Evan's tongue slipped out, teased at Brennan's top lip and, when Brennan opened for him, lightly touched the tip of Brennan's tongue. Brennan surged in, kissing passionately and moaning. Alek nipped gently at the shell of Evan's ear and his hand snaked across their bodies, wrapping behind Brennan, overlaying Evan's hand on Brennan's backside.

The song ended, fading into the next, and Evan broke the kiss, breathless and dizzy. Brennan's hand slid up under Evan's shirt, caressing his bare skin and they just kept dancing. Alek's mouth latched on below Evan's ear, and Evan's eyes cracked open just enough to see Brennan watching Alek suck a mark to his skin. Evan tilted his head to give Alek more room and his cock twitched inside his jeans. Brennan's next push against him was more pointed and fervent, grinding right against Evan's hard-on.

Evan could feel how easy it would be to keep going. Out of the corner of his eye he could see Luka sitting on the counter and swinging his feet, drinking a bottle of Brennan's spring water, and watching the three of them like a hawk.

Surprisingly, it didn't bother Evan at all, being on display like that for Luka. If they had suddenly lost the pretense of the dance and just devolved into sexual deviance right there in the middle of the kitchen floor with a captive audience witnessing the whole thing, well, that would've been okay, too.

Evan cleared his throat and twisted away, away from Alek and Brennan as well. "Just gimme a sec, okay?"

Concern darkened Brennan's bright eyes but Evan gave him a slight smile to assure him he was all right.

"Hey, Bren, you crazy little fucker!"

Brennan's eyes narrowed with clear mischief. A fiery look was aimed at Luka from over his shoulder. Evan watched as Brennan spun and jumped onto Luka after he had slipped down from his perch. Brennan wrapped his legs around Luka's waist. Luka held him there with two hands cupped under Brennan's ass as Brennan bounced to the music, writhing like a cat. Luka laughed and kissed him passionately.

"Your brother is... not shy. And a little crazy," Alek chuckled.

"Yeah, well, likewise. You're um, sweaty," Evan said, grinning after he said it.

"Oh yeah. Sorry. I might need to use your shower before I head over to work for a few hours," Alek muttered, looking down at himself.

"You seriously didn't have to do yard work."

"I have no idea what you're talking about," Alek replied with feigned ignorance, planting his hand on his narrow hips. Evan simply plucked a blade of grass from Alek's sweat-damp shirt and handed it back to him.

"So, you really have to work today?"

"Just for a few hours. I'd like to come back tonight, if that's okay. I think Luka's planning to spend the day here, so you'll have company. Did Bren get you some breakfast?"

"Yeah," Evan murmured. "Thank you for that. You really didn't have to do that either."

"I wanted to. How are you today?" Alek guided Evan back toward the doorway, away from Brennan and Luka, lowering his voice.

"I'm good. Look, I'm sorry for laying all of that on you last night. I don't want it to change how you think of me. I'm not gonna break and I'm not, you know — weak."

"I know you're not," Alek said quietly, frowning. "But it's part of who you are, and I'm glad you told me. I want you to be able to tell me anything. How are you and...." He nodded to the other pair, still dancing, kissing and laughing, oblivious.

"Well, it got weird," Evan admitted. "But the weirdest part of all might be how comfortable it was. It shouldn't feel that good to get off on your brother, right?"

"What happened?" Alek asked confidentially, leaning in closer and glancing over to Brennan.

But Evan shook his head, not willing to talk about it yet or there, with Brennan so close by.

"He loves you so much, Evan. It's so apparent. There's this insane level of chemistry between you two. We talked about this, remember? No judging. You do what feels right to you. I just ask that you're honest with me about it."

Evan hung around Alek until he was ready to leave, lingering in the bathroom while Alek took a shower and reclining on the bed while he got dried off and dressed. Evan stayed quiet, just enjoying being near his lover and enjoying his company while he could. Alek didn't press Evan on the Brennan issue, for which Evan was grateful. Evan knew he needed to figure things out for himself before he brought anyone one else into it all. He was willing to tell Alek something happened, but not to analyze it with him.

Alek took his duffel bag with him, saying he intended to pack it with fresh supplies from home before returning after work, but it made Evan nervous to have Alek collecting all of his things and leaving nothing behind, with no concrete reason to return. Luka even had his own car there, and was perfectly capable of taking off, not needing Alek to come back and give him a ride. What if Evan had really disturbed Alek with the confession about his suicide attempt? What if, despite his assurances, Alek really was put off by Evan's attraction to Brennan and he was just being polite until he could get away, scot-free? These questions swirled around inside Evan's head, swarming and multiplying until they were all he could think about, blocking all sense and reason.

They walked to Alek's truck and Evan could still feel the throbbing deep inside his body from where Alek had been inside him the night before, but the ache in his heart was more acute. He tried to block it out, to let on nothing of what was happening inside.

"So, I'll see you later, right?" Evan mumbled, plucking a cigarette from the pack he'd stuck in his back pocket and cupping a hand over the end as he lit it. He sucked in a lungful of smoke and held it in.

Alek threw his bag into the passenger side footwell and folded his arms across his chest, frowning slightly with disapproval at Evan's smoking.

"Yeah. I'll probably be here around midnight."

Evan blew out a long tendril of smoke and let the lit cigarette fall to his side as Alek's frown deepened.

"That's really bad for you, you know."

"Yeah," Evan mumbled. "I know I said this already, but I swear I'm not as pathetic as it sounded. I mean, I understand if you're not interested as much anymore. You don't owe me anything."

"What are you talking about? I just said I'm coming back later."

"I know what you said. I'm just giving you an out if you need one." He scratched the side of his nose with his thumb, the cigarette pinched between two fingers. It was to disguise the sudden wave of emotion choking him, squeezing his throat closed and burning in his chest. He couldn't read Alek's expression. At first he seemed shocked, then angry, then upset. "So, if you change your mind, I just wanted to say thank you for listening and for everything you've done."

Alek hissed through his teeth and his expression clarified into pure heartache. He slung an arm behind Evan's neck and hugged him to his chest, sighing thickly into his short hair. "*Stop*. Stop saying goodbye. I'm not leaving you. I meant it when I said I love you. You couldn't get rid of me now if you tried."

Evan tried to believe it as Alek held him, feeling how solid and real Alek was.

When Evan said nothing and only tried not to return Alek's embrace in case it was the last one he was going to get, Alek growled, "I swear to fucking God if I ever meet your dad, I'm gonna punch him right in the face for what he did to you. He sure did a piss-poor job taking care of you."

"He tried his best."

"Well, his best wasn't good enough. I will *not* take off and leave you alone like he does. Got it? If you need anything today, call my cell or talk to Luka. Please. I'll see you in a few hours."

He planted a soft kiss to Evan's forehead and took a good look at his face, cupping it in his hands. Evan gazed up at him hopefully and said, "I love you."

"I love you, too. Take it easy, okay? I might bring over my pillow and some other stuff tonight. You were totally hogging the pillows last night, so I think I need to improvise a little."

Embarrassed, Evan bowed his head. "Was not," he protested.

"No, you totally were," Alek insisted with raised eyebrows. "It was terrible. How dare you, Evan."

Evan rolled his eyes and repressed a grin. "Dork. Go to work."

Climbing in behind the wheel and rolling down the windows, Alek called, "If our brothers are humping like rabbits again, throw a bucket of cold water on 'em for me!"

"Done!"

Evan waved as Alek reversed out of the drive and coasted away down the road. Alek honked twice before turning and disappearing from sight.

After a quick glance back over his shoulder at the house, Evan made himself comfortable on the front stoop and enjoyed the rest of his cigarette. When it was burned down to the filter, he crushed it out and tossed the pack into the garbage, wanting to make Alek happy, and proud of him.

# Chapter 24
# Avoiding the Issue

While Luka showered off the sweat from doing both the yard work and dancing, Brennan did a load of laundry. As he gathered dirty clothes, he peered out through the windows at Evan, who although Alek was long gone, was still outside, tinkering with and washing his car. It reminded Brennan of how Evan behaved that morning, lingering in bed long after Alek had left it. Savoring the remnants of Alek's aura in the room, cherishing the note Alek left and clinging to the sight of Alek's things sitting there in Evan's room so boldly, like they belonged there, as if Evan had found a strange new reality with something very precious—someone who didn't owe him anything at all, but cared anyway. And now that Alek's things, his truck, and his self, were gone, Evan was lingering in the yard Alek worked to spruce up that morning in order to lighten Evan's load.

Brennan watched as Evan treasured it like a gift, spending all day amidst Alek's handiwork, the sinking sun baking into Evan's tan skin and shining gold in his hair. It spoke to a deep sentimentality in Evan's personality and reminded Brennan of their mother, and how the little things, like small acts of kindness, were always the most important to her.

After gathering some used clothes in his own room, both his and Luka's, Brennan went to Evan's room, grabbing the bed sheets which were soiled by the intimate moment shared by them a handful of hours ago, a moment still looming large and bright in Brennan's mind. Brennan also collected the clothes Evan wore the night before on his date with Alek. They all got tossed and mixed together in his basket, which he took to the washer and dumped in. And if

Brennan took a few seconds to inhale Evan's musky scent from one of the t-shirts, then, well, no one really needed to know about that, did they?

Around late afternoon, Evan came inside in a hurry, half-drenched in sweat and sudsy water from washing the car. He went straight to the living room where Brennan and Luka were cuddled up together on the couch and watching golf. Dripping all over the wooden floor, Evan said breathlessly, frantically, "I'm not home. Okay? I'm out. Went to town or something. Got it?"

With a nervous glance over his shoulder at the front door, he fled to his bedroom, leaving them confused until there was a knock at the door and Jimmy's voice called for someone to answer. It carried in easily through the opened windows. Brennan hopped up and went to answer it.

"Hey Jimmy. What's up?" he asked, cracking the door open and leaning against it, intentionally blocking Jimmy's view of the inside of the house.

"Where's Evan? I've been trying to call him and he won't talk to me. I'm worried."

"Evan's fine. He went for a walk into town. I'll tell him you stopped by, though."

"Why isn't he answering his phone?"

"He, um... he's been with Alek, so he probably turned it off and forgot about it. Seriously, don't worry. I've been keeping a really close eye on him."

Jimmy looked doubtful but nodded, hands shoved deeply in his front pockets. Turning his head, he glanced at the water dripping from Evan's freshly-washed, prized Chevy onto the driveway, at the sponge left lying on the asphalt and hose abandoned in a messy heap.

"Okay. Thanks, Brennan. How have you been? Good? You look good."

"Thanks," Brennan smiled happily. "I am. Things have been looking up."

"I'm glad to hear it. I'll catch you later, I guess. Have a nice day," Jimmy smiled distractedly back. With a small wave, he walked back toward the road and out of sight.

Seconds later, Brennan had shut and locked the door and was passing by Luka with his questioning expression, holding up a finger to him as he stomped into Evan's room.

"What was that about? Since when do you avoid Jimmy?"

Evan sighed and stopped his pacing in the middle of the room. "I knew he was gonna ask me about how things have been with you, and I can't lie to him. I just can't. I'm incapable of it. The only reason I'm alive and standing here right now is because of him. I can sometimes avoid talking about shit, but what if he saw on my face the *truth* about how things have been with you? You really think an ex-preacher's gonna understand about how I feel about you and the *filthy fucking things* I want to do to you every time I see you? You're my *brother*, Brennan."

"Jimmy cares about you, Evan. He'd never do anything to cause you harm or make you feel bad about yourself. You have to know that." Brennan clung to the rational argument, but the part of Evan's tirade that really stuck in his head was the last part, and the implication of what Evan wanted. It made Brennan's blood rise. Questions sat on his lips: *What kinds of things, Evan? What would you do to me? How far will you let this go?*

They locked eyes and the moment drew out until Evan blurted, "Where are my sheets and my clothes?"

"Being washed. They were dirty."

*Filthy fucking things... Hell yeah, they were dirty,* Brennan thought.

Evan bowed his head, arguing, "I can do my own laundry."

"I was doing a load anyway. It's not a big deal."

"Maybe I don't want you going through my things! Maybe I don't want you in my business and cleaning up my messes. I just—you know what? I can't do this. I can't. Please go. Please leave me alone for a while," Evan sighed tiredly, turning his back on Brennan.

"Why?" It sounded hurt and small.

"I think you know why."

Brennan hovered in the doorway anyway, fighting the natural, magnetic pull that wanted to draw him closer to his twin. "Come and sit with us," he offered. "Relax for a little while. Luka said he wanted to hang out with you and I think it could be fun. You two should get to know each other better. You—"

"I'm not done outside yet," Evan interrupted.

Brennan fell quiet and nodded once, muttering, "Of course not."

Evan turned at that, but Brennan was already starting to leave. All Evan got was a fleeting glimpse as Brennan went back to Luka.

It had been a long, weird day and, after eight hours slaving over a hot stove, his back stiff and generally exhausted, Alek pulled up to the Savage-Holt household. Taking his things from the truck, he headed to the front door.

Alek had a semblance of an idea of what the evening had been like for Evan, Luka and Brennan, since he was texted throughout the afternoon and night by both his brother and his boyfriend. It was still a surprise, though, when, standing in the foyer, bags and pillow in hand, he saw Evan, Luka, and Brennan seated on the couch in that order and looking quite cozy. Bitter envy froze Alek to the bones, giving him a much needed boost of energy but also causing him to hate his beloved brother a little for how comfortable he looked with Evan.

Evan had a number of empty beers lined up in front of him on the coffee table and Luka's arms were slung behind both Brennan and Evan's shoulders. Brennan also had a drink in hand, something dark amber and on the rocks. There was a pronounced scowl on Evan's face but he was leaning into Luka, whose hand was resting on Evan's chest, his thumb idly stroking over it. Luka's other hand was fingering through strands of Brennan's hair. An old B horror movie was playing on the television in front of them, but none of the trio appeared to be truly watching.

"Oh hey, Aleksy. How was work?" Luka said easily, catching sight of him.

"The usual. Lots of drunk people. A bunch of them were packing though. Always makes things more interesting. We're thinking we might need to hire more security."

"You should be careful."

"Yeah, I know. Always am. How are you?"

"Can't complain," he smiled, his hands lifting for a second to punctuate the boast, gesturing to the gorgeous twins flanking him and cuddled up to him. There was something else there in his eyes, though, other than pride or contentment. Something darker, brittle, and well-enough camouflaged that Alek knew it was a message just for him.

Evan finally looked over at Alek, and happiness subtly washed over his previously gloomy expression. He was trying to be cool, Alek realized, but it was crystal clear how glad Evan was to see him.

"Hey. Welcome back," Evan said quietly.

"Glad to be back. Luka, can I talk to you for a second in the kitchen?" Alek nodded toward the back of the house. Luka mumbled an assent and moved to join him, excusing himself.

"Hey, get me another one of these while you're up?" Brennan asked quietly, swirling his glass.

Luka leaned in to answer him, lowering his voice discreetly. They all heard him anyway. "I think maybe you should cool it for a little while. Those are pretty strong."

"Are you my daddy?" Brennan shot back. "You giving me orders now?"

"No," Luka replied shortly, lips pursing with frustration.

Evan was looking at the TV screen, apparently tuning them out as he sipped his beer.

"Then please, would you be so kind as to get me another rum and coke. Thanks."

He was hiding it better than Alek would have guessed, but he was clearly buzzed. His words were crisp enough, but there was a shine and fuzziness in his eyes. Though not yet full-on drunk, Brennan was getting there fast. Alek's time as a bartender had made him proficient in picking up the telltale signs, and if Brennan was parked on a barstool as a customer, Alek would have been cutting him off for sure.

Luka straightened and quickly joined Alek. They walked back into the kitchen after Alek dumped his things inside Evan's room.

"What's going on?" Alek asked once they had slightly more privacy.

"Jesus Christ, man, you can cut the tension in there with a knife. They had an argument. I don't know what about. And it's just been getting more intense by the minute. I've been trying to cool them down, but they aren't talking to each other, just to me. Evan's pissed off that Brennan is drinking. I guess he's never had alcohol before. And to be honest, *I'm* kind of pissed at him, too. I don't know what he's trying to prove, but he's really determined to get bombed."

"Maybe we should give them some time alone to work it out," Alek sighed. He grabbed a seat at the kitchen table and slumped down in it. Luka joined him.

"How're things with you?"

"Eh. Same. Work was too slow, then too busy. Kept one eye on the guys carrying weapons and still tried to keep up with everything. Katie was all in my face about shit. When I went home to grab my stuff, Presley's room was empty again, and Carter's door was shut." Alek gave Luka a pointed look. "Guess they figured we'd both be safely out of the way tonight."

Luka stared at his hands laced together on the tabletop, saying nothing.

"I wish they'd at least be honest with us. I mean, Pres talks to you. He knows you know. They know *I* know, why can't they just fucking admit it?"

"Because they can't," Luka said softly. "And they shouldn't have to. It's their business. They aren't like us. They care what people think and say about them."

"Is it just screwing around? Because I get a vibe from them sometimes like maybe it's not. Like they're lying to themselves, too. Carter gets so fucking protective of him. That means there are emotions involved, right?"

"I don't know, man. I don't know how deep it goes."

Alek fell quiet, looking off towards the living room, trying to pick out the sounds interspersed with those coming from the television.

"You ever seen 'em together?"

"Presley and Carter? Yeah, just once."

Turning toward his brother, intrigued by his uncharacteristic silence, Alek waited for further explanation. "And?"

"I don't know. It was hot. I was just going downstairs to get a midnight snack, couldn't sleep. The usual. I was in the hallway and heard moaning, so yeah, I stopped to look. Carter was just, you know, *really* giving it to Presley, and Pres caught me watching. He looked *freaked* that I saw. But he didn't say anything or tell Carter to stop, so I just kept on movin' along. That's why he talks to me about it sometimes. It wasn't really something he chose to confide in me."

"Hmm," Alek hummed pensively, thinking it over. The whole thing made him sad. Knowing things were off between Brennan and Evan just added to it. His hand snaked over and overlaid Luka's. Pivoting his wrist, Luka took Alek's hand, holding it, stroking gently over his wrist with his thumb.

"You can't fix everyone, you know. Can't always help 'em either. Sometimes they've gotta want to be helped first."

Alek smiled, chuckling softly. The grin faded completely away. "How'd you get so damn smart?"

"Well, I do have this awesome brother to show me the way," Luka winked.

Alek sighed, then groaned, "What do we do about them?" He nodded to the front of the house.

Luka shrugged helplessly. "Honestly? No idea."

# Chapter 25

# Hard Choices Made Easy

When it was clear Luka and Alek weren't going to be returning anytime soon, Brennan was the first to break the ice. Evan had been staring at the TV screen with glazed eyes, on edge from the built-up, frustrated sexual tension, paralyzed by the weight of what they'd done and what he knew still could happen.

Evan finished his beer and set it down next to the other empties. Brennan took another deep drink from his glass. Evan knew Brennan had to be buzzed out of his mind with all of the alcohol he'd had. He turned to Evan, sitting sideways on the couch with his left leg folded in front of him, and, made braver with the help of the booze, stopped holding back.

"Why are you pissed at me?"

"Why are you so dead set on getting shitfaced?" Evan retorted.

"Answer mine first," Brennan dared.

Evan huffed, slouching down farther on the cushions and wishing secretly Luka would come back and be the warm, incredible-smelling, solid barrier of pure, chiseled muscle between them for a little longer. Then he remembered Alek was there too and felt instantly guilty for thinking of Luka first. He blamed it on the beer.

"Just answer the damn question, Evan. Why are you pissed at me?"

"I'm not mad at you, okay?" Evan hissed sharply. "I'm mad at myself!"

"Why?"

Their eyes met for the first time in hours.

Neither of them looked away.

Brennan added softly, "Is it because of what we did? Do you regret it that much? Because I don't. Maybe I should, but...." He shrugged. "I still want you."

"Bren," Evan groaned, his expression falling. "Are you saying this stuff to make me feel better? Because if you are, don't. Don't sugarcoat this. I know I'm fucked up, okay? I do. The last thing I want is to bring you down with me."

"God damn it, Evan! No, you know what? Fuck it!"

The outburst was sharp, determined, and got Evan's attention. Startled, he tried to sit up straighter just as Brennan pivoted, swinging his right leg over Evan's thighs and straddling him, sat on top of him. He rested his arms over Evan's shoulders, his eyes growing darker, heavy-lidded. His fingers twisted up into the hair at the nape of Evan's neck and his hips rolled forward once.

"What the hell are you doing? You're drunk," Evan argued, his own head swimming, his reflexes dulled. Intending to push Brennan off, his hands palmed Brennan's ass instead, and when Brennan rocked forward, deliberately, into Evan's crotch, Evan grunted softly. Sighing, Brennan dipped his head to catch Evan's mouth, suckling lightly at his lower lip as the fingers of his right hand searched upward under Evan's shirt, moving lightly over his stomach and chest. His thumb rolled over Evan's hardened nipple right as he thrust forward again, with more force this time. Brennan's tight, nimble body undulated, and Evan made a soft, needy sound, squeezing a double-handful of Brennan's backside as Brennan started to pepper kisses back along Evan's jaw and down his neck.

"We've gotta stop," Evan panted. But Brennan was fiddling with the button of Evan's fly and a hard shiver ripped through Evan, leaving him tingling, aching.

*Is this happening? Is it really happening? And where's Alek? Where's Luka?*

"No, we don't," Brennan shot him a dark look through fallen bangs. "*We* make the rules. Nobody else. Just us. Can I taste you? I just wanna taste you."

Slowly, he tugged down Evan's zipper. It was loud in the room, the small metal ticking of the teeth coming apart. Frozen, shocked, confused, and horny, Evan sat there as Brennan slid backward off his lap to the floor and guided Evan's legs apart, making room for himself there. With the jeans now opened, Brennan held Evan's stare and quickly, firmly, tugged on the sides of them, yanking them down a few inches—just enough. Evan's mouth worked soundlessly for a moment as Brennan's hand circled his dick, squeezing lightly, guiding it upright, and stroking him so very slowly and tenderly.

"You lose the underwear for Alek? That's so fucking sexy."

Evan's head fell back against the couch as he chose not to watch. He ground his teeth together as Brennan lazily tugged him to full hardness. Fingers dragged along his shaft, flicking over the ridge of the head and across the tip as a few clear drops wept from the slit. Rubbing through the fluid, Brennan smeared it down over the throbbing, swelling flesh.

Breathy and helpless, Evan asked, "Why are you doing this?" "Because I want to," Brennan answered, sounding wrecked, his voice rough and throaty. He leaned in and licked a long, wet stripe from root to tip, curling his tongue around the underside of the ridge, then placed a sucking, wet kiss to the tip of Evan's cock. Evan gasped loudly, almost violently. His hands curled into fists at his sides. Desperately wanting to touch Brennan, he didn't allow himself to give in to the urge. His dick was so hard it felt like he was dying. All he could make sense of was the smooth, soft texture of Brennan's full lips, the wet heat of his tongue and the raw lust in his voice as Brennan said, "And because you're letting me."

Evan's hips chased up reflexively as Brennan sucked him down, slow and deep, all the way to the root, taking him back into his throat, and, just as slowly, pulling completely off with a slurp.

"Holy *fuck*," Evan whined.

"Tell me to stop. You want me to? You want me to stop?" Brennan licked him again, and Evan noticed how Brennan was palming himself through his pants, kneading his erection, encased in his tented pants. Brennan was just as hard as Evan. The realization of that was like a lightning bolt frying Evan's brain.

"No," Evan moaned.

"Good," Brennan sighed. He shifted higher, not sitting on his heels anymore, but kneeling upright so he could lean over Evan's lap and suck him faster. One of Evan's hands tangled in Brennan's hair at the back of his head, guiding him and his speed. Shuddering and frantic, Evan's felt the tight coiling way down low in his body, chasing toward a quick climax.

"Oh my god. Oh my *god*," Evan gasped. Every ounce of sense and reason was gradually being sucked out through the tip of his cock as Brennan hollowed his cheeks and hummed with pleasure.

Nothing else existed.

That's why he didn't hear Alek and Luka enter the room or notice their presence until Alek was right there next to him on the couch, claiming Evan's mouth in a deep, searching kiss, tongue-fucking him into delirium.

Evan moaned, shaken, but kissed Alek back fervently, grabbing tightly onto Alek's shirtfront with his free hand to keep him there. Alek caressed through Evan's short hair, over his flushed skin and hushed, "It's okay. It's okay. I'm right here, not going anywhere. Feels good?"

"Alek, oh *god*. I'm so sorry."

"Shhh."

Evan stroked over Brennan's cheek, feeling the wetness of saliva running down his chin, and moaned into Alek's mouth through their next kiss. Brennan's mouth was sinful, hot, velvety perfection, better than Evan dreamed it would be.

"Bren, switch with me," Alek rasped.

"Okay," Brennan said hoarsely, letting Evan slip, sloppy wet, from between his reddened lips, taking one more greedy lick over the head before shifting up beside Evan on the couch as Alek sank down to the floor. Cradling Evan on his tongue, Alek closed his lips around him and slid Evan's steely girth back along the muscle until his dick filled up Alek's mouth, his lips stretched tight around the circumference. Then he sucked and fondled Evan's balls, drawn up tight to his body.

"Bren," Evan rasped. He cupped the side of his brother's face when he moved in close, licking the salty, thick taste of pre-come back over Evan's tongue. Frantic, Brennan struggled to free himself from his drawstring pants.

Luka, hovering nearby, folded his arms and watched the action.

Brennan pulled his cock out, begging shamelessly, "Evan, touch me. *Please.*"

Growling, Evan nipped at Brennan's plump lower lip and wrapped a fist around his brother's cock, pumping him, setting a bruising pace that had Brennan bucking into his hand. He started to keen between kisses.

Inhaling sharply, Evan broke the kiss for a second as he tensed up, right at the edge. Frowning, mouth fallen open wide, hips coming forward, chasing the brutal suction of Alek's mouth, Evan felt Brennan nuzzle his ear and say, "Lemme hear you come."

Evan cried out, pushing helplessly into Alek. Alek's hands locked down around Evan's hips, holding him. Brennan swallowed the sound of Evan's anguish in a soft kiss, heat radiating from him, caressing Evan's lower abdomen as the muscles tensed.

His pace slowed temporarily by the distraction of his orgasm, Evan resumed jacking Brennan, working him quickly to his own release. Managing to glance down at Alek, then over at Luka, locking eyes with him, not looking away, Evan rasped, "Alek, wanna watch you suck Bren."

Part of Evan understood what he was asking, that if it happened, turnabout was fair play. That was why he looked right at Luka when he said it.

Alek pulled off of Evan, wiping a hand over his mouth. Turning to Luka he asked seriously, "You okay with that?"

"Yeah," Luka nodded, biting his thumb with a piercing stare at Evan. For a long moment, it was just the two of them—Luka and Evan. Luka's predatory gaze skittered down over the debauched vision of him, milked dry, flushed and breathless in a post-coital, blissful daze. A wave of heat and bashfulness rocked Evan and he forced himself to look away.

Brennan twisted, sitting back on the couch and hissing through his teeth as Alek's hand gripped tightly just under the head of his straining member. Closing his lips around Brennan, Alek took him in as deeply as he had Evan, giving him intense suction. Delicate crinkles formed in Brennan's brow.

Shifting closer, turning sideways on the couch, and breathing hot against Brennan's face, Evan caressed over his brother's cheek and whispered, "Love you... so much...."

Brennan gasped sharply and writhed. He turned his face toward Evan and whimpered as Alek pulled off, pumping him until he came. Once Brennan was spent and Alek was crawling back up Brennan's body, Evan chased the lingering flavor of Brennan in Alek's mouth, kissing him and moaning.

Evan's head was still spinning, and he couldn't tell if it was from the blowjob or the booze. It all seemed like a dream, like it hadn't really happened at all. He blinked and he was lying down lengthwise on the couch. Alek was zipping him up just enough to keep him decent, but not bothering with the button of his fly.

He blinked again and Brennan was sitting on the chair across the room, straddling Luka's lap, facing Evan and leaning back into his boyfriend. Luka was whispering something into Brennan's ear and unabashedly palming Brennan's spent cock and balls, now tucked back inside his pants, squeezing him in gentle pulses and thrusting up sharply into his backside every now and then. Brennan looked dazed and unquestionably happy. Boneless, he let Luka do whatever he wanted with him.

It was so unreal, Evan wondered if he'd passed out next to Luka on the couch, waiting for Alek to get back, and was dreaming the whole thing.

But the weight of Alek when he laid half-atop him, gazing contentedly down at him and touching him with gentle little caresses, seemed real enough.

"Hey," Alek grinned. He tried to shift slightly to the side, then resettled. "Can't leave you for a minute, can I?" Alek teased.

"Mm. You're amazing. That was amazing," Evan smiled.

The room was darker than it was before. Light had been filtering in from the hall and kitchen, but now it was gone, shut off, leaving them with only the bluish glow from the television to see by. Evan's gaze flicked to the side, over to the large chair brought to the house by his brother and the debauched sight of him being groped in it, then came hurriedly back to Alek. All he made out in the split-second glance was how Luka's hand was now inside Brennan's pants, pushed very low and working under the fabric. Brennan's legs were drawn up, braced on the front of the chair, his hips tilted. His breath catching, Evan forced himself not to look again.

"You wanna watch? It's okay," Alek assured him.

"They're not—?" Evan started. He glanced back at the chair. Luka was sucking on Brennan's neck and there was no doubt what he was doing to Brennan from the expression on Brennan's face alone. Evan swallowed thickly and felt his heart jump in his chest.

"I'm pretty sure they are." Alek raised the volume of his voice and asked without looking around, "Is it okay if we stick around or you want us to leave?"

"Stay," Brennan rasped. The hand working between his legs snapped inward and Brennan made a small, startled, half-gasp, half-whimper. His legs fell open wider and his breath quickened.

Luka locked eyes with Evan, who had been watching Brennan with wonder. Tossing the hair back from his face, Luka grinned, daring Evan with a look to not watch, and somehow suggesting even filthier things without even saying a word. Luka stared right into Evan's eyes and pumped his fingers deeper into Brennan, causing him to exhale sharply and writhe. It was like Evan could feel it as if he was Brennan—Luka fingering him open, getting him ready and taking him apart.

Leaving never occurred to Evan after that; he was too entranced to move a muscle. As Luka withdrew his fingers from Brennan, he whispered something to his lover who reared up enough to shift his pants down in the back. When Luka freed himself, slicking on a condom, he held Evan's stare.

Almost unable to catch his breath, Evan felt Alek rest a hand over his heart, tracing gentle arcs there as he kissed a line up Evan's neck and teased his earlobe with teeth and tongue. Evan held on to Alek and tensed bodily as Brennan, with bowed head and closed eyes, was guided down onto Luka by Luka's big, thick hands braced on his hips. Then Luka thrust upward—sharply. Brennan made a soft, desperate cry, his face creased with fine worry lines, his full lips parted around small, continuous gasps. Luka sighed, breathing roughly against Brennan's sweat-streaked neck. Slowly, Brennan sank the rest of the way down until he was flush with Luka.

"Bren, look. Evan's watching us," Luka urged, but Brennan didn't, or couldn't. He knew Evan was watching. Perhaps the knowing was enough. Seeing it might have been more intense than he could handle yet.

As soon as Brennan started to move, working himself on Luka, bouncing on his cock slowly at first, circling his hips in little swoops, Evan closed his eyes. A shiver raced through him and he turned toward Alek. Alek moaned softly and grabbed for Evan's outer leg, guiding it up and hooking it behind Alek's back. The lay tangled there, listening as Brennan and Luka made love, the soft slapping of flesh against flesh, the gasps and groans.

Sometime after they'd finished, Alek whispered into Evan's ear, "Bedroom?"

Nodding his assent, Evan let Alek lead him from the room, his eyes downcast until they were alone and tumbling together to the bed.

Alek slid in under the covers in Brennan's bed and got comfortable, fluffing the pillow and sighing as he stretched out. He rolled over and waited, awake enough at the moment to begin to feel the stirrings of his thoughts reviving as well.

A warm, solid body pressed up behind him. An arm wrapped his chest in a lover's embrace.

"Did we do the right thing?"

"We'll find out, I guess," Alek admitted softly. "Was this your idea?"

"What do you think?"

"Hmm."

"How's Evan?"

"He's okay, actually. Quiet, but okay. Brennan?"

"Determined. But I guess you figured that out already, since he kicked your ass out of bed. I don't think he's going to stop until he has what he wants. The only one who can stop him now is Evan."

"How do you feel about that?"

"I don't know. I understand. But I told him what happened, you know. With us. That night. He knows no means no. So, don't worry about Evan."

A pain stabbed at Alek's heart. He winced noticeably.

"Aleksy," Luka sighed, kissing his shoulder. "When are you gonna stop beating yourself up over that?"

"Never."

"But I forgive you," Luka hissed, sounding hurt. "You know that."

Alek pulled Luka's arm tighter around him, unable to reply with words. They'd discussed that night so many times, words were meaningless anymore.

"How can we let them make the same mistakes we did? How can we do that if we love them?"

"We can't decide this for them. This is happening whether we're involved or not, so it's safer for them if we are involved. You were there, tonight. You saw. Hell, you tasted them, too. It's too late. I think it was too late even before we met them. They would have gotten here, one way or another."

"Would they? Really?"

Stillness blanketed the room for long moments, until Luka's parted lips dragged gently up the back of Alek's neck, skimming over the skin. He whispered, almost too softly to hear, "*We* could stop, you know. We could put an end to this. Once and for all."

Alek arched. Luka's bitten-short fingernails scratched roughly over Alek's abdomen. "What do you say, Aleksy? Should we stop? Because it's *wrong.*"

"Shut up," Alek hissed. "Just... shut up..." Spinning in Luka's arms, he tucked himself as deeply into the embrace as he could get, losing himself in the safety of hard choices made and set in stone long, long ago.

# Chapter 26
# Forbidden Love

It was sometime in the middle of the night when Evan, who had fallen asleep with Alek, woke to find his own reflection gazing sleepily back at him when he opened his eyes.

Evan mumbled, "Bren?"

Brennan wove their fingers together, their hands linked on the soft bedding between their chests.

"Yeah. Go back to sleep. I just wanted to be near you."

Evan frowned deeply. He shifted slightly closer to his brother and got a better grip on his hand.

"I just wanted you."

"Feels better when you're close," Evan muttered in agreement, his voice thick with sleep.

Seeming not nearly as drowsy as Evan was, Brennan appeared to measure Evan's every reaction. Placing a tender kiss to the center of Evan's forehead, Brennan followed it with more kisses that traveled down the side of his nose to his mouth.

"Why... *mm*... why do we keep... kissing, and... what...."

"Feels better when you're close," Brennan replied, echoing his brother but the words now laden with subtext. The soft, wet sucking sounds of their kisses were overloud in the room. It went on and on, deepening, becoming more passionate, fervent until Evan stopped to catch his breath.

Brennan told him, "Roll over."

Evan grumbled in question, but did it anyway, tucking the pillow under his head and curling up. Brennan spooned behind him.

Then, suddenly, Evan wasn't so sleepy. He kept perfectly still.

After another moment, he pressed back slightly into Brennan, wanting more contact, and getting it. Evan could feel the hard line of his brother's swollen erection nestled in the crease of his backside. It sent a thrill rippling through Evan's gut, and he closed his eyes, focusing on the obscenely intimate touch. Just like that, as if joined psychically, Brennan moved. It was subtle but real as he rocked forward against Evan, thrusting gently up and through the crevice. Brennan exhaled sharply and Evan could feel Brennan's full, warm lips tickling at the back of his neck, right along his spinal column.

Grasping Evan's shoulder, Brennan oh-so-quietly moaned Evan's name. It was enough. It was what made it happen—the raw, needy, complex ache in Brennan's sweet voice. Evan felt how Brennan had chosen this. It wasn't an accident of circumstances. Brennan came to Evan's bed. He left Luka's side, asked Alek to leave, and took his place. There was no doubt about why this was happening.

Evan hooked a thumb in the waistband of his boxers, the only thing he was wearing, and tugged them slowly down so the elastic band hugged just under the curve of his ass. Evan's stomach fluttered with jittery nerves and he held his breath.

Exhaling roughly, Brennan caressed down to the bared skin. He hesitated, resting his hand on side of Evan's buttocks and asked, "Yes or no? Evan...."

"Yes," Evan sighed. In his heart, he prayed for the mercy of whatever god might have been watching over them, knowing it was never really a choice. He'd wanted this since he first laid eyes on the beautiful creature now sharing his bed. Evan was Brennan's and if Brennan wanted to claim him, Evan would let him.

After a pause in which he seemed to steel himself, Brennan pushed at Evan's left hip, guiding him onto his stomach instead of his side. Evan trembled, his breathing suddenly labored. He knew there was no way Brennan was turning back. He traced down Evan's crack and found his opening, pushing two fingers through. They went in easily, and Brennan choked off a moan. "You're still loose. Alek—he took you, didn't he? Before you fell asleep. *Evan.*" He greedily stroked Evan's inner walls.

Unconsciously clenching around Brennan's fingers, Evan's eyes rolled up in his head and he swallowed back a guttural, wrenching groan. It was so wrong, so dirty and he was losing his mind from how much he was getting off on it. His body decided for him, his ass pushing up off the bed and hips tilting, back bowing as he took more of Brennan's fingers. Hand splayed on the bed, Evan felt the fingers spread apart inside him and panted with helpless, low grunts.

Brennan's fingers plunged deeply, twisted and bent as they pulled back out, prying Evan open wide. No sooner were they plucking free of Evan's rim than he felt Brennan's thickness there, thrusting up through his crack again, but skin on skin now, nothing keeping them apart, not anymore. The silken head caught on Evan's hole on the next thrust and Evan keened. Brennan spit on his hand and pushed Evan's underwear down the rest of the way, kicking them free of his feet. He spread Evan's legs apart by nudging at the insides of them with his knees and settled there, lining up, his stiffened flesh fitted gently against Evan.

"*Brennan....*"

When it happened, at first Evan was simply blank. He had no thought, no reaction other than the burning of the stretch as Brennan entered him, filling him too full, too fast. With no experience on how to make it easy on his lover, Brennan initially thrust too hard, trying to go deep, and it hurt a little. He thrust into Evan like he wouldn't stop until he had taken everything, and all of him. So Evan gave in to him. But he begged, softly, "Easy. Easy." And, right away, Brennan moved more gently, more shallowly.

Relaxing into the push and pull, he felt Brennan slide further and further into him. It was when Brennan tugged almost all of the way back out, the head of his cock catching on Evan's outer ring of muscle before he plunged back inside, that jolted Evan back to his senses. The blankness was gone, just like that. Brennan thrust again, and the friction of him sliding against Evan's inner walls, the desperate, scorching, sexy and shattered mewls coming from Brennan as he moved in a gentle easy rhythm, curling his arms around Evan's shoulders, and nuzzling against Evan's neck—it took Evan apart. There was fear but desire was much stronger. Evan came hot and messy over the bed sheet under him, rutting into the mattress counter to Brennan's thrusts and tugs. It shocked Evan, catching him unawares. His orgasm was like cleansing fire, burning everything away but Brennan.

Only seconds later, Brennan cried out. It was tender and beautiful, and Evan could feel Brennan's tears dampening the shell of his ear. One fell and landed on Evan's cheek, trailing down his skin. Even after he was spent, Brennan stayed there, in Evan, molded to his back in the most intimate of ways and hiccupping softly with his fading tears.

Sounding terrified, Brennan asked faintly, "Did I just lose you?"

"You're never gonna lose me. Not ever," Evan whispered, finding Brennan's hand and holding it.

"Promise me."

"I promise."

The light was surprisingly bright in Evan's bedroom, since it faced east. The morning sun hit it directly as soon as it was over the horizon and had cleared the tree line far across the fields surrounding the house. It trickled in around the curtains' edges and glowed golden-white. The rumpled sheets on the bed, tangled around their nude, entwined bodies were a crisp white, in contrast to the slight suntanned hue of their skin. Both of them were awake, lying together with nowhere else they wanted to be, simply enjoying the comfortable warmth of the air and each other.

Brennan was still curled up around Evan, possessively so. His right arm was folded under Evan's head, his bicep functioning as Evan's pillow. Evan was brushing the backs of his fingers along the underside of it, idly. His other hand was wrapped behind him, draped atop Brennan's upper thigh, enjoying the soft texture of the fine hair dusting it. But the focus of Evan's attention was the particular way Brennan's left hand was braced against him, just below his navel, his pinkie finger nestled in the nest of soft curls of Evan's pubic hair, his thumb caressing the taut skin under his belly button. Only Evan's lower legs were covered by the sheet, and Brennan was bare from mid-thigh down, his hips tucked up snugly against the curve of Evan's backside, his chest flush to Evan's back. Every now and then Brennan dragged his lower lip lightly over the smooth patch of skin behind Evan's ear, making Evan's eyes close in pleasure.

Unsure how long, exactly, they'd been there just like that, soon they both seemed to realize at almost the same time, that they were no longer alone. In the shadows of the doorway leading out to the hall was a tall, broad-shouldered figure with cascading, long dark hair that was tucked behind his ears. Dark, piercing eyes peered from the gloom, seeing everything, every detail. His jaw was shaved smooth, and the figure was wearing a non-descript pair of cotton shorts and a tank top with sneakers.

Evan didn't have any idea if it was Alek or Luka. The silence drew out as they laid there, displayed, staring back, and waiting.

The figure stepped forward, leaning against the door frame.

"I'm headed out for a run. You wanna come with?"

Evan felt more than heard the soft exhale of Brennan's amusement, and the way his lips curled up at the ends as he sucked a kiss softly to the side of Evan's neck.

"I think it's for you," Evan said.

"Unless it's a trick," Brennan hummed. With the tip of his tongue, he traced up the sweeping arc of Evan's neck, his breath quickly heating the cooler, dampened skin. Brennan's left hand shifted, stroking down the inside of Evan's thigh then slowly back up, his knuckles dragging gently over the softness of his brother's genitals before reclaiming the spot centered on Evan's pelvis.

"You two look awfully cozy," Luka observed with a raised eyebrow, stepping closer.

"Wanna join us?"

He appeared to think about it before answering with a dark, heated look, "Maybe later. So, what d'you say?"

"Yeah, gimme a sec to get dressed. I'll just shower after." Brennan surged up, leaning over Evan to catch his mouth in a brief but tender kiss. "You don't mind, right?"

"Nah, go ahead."

Brennan dashed, naked, past Luka to his room. Luka lingered behind, still watching Evan. At first, Evan managed to hold his gaze, but then bashfulness won out. Seconds ticked away and Luka didn't leave, didn't move. Then, he asked Evan quietly, "He treat you good?"

The question affected Evan in a surprisingly intense way, making him feel more self-conscious than ever. "Yeah," he rasped, grabbing for the sheet, though he knew it made no difference. Luka had been staring at him for a while. He'd seen it all.

"I know it was his idea. You must trust him a lot, to give him that much power over you."

"I do," Evan answered after a pause, without having to think about it long. "With my life." He realized he did trust Brennan that much.

"It was kind of hard on me, mentally, when Alek first went that far with me. He led and I followed, and I just let him do what he wanted to me, because I loved him. It was different circumstances, of course, but I just want you to know that if you want to talk about it or anything, I'm here, and I understand."

The kindness and concern in the words hit Evan strongly. He nodded and said, "Thanks."

"You okay if I...?" He gestured back over his shoulder. "Alek's around here somewhere. I'll tell him you're up."

"Yeah, I'm good," Evan told him. As Luka smiled in goodbye, turning away, Evan added, "Hey, Luka?"

"Yeah?"

"Are you cool with this?"

"I am," he nodded. "You need each other. I get that. And I appreciate it."

"I guess you do. And, um...."

"...What?"

In a small voice, Evan asked, "Are we gonna be okay? Me and Bren?"

"Yes," Luka answered, his expression anguished and overcome in a way that made Evan's heart beat faster. "I promise."

"You really think so?"

"I do."

"Okay. Thanks."

Luka only made it three steps away from Evan when the extremity of his emotion stopped him in his tracks. He clapped a hand over his mouth, moaning softly as he seemed to try to force it back down, but it wouldn't go. He pivoted on a heel and crossed to Evan, whose eyes widened the closer Luka got. Luka placed a soft kiss to the center of Evan's forehead, whispering, "You're gonna be okay. Make your peace with it. This is between him and you, and the four of us, and no one else. Other people will judge you for it if they figure it out, and they won't understand, but they don't have to. Alek and I are living proof of that. We take what we need. No regrets. No apologies. Got it?"

"Yeah."

Luka squeezed Evan's hand briefly, then went, for good this time, leaving Evan bewildered, but sated and grateful.

The room grew even brighter, and Evan began to eye the free weights in the far corner by his dresser, feeling guilted into doing some sort of morning exercise himself. His stomach was growling too and, worst of all, he *really* wanted a cigarette.

Alek appeared before Evan could decide what he should do, coming quietly into the room and planting himself on the floor right by the side of the bed where Evan lay, leaning back against the nightstand and stretching out his legs. Evan dropped his hand over the side of the bed and Alek took it, linking them.

"Morning, sunshine."

Evan smiled helplessly, but his raging confusion quickly melted it away.

Watching him from the corner of his eye, Alek seemed to take it all in, but for the moment, said nothing.

When Evan groaned, Alek raised his eyebrows in question.

"I just really want a smoke. It sucks."

"Why?"

"Trying to quit, I guess," Evan mumbled. He glanced up at Alek, to see his reaction.

Alek looked pleased. "It'll be a hard habit to break. Worth it though."

"Yeah," Evan sighed. He didn't quite know what Alek knew, or what to say, so he settled on, "You can ask if you want."

Turning to look squarely at Evan, Alek reached up with his free hand, cupping Evan's face.

"How far did it go?"

"Pretty far," Evan admitted quietly. "Bren and Luka should probably get tested, if they haven't. Bren didn't use a condom. Or pull out."

He couldn't look at Alek. He couldn't breathe either, but Alek's hand stayed there, holding Evan's face. It felt good, like forgiveness.

"I'll let them know. Did you say yes to him?"

Evan nodded.

"Do I need to worry about you?"

"I wanted it, okay? I asked him to go through with it. It was consensual," Evan answered defensively.

"That's not what I meant," Alek countered gently. He gripped Evan's hand more tightly. "Do I need to *worry about you*?"

Evan's lips shaped the word 'no,' but there was no sound behind it, only a restless storm of emotion.

"You fuckin' be honest with me, Evan," Alek growled.

"Okay! You want honesty? I'm glad Bren got rid of my gun."

The air left Alek's lungs in a rush, and he had this bad look in his eyes like he was falling, tumbling, slipping into quicksand.

"Why?" Alek hissed.

"Because. I mean, I accept this—who I am, that I want him like this. I ain't hiding from it. But...."

"*Tell me*," Alek growled viciously through gritted teeth, his eyes damp now.

"But if I wasn't here, he wouldn't be able to do this. He wouldn't be guilty of it, or want this."

"What? To love you?!"

"I wouldn't do it," Evan insisted, embarrassed and shamefaced. "But I'm still glad the gun's gone."

He was convinced Alek was pissed at him, so he tried to explain. "Look, I've told you how hard it is for me to talk about this kind of stuff, so it's a big deal that I can even admit that to you. I'm trying to deal with it, okay? I'm trying. I realize how much Brennan needs me to be here for him. He's counting on me. And you, Aleksy," Evan sighed, choking up. "How could I do that to you?"

It was a struggle for Alek to compose himself. First, all he could do was lean with his face pressed against the bed, gripping Evan like he might disperse into thin air if Alek wasn't careful. Eventually, Alek began to breathe more evenly, and finally found his voice.

"I'm getting you out of this bed, you hear me? You're getting up and showered and dressed. If you want, we'll get breakfast out somewhere. Then I'm taking you to my place. We'll hang out there. Maybe with Presley and Carter. After that, I don't know. We'll take it from there."

"Okay," Evan said softly.

Alek dug his phone out of his pocket and stood, throwing the sheet back off of Evan and taking his hand to pull him up out of bed. Putting the phone to his ear, Alek said, "Yeah. I'm taking Evan to our house for the day, but you've got a job. Take Bren to the clinic and both of you get tested. Today. From now on, all of us are going to be more safe and careful. Call me later, okay? Yeah. Me too. Bye."

Brennan's entire being had been reduced to the pounding of his heart in his chest, pumping his blood hot and fast through his body. Everything from the top of his head to his fingers and toes tingled and pulsed. His breath was ripping from his lungs which were on fire. For most of the ten mile run, he managed to keep up with Luka, but it took its toll. They finally got back to the house and Brennan collapsed on the freshly cut lawn, sprawling on his back. Covered from head to toe in dripping sweat, making his hair stick to his forehead in slick tendrils, flushed from the exertion, he knew he probably made quite the picture.

Luka, however, was doing fine. Bracing his hands on his knees, easily catching his breath, he gazed sweetly down at his boyfriend.

"You're giving up already? We're only half-done! Get yer ass up, young'un!"

Brennan had just enough energy left to flip Luka off, double-fisted and wheezed out a groan of complaint.

Chuckling, Luka peeled off his tank and used it, balled up in one hand, to mop his face dry. It earned him a death-glare from Brennan, squinting up at Luka who was bare-chested, glistening and perfect.

Brennan rasped, "What is this, payback?"

"I prefer to think of it as a physical challenge," Luka smirked.

"Did I pass?"

Pursing his lips thoughtfully, Luka deigned not to answer and grabbed Brennan by the hand instead.

"C'mon. Let's hit the showers. We got things to do, places to be."

Leading the way, Luka headed right for the bathroom, shedding the rest of his clothes on the way. With a mere backward glance, he stepped into the shower and turned the water on full-blast, not waiting for Brennan to join him. Brennan hovered by the sink, looking at himself in the mirror. There was a sense of calm rising in him, as his heartbeat settled to a more normal pace and the roar of his blood quieted. He felt different, and half-expected to look different, too. But there he was, same as ever.

Removing his glasses, he looked again. His reflection was foggier, unfocused.

*I had sex with him*, he said to himself, like he couldn't quite believe it. It felt like a dream, but it was real enough come morning. Now, he had to live with the consequences. He had to face Evan and himself, not to mention the man currently in the room with him and Evan's significant other as well.

It was all tangled, but none of it mattered. All that counted was what Brennan felt in his heart. He blocked it all out and looked within, tuning in to nothing else but that. What he found there was this: not only did he not regret it, but he knew it was only a beginning, that being with Evan had sated some need he never knew he had, something practically impossible to give name to or label. Part of it was a satisfaction at striking back at their parents by claiming each other for themselves, on their own terms and no one else's. Part of it was selfish, wanting all of Evan—body, soul, emotion, desire. Stripping Evan of his power, dominating him, claiming his body and getting him off pleased the part of Brennan that had grown so fearful he would lose Evan. If Evan belonged to him, then nothing could go wrong. But it wasn't as simple as that. There was fear he went too far, and he may have pushed Evan away by crossing that line. He may have pushed Evan so far he'd go back to the darkness, and for that Brennan would never forgive himself, but it was a risk he had to take.

Having always been the good son, the dutiful son, the caregiver, but also the one left behind, the one expected to take on responsibilities far grander, far graver than someone his age should have been expected to, it energized Brennan on a profound level to do what he had done. It made him feel in charge of his life, and capable of choosing what he wanted, no matter what. The death of his mother left him feeling hollow and powerless. Now he felt full and invincible. Yes, the fear was there, too; fear for Evan more than for himself, but the fear was also strengthening.

All of this churned away in Brennan's head as his imperfect eyes gazed blankly at the visage of his face, the one he shared with his new lover.

From feet away he heard, "You joining me or no?"

He roused himself and answered, "Yeah. I was just thinking."

Luka shut the water off, pushed the shower curtain aside and grabbed for a towel to dry off. The seriousness of his expression informed Brennan of all he needed to know.

"It's all yours. You want me to wait for you, or give you some privacy?"

Brennan deliberated, then said, "Wait. I'm guessing we need to talk about this anyway." He pulled off his shirt and pushed his shorts down, stepping out of them. Moving past Luka, he got into the shower and sighed when the water sprayed cool against his overheated skin.

"I can't tell if you're mad at me or what, for taking that from Evan, like Alek took it from you."

"I'm not mad. Sad maybe, but it's different for you two. I realize that. And he was your first. I get that too, what a big deal it is, and how cool it is to have that with someone you love, who also loves you back. How was it?"

Brennan smiled. He couldn't help it, the memory of the night before made him too happy not to smile.

"It was amazing. I don't know, I was just watching him sleep. We started kissing and I just needed to be inside of him. It was totally different than anything I've experienced before, because it wasn't even really about sex, if that makes any sense. I think I needed to make him see he could trust me that completely."

Hurriedly, he finished soaping up his body and rinsed it all away. When he emerged from the shower not a minute later, finding Luka still standing there, impassive, patient, something about him—his size, his resoluteness—made Brennan's stomach flip-flop and his nerves alight.

He reached for a towel but Luka caught his arm, pulled him away from the tub, spun him and pushed him back against the wall. In a smooth movement, he trapped both of Brennan's wet wrists in one strong hand and pinned them to the wall above his head. Slipping a knee between Brennan's dripping thighs, Luka held him there. Brennan wriggled a little, his heartbeat quickening, lips parted and soft, eyes watchful and wary.

With his free hand, Luka caressed down then back up Brennan's damp body, leaving a trail of goosebumps in the wake of his fingers. Feathering his fingertips all the way up to the divot under Brennan's lower lip, Luka watched him, his reactions, then asked, "If I told you I want you to stop, and never be with him again, would you do that for me?"

Brennan took a deep breath that caught a little on the inhale. He shivered as Luka's hand moved down over his side, through the drips of water coursing over his skin.

"Yes," Brennan sighed, not knowing if he meant it or not, arching into Luka's touch, getting hard.

"Do you want to be with Evan again?"

Brennan remembered the particular feel of Evan, gripped around him, the way Evan had moaned, and stiffened even more. He nodded, not trusting his voice not to shatter apart on the admission.

"I would give up Alek for you. You know that," Luka reminded him.

Flushing and becoming meeker, Brennan turned his head to the side as Luka caressed with the backs of his knuckles down the side of his throat, watching as Brennan swallowed thickly.

"Maybe you don't need me at all. Maybe you just need him."

Brennan winced and tugged against Luka's hold on his wrists, wanting to touch, to embrace him, to prove himself. But, renewing his grip, stretching Brennan out even more, Luka observed Brennan's fight and easily contained him. "Luka... Luka, *please*," Brennan begged. "I'll be so good for you. I'll be whatever you want me to be. I'll do anything. Let me prove it to you. Let me show you how much you mean to me. *Please.*"

Luka leaned in, almost close enough for Brennan to reach him in a kiss. Chasing forward, Brennan sought Luka's mouth but it was still a breath away. Luka let him try, though, sighing against Brennan's lips as he worked to reach him and failed. "*Please?*"

"You put him in real danger by fucking him without protection," Luka replied softly. "Hell, we've all been way too sloppy. Now, you and I need to go and make sure we're both clean. We should have done it earlier. It's too late now, though. But I want your word, Brennan, that from this moment on, when it comes right down to it, *I* come first for you. Evan is family and he's part of you, but *I* am your boyfriend. You need to respect me enough to give me that much, and honor my feelings, because I've already given that honor to you. Otherwise, I'm done. I'm gone. Because once we start going down this path, it's gonna get messy, and I need to know we're on the same page. Are we?"

"Luka," Brennan pleaded, fighting not to cry. "Don't leave me. I love you. I love you *so much.*"

"Will you stay safe? Will you be more careful?"

"Yes! I swear I will. And I won't do anything you aren't okay with. I'll talk to you and be honest with you about all of it. It'll be your call. I'm yours. Okay? I wanna be yours."

Luka stared at Brennan's quivering lower lip, trapped now between his teeth, unable to meet the wide, scared blue eyes trained on him.

"I've never cared about someone as much as I care about you. Ever."

"Luka let me... let me go. Let me prove it to you. Let me...."

Luka let go of Brennan's arms and braced his hands against the wall as Brennan fell to the floor. Sinking to his knees before Luka, Brennan proceeded to reverently worship Luka with his lips and tongue, letting Luka fill his mouth and slide deep, lodging in his throat, not holding back anything, and lavishing everything he had on him. Luka bit down on the back of his arm to muffle the anguished cry accompanying his release, quaking as Brennan wrung him out until he was pulsing dry. Even when it was done and Luka was coming back down, Brennan continued to pepper kisses over Luka's thighs and pelvis, nuzzling against him and begging, just *begging* shamelessly for Luka to be happy with him.

It was a while before Luka found his voice. When he did, what he said was, "Just don't break my heart, okay? I know how tempting this thing with Evan is for you, the comfort he gives you. But I need you too, Bren. I need you to love me back. *Please*."

Luka listened to the professions of love by the boy at his feet, clinging to him so desperately, as Brennan swore with all his heart he would, and meant it. He just needed Luka to give him time to prove it.

## Chapter 27

# The Beginnings of Bravery

While Brennan and Luka were on their way to the clinic, Alek and Evan rolled slowly up the driveway of the house Alek and Luka shared with their roommates. They'd come from a restaurant where they had breakfast. Before that, Evan had taken Alek by the homeless shelter where he volunteered.

One of Evan's friends, someone he'd known for years through Jimmy, had been there—an elderly Puerto Rican man named Pedro who was busy chopping up a huge bag of donated potatoes for a large batch of stew. After introducing Alek to Pedro, Alek had been immediately recruited to help prepare the food. Bewildered but more than willing to assist, Alek washed his hands and had been pointed to a cutting station. Upbeat music from a local Spanish language radio station played loudly throughout the space, echoing off the cement block walls. Alek broke into amused laughter when Pedro began dancing while he worked, humming along with the melody.

Meanwhile, Evan slipped into the cafeteria-style room in which the food was served. Some cots lined the walls but most of the floor space was packed with long tables and benches. With a clear view through the pass-through window, Alek watched as Evan was called over by a man with a long silver beard and wearing a black bandana tied around his head. Clad in a well-worn army jacket decorated with many patches, he reached out and eagerly shook Evan's hand, clapping him soundly on the shoulder, too, for good measure.

"Evan! Man, what're the odds. Jimmy here too today?"

"Nah, just me, but I brought a friend. He's working on getting lunch ready."

"Fantastic! Damn, but I'm glad to see you. Listen, I don't wanna be any trouble for ya. I know you're busy, but Lucy's been wheezing and coughing for weeks. I left her right out front. Do you think you could—?"

"Yeah. Of course. Come on. Let's see what's up with her. You haven't been riding her too hard, have you?"

"You kiddin'? I'm always as gentle as could be. I take care of my baby girl."

"Mm-hmm," Evan smiled. "Is that why I heard an engine revvin' like hell when we pulled up? Sounded suspiciously like—"

"Shit," the man frowned.

Evan laughed brightly. Leading his companion with one hand braced on his back, they headed toward the parking lot.

A half hour later, Evan reappeared with engine grease smeared over his hands. Walking through the kitchen to the sinks, he grinned at Alek.

"Lucy?"

Evan chuckled, "Yeah. You heard that, huh?"

From the other room, a chorus of voices started calling Evan's name. "Evan? Evan's here. Oh man, I gotta talk to him." "Evan! Hey Evan!" "Yeah, you got a minute?!"

"Gimme a chance to get cleaned up!" Evan shouted back. "I'll be right out!"

Pedro chuckled and kept dancing. "Evan's very popular here," Pedro winked at Alek. "Everyone's always really happy to see him, just like I am. He's good to talk to, you know? He listens and he doesn't judge people. He's a good boy."

Alek locked eyes with Evan from over his shoulder, busy scrubbing his hands under the tap with thick sudsy soap. Evan pretended he didn't hear but warmed at the pride glowing in Alek's eyes for him.

That had been two hours earlier. Now, with stomachs full of some of the best omelets, sausage and biscuits either of them had ever had, served up at a small place by the shelter—one of the restaurants Evan knew to regularly donate surplus to the needy—they were just looking to relax.

Walking from the truck to the front door, Evan steadily lost some of the confidence he felt at the shelter. Fidgeting, Evan stuffed his hands deeply into his pockets one moment, and the next was rubbing nervously over the back of his neck like he had an itch he couldn't quite scratch. Evan stayed behind Alek, chewing a piece of gum from the pack Alek bought him at the diner's register when Alek noticed what a hard time of it Evan was having with resisting his urge to smoke.

Alek took him by the hand, and gave him a level look.

"Hey, don't sweat it. You've already met these guys. They're cool. It's no big deal," Alek assured him.

Evan rolled his eyes. Their linked hands felt like a big, neon sign announcing his status as Alek's bottom boy. But he was also wholly unable to find voice to protest or bring himself to pull away. Evan let Alek lead him inside.

The house was fairly quiet. A TV was playing somewhere nearby. There was a low, unidentifiable rustling, possibly accompanied by muffled voices.

"Hey! Anybody home?" Alek called, hanging his keys up on a hook by the door. With an incline of his head toward the living room, he guided them deeper into the house.

Someone answered, "Alek? That you?"

There was no one in the living room when they got there, but Carter appeared behind them in the hall.

They turned toward him and Alek said, "Hey. What's up? Carter, you remember Evan?"

Evan noticed the quick once-over Carter gave him, head to toe, like he was making note of absolutely everything from his and Alek's linked hands to the hang of Evan's clothes on his frame to the size difference between him and Alek. Smiling politely but awkwardly, the most Evan could handle was a muttered, "Hey."

"Of course I remember. Nice to see you again, man," Carter said, extending a hand.

Thinking it would be too weird to shake Carter's hand while holding Alek's, Evan slipped free of Alek and gave Carter a firm, manly grip. Undeterred, Alek draped an arm over Evan's shoulders and said, "Yeah, I think we're just gonna hang out here for a while.

That cool with you?"

Horribly, Evan felt himself blushing, his face getting redder by the second as his hands found their way back into his pockets. It was the most innocent conversation in the world, but it just seemed to him like Alek was declaring his status as the owner of Evan's ass. And, the more Evan blushed, the more it seemed like Carter was smirking at him.

"Sure. It's your house, too. Hey, I think the Mets are playing the Phils. Not sure what time, though. I was gonna check it out. Grab some beers."

"Awesome. Hey, is Presley here?"

"Yeah, he's um... sleeping." Carter tucked his long hair back over an ear and unintentionally revealed a large, fresh hickey on the side of his neck.

A few minutes later, Evan had been left blessedly alone with the television and remote while Alek and Carter had gone into the kitchen to go over the monthly utility bills. Evan was still trying to figure out how to navigate the satellite's menu when he felt the couch shift as Presley flopped down next to him.

"Evan, right? What's up?"

"Oh. Hi. Yeah. Alek, um... I'm just here because... I mean, we've been spending a lot of time at my place, so Alek thought... I can't really figure out how to change the channel."

Presley took the remote from Evan and flipped through the stations. "What're you looking for?" "Anything besides this infomercial, pretty much."

Presley flashed Evan a smile. "So you and Alek, huh?"

"Yep."

"How's that goin'?"

"Uh, good? Goin' good. He's a good guy."

Shooting Evan a no-holds-barred, are-you-shitting-me look, Presley prodded him with, "But you guys are together, right?"

Evan pressed his lips together and bit at them. "Yeah. We are."

"I mean, it's not like a secret, right?"

"No," he scoffed, wanting to curl in on himself and die, but trying to man-up and act cooler than he felt. "It's not."

"Hey, I'm not trying to freak you out or nothin'. I was just curious. Alek's not really one to bring a boyfriend home to watch TV, if you know what I mean. So *you* are just kind of... interesting."

Smiling shyly and ducking his head, Evan glanced over at Presley then back at the screen. It was the Discovery Channel and they were doing some sort of experiment with rockets.

*Perfect,* Evan thought. *More phallic symbols. Not awkward at all.*

"Have you met Luka yet?"

For a second, Evan was bombarded with the very vivid memory of lying in bed that morning, naked, with Brennan, and Luka standing in the doorway, watching. Then he got another flash of the night before. It was hazy but clear enough to jolt him—Brennan sucking his dick and Luka watching that, too.

Clearing his throat loudly in an attempt to cover a small, sharp, breathy exhale, Evan said, "Yeah, you could say that. I was pretty surprised that Alek has a twin. But Luka's cool."

"Yeah, he's cool all right." Presley gave Evan a sidelong glance as if he was thinking about how close the Popović brothers were, and what that might imply for someone like Evan. Unsure whether it would be less questionable to meet that sort of look head-on or to simply avoid it, Evan stared right back at Presley for a long moment before his conscience won out and Evan dropped his gaze.

Silence fell between them. Evan wondered if Presley was speculating what sort of kinky shit he and Alek had gotten up to. It made him want out of there, and he almost got to his feet when Presley said, "I'm a little closer with Luka than Alek. He's my boy, you know? We go back. He's got some uh, interesting personal boundaries, which you may have discovered already, but that's all surface. Both Luka and Aleksy—they're good guys to have on your side. When they like you, and I mean, *really* like you, then you're pretty much golden. They'll go out of their way to get your back. You feel me?"

"Yeah," Evan nodded. He smiled genuinely and truly relaxed for the first time since leaving the truck. Presley wasn't judging him, Evan realized. Presley not only seemed to understand, he was actually trying to make Evan feel more comfortable. And it was working.

Digging a fresh piece of gum out of his pocket, Evan muttered,

"I'm trying to quit smoking. It's not really going well."

"Well, I think I might have some nicotine gum. You're welcome to it. It works a little better than that shit," he gestured to Evan's spearmint gum. "Trust me." "You quit too?"

Presley nodded, "I did. Carter asked me to, so I couldn't say no. Said he was concerned about my health. Then I started feelin' all guilty and, well, you know how it goes."

Astonished by the confession, Evan's eyes widened subtly. *He's confiding in me*, he thought. *He's telling me stuff he might not even tell Alek.*

"He must care about you a lot," Evan observed quietly. "I could see it at the bar too, when that dude punched you. Carter looked freaked."

"Yeah, yeah. It's complicated."

"Hey, I know from complicated. Believe me. I think complicated is my middle name."

Chuckling, Presley stood and, for a second, gripped Evan's shoulder. "I'm gonna grab you that gum."

"Thanks. I appreciate it," Evan replied, smiling to himself.

Brennan, slouched down beside Luka in his truck, folded and re-folded the receipt from the health clinic. It was a relief to know both he and Luka were disease free and he hadn't unwittingly given any-thing to Evan or Luka or Alek.

*I'm supposed to be smarter than that*, he berated himself. *I'm sup-posed to be good at taking care of people, and especially the ones I love.*

"I've been really selfish, haven't I?"

"You've been going after what you want," Luka clarified. "And now you kind of have it, so you've gotta step up to your responsi-bilities if you want to keep what you have."

"I know. I'll try. I really will. But there is this one thing that I keep thinking about, something Evan can't know."

"What is it?"

Brennan sighed. "Charlie's trying to come down for a visit." He looked right at Luka, eyes open and aware. "What the hell do we do if Charlie shows up? I mean, avoiding Jimmy is one thing, but—"

"You need to talk to Evan. There's gotta be boundaries, ways to deal with this stuff between you while you figure it all out. Alek and I went through the same thing. You need to be brothers first. The rest of it you might need to keep to yourselves."

"We're going over there, aren't we? To your place?" He knew Luka spoke to Alek on the phone again, and that something had been decided between them.

"Yeah. We need to talk. All four of us. No more games. No more secrets."

Brennan nodded, frowning slightly. Luka reached across the space between them and took his hand. "Okay. No more secrets."

## Chapter 28

# No More Secrets

Meanwhile, inside the house and in a heated debate over the superiority of classic Fords versus classic Chevrolets, Carter and Evan went back and forth arguing their points. Whenever Alek or Presley tried to chime in or change the topic they were met with only a vehement shushing from Carter. It was a little annoying at first but quickly became endearing as Carter guarded Evan's attention carefully, wanting it all for himself.

"Are you kidding?" Evan gaped. "Any Ford built before 1984 is ridiculous, unless you give the engine a complete overhaul. The transmission's for shit, the cooling and oiling systems are a mess."

"Well, Mustangs are a hell of a lot better than the Camaro."

"On what planet? Maybe if all you're using it for is to pose in front of and look pretty. Some of us like to drive something with a little horsepower under the hood."

It went on and on. Once in a while, Alek and Presley shared an amused look before returning their attention to the game. This was why no one seemed to notice right away when Luka and Brennan wandered in through the front door and appeared in the hall adjacent to the living room. Brennan had an arm comfortably looped behind Luka's lower back and leaned against him. Running his fingers back through his blond tresses, he watched Evan, took a curious look at the roommates and waited for Luka to introduce him. Luka cleared his throat loudly when there was a lull in the conversation, holding Brennan snugly to him in a one-armed embrace.

Finally, Presley noticed them. He gawked, glancing between Brennan and Evan, "You've gotta be kidding me. This? You two with the... how in the *world* did you two find another set of gay identical twins?"

"It was totally unintentional. I swear. These things just happen sometimes."

"No, Luka, these things don't just happen. Unless you've made a pact with the devil or some shit. You got somethin' you wanna confess?"

Carter, who was halfway through making a salient point having to do with aerodynamics, stuttered and his mouth snapped shut. He glanced from Evan to Brennan to Evan to Brennan to Alek and sighed, "Seriously?"

Alek shrugged with a smirk that only lingered for a brief moment. Becoming somber, he turned to Luka to ask, "You guys make out okay?"

"Yeah," he replied shortly. "Everything's good. Hey um, Presley, Carter, this is my boyfriend, Brennan Holt, Evan's brother."

"Very nice to meet you," Brennan smiled, coming forward to shake each of their hands. "Luka has told me so much about you guys. I think it's great that he has such good friends around him." Pausing by his brother, Brennan murmured to him, "Evan."

"Bren. How was the run?"

"Exhausting. But good. Really good."

For a long moment they held one another's gaze, tuning in to each other and saying a lot more than their words were able to. There was evident heat there but it was buried beneath layers of concern, questioning, peaceful contentment and just a hint of tense trepidation.

"Wait a minute. Brennan, did I see you at the gym the other week?" Presley asked as Luka migrated back over to Brennan's side, taking his hand. There was not a hint of Evan's bashfulness in Brennan, and he stared right at Presley, almost in a challenge. It was probably why Luka seemed to be the better match for Brennan, and how, in their own, quieter ways, Alek and Evan suited each other as well. "Ooh!" Presley pointed at Brennan, sitting up straighter and bouncing a little on the couch with his excitement. "The blond pescetarian without any clothes on!"

"What the *hell* are you talking about?" Carter asked him.

"Yeah, that's where Luka and I met," Brennan said. "You two work there together, right?"

"Yeah, we do." Presley shook his head and looked at Evan, saying, "Damn. I *knew* you looked familiar."

"I hate to cut this short," Luka interjected. "But Alek, Evan, can we talk to you guys upstairs? Carter, Pres, you don't mind, right?"

"Naw, man. Go right ahead." They could see how solemn Luka was, and knew how rare it was for him to act so reserved. "Everything okay?"

"Yeah, don't worry about it," he retorted coolly, probably rousing their suspicions even more.

Once in Luka's room, Brennan and Evan sat side-by-side on the bed, so close their thighs touched. Evan was the one to sit down first, and Brennan sidled up to him. Slipping a hand around Evan's knee, Brennan grasped it, his fingers sliding down into the warmth between Evan's legs. Evan folded his arms, hugging himself and trying not to scratch nervously at his skin. He would have killed for a cigarette and the craving was making it hard to sit still. Luka and Alek slid the padded weight bench in the corner over so they could sit across from Brennan and Evan.

The more fidgety Evan got, the more tightly Brennan grasped him.

Unsure what to make of all of this, calmed only by Brennan's presence, but also, conversely, on-edge *because* of Brennan's presence, Evan tried not to guess what the 'talk' was going to be about. Not even knowing he was doing it, he started to scratch at the inside of his left arm, leaving red lines behind. His expression darkened and he slumped down. He didn't want to talk; he wanted to get out of there. He wanted to jog down to the nearest convenience store and buy a fucking pack of cigarettes, not analyze his problems. There were way too many of those to even begin to want to think about them, let alone share them with three people who had completely infiltrated his life and his heart. Evan's instinct had always been to push things down, to act without thinking about what he'd done. Afterward, he'd run or hide or keep himself busy with cars or helping other people as distraction. It felt unnatural to try to look within and face what was there. All that had ever brought him was pain.

Evan realized Brennan's thumb was stroking gently back and forth over the inside of his knee. He tuned in to the way it felt to be touched so intimately by Brennan, to feel him there, next to him. It gave Evan strength and made it a little easier to bear when Luka and Alek sat down across from them and Luka said, "We need to talk. About a lot of stuff. There's been too much discussed secretively, stuff that affects all four of us now, and I need to know we're all on the same page."

Alek leaned forward, resting his elbows on his knees. He caught Evan's gaze and held it. "So, where do we start?"

"Brennan starts," Luka said simply.

Sighing, Brennan turned to face Evan, tucking his left leg up in front of him. Softly, he urged Evan, "Look at me. Please."

A cold bolt of fear shot down the center of Evan's body. It tightened his chest, turned his stomach, and knotted up his gut. Everyone's eyes were on him. Evan could feel it, so he turned to Brennan in an attempt to narrow his focus. But he found he couldn't meet his brother's eyes. He stared at Brennan's lap instead and kept scratching at his arm. The skin there was inflamed and raw when Brennan pried Evan's fingers away from the spot. Cupping a hand under Evan's jaw, brushing his fingertips over Evan's cheekbone, Brennan frowned with concern as Evan battled to bottle up everything. Some of Evan's shame and pain slipped out anyway in the shape of his lips, in the wetness of his eyes.

"This is why we have to talk," Brennan hissed quietly. "*I* did this to you, didn't I? Evan, I'm so sorry. I should have treated you with more respect. It was so careless of me to take you like I did without stopping to find protection and to make sure it's what you really, *really* wanted."

"You didn't." Evan exhaled roughly. "You didn't make me this way. I've always been this way! I've always—"

"Shh." Brennan touched their foreheads together, winding his left hand inside of Evan's and still stroking his cheek, brushing away a tear that trickled down it.

"We all know what happened," Luka said solemnly. "That's why Bren and I went to get tested. They didn't find anything. We're clean. Are we all agreed we're only going to be sexually active with the people in this room?"

"Yes," Alek said, grasping Evan's knee as another tear slipped from under Evan's eyelashes.

"Yes," Brennan agreed.

"...Yes," Evan whispered, bowing his head as Brennan watched him like a hawk.

"Good. I do too." Luka looked sidelong at Alek, then spoke directly to Evan. "Okay. Another thing that has to be said aloud is that we all know about your past, Evan. We know what you went through and that you tried to commit suicide. I want you to try to tell us why you would do something like that, because we all care about you and don't want to ever lose you. Okay? Please?"

Alek's face worked. He eyed his brother with astonishment, but said nothing, only nodded and refocused on Evan.

Evan sighed and cleared his throat. He pulled away from Brennan and tried to tug his hand free. Brennan didn't let him. "Christ, I need a cigarette. I—I don't want to do this."

"You can't hide this stuff anymore," Alek said gently. "It's tearing you up inside, baby. Please. It's just us. We're not going to judge you."

Evan spat it out, wanting to get it over with fast. "It was *you*, okay?"

He looked up at Brennan at last.

"I needed you and you weren't there. You were never there and I couldn't do it on my own. There was this whole part of me that just... *wasn't*. It was like I was trying to live with only half of my soul and where the rest should have been was this void I couldn't ever fill. So yeah, I gave up. I didn't tell anyone, I just decided it was time and tried to off myself. And I never told Jimmy or Dad why when they brought me back. And I didn't tell you, either. But now I... I mean, you're *here*. You're right fucking here, Brennan, and I'm so scared I'm going to lose you again somehow. And I just... I want to just devour and cherish every part of you while I still have you. It's fucked up but I don't care. I really don't."

Taking a deep inhale, Brennan let it slowly back out, and it caught. His expression twisted, and he dropped his gaze.

Luka spoke up, determined, "So, when Brennan had sex with

you it was completely consensual?"

"Yes," Evan rasped. "Of course it was."

"You didn't do it because you felt obligated; to prove how much you love him?"

Evan's head snapped around, looking sharply at Luka, catching sight of the pain in Alek's face, too.

"No, it wasn't like that. I mean, yeah, he can have whatever he wants from me, he can take it all if that's what will make him happy. But I wanted it. Trust me. And I'm sorry it was different for you guys. If I could undo that, I would. In a heartbeat."

"You can't undo the past," Luka said sadly. "You can only go forward."

"You want me to say it?" Alek croaked. "I'll say it. I forced myself on Luka. He wasn't ready, and I was too fucking high to realize how upset he was. I can never take away the pain it caused him, and I will be paying for that every day for the rest of my damn life. That's why we want better for you two."

"You have a chance to be together *and* be as happy as Alek makes me, right from the start," Luka said, wrapping an arm around his brother. "That's why it's important to be safe, to be open and honest about everything, but especially the hard stuff, and to lay off on the drinking."

"Okay," Evan nodded. "So are we done now? Is that everything? We cool? We can kiss and make up and go on with our fucking day so I can get a damn cigarette?"

"Addict," Brennan *tsked*. His mouth curled up in a crooked smile right before he leaned in and kissed Evan softly on the lips. "Maybe you just need some distraction to keep your mind off the smoking."

"Please, that's not a kiss," Luka scoffed, grabbing Alek with both hands and claiming his mouth passionately, kissing him thoroughly. Brennan and Evan stared, watching their jaws work as Luka tilted his head to get deeper, moaning as Alek twisted around to face his brother and gave it good right back to him.

When they parted, Luka gasped breathlessly, "*That's* a kiss."

"Fuck yeah," Evan gaped. "Please don't stop on our account."

Alek's focus shifted instantly from his brother to his boyfriend, his eyes narrowing darkly.

"Oh shit," Evan gulped, scooting back a few inches on the bed right before Alek tackled him backward, flattening him. He'd expected Alek to maybe kiss him, but when Alek latched onto the side of his neck instead, nipping and sucking hard, Evan's mouth fell open widely in an aching moan, his fingers chasing up to tangle in Alek's hair.

"Nice," Luka grinned. He turned to Brennan, who was up on his feet, circling where Luka sat on the bench. "You want some of that too, you little toppy bastard?"

"What do *you* think, smartass?" Brennan asked slyly, grabbing a handful of the hair at the nape of Luka's neck. Yanking on the hair to get Luka's head tilted far back, the long, thick column of his neck straining, Brennan gave Luka a hard, dirty kiss.

"I think you're *way* overdue for another spanking," Luka told him. "Put your fine ass in line."

"Oh yeah? Is that what you think? I'd like to see you try."

"I'd like to see you try, too," Evan said roughly from the bed, raising a hand.

Alek raked a hand down Evan's body. Evan twisted and writhed, choking off a surprised sound, and Alek growled, "I guess we know what we're doing tonight then. Sounds like fun to me."

"Did you see that? With Evan and his brother?"

Carter blinked, hesitated, and nodded. "Yeah."

"Remind you of anyone? Certain overgrown people who get way too handsy with members of their own family?"

Carter chuckled. Then, growing pensive, asked, "You think we should say something? Warn the young'uns in case our boys are the ones eggin' 'em on?"

Presley sighed. "Nah. You know what, they might have questionable judgment when it comes to each other, but I don't think they'd do anything to harm someone they cared about. And the new lovebirds seem pretty serious. Just the fact that they introduced 'em to us says a lot."

After a pause he continued, "I'm happy for 'em, you know?

Having something so special you just want everyone to know about it, because they're that proud of the way they feel. That's a good thing. I hope it works out for 'em."

They were sitting beside each other on the couch. Carter shifted closer to Presley and propped his feet up on the low coffee table. His arm was slung behind Presley's neck and after a little while, his fingers started to move, brushing in a gentle, repeating arc over the side of Presley's neck. It was a casually intimate sort of touch and unusual for Carter to do such a thing without wanting it to lead to something more. They'd never been the types to go for cozy, cuddly gestures. But it felt nice enough that Presley didn't move away. When the clear sound of voices and footsteps sounded in the hall upstairs and descended toward them, Presley waited for Carter to spring away; expecting him to slide to the far end of the couch and pretend like nothing was going on.

The voices got louder and the lower halves of Luka and Brennan's bodies became visible in the stairwell, and Carter not only hadn't moved away, but was still stroking the side of Presley's neck. Presley became very, very confused.

Soon, all four of the other men, their roommates and their new boyfriends, were standing mere feet away. Presley froze, his heart pounding. Carter's thumb dragged slowly down over a tendon in Presley's neck.

Alek asked, "You guys in tonight? We're gonna go play some touch football if you're interested in joining. It'd be more of a game if we had bigger teams. We're gonna go pick up some salmon steaks and prime rib to grill up later."

Presley couldn't answer, his brain was flooded with nothing but, '*Oh my god, oh my god, oh my god*,' so Carter answered for him.

"Sure! Sounds great."

"Cool!" Luka smiled. "Hey, while we run out for supplies, you mind checking the garage for the football? If you don't find it, text me and we'll just buy another one."

"Yeah, no problem. I think I saw it by the tool bench."

"Awesome. Okay, we'll be back. You two behave yourselves while we're gone," Luka winked.

Moments later, after Evan and Brennan waved goodbye on their way out, the pair on the couch were left alone once more. Presley clenched his jaw and took a deep breath.

"Okay, what the hell was that?" He sat bolt-upright and faced Carter, whose hand finally fell away.

"I'm not an idiot, you know. I am proud of you... and us. I just thought it'd be easier if we had privacy."

"Easier for whom?"

"...Fair enough."

"So that was your grand gesture? That was you making a statement?"

The door creaked open and Luka appeared in the hall again. "Hey, guys, forgot my keys."

Carter, scowling with defiance, surged forward, kissing Presley squarely on the mouth.

"Okay. I'ma just... get my keys and... yeah. Get a room."

"No problem," Carter growled. "Don't mind if I do."

Once the door slapped shut again, Carter asked, "That grand enough for ya?"

"Mm-hmm," Presley grunted, weakly.

# Chapter 29

# Foursome

"What are you thinking about?"

The question, asked by Evan in a lust-roughened, gravelly voice, was posed with a desperate sense of urgency, in an attempt to distract himself from what else was going on in the room. He was on the chaise in Brennan's bedroom, beside Alek, who was reclined with Evan draped over him, boneless and happy.

"You mean besides the spanking?" Evan could hear the sly smirk in Alek's tone. The tips of Alek's fingertips skittered down the right side of Evan's chest, flicking over his nipple, which was fully hard just like Evan's cock. "Take off your shirt."

Evan didn't even think about it, he just did as Alek asked, letting the t-shirt fall to the floor. Alek guided him right back again, against his chest. Alek's fingers immediately began to play at Evan's nipple, tweaking it, and rolling it. It got Evan arching, his breath catching. From the bed, just a few feet away, came sharp grunts and slaps as Luka continued to spank Brennan's bare ass, which was already a deep pink color. Brennan, who had been instructed to grip the bed's headboard and bend sharply at the waist, took it well. At first the only reaction he'd given was to clench up after the first series of blows, but as the gentle but continuous flogging went on, small cries began to mix in with his jagged breaths.

Alek eye-fucked Brennan and the inflamed skin of his bottom. Evan couldn't blame him. The blond young man was perfectly naked, perfectly beautiful and perfectly identical to Alek's own lover, especially if you squinted. In the relative darkness of the room, Brennan's glasses were the main thing that gave him away.

But Alek also seemed to notice every little piece of evidence signaling Evan's near-suffocating lust, stirred by watching his brother and Luka. All day long, Evan had been quiet and reserved. In response, Alek had been careful not to leave Evan alone, to keep him company, keep him laughing or engaged in conversation or at the very least distracted from his thoughts. The constant, devoted attention made Evan feel nothing but loved. The best part about the attention, though, was Evan felt he could enjoy it without needing it to get by. He loved how he had people who put his wellbeing at the top of their priority list, but simply having their affection did more for him than any gift or act could.

When the four of them returned to Evan and Brennan's home, and had all retreated to the bedroom together, Evan had fallen even quieter. It started with Brennan getting spanked. Evan had been merely slightly flushed when it began, and his coloring could have been interpreted as stemming from embarrassment as well as interest.

After a little while, Luka slowly twisted a butt plug up into Brennan's carefully lube-slicked hole and Evan turned the corner. Now, as Luka rubbed a hand roughly over the abused swell of Brennan's backside, pushing at the plug's base and kneading handfuls of throbbing flesh, Evan knew he was pretty much a wreck. His jeans were obviously tented by his erection but his whole body was jittery with amorphous need—for what or for whom, he didn't even know.

Evan's breath quickened and his skin was slick with a light layer of sweat despite the shower he had not long after their game of football and dinner. When Alek twisted Evan's nipple and rubbed a hand underneath the front of Evan's pants waistband, Evan sucked in his stomach and pushed his hips up greedily into the touch, trying to relieve some pressure. His mouth fell open briefly in a sigh. Alek's hand pushed lower inside Evan's jeans, meeting no resistance as he circled the base of his cock and stroked the root with a thumb only to draw back, rubbing over the smooth skin of Evan's pelvis. He tugged gently at the soft curls of Evan's pubic hair, then withdrew his hand completely without providing any other sort of relief.

"Fucker," Evan complained.

Alek laughed darkly. "You want to know what I'm thinking,

huh? Well, I *was* thinking about how freely Carter was slapping Presley's ass in a not entirely sportsmanlike way during our game earlier, but now I'm just thinking about sucking your cock."

Evan groaned, shivering as a particularly sharp strike of Luka's open hand to the underside of Brennan's bottom was followed by a wrenching cry from Brennan. "Please."

"You want it? My lips wrapped around you? I'd tongue your slit while you watch your brother writhe on the end of Luka's fat cock."

"*Yes*, fuck. Please."

Alek grasped each of Evan's arms, guiding them up above his head. Crossing Evan's wrists, Alek circled them both with a hand, pulling Evan back, strung out over the breadth of Alek's chest with Alek's mouth tucked in the crook of Evan's neck. Reaching down between Evan's legs, Alek smiled as Evan let his thighs fall open widely and he thrust up, wanting to be touched. Alek didn't give him what he expected though, grabbing Evan by the balls through the coarse denim. Evan wriggled and gasped loudly as Alek tugged and squeezed lightly.

"Or maybe I should string you up right next to him, and spank you, too. What do you think, Jailbait? I *know* you've been bad. Maybe you should be punished."

Luka glanced back over his shoulder, taking a long moment to watch Evan twist and undulate. After giving Alek a heated look which said Luka would quite enjoy Alek's threat, Luka reached for the plug stretching Brennan out. Gripping it by the base, he tugged on it, extracting it very, very slowly. Brennan pushed out his ass and exhaled sharply. His eyes slipped momentarily shut. Then he turned to look at his brother.

Brennan stared at Evan whose feet were flexed, his legs restless, and looking for some kind of purchase on the slick wooden floor or the edge of the chaise as Alek held him by the wrists and the balls. Evan curled up one leg at a time toward his body as Alek kept his tight hold on his sac. His mouth falling open around his gasps, perfect echoes of Evan's, Brennan cried out with ache at the sight.

"Open his pants," Brennan gasped. "I wanna see how hard he is."

"He's pretty hard, aren'tcha, Jailbait?" Alek grinned. "Should we show 'im? Let's show Bren how much you get off on staring at his pretty pink ass."

"*Alek*," Evan pleaded.

Keeping his unrelenting hold on Evan's wrists, Alek popped open Evan's fly and inched his jeans down on his narrow hips, just enough so his cock was able to spring free, straining up tight to his belly, flushed red and dripping wet with pre-come. Just as Luka inserted three lube-slicked fingers into Brennan, Alek hooked the hand around the base of Evan's sac, pulling on it, stretching Evan's testicles away from his body. Evan gasped loudly, hips chasing upward off the chaise, into Alek's hand. His cock seeped clear fluid and Evan stared at Brennan, looking back at him and biting so sweetly on his bottom lip as Brennan took Luka's pumping fingers, moving in and out of his hole.

Moaning wantonly, Evan shuddered in Alek's grasp.

"Bet you'd come if I so much as blew across the end of your dick right now."

On the bed, Brennan spread his legs wider and rasped, "C'mon. More, I need more." Luka just shook his head and tugged his fingers free of Brennan's shiny-wet hole, enjoying one more open-handed rub over the sore, inflamed skin of his bottom. Brennan sucked in a breath through gritted teeth at the touch. Directing a hard slap to the spot, Luka watched Brennan's butt jiggle and hummed at the sound of Brennan's surprised yelp.

"You want more, Cupcake?"

Bracing a splayed hand against Brennan's lower abdomen to hold him still, Luka lined himself up and drove into him. He breached the snug outer ring of Brennan's sphincter and put gentle force behind his thrust, making Brennan take all of him.

Brennan dropped his head between his arms and groaned. When Luka caressed the reddened surface of his behind, Brennan's emoting took on a sharper edge, but he didn't wait any longer, he started to move, pulling forward slightly before pushing back onto Luka, building a rhythm, but starting with shallow movements. Luka roused himself, stopped just watching Brennan move on him and took control, holding Brennan by the hips and driving into him deep and hard.

Evan tried not to watch, but he couldn't not watch. At least his angle wasn't giving him the best view, which he was grateful for until Alek said, "Sit up. Sit on the edge of the chair."

"Why?"

"Just do it."

Evan sat, his arms free at last and he moved to touch himself once he was seated but Alek caught his hand first. "Don't even think about it."

He pulled Evan's arms behind his back and used a discarded belt on the floor to bind his wrists together. When that was done, he adjusted Evan's pants so they were too low to help him rub against to get off. Sitting behind Evan, Alek asked, "So what do you want? Tell me. And be creative."

"Creative, huh?" Evan said with a wicked gleam in his eye. "Anything?"

"Anything. As long as it's okay with Bren and Luka."

"Okay. Then I want you to fuck his brains out," Evan rasped.

"Who?" Alek asked, glancing at the bed. There was a hopeful note to his voice when he added, "Bren?"

"No. Luka. That's what I want."

Alek teased his lower lip between his teeth and leaned in for a kiss. "You dirty boy."

He stole Evan's breath, kissing him roughly and left him there, panting, to go to Luka.

Luka went perfectly still when Alek crawled onto the bed and pressed up behind him. Alek circled an arm around Luka's sweat-slicked, thickly-muscled chest. "This okay with you?"

"Yeah," Luka nodded after a moment, leaning back ever so slightly into Alek's touch, holding on to Brennan and looking directly at Evan. Understanding passed between them and feelings of empathy as well as affection bloomed in Evan's heart for Luka.

Evan could tell Luka saw how Evan didn't want to be the only brother taken in the way Brennan had taken him. He wanted, possibly *needed* to witness the extent of the sexual intimacy so far only spoken of, and not demonstrated by, the other set of brothers. "How about you, Bren? You cool with this?"

"I'm only cool with it if you turn me around so I can watch, too," Brennan rasped, flexing his back and shoulders, grunting as Luka tugged free of him.

"So, you wanna be in the middle, hmm?" Alek grinned, slicking lube onto his hand and pressing two fingers into Luka.

They all watched as Luka's chest heaved and his skin flushed darker at their collective, focused attention and Alek's intimate touch. Brennan lay down on his back and Alek pressed Luka forward with a hand to his middle back, bending him over. Brennan spread his legs and kissed Luka's gasps away. Luka palmed Brennan's ass and slid, slippery and easily, back into his lover. He rocked gently into Brennan with shallow movements as Alek quickly stretched him out, corkscrewing his fingers within the snug passage. When Luka heard the condom wrapper being ripped open, he wound his arms more closely around Brennan, closing his eyes.

Brennan lay back to give him air. Tiny, delicate frown lines appeared in Luka's brow and his lips sealed tightly together. Alek lined up and pressed against Luka, the thick, bulbous head of his dick demanding entry.

Evan stared fixedly at them, seeing everything. Alek looked his way, caressing over Luka's side. Driving his hips forward, he thrust into Luka.

Luka cried out. "Fuck! Easy! Easy. Been a while."

Alek hissed between his teeth and tugged back an inch or two. He pressed more gently deeper, slowly sinking into Luka completely.

Luka moaned thunderously by Brennan's temple. Evan watched raptly as Luka lost himself in what he imagined was the blissful sensation of Brennan gripped like a glove around his cock and Alek driving ever-deeper into him at the same time, pushing him with every thrust farther into Brennan.

Luka relaxed, letting Alek take over, moved by him, kissed and caressed by both of them. It was intense. Evan had never witnessed nor shared anything like it with people he knew to truly love him, albeit in different ways. And that wasn't all. Luka's complex yet unconditional love with Alek and his budding, profound love with Brennan only imbued every moment, every touch, with meaning and wonder.

As soon as Alek set a steady pace, he angled Luka a little differently. On Alek's next thrust, Luka exclaimed and gritted his teeth, putting his own force behind his thrusts in and out of Brennan as Alek sent him racing towards climax. Suddenly, Luka choked off a jagged moan as he orgasmed, shuddering in Brennan's arms.

Alek pulled out and Brennan guided Luka down to lay over him while he recovered. "I should... you haven't..." Luka gasped. "We didn't finish."

Brennan whispered, "It's okay. Relax. It was perfect. You were perfect. Just when I thought I couldn't love you more. You were so sweet with him, Luka."

Luka nuzzled into Brennan touch and only looked around once he heard what was going on over on the other side of the room.

Stripping off the soiled condom, Alek approached Evan. Without prompting or even so much as a word, Evan, with his wrists still bound, fell to his knees, sliding from the chaise to the wooden floor below.

Alek sighed heavily at the sight of Evan wrecked with desire and needing nothing but Alek. Evan's mouth fell open wide, his tongue extending out hungrily to meet Alek when he stepped up close and held Evan's head in a hand, caressing over his cheek. Cradling Alek's cock on his curled tongue, wrapping the muscle around him, Evan let him slide as far back as he wanted, closing his lips up around the shaft and hollowing his cheeks as he sucked. He tried to stay relaxed. For the first few pumps of his hips, Alek managed to hold back, but one glance down at Evan, his lips stretched around the dark, swollen cock and wanting nothing but to please, seemed to end Alek's self-control. He pulsed over Evan's tongue, pre-come coating it. Alek thrust, sliding deeper, nestling in Evan's throat and stuffing it full of him.

Evan made a startled grunt but took it, his eyes streaming as Alek pulled back only to thrust right back in, riding the tight suction from his mouth.

On the bed, Brennan was watching avidly, moaning a little at the sight coupled with his own unquenched need. Luka brushed the backs of his fingers over the inside of the protrusion of Brennan's hipbone and peppered soft kisses to his neck and chest.

Evan whimpered and struggled to take Alek's forceful thrusts. But then Alek pulled out completely, leaving Evan sucking in a large gulp of much-needed air, his chin wet with saliva, and lips darkly swollen. With his huge hard-on straining between his legs, Evan was possibly at his most debauched. With only two squeezes up to the tip, Alek's cock erupted, shooting come onto Evan's quivering lips, his chin, cheeks, and some hot droplets even falling onto his eyelashes. Evan breathed roughly and waited for every last drip to fall from Alek.

"Jesus fuck. Stand up, baby. C'mere." Alek kissed the mess of Evan's mouth and began to wipe Evan's face clean. He freed Evan's hands from the belt binding them. "Thank you. I love you so much. Fucking worship you."

Evan grunted brokenly and kissed Alek back, brow furrowed and savoring the tender words, though without the breath to reply.

"What do you want? Name it." He caressed Evan's stomach, down past his navel, but didn't touch his erection, not quite. "You want Brennan?"

Evan started, pulling back. He asked himself, *Do I?*

He couldn't speak. One moment, he was staring pleadingly up at Alek, who owned his heart, and the next, he was walking to the bed, to the man who owned his soul. One brief look at Luka and Evan knew it was okay.

"Yeah," Evan answered, nodding. Feeling nothing but overwhelming thankfulness, for so many things, Evan held Luka's gaze and moaned his name. It was barely a whisper, a plea. Evan didn't want to have to act on his own. He needed Luka's help to take the next step. "Can you—?" "Yeah. C'mere. Lie down," Luka said, taking Evan by the hand and making room for him to lie back on the pillows. He stroked Evan's straining erection slowly, causing Evan to gnaw at his lips to hold back a gut-deep moan at being touched like that by him for the first time.

"Bren," Luka beckoned, watching Brennan battle with his emotions as he got up on his knees and moved to straddle Evan. His eyes slipping shut, his lips pursed, Brennan made a pleading sigh as his hand and Evan's found each other. Their fingers wove together and

Evan rested his other hand lightly on Brennan's inner thigh as Luka aligned Evan with Brennan and, gently but firmly, pushed Brennan down onto Evan.

Toes curling and fingers clawing around Brennan's hand, Evan inhaled sharply through his nose and reacted helplessly. He thrust desperately up into Brennan as soon as he got the first taste of the feel of him, soft, tight and hot, hugged around Evan's aching cock.

"Bren. *Oh god.*" Evan's deep voice shattered on a cry.

Luka kissed the side of Brennan's neck and guided the movements of his hips, caressing him as he rolled them in tight little swoops and circles. Moving on Evan, Brennan worked him to the knife's edge of oblivion, teetering on that very edge himself. He tried to make it last, but Evan could tell how desperately he needed to come and Brennan keened, leaning forward so he could fuck himself down onto Evan faster and harder, bouncing on him, taking him deeper.

Luka caressed him, rubbing over the place where Brennan and Evan's bodies joined. Alek was there, kissing Evan and swallowing the feverish noises erupting from the back of Evan's throat. It only spurred Brennan on. Rolling his hips forward, his dick dragging a wet line over Evan's rock-hard abdomen, Brennan's mouth fell open in a gasping shout.

He came suddenly. His orgasm was ripped from him and he ground down against Evan, fucking himself against him while Evan clawed at his hand, at his body too. Evan wrapped his hand around Brennan's cock, pumping him through his climax, milking him dry and driving his own cock up into Brennan like a man possessed. Evan came seconds later, as Alek kissed him dizzy and Brennan's gentle but deliberate bounces up and down on his dick wrung every last drop from him.

Evan didn't realize he had passed out until hours later, when he woke up in his own bed, in the warmth and comfort of Alek's arms, held close and with nothing but peace and satisfaction in his heart.

Thinking of Brennan, and Luka, and how happy they all were, in different bedrooms in the very same house, Evan smiled to himself. He looked forward to what the next day might bring and pulled the strong, enveloping arms of the man he knew he belonged to more snugly around him. There were still trials left to endure and secrets to either confess or make peace with, but for now it was enough to be understood, to love and be loved, gratefully.

If you enjoyed this story, you can sign up for a free membership at ForbiddenFiction and discuss it with other readers and the author at the *My Brother's Lover* story page at http://forbiddenfiction.com/library/story/LK1-1.000154.

We do our best to proof all our work, but if you spot a text error we missed, please let us know via our website Contact Form at http://forbiddenfiction.com/contact.

# About the Author

**Lynn Kelling** began writing in order to tell stories that weren't afraid of the dark, didn't hold anything back and always strived to be memorable, forging lasting attachments between character and reader. Her inspiration comes from taking a closer look at behaviors and ideas lurking at the fringes of life—basically anything that people may hesitate to speak of in mixed company, but everyone wonders about anyway. Her work is driven by the taboo in order to expose the humanity within it. Lynn is an artist, designer and lover of any form of creative self-expression that comes from a place of honesty and emotion, whether it's body art or opera. She has had multiple novels published, has written over fifty works of erotic fiction of varying lengths, and always has several novels in progress.

# About the Publisher

**ForbiddenFiction.com** is a publisher devoted to writing that breaks the boundaries of original erotic fiction. Our stories combine intense sexuality with quality writing. Stories at Forbidden Fiction.com not only arouse readers through sensations, but also engage them emotionally and mentally through storytelling as well-crafted as the sex is hot.

ForbiddenFiction.com is also designed to be a social reading environment. You'll have fun even if just reading the latest post each day, yet you will have the chance for so much more. Readers and authors can be part of ongoing discussions of specific works and individual authors as well as more general topics.

Sign up for a FREE Membership today at ForbiddenFiction.com